# tempt
## me
### tonight

By Toni Blake

TEMPT ME TONIGHT
SWEPT AWAY

# tempt
## me
## tonight

## toni blake

**AVON**

*An Imprint of HarperCollinsPublishers*

HarperCollins books may be purchased for educational, business, or sales promotional use. For information please write: Special Markets Department, HarperCollins Publishers, 10 East 53rd Street, New York, NY 10022.

FIRST EDITION

*Interior text designed by Diahann Sturge*

Library of Congress Cataloging-in-Publication Data

Blake, Toni, 1965–
    Tempt me tonight / by Toni Blake.—1st ed.
        p. cm.
    ISBN: 978-0-06-113609-2
    ISBN-10: 0-06-113609-3
    I. Title.

PS3602.L349T46   2007
813'.6—dc22          2006037649

07 08 09 10 11 JTC/RRD 10 9 8 7 6 5 4 3 2 1

To my dear friend, Renee Norris,
for all she does for me,
and for everyone else, too.
I am blessed to know you.

# Acknowledgments

They say it takes a village to raise a child. *I* say it takes a village to help write a good book! My sincere thanks goes to:

Robin Zentmeyer, for early brainstorming, and for the idea of the chapter headings.

Attorney Glenda Edwards, for being my advisor and brainstorming partner about the legal aspects of the story.

Attorney Rodger Moore, for answering a few other quick questions.

My mechanic buddy Steve, for so kindly helping me provide accurate details about Joe's work.

Lucia Macro and the fine folks at Avon Books, for all the great stuff they do for me.

Meg Ruley, for early feedback and also for just being a plain fabulous agent.

And finally, to Renee Norris, whose input on this book was vital. Thank you, Renee, not only for taking an early look at the first fifty pages and brainstorming changes with me, but for giving me thorough input after reading the rough draft—and then reading the whole thing *again*! And on top of all *that*, you introduced me to the Shelby Cobra, too. You rock.

# Prologue

*14 years ago*

Tendrils of longing curled through her, hot and thick as the August night—and when his palm slid to her breast, that made it even *better*. She wanted this—wanted *him*. *Tonight's the night*. She'd said those very words to him today on the phone and they echoed through her again now.

Her breath turned ragged as he began to knead her—slowly, so slowly—through her thin summer top and bra, raking his thumb across her sensitive nipple in rhythm with his kiss. The back of her neck tingled, and a tender little bite on her lower lip sent the sensation skittering lightning-fast down her spine. She forgot to feel the humidity pouring in through the open car windows, forgot to feel her usual fear—and the whole world narrowed until only the two of them existed. His hands, her body. *Mmm, yes. Tonight's the night.*

An old country song played low on the radio, promising that heaven was just a sin away, and crickets chirped in the trees as she whispered his name. "Joe." It said everything. *I love you. I feel so close when we touch like this.*

As his fingers closed over the hem of her top, his breath, too, came hard, needful. He pushed the fabric inch by agonizing inch up over her chest, then lowered one short but tantalizing kiss through the lace of her bra. *Oh God. Yes.*

Pungent summer scents swept through the car on a warm breeze, nearly swallowing her, and she thought, *Please, oh please*—until finally he undid the bra's front hook, using both strong hands to spread the lace and take her in his grasp. A fresh moan escaped her.

"Trish," he murmured throatily. "God, Trish."

And then came the lovely suction of his mouth at her breast, making her whimper and pant, sending sweet aches to the small of her back and the juncture of her thighs. Shifting in the reclined front seat of his '85 Trans Am, she parted her legs and let him lean into her, so that what had pressed rock-hard against her hip a moment before now settled firm and solid between her thighs. Heaven *was* just a sin away—she could feel it tempting her.

Steamy, excruciating moments later, his work-roughened fingers stroked high on her inner thigh, soon easing their way past the hem of her shorts, and she kept thinking of saying no, but her body was still begging, screaming—*yes!*

They both trembled when he touched her there. It wasn't the first time, but it always seemed new. She could feel her own wetness. His fingers strummed her, and without quite meaning to, she began to move against his hand. When the car seat started to squeak, embarrassment bit at her, but it wasn't enough to stop her.

Until he unfastened the snap on her shorts and slid the zipper down. "Let me take them off."

His voice echoed low, persuasive, and she wanted to—oh Lord, how she wanted to. But she suddenly wasn't sure—even now. What if it changed something between them? Especially now that she was leaving? What if it hurt, or was horrible and ruined their last night together? They'd be *back* together, in just a couple of weeks, but tomorrow both their lives would change—things would never be quite like *this* again. Let him take them off and there was no going back.

Her chest tightened as she released a heavy breath. Uh-oh. Maybe tonight wasn't really the night, after all.

"*Joe.*" Not a passionate declaration this time—instead, a plea of doubt.

"I love you, Trish." His voice wafted over her, just as intoxicating as his touch.

*Why can't you do this? Why can't you give yourself to him?* "I love you, too."

"I want you so much. I've wanted you forever." She'd never heard such deep emotion in his words—but then his voice shifted, sounding confused. "And I thought you said . . ." *That tonight's the night.* She wanted to smack herself for feeling so sure earlier.

Her throat quivered when she tried to talk. "I know. But now I just . . ."

Above her, he released a heavy sigh. She hated that—hated bringing them to this grinding halt, like always. But she especially hated it now. *Why did you have to promise him on the phone?*

"Trishy, you're leaving tomorrow."

As if she needed reminding of that. She'd been sure her imminent departure would finally make her ready. But now the same old fears lingered, tightening up everything inside her. She took a deep breath and tried to summon just one word. *Okay.*

But instead, she heard herself pointing out to him, "I'll be back in two weeks. Two short little weeks."

"For the weekend," he countered. "And then you'll be gone again."

"Joe, I love you. But . . ."

"But what, Trish? Why won't you be with me? I just want to show you how I feel. I just want to . . . be inside you."

She clenched her teeth. That almost got her, almost made her forget, once more, about anything but him and her and their bodies moving together. They'd gone so slow for so long—he'd been so patient. Joe Ramsey could have any girl he wanted, yet he'd waited for *her*.

*Don't be afraid. Let this happen. If you're not ready* now, *when* will *you be?*

Make *tonight the night.*

Yet tears formed in the corners of her eyes. "I want to. I just . . . can't."

Easing back slightly, he ran one hand through his dark hair and closed his eyes, clearly trying to fight his frustration. A heavy male sigh permeated the thick night air.

Lying beneath him, she began to feel naked—and more sad than excited now. "I'm sorry," she murmured as she nervously reached to pull her bra back together.

Just then, the bright beams of headlights lit up the car's interior. "Shit," he whispered, raising to squint out into the glare. Trish struggled to get her bra fastened and her top back down as pure dread pummeled her. Who on earth could be out there?

A few seconds later, a face appeared in the window—Beverly Rainey, a racy, older girl Trish only knew in passing. "Joe? Is that Trish Henderson in there with you?"

They both sat up, and Trish wanted to snap, *Of course it's me.*

They'd been together for three years and everybody in town knew it. But she held her tongue and simply tried not to look too disheveled.

"*Yeah*, it's Trish," Joe said in a tone that made her feel vindicated.

"I'm sorry to bother you two—but Trish's dad is calling around, looking for her. He called up to the Dairy Queen while I was sitting outside with Rusty Tanner and some other guys."

Trish's heart leapt, making her forget Beverly Rainey was still referring to her in the third person. "*Why?*"

"Apparently you missed your curfew?" Beverly said uncertainly.

Trish glanced at the tiny clock on Joe's dashboard, then gasped. How had they lost track of time? She was almost an hour late! She swung her gaze to Joe in the darkened car. "It's nearly two. We've gotta go."

"Damn," he muttered.

Joe rushed to start the engine as Trish reached for the lever that would raise her seat. Neither remembered to thank Beverly for coming to find them as he gave the Trans Am some gas and shot out onto the gravel road rimming Crescent Lake.

The ride stayed mostly silent as they turned out onto a dark two-lane highway, soon racing over the winding country roads that led to Trish's house. "I'm sorry, Joe," she said.

He gave his head a short shake. "It's all right."

But it didn't *sound* all right.

Then he started punching buttons on the radio until he found something fast and hard by Lynyrd Skynyrd and turned it up loud enough to discourage conversation. Trish's heart beat like a hammer in her chest as he took a curve a little too fast. Darn it, why couldn't tonight have been the night?

When they finally pulled into the gravel driveway next to the big white farmhouse where Trish had grown up, Joe said, "I'll go in with you, try to explain."

Yet she shook her head, letting out the breath she'd been holding. "If I'm going off to college tomorrow, I need to start handling some things by myself." Which was true—but the real reason was her dad. He'd never been crazy about Joe, or any of the Ramseys for that matter, and it seemed like a bad idea to put them face-to-face when her father was mad. Things felt messed up enough already.

"Are you sure?"

She nodded at him in the dark, then realized for the millionth time how *perfect* he was, and she found herself longing for a million different things—that they were older, that she wasn't afraid, that college was already over and she was back here with him, ready to start their real life together. She grabbed his hand and their eyes met in the faint glow from the porch light. "Joe, I'm really sorry. About before."

She heard his sigh and wished she could see his expression better. "It's okay," he said, but his reply still sounded stilted.

She forgot that, though—forgot everything negative—when he reached under his seat to pull out a small white box. "Almost forgot to give this to you."

She smiled softly, then drew off the lid to find a dainty chain sporting a pretty silver pendant in the shape of a cat.

"To remind you of Pumpkin—and me."

Her heart warmed and everything suddenly felt okay. She'd probably told Joe fifty times how much she was going to hate leaving behind the kitten he'd given her. Grasping the chain tight in her fist, she threw her arms around his neck. "I love it! I love *you*. And I can't wait to see you in two weeks."

"I love you, too, cupcake." Lifting a warm palm to her cheek, he gave her a long, deep, soul-stirring kiss—the kind that would keep her awake all night just remembering it. It moved through her with slow heat, making her decide sex couldn't be any better than this.

As she grabbed onto the door handle, he said, "Wait," then reached over to gently zip her shorts back up.

"Oh God," she said, filled with the simultaneous terror and relief of realizing she'd nearly walked in the house that way—and equally filled with the rippling awe of having his touch there again, even if only briefly. Okay, so maybe sex *could* be better. She'd find out with Joe soon, she promised herself. *Really* soon. Heck, after two weeks away, she'd probably throw herself on him.

After the kiss, he raised his hands to her hair, trying to smooth it, and she realized she must look a mess.

"Is it awful?" She peered over at him, trying to comb her fingers through it. It was bad enough she was late—she couldn't come in looking like she'd just had sex, especially since she hadn't. Quite.

"It's *windblown*," he supplied with a small, sexy smile. "We had the windows down—it's a hot night."

The hottest. In every way.

She squeezed his hand, leaned over for one more quick kiss that sizzled down through her like a lit firecracker, then got out and slammed the door. Watching him back out of the driveway to take off down the road, she clutched his gift tight in her hand, cherishing it already.

Tonight hadn't been the night. *But soon, Joe. I promise.*

A few hours before Trish was ready to leave for the University of Indiana, a knock came on the door and she opened it to find her best friend, Debbie, standing on the front porch. "Hey," Trish said, smiling. Debbie must have come to see her off—she even held a small, slightly wilted-from-the-heat bouquet of wild daisies and Queen Anne's lace. As Trish took it from her, she used her free hand to hold up the little kitty pendant at her throat. "Look what Joe gave me."

Only thing was—Debbie wasn't looking at the necklace, and she wasn't smiling back.

"What's wrong?" Trish asked.

Peering at her through thick glasses, Debbie bit her lip. "I hate this."

"I know, but time will fly and we'll talk on the phone and everything will be fine."

Yet Debbie shook her head, eyes pensive beneath teased brown bangs. "No, that's not it. I hate that I have to tell you something awful—just awful, Trish."

Trish drew in her breath and set the flowers on the table by the door. "What are you talking about?"

Debbie took both her hands and squeezed tight. "It's Joe."

Trish's heart seized. "God, was he in an accident? Is he all right?" She'd *known* he was driving too fast last night.

But Debbie just grimaced. "Trish, he . . ." She stopped. Sighed. "Last night he had sex with Beverly Rainey."

The words pierced her like a bee sting, sharp and shocking— but since they weren't true, she shook her head. "No, he was with *me* last night. We just ran into Beverly down by the lake."

Yet . . . Debbie *still* wasn't acting relieved along with her. Instead, her mouth stretched into a grim, straight line across her face. "No, Trish," she said softly, continuing to hold her hands. "*After* that. After he left you, he . . . hooked up with Beverly."

Trish shook her head *again*. "Joe would never do that to me."

But the mournful look in Debbie's eyes slowly began to bore into her, began to make her wonder, make her fear . . .

Light-headed, she let go of Debbie to grip the doorjamb.

Her knees went weak as more words spilled from Debbie's lips, words she could barely absorb—something about Beverly having beer, and about her telling everyone at the DQ today that she did it with Joe Ramsey last night. "Kenny asked him," Deb gently continued. Kenny was Debbie's boyfriend and Joe's best friend. "Joe didn't deny it."

Trish stood very still, her chest throbbing, her throat clenched. She tried to speak but couldn't get anything out. She loved Joe. With her whole heart. He loved her, too—didn't he?

And yet the guy she'd been planning to marry . . . *had given himself to someone else?*

This couldn't be real.

She held the doorframe tighter to keep from going down.

Debbie leaned to look inside the house, to make sure they were still alone, then went on somberly. "He told Kenny he fucked up. Kenny said he was really upset, quiet, that he was holding his head in his hands."

Trish let out a shaky breath, still trying to grasp, believe . . . the impossible. Joe had really cheated on her?

No. No—he couldn't have.

And yet, if he'd practically admitted it . . .

Her gaze drifted blankly down her friend's tank top, to her tennis shoes, to the bristly welcome mat below. Then her knees gave out and she sank to the hardwood floor. "Oh God."

"I'm so sorry, Trish," Debbie said, kneeling down in the doorway with her. "So, so sorry."

Deb's arms closed around her, but Trish could barely feel them. Because all the bones in her body seemed to be dissolving away to nothing. Because her chest was caving in. How could this be?

That's when everything inside her burst loose, like a dam breaking, and tears flowed hot and thick down her cheeks onto Debbie's shoulder as she collapsed a little deeper into her friend's supporting arms. *How could you, Joe? How could you?*

"We need to think through this," Debbie finally said through her own tears. "We need to figure out what you're gonna do."

But Trish didn't want to think. Thinking *hurt*. She didn't want to think about Joe with another girl. She didn't want to think about how her heart was shattering. Instead, she wanted to run.

And fortunately, she had someplace to run *to*. College. Two hours and a world away. She swallowed hard and shook her head. "I just want to go. I just want to get out of this stupid town and never think about this again."

Debbie's face scrunched with confusion. "That's impossible."

Yet Trish shook her head, resolute, even if a bit unbalanced at the moment. "No, it's not. And it's exactly what I'm gonna do. *I don't need him.* I . . . I *hate* him. How could he do this to me?" She met Debbie's gaze, helpless and incredulous all over again.

Deb's cheeks still glistened with tears, and her voice sounded sad and small. "I don't know, Trish, I don't know. But . . ." She sighed. "God, what should I tell him? He'll ask me if you know."

Without warning, something ferocious rose up in Trish, some part of herself she'd never encountered. "Tell him I never want to hear from him again for as long as I live!"

Debbie blinked behind her glasses. "Really? That's what you want me to say?"

What else *could* she say? "Yes. Because nothing could fix this. Ever." She let out a heavy breath.

And then she began to sob—a sound that grew from deep inside as despair started to consume her. She hugged her knees and rocked back and forth, wetness streaming down her cheeks, and Debbie rocked with her. *"How could you, Joe? How could you?"* she heard herself whisper.

She'd never thought, never even imagined . . . She'd always *trusted* him. Without question or doubt. Completely. *Blindly.* She'd never dreamed he could ever . . . she'd thought it was only *him and her, in love, forever.*

That same question kept playing over in her mind like one of her mom's old records with the skips in them: *How could you? How could you?* But as a few minutes began to pass, as it started to sink in deeper that this was *real*—it had really *happened*—the only answer she could come up with was sad but simple: He just didn't love her the way he'd always promised he did.

And nothing in her life would ever be the same again.

**Plea:** an accused person's answer to a criminal charge. For example: not guilty; guilty; no contest; <u>or</u> an appeal, an earnest request.

# One

Halfway between Cincinnati and Indianapolis, south of I-74, set God's country. Trish supposed many thousands of rural or dramatic landscapes had been referred to using those same words, but she hadn't known that when, at the age of seven, she'd sat perched on her Grandpa Henderson's knee and he'd told her she was looking out at God's country in all its splendor. All she'd seen was a wide cornfield, a line of trees, and the horizon, feeling—even then—the vague urge to somehow look beyond it all, to whatever was on the other side of the picture. And she never came home to Eden, Indiana without remembering the love of the place she'd seen in her grandfather's eyes on a day when she'd really been much more focused on the fact that she'd scuffed her new black patent leathers coming out of church. A girl had to be concerned about her shoes, after all.

She wondered now if Grandpa Henderson, God rest his soul, would see the irony or humor in the fact that she was driving toward a *bar* on the outskirts of God's country—the Last Chance Tavern. Last chance for a beer before entering God's country, she supposed. Or before leaving it.

"Here  turn here," Debbie said next to her.

Trish's stomach churned lightly as she angled her Lexus into the wide gravel parking lot dotted with cars and a few pickups. She really *didn't* want to be here. "And we're coming here, again, why?"

Debbie shoved a lock of thin brown hair from her face. "Kenny wants to see you, and it's pool night."

Trish nodded dryly, resisting the urge to point out that Kenny had the entire next week to see her. "Well, we wouldn't want Kenny to miss pool night."

Debbie blinked, looking miffed. "Kenny works hard and looks forward to Friday nights when Mom keeps the kids."

"Sorry." Trish sighed, feeling at once guilty and justified. She didn't want to be here because she simply didn't *fit* here any more. She knew it to the marrow of her bones—but despite the fact that she regularly dealt with hardened criminals from all walks of life without flinching, she felt an absurd dread faced with strolling into the Last Chance. She scrunched up her nose. "I guess I just would have enjoyed . . . dinner or something— more than this."

"You can come over and watch the boys hurl mashed potatoes at each other one night next week if you want. But Friday night is pool night."

Trish parked beneath a security light mounted on a large pole, choosing a spot a few car widths from a large pickup sporting mudflaps embellished with chrome silhouettes of naked women.

She tried not to let Debbie see her grimace, but those mudflaps always gave her the creeps. It was as if they said women were just nameless, faceless sex objects. *Bleck*. Then she flinched slightly. *Please don't let that be Kenny's truck.*

As she got out, pushing the button on her keychain to lock the doors, Debbie made a face over the roof of the car. "This is home, Trish—not Indianapolis."

Trish raised her eyebrows. "No one steals things from cars here?"

Looking as smug as Trish felt, Debbie shook her head. "No—they don't."

Which was when it hit Trish—they probably didn't. Even now. Not in Eden. There might be bars and chrome women on mudflaps, but she supposed that, in a sense, it really *was* still God's country. "Oh. Guess I forgot that for a minute." But she still left the car locked.

Over the years, *home* had become an entirely relative term in her life—this was where her parents lived, and where Debbie lived, but it wasn't *her* home anymore. She'd been back countless times over the years—every Thanksgiving and Christmas, sometimes for a Sunday dinner with relatives—yet this was different. This was the first time she'd actually come to *stay* for awhile. A week or so. This was the first time she hadn't just whizzed in and out of town for a day, or maybe an overnight stay that included a quick visit with Debbie and Kenny. This was the first time she'd be here long enough that she'd have to *see* people. People she hadn't seen in forever. People she'd never expected to see again. *Double bleck.*

"Rowdy Lancaster owns this place now," Debbie pointed out as they trod through the gravel toward the front door of the flat, one-story building painted a dull shade of brown. Through cloudy windows glowed mini-Christmas lights strung around neon beer signs, and a muted Garth Brooks song echoed through the walls.

She remembered Rowdy as a good-natured boy with red hair who'd raised 4-H award-winning calves in high school. So maybe saying hello to him wouldn't be awful. "I always liked Rowdy," she offered, trying to cheer herself up. Then, three steps from a heavy-looking steel door sporting the stenciled words LAST CHANCE, she posed the question she'd been trying to be too mature to ask. "Who else will be here?"

Debbie began rambling off a list of names that conjured vague images from high school, explaining that a couple of them worked at the plant with Kenny, and concluding with, "That's pretty much our Friday night crowd."

And Trish's stomach hollowed. At the strange realization that . . . life had gone on here. All the same people were still here—only grown up now, living their lives. Debbie and Kenny had a "Friday night crowd" made up of people Trish barely knew, only remembered dimly from her past. How had that happened? How had she ended up knowing so little about her best friend's life?

It wasn't as if she'd thought life in Eden had come to a grinding halt at her departure, but she supposed she'd been so caught up in her own existence all this time that she'd somehow forgotten everything else. And walking into the Last Chance was going to give her a taste of something she hadn't thought about in a very long while—the life *she'd* once planned to lead here. *Bleck to the tenth power.*

Not that Eden was an awful place. It was quaint in its way. But *its* way wasn't *her* way and hadn't been for a long time. It was hard to believe she'd *ever* belonged here.

Trish flicked her gaze to Debbie then, hating herself for even letting this enter her mind, but . . . "Anybody else I know?"

"I wouldn't expect Joe to be here, if that's what you're wondering."

She shrugged. It was *exactly* what she was wondering. "Not that it really matters," she assured Debbie. And it didn't. As life had worked out, she hadn't seen Joe Ramsey since she'd left for college and that suited her fine. After mailing off a long, angry letter to him a week after departing for IU, in which she'd reiterated the "never want to hear from you for as long as I live" part, she'd done exactly what she'd told Debbie she was going to do—she'd moved on. It hadn't happened overnight, of course; he'd broken her young heart, which had taught her to guard it a lot more closely. But she *had* long since gotten over him—she just didn't particularly wish to run into him in a bar nearly fifteen years after he'd made a colossal fool of her.

*And for heaven's sake, why does any of this even matter? Just go in, have a glass of wine, talk with Kenny—then claim exhaustion and leave. Getting this evening behind you will put you one night closer to going home—to your* real *home, your real life.*

Having steeled herself with that little pep talk, she boldly grabbed the door handle and pulled.

Garth's "That Summer" filled her ears as she followed Debbie inside. A long bar lined the left wall, two pool tables sat in the back near an old-fashioned jukebox, and the rest of the room was dotted with mismatched tables and chairs. Few of the tables were occupied, but a small group stood around watching Kenny and an older version of a boy she recognized from high school shoot pool. Light laughter rose at something Kenny said.

Trish spotted Rowdy behind the bar then—older, too, but still red-haired, although it looked thinner than when she'd known him before. He chatted with a dark-haired guy seated on a stool across from him, and her eyes stuck on the tattoo of a cobra coiled on the guy's muscular biceps, which moved slightly when he lifted his beer bottle for a drink. Something inside her stirred unexpectedly, making her wonder when she'd started finding snake tattoos sexy.

She usually thought anything having to do with snakes was pretty ooky, and if she were going to get something permanently engraved on her arm, it would not have been a member of the reptile family. But something about *this* snake seemed to appeal to her inner biker chick. Although it was the first time she realized she *had* an inner biker chick.

It was only when the tattoo guy glanced in her direction that she nearly fainted.

Joe.

His warm gaze locked on her instantly and she knew he was just as surprised to see her as she was to see him. She couldn't blame him—it had been almost half their lives ago that they'd spent long summer nights writhing against each other in that old Trans Am, or anywhere else they could steal a few minutes alone, and suddenly, here she was, walking into the Last Chance.

Of course, nearly fainting wasn't just about seeing Joe. It was about seeing Joe looking like the hottest thing ever poured into a pair of faded blue jeans. It was about his thick, dark hair—just as lustrous as when she'd last run her hands through it. It was about his jaw, covered with heavier stubble than when he'd been a boy. It was about broad shoulders and well-muscled arms and suddenly being faced with an all-grown-up version of Joe Ramsey who could probably get a woman on her back with no more than a look—the look he happened to be casting in her direction right now. Oh boy.

"Don't kill me," Debbie begged next to her, voice quiet. "I didn't know, I swear."

Trish switched her gaze to her friend and spoke low, through clenched teeth. "Too bad. You're dead."

Debbie tried to look hopeful, although her eyes were still bolted open too wide. "You look great, though—if it helps."

Trish glanced down at her capri pants and sandals, fleetingly wishing she'd paid more attention to what she wore tonight. Not that she cared what Joe Ramsey thought. She most certainly didn't. But thank God she at least had on a pretty top that showed a little cleavage.

At the other end of the bar, Joe set his beer down and leisurely pushed to his feet. Wow. If the profile had been good, the full frontal was no less than devastating. A snug white T-shirt bearing the Porsche logo stretched across his chest. He was bigger than in high school—not muscle-bound, but the kind of guy you knew could win a bar fight hands down and probably *had* won a few. And his eyes—oh God, his eyes were still just as blue, even from across the room. She stood frozen in place as he moved toward her, trying like hell to look as confident as she'd planned before coming inside. Of course, that had been before Joe.

His gaze paralyzed her further. "Hey, cupcake."

Damn, his voice had gotten deep. And the old pet name was almost enough to bury her.

"Hey," she managed. *Why couldn't you be fat and bald and ugly?* And why on earth hadn't Debbie told her? Debbie had told her a considerable number of things about Joe over the years, but she'd neglected to mention that he'd turned out sizzling hot.

He looked to Debbie. "Deb."

"Hey, Joe." Debbie lifted a hand but looked uncomfortable, even though Trish knew Debbie saw him all the time.

The most gorgeous blue eyes God had ever made turned back to Trish, reminding her once more—this really *was* God's country. "Been a while."

A lifetime. *Are you thinking of it, too? That last night? Hell, that whole last summer. All that kissing and touching.* "Yeah."

"I'm gonna go talk to Kenny," Debbie said in a rush, then flitted across the room before Trish could stop her. She firmly planned to murder Deb for leaving her, but she had bigger things to deal with at the moment.

"What brings you to town?" He spoke in so unhurried a manner that Trish thought she must have imagined his surprise at seeing her—he was utterly cool and collected, his every word somehow seductive.

She swallowed, trying to clear the nervous sludge from her throat. "Just here to help my parents with some legal issues."

He tipped his head back lightly. "Heard they're selling the diner."

She nodded. "Retiring. They'll just be running the farm now." Her dad had always kept a herd of beef cattle in addition to running the restaurant on Main Street.

"So . . . Deb says you live in Indy."

Another numb nod on her part.

"And you're a lawyer, right? She said you work at a big firm downtown. Sounds like things turned out good for you."

"Yeah." *Although you wouldn't know from my sparkling conversation that I have half a brain in my head.* Time to rectify that, act more like a normal person just running into an old . . . *friend.* "She tells me you bought Shermer's Garage." He'd always loved cars and had worked there repairing them in high school. It's where he'd gotten the money for the used Trans Am.

He nodded. "I specialize in foreign makes now, though."

Yeah, she knew that, too. Given that he was still Kenny's best friend, it was impossible not to know things about him. Not that she'd asked. Okay, maybe she had. Occasionally. Just casually, whenever his name came up.

But she didn't see any reason to act like she and Debbie sat around talking about him all the time, so she didn't admit she knew. And she even considered telling him she was happy he'd done well for himself—but instead she simply forced a small smile and said, "That's great. So . . . how's your family?"

He shoved his hands in his front pockets and she cringed inside, remembering. His mom had died. Less than a year after Trish had left Eden. A bad car accident. She'd cried for him when she'd heard.

"I'm sorry," she said quickly. "I mean, Debbie told me about your mom back when it happened." For some reason, she couldn't quite meet his eyes any longer—the topic was too awful, and she'd just tossed it carelessly out between them without meaning to.

"It's okay, Trish—it was a long time ago."

She raised her eyes automatically—it was the first time he'd said her name. She sighed, bit her lip, and tried to move on. "Your dad? Your sister? She must be all grown up now. How are *they?*"

"Dad lives in Florida—he remarried. And Jana just moved to Ohio. She got a job there and met a guy. She's twenty-five now." He didn't look particularly happy about any of it, but Joe's family life never *had* been particularly happy, and she regretted bringing it up.

Time to go. "Well . . . it was, uh, nice to see you." She pointed absently toward the pool tables. "I'm gonna go catch up with Debbie and Kenny."

She started to walk away—when a warm vise closed around her wrist, stopping her. She glanced down to see Joe's large, tanned hand—and dear God, moisture surged between her thighs, just from that.

She jerked her gaze up to his, still deep blue and penetrating.

"It was nice to see you, too, cupcake."

Their gazes held for another scintillating moment.

And then he let her go, and she was treading across the floor, but she didn't feel it beneath her, didn't feel the greetings suddenly being passed her way by old friends or the hug from Kenny—all she felt was Joe's stare on her backside and the tingling sensation still pulsing in her panties. And there suddenly wasn't a *bleck* to be found in her mind. Nope, it was all about *wow* now. And *mmm*. And maybe *ah*.

And as she went about returning all the hellos and trying to make sure she called everyone by the right name as she answered questions about her job and her life, she kept hearing the words her father had imparted a very long time ago, when Joe had first kissed her in the bleachers at a basketball game and asked her to the fall dance. *That boy's trouble. Pure trouble.*

He'd been so right. *And in more ways than you even know, Dad.*

Who'd have thought *now*, though, at the age of thirty-two, Joe Ramsey would still be dealing out trouble to her? Yet here it was—a *lustful* kind of trouble, and an innately *adult* kind of lust, filling her body with a more consuming need than she'd felt in . . . oh God, maybe ever. How the hell had *that* happened?

"Wanna play, Trish?" Kenny asked.

She flinched, but then saw he held up a pool cue. For a second, she'd had the crazy notion he could read her mind and knew she was thinking dirty thoughts about his best friend. She lifted a hand to wave off the cue. "No, no thanks—I'll just watch."

"Aw, come on—I've already beat on *these* two guys." Wiping thinning blond hair off his forehead, he motioned to his previous opponents, the vaguely familiar one donning a John Deere T-shirt, and another guy wearing a Ford cap over scruffy brown hair. She began to feel a bit overdressed, even just in capris and a silky camisole. "And I beat all the girls *last* week. I need some new blood."

She laughed lightheartedly but was secretly thinking—*No way in hell*. She'd never played pool in her life, so she wasn't about to start now in a room where she already felt uncomfortable. "Well, if you've beat all of *them*, you'd definitely beat *me*. Afraid I'll have to be a spectator."

"*I'll* play you again, honey," Debbie offered, wrapping both her arms around one of his. She smiled up at him so dreamily— still, after all this time—that Trish suffered a small twinge of wistful jealousy over their happiness.

Kenny touched his finger to the tip of Debbie's nose. "I've got different games planned for you later, lambchop," he said on a slightly intoxicated chuckle. "But you're no competition when it comes to pool. I need to find somebody I've never beat before. New blood. Fresh meat." He spread his arms to the bar at large, starting in with more bravado. "Come on, who wants to get their ass whipped in a friendly little game of pool?"

"You've never beat *me*."

Trish looked up to see that Joe had ambled across the room to make his way into the crowd. Crap. She'd thought she'd escaped him. Now, as she studied him, she wondered if anyone could see the waves of pure desire radiating from her. Or the fact that she was starting to sweat. She wondered if her nipples were showing through.

*That boy's trouble.*

*Pure trouble.*

Kenny was laughing uproariously. "I've beat you plenty, man. Probably a million times."

Joe pulled back as if surprised, a grin tugging at his mouth. "You've had one too many, buddy. You're thinking of somebody else."

But Kenny shook his head, trying to hide his own smile. "Come on now—admit it. I've beat the hell out of you at least twenty times at this very table."

And Trish realized that as much as things changed, they stayed the same. Back in high school, Joe and Kenny had shared a running joke where they each claimed to be superior at whatever sport or game or skill arose. And on it went.

"Nope. Give me that cue and I'll prove it," Joe said.

"Careful, guys," Debbie chimed in. "There are witnesses tonight—we'll all *see* who actually wins."

"That's the point," Joe replied, snatching the stick from Kenny's grasp and reaching for a square of chalk. "Pretty soon, these guys'll be wanting to hang with *me* on Friday night." He motioned to Kenny's pool buddies, no longer holding in his grin—and dear God above, Trish had forgotten how powerful it shone at full wattage. Yow.

As Kenny racked the balls and Joe took another drink of his beer, Trish moved toward Debbie, grabbed her wrist, and pulled her aside. She'd just made a decision. For the good of her mental health. She couldn't stay here and keep torturing herself. It was like watching them make those enormous slabs of fudge through a window at a candy shop—but being allergic to fudge. Why watch Joe Ramsey move around that pool table in those perfect blue jeans with that snake twitching on his arm every time he made a shot when he was a total impossibility in her life?

"What's up?" Debbie asked, all innocence, lifting a finger to push her much-daintier-than-in-high-school glasses up her nose.

"I'm taking off."

Debbie blinked. "We just got here. You haven't even had a drink."

Oh yeah, *that* was what she needed right now—alcohol in her system, something to blur her judgment. "I'm exhausted. It just hit me. And I really need to start looking over the requested contract changes for the diner. I'll call you tomorrow. We'll plan that potato-hurling dinner you offered me. I don't get a lot of potato-hurling in my world, so it'll be good for me."

Slowly, Debbie's mouth unfurled into a suspicious grin, and Trish realized maybe she'd been talking a little too rapidly, overexplaining her departure. "Is it that horrible?" Debbie asked.

She played dumb. "Is *what* that horrible?"

"The effect he still has on you."

Deciding denial was futile, Trish let out a short little conceding *harrumph*. "Why didn't you tell me?"

Debbie tilted her head, still smiling. "About?"

"You know good and well what about." She glanced back to the pool table in time to see Joe draw back his cue and break, the balls scattering with a clatter. As predicted, the snake on his arm rippled, and for some reason, it made her flinch between her legs.

Debbie no longer feigned ignorance. "I didn't see the point. Didn't figure you'd enjoy knowing he was God's gift to women."

True enough. Yet Debbie had never exactly been known for keeping anything to herself. "Maybe not, but . . . since when did you learn to keep secrets?"

Deb sighed. "Maybe I was just trying to look out for your feelings or something—ever think of that?"

"Oh."

"And besides, the fact that Joe is God's gift to women isn't exactly a secret around here."

Trish spoke quietly, voicing the thought that had just occurred to her. "I bet there are a lot, huh?"

"Women?"

Trish nodded.

And Debbie's eyes grew predictably wide as she said, "Well, *yeah*. I mean, look at him. He practically has to beat them off with a stick."

Trish looked—again. This time he was smiling as he said, "Four in the corner," then plunked the solid purple ball easily in the pocket.

"Easy shot, compadre," Kenny said. "Snake didn't even dance."

So Trish wasn't the only one who'd noticed how *active* Joe's tattoo could be. She turned back to Debbie. "Does he? Beat them off?"

Deb tilted her head. "Not really. Not that he tells me about his sex life, but . . . his bedpost definitely has a lot of notches."

*Swell.*

Not that she knew why she cared. In fact, she didn't. This was ridiculous. This whole *night* was ridiculous. "Well, anyway, I'm going. Tell Kenny I said bye and that we'll visit longer later."

Only Debbie grabbed her arm. Seemed *everybody* was grabbing her arm since she'd walked in here. "You shouldn't go. It'll look like you're running."

*That's because I am.* "I couldn't care less."

"Come on, Trish—don't be this way. Get over the past."

But the past wasn't the problem. It was the present. The present lust thrumming through her veins and into her most sensitive areas. The present fear that if he touched her again, she'd dissolve. She'd *known* she should have refused Debbie's invitation tonight. "I'm over it. That doesn't mean I want to socialize with the guy."

Debbie started in with a knowing, repetitive nod. "Oh, I think you'd like to socialize, all right. I think you'd like to socialize him right into bed."

*Which is why I need to leave.* "You're out of your mind," she said instead.

"Look, if you just stay and see that you can have a good time in the same group with him, think how freeing that'll be. Because say what you will about how over it you are—we both know what a huge deal it was when it happened, and we both know it's what got you in the habit of not coming home very often. It's time you face this demon."

Damn it. Debbie was right. Although it wasn't that Trish had spent fourteen years away from Eden in order to avoid Joe Ramsey. Almost from the day she'd decided to pursue law, it had become her life—her work kept her in the city a lot, most recently because she was busy trying to make partner. But Joe *was* the main reason she'd stayed away in the beginning, and it had started a pattern.

And hell, if she stayed a while, maybe he'd do something to make her really dislike him. Really disliking a guy could kill lust fast. Or maybe he'd become drunk and disorderly—another thing that could squash her attraction to him in a heartbeat.

So she would force herself to stay, watch the guys play pool, act like a normal person, and face her demon.

She just wished the demon weren't so darn sexy.

\*　　\*　　\*

Twenty minutes later, Trish had watched Joe and his snake beat Kenny twice. Of course, Kenny was drunk, so that obviously made Joe's work easier.

But she hadn't really been watching the game. She'd been watching Joe's body as he bent over the table, stretching out long, muscular, and lean, his butt appearing just as firm in that denim as she remembered it from all those years ago. She'd been watching the confident little twitch at his lips—too cool to smile—each time he made a shot. And she'd been watching his eyes—focused, sparkling when he laughed—and she'd found herself annoyingly disappointed that they never raised back to her, not through the whole two games.

Debbie had strayed to the bar at some point for a beer, but Trish had insisted she didn't want anything to drink. Intoxication and Joe Ramsey just didn't mix.

"I'm going to the bathroom," she announced to her friend.

"The window's too small to climb through, just so you know."

Trish ignored that and retreated to the small, dank room. She found herself looking in the pockmarked mirror, freshening her lipstick, trying to fluff her blond hair and hoping the darker roots weren't showing too badly. Then an irritating thought hit her—*Why on earth do you care? And what does it matter that he didn't look at you when he was shooting pool? You said it yourself—he's not even a remote possibility.*

Fortunately, she came up with a satisfactory answer. *I just want him to think I look good.* No crime in that. Who *didn't* want their old boyfriends to think they were hot?

So that meant it was perfectly okay to add a little mascara, too.

When she exited the bathroom, she found the pool area deserted, then realized her group—although she hesitated to think of them as *her* group—had pulled together a couple of small tables and sat down around them. One chair in the circle was empty—and it was next to Joe.

She glared at Debbie, who grinned and shrugged. One more reason to plan a painful demise for her friend. Since nothing could happen between her and Joe. Since he was fudge and she was allergic.

Joe had turned his chair around backwards to straddle it, balancing his muscular arms across the back. Trish drew in a deep breath, pulled out her own chair, and took a seat, careful not to bump him. Bumping, though, she discovered, really wasn't necessary to create trouble here—just having him that close to her made her *feel* him, smell the musky scent of him. She found herself glancing down at his thigh, the denim stretched snug across it. She flashed back to all the times it had been pressed between *her* thighs.

"So you're a big lawyer in Indy, huh?"

Trish cringed, yanking her gaze upward to the scruffy brown-haired guy she now realized was Tommy Hudson from their class, his cap shading his face. *Act normal. As opposed to overwhelmed with carnal desire.*

She tried for a laugh. "Well, I don't know about big."

"Oh, don't be modest," Debbie said. "Trish works for Tate, Blanchard & Rowe downtown and has been named Best Up-and-Coming Attorney in Indiana by . . ." She looked at Trish. "What's the name of that magazine?"

Trish shook her head. "Not important." She felt far enough removed from these people as it was—she didn't want to distance herself even further. "I'm just thankful to have a job I love."

Everyone nodded, but no one responded, and Trish feared even *that* had been the wrong thing to say. At least three of the table's occupants worked at the local food-processing plant—they probably weren't doing a "job they loved."

"I know what you mean." The deep voice came from her right, and when she turned to Joe, she was startled again to find how close he was—their faces mere inches apart. His eyes met hers briefly, then he shifted his gaze to the rest of the group. "Makes earning a living a lot easier if you like what you do."

He was rescuing her, she realized. Reminding them all that *he* did something *he* loved—that attaining your goals wasn't reserved for the uppity girl who'd left town and never come back.

Joyce Carnes, another girl from school, there with one of Kenny's buddies, added, "I just got my hairdresser's license. I'm cutting hair down at Sophie's, and so far, it's a whole lot better than the factory." The one that made the tin cans for the food-processing plant, Trish presumed.

She smiled, happy for Joyce, and happy that Joyce was making her feel more normal. "That's great—how long have you been at it?"

"Three months—and I don't even mind getting up in the morning anymore."

"You guys need another round?" Trish looked up to see Rowdy Lancaster. "Hey there, Trish—remember me?"

She nodded. "Of course. How are you, Rowdy?"

"Fair enough. This place keeps me busy, but I like it. What can I get you to drink?"

"A glass of Merlot would be great."

Rowdy pursed his lips and the table went silent.

Finally, Joe said, "Don't think Rowdy has that."

Not just Merlot, he meant—wine, period. She looked up at Rowdy again. "How about a cosmopolitan?"

Rowdy blinked, looked slightly confused, then shook his head.

*You're not in the city anymore.* She made her next choice more carefully. "A screwdriver?"

Rowdy grinned. "Vodka and OJ, coming up." He looked around the table. "Another beer for everybody else?"

And Trish sighed. She was the odd man out here, no disguising it—the freak-of-nature lawyer in capri pants who didn't drink beer. She planned to slug down her drink quickly and get the hell out of here. An hour of this agony was enough—enough to "make nice" with Joe, enough to please Debbie.

Just then, the jukebox spouted out a new song—some country ballad Trish didn't know. "My song!" Debbie screeched, and Trish laughed inside. Ever since high school, any song that Debbie liked she claimed as her own. She must have thousands by now. Debbie grabbed Kenny's arm. "We have to dance!"

Kenny rolled his eyes yet took his wife's hand and pulled her to her feet as he glanced to the rest of them. "Gotta keep her happy." He tried to look put upon but failed.

Before Trish knew it, the other two girls at the table had cajoled their men up to dance, as well. Which left . . . her and Joe. Sitting elbow to elbow, shoulder to snake. She couldn't remember the last time she'd felt this awkward, but it had probably been in high school. "So . . ." she said.

He rested his chin on his crossed arms and looked at her. "Little weird, huh?" he asked, offering half a grin.

*I'd go so far as to say surreal.* But she just nodded, returning a small smile. "Yeah."

His gaze dropped to her wrist, to the thin gold bracelet she wore. Tiny gold cat charms hung from it at one-inch intervals. "Still got a thing for cats, huh?"

Everything inside her tightened as she was forced to remember that cat necklace he'd given her. Despite what had happened between them, she'd worn it anyway, because she'd liked it, and because it had seemed like a good way to tell herself he didn't matter—as opposed to throwing away a perfectly good necklace. It had started a trend in her life—friends had started giving her cat-themed jewelry and eventually home décor, and they still did. She owned black cat bookends, she hung her bathrobe on a pewter cat whose tail formed a hook, and a big rustic folk-art print of an orange tiger cat hung over the dining table in her downtown loft. And never before this moment had she realized—let herself acknowledge or remember—that it had all started with the little keepsake Joe had given her that last night. Whoa.

"Yeah," she said, hoping her strange reaction hadn't shown in her eyes. "I guess I do."

"Do you have any? Cats? At your place in the city?"

She would have liked to, only . . . "I'm not home enough. But Mom and Dad still have Pumpkin's two kids—Pickles and Morris. Good mousers, my dad says. Although they're getting old now."

The look in his eyes told her he was remembering the cat necklace, too. And the kitten he'd given her. Then the corners of his mouth quirked softly. "I didn't know Pumpkin had kids. In fact, I didn't even know Pumpkin was a girl."

She remembered how hard it could be to tell with kittens sometimes, then laughed lightly. "Yeah, I got an angry phone call from my mom at college, telling me *that cat* I'd left behind was pregnant. Although they managed to give away all but the two, who are both boys, so no more surprises since then."

Joe smiled, but then sighed, letting the amusement fade from his eyes. "Truth is, cupcake, I'm glad to have a minute alone with you." Like before, the old nickname seemed to bore into her, reattach her to him somehow.

"Oh?"

He spoke slowly. "I've never had a chance to apologize."

She broke eye contact, heat ascending her cheeks. Oh, hell— was it possible she still felt that awful hurt? Or was she just embarrassed all over again remembering the betrayal? She spoke kindly but firm. "It was a long time ago, and I got *over* it a long time ago, so there's no need."

"There is," he insisted. "For me, anyway. I . . ." He shook his head, as if at a loss. "I'll never know what got into me that night."

She cautiously returned a soft gaze to his, even managed a grin. "I do. Beer. And hormones."

He shrugged concedingly. "Guess that pretty much sums it up." And she didn't realize she'd quit looking at him again until he lifted her chin with one bent finger. The touch moved through her like liquid as their eyes met. "I wished for a long time I could tell you how sorry I was, but you said you didn't want to hear from me and I took you at your word. Now that you're here, though, I can finally tell you. I'm sorry, Trish."

The words hung between them like something volatile, alive. Part of her wanted to *really* talk to him, really discuss it like two normal, mature adults. But a bigger part of her couldn't go there, couldn't give the past that much presence in her life today. So she took the easier road. "It's all right, Joe. It's ancient history and there's no reason to dredge it up. Life went on and we're both fine. Right?"

He took a moment answering, those warm blue eyes nearly drowning her. "Right."

Fairly desperate to lighten the mood, she pointed at the snake curled on his arm. "What's this?"

He glanced down at it, then at her, amused. "It's called a tattoo."

She raised her eyebrows. "But . . . a snake? Why a snake?"

"Not just a snake," he pointed out. "A cobra."

She could tell from his tone of voice that it actually meant something to him, but she still had no idea what. "What's so special about cobras?"

"I have one. Not a snake—a car. I've spent the last eight years restoring a 1967 427 Shelby Cobra. I just put the finishing touches on a few months ago."

A Shelby Cobra. Trish wasn't sure, but she thought one of the top partners in her firm had fought over the same model of car in his divorce settlement—and if so, it was a fairly valuable vehicle. Just how well *was* Joe doing for himself? "So you celebrated by getting a tattoo?" she asked with a half smile.

"Not exactly. Got the tattoo about five years back. Remember Billy Sturgis? We were out drinking one night over near Cincinnati. Tattoo place was next to the bar, so we both decided to get one. I was deep into the restoration then, so the cobra made sense."

"What did Billy get?"

The corners of his mouth quirked. "Not a damn thing. I went first and he backed out after he figured out it hurt."

Just then, Debbie's song faded into another slow country tune, one Trish actually knew—a sexy song by Billy Currington called, "Must Be Doing Something Right." Joe reached for her hand, closing it in his. "Dance with me."

Oh boy. The request, the warm hand—together, they were as paralyzing as when she'd first seen him tonight. But she had no intention of dancing with him. Dancing would mean touching, swaying. You couldn't dance to *this* song *without* swaying.

Just then, Rowdy arrived with a tray full of beer bottles and one lone mixed drink, and she thought, *Saved by the bartender.* When he set it before her, she drew her fingers from Joe's and took a long sip. She still didn't want to drink much, but she needed a little fortification, and it gave her something safer to do with her hands.

Yet as soon as Rowdy departed, Joe took the glass right back out of her grasp and set it down, then drew her to her feet as easily as if she'd been a rag doll without a brain.

And she let him. Just plain let him. Because it was so easy. And who could resist a nice, sexy slab of fudge—allergic or not? Simple as that, she let him pull her a few steps from the table; she let him take her in his arms.

Clearly, Joe Ramsey had never learned the art of dancing any differently than he had in a dark high school gym—his hands settled low on her hips and their torsos pressed gently together. Her arms came to rest around his neck, same as if she'd last danced with him like this yesterday.

And her body was *responding* just as it had in high school— only much stronger. Back then, she wouldn't have believed a girl could yearn for a guy's touch more intensely than she'd yearned for Joe's at the time—but she'd been so very wrong. The small of her back ached with pleasure and need, delivering the urge to crush herself against him—but then she realized they were *already* pushed pretty tightly together, her breasts to his chest, their pelvises aligned. When had *that* happened? And why hadn't she kept a reasonable distance between them?

*Because you're melting. And because you're beginning to lose complete control over this situation. He's fudge, after all.*

"This is nice, Trish." Yet he hadn't said it like it was nice. He'd said it like he was turned on, his voice low and smoldering.

"Yeah." Had she just said that? Oh God—she had. Although, to her horror, she hadn't really *said* it so much as *breathed* it.

And then things somehow turned very slow and hard to fathom.

She knew only his hands, caressing her back, all over.

His breath, coming heavy and deep in her ear, on her neck.

His hips, beginning to move, ever-so-gently, and sexy, against hers.

And not just his hips. Oh my—she could *feel* him. Hardening against her. Softly grinding. Darkness hid the sight, leaving the intimate friction a secret only the two of them shared, and her eyes fell shut, absorbing the sensation. This was *way* better than fudge.

She needed more of him now. Not just that rock-solid part, but the rest of him, too. She needed to run her hands over all these muscles he hadn't possessed when they were young. She needed to touch the stubble on his face, kiss his mouth—hard.

But—dear God—where had her sanity gone?

*Push him away. Say you've had enough dancing, you need to go buy some fudge, anything.*

Yet an overwhelming magnetism had come into play now, one she couldn't break free of. Especially when he peered heatedly down at her, then brushed an agonizingly soft kiss across her lips.

She made a sound. Like a moan. Low but potent. She hated that she'd let it leak out, but like everything else tonight, it seemed beyond her control. That tiny little kiss had just stirred her more deeply than *sex* with *some* men.

"Damn, Trish, I'm sorry—I didn't plan it like this." His voice was like a hot breeze. "But some things never change, I guess."

Oh Lord. What the hell to say to *that*. She had no idea.

He pulled back slightly, his blue eyes gone dark and completely possessive as he said, "Come home with me."

*Whoa*. Come home with him?

She understood how he'd gotten all those proverbial notches in his bedpost—he might not know how people outside of Eden danced, but he was clearly schooled in the art of seduction. And she was completely aroused by everything about him—yet it wasn't that simple. There was no way she could let him seduce her like this, just no way. Betrayed once because she wouldn't do it, then bedded for a night because now she was grown up and she would? A few short minutes ago he'd been earnestly apologizing for the past and now he was asking her to sleep with him? She was not the chaste, untouched girl she'd been in high school, but she couldn't become just another conquest for him, either.

"No," she said, proud she sounded so darn sure.

He didn't look surprised, just disappointed. And, as he always had, he used his eyes to plead with her, to look sincere and sexy all at once. "Come on, Trish. Let me show you what you missed."

Oh. *Ouch*. His words swept her smoothly back to a very old passion in the midst of this very *new* passion—and it would have been ridiculously easy to give in.

But it was a matter of pride. And principle. She'd gotten *over* the past, yet she hadn't *forgotten* it. And to let him seduce her—to let him hear her say no, yet then convince her to say yes—seemed like the ultimate way he could conquer her. Even if conquering was the last thing on his mind, she would still feel that way. She couldn't let him make her feel so conquered again.

She pressed her palms to his chest, an attempt to put a little distance between them. "For your information, I've already been shown *plenty*. I'm not eighteen anymore." *So there. I've had sex. With lots of other guys. Well, some. But either way, you ceased being the center of my sexual universe a very long time ago.*

Yet her attempt at separating them had failed woefully because their hips remained glued together and their bodies still moved slowly to the music. And his voice was little more than a growl when he said, "I could show you more."

Oh my.

She believed him. Completely. And the juncture of her thighs tingled madly. *Welcome back to my sexual universe.* She'd never in her life indulged in a one-night-stand, but if Joe were a stranger, tonight she would've—the animal attraction was that potent.

Only he *wasn't* a stranger. *You have to remember that. This is Joe. The Joe. The first-love, cheating, heartbreaking jerk Joe.* And she simply couldn't let him have his way with her *now*. It would only add insult to that long-ago injury. "No thanks," she said, trying to sound far cooler than she felt.

Above her, he let out a thwarted sigh, even as his erection settled deeper against her. "How long are you in town?"

She sucked in her breath. He was so hard. Then she bit her lip. And kept dancing. Moving with him, *against* him. "I'm not exactly sure. A week or so."

"Let me see you again."

Oh God. "No."

"Why not?"

She sighed, exasperated . . . tempted. "I don't have to give you a reason."

"No," he said slowly, "but the way you're dancing with me makes me think it doesn't have anything to do with not wanting to be near me."

His words weakened her even more. He could see through her. And despite herself, she kind of wanted to let him see *all* of her.

Except—she couldn't, she just couldn't. "This can't go any further."

His voice came low and persuasive. "I don't know why not. We still have every ounce of chemistry we ever had."

Part of her wanted to just tell him the truth—*You can't have me because you hurt me once, and you don't deserve me. And after all we shared back then, I refuse to be simply another notch added to your bedpost, one more instance where you do whatever feels good without caring who gets hurt.*

But she'd told him she was over that, and she was. She didn't want to start bringing emotions into this. She liked letting him see the confident, assured woman she'd grown into, and she wasn't going to let him take that away. And she was going to start hiding the lusty part of herself better, too.

"You're right," she finally admitted. "We have chemistry, always did. But going to bed with you is the last thing I came home for. And I hear you show a *lot* of women what I missed, so if you need it tonight, I suggest you get it someplace else."

Wow, she'd sounded good saying all that. Now she only had to grab her purse and leave and this would be over. No more fudge, and once it was no longer right in front of her, she'd be glad she'd resisted.

So, breaking free from the dance, she snatched her bag and turned to go. But she hadn't counted on him blocking her way—a solid wall of heat and sexuality. She lifted her gaze from his broad chest to his determined expression.

"You still think I'm a rotten guy."

"No, actually, I don't. But that has nothing to do with sex."

He spoke quietly enough that no one else could hear. "I want you so much right now I can barely breathe."

God, his words nearly made her *own* throat close up. She never could have imagined when she'd first seen him on that bar stool that something like this could happen—and so fast she'd barely had a chance to think. It would still be easy to give in. To just say, *Take me home. Have your way with me.*

But how would she feel afterward?

Weak. Used. *Conquered.*

Even if he didn't mean it that way.

The fact that they shared a turbulent history changed everything.

So she said, "It's not gonna happen," instead.

"You want it, too," he insisted.

She tried to be pissed at his arrogance, but the truth in it—his innate knowledge that they were both sharing the same burning desire—somehow just excited her that much more. Damn it. "Do you hear yourself?" she asked anyway. "When did you get this ego?"

*Probably as the notches had started accumulating.*

Yet his eyes went a deeper shade of blue. "I don't need an ego with you, Trish. It's just the way things are. We still want each other."

She swallowed, hard—but forced herself to stay strong. "I'm leaving. Move, please."

Despite her demand, he still stood confident before her, looking so brutally sexy that she could barely catch her breath. "We both know this isn't gonna go away."

She couldn't break the gaze for a moment. And she also couldn't deny what he'd just said.

But she *had* to deny it. She had to end this. "It just did," she said. Then she pushed past him, ignoring Debbie's questioning eyes as she strode past her and Kenny to step out into one more hot summer night in Eden, Indiana.

Free at last, free at last.

But maybe you were only as free as you felt.

And at the moment, she felt completely captivated by Joe Ramsey.

**Witness:** a person who testifies to what they saw, heard, observed, or did, in a court of law; _or_ to see, hear, or know by personal presence and perception.

# Two

The next morning, Joe slid onto his usual stool at the Waffle House, regretting the night before. If he'd been a heavier drinker, he'd be battling a pounding head and blaming last night—like one other night, long ago—on too much beer. As it was, he had nothing to blame it on but his dick.

Beverly turned toward the counter, red-dyed hair pulled back in a low ponytail. "Morning, Joe. Usual?" She wore a flirtatious smile.

He didn't smile back—he never did with Beverly—but gave a short nod, then listened as she spouted off his regular order of eggs, sausage, and hash browns to Floyd, the elderly cook who'd been manning the griddle for as long as Joe could remember.

"You look tired," she said, placing a fork atop a small napkin in front of him, then pouring his coffee.

"Late night." Not really, but it felt the same. He'd headed home soon after Trish had left—just hadn't gotten a hell of a lot of sleep.

She cocked her head. "Anybody I know?" She tried to sound casual, but he knew better.

And he figured *this* oughta knock her socks off. "Trish Henderson."

Bev's eyes widened, as expected, and her back went stiff. "Really? Trish is in town?"

Another short nod. "Yep." No more details, though, because it was none of Bev's business. Time to change the subject. "Carissa need anything?"

Carissa was Beverly's thirteen-year-old daughter, who she'd quietly let people assume Joe had fathered all those years ago after their one night together. He'd had reason to question it, so he had, and the DNA had proved he was right—yet he'd already taken on a role in Carissa's life by then, so he'd never exactly left it.

Most people who didn't know the DNA results—which meant almost everybody—thought he was a jackass for not claiming her, and maybe he should have. Maybe he should have just told the lie, been her dad. But those days had been strange, murky. His mom had just died. His dad had just left. And he'd been watching his little sister suffer the losses.

Still, he hadn't wanted Beverly's daughter to go through life without any sort of father figure, so despite never naming himself as her dad, he'd stuck around. He'd been trying like hell to do the right thing, maybe in some effort to fix everything else that had been so royally fucked up at the time.

Now he didn't think through all those whys and ifs anymore— he just made sure Carissa had what she needed when Bev's waitress salary didn't stretch far enough. And as for the people who criticized him—screw 'em. It was none of their business, just like last night was none of Bev's.

As usual when Carissa's needs came up, Beverly looked sheepish. "School's starting and I guess she could use some new blue jeans. And she's joining the chorus and needs a nice pair of black pants."

"School supplies?"

She shrugged, still reticent but practical. These were the only times he felt bad for her, since he knew she didn't like asking for money. "I'm sure she'll need some. She has to have some special calculator for advanced algebra."

He gave another quiet nod. "I'll drop a check by."

Her eyes looked more doleful now than flirtatious. "Thanks, Joe."

"Order up!" Floyd called behind her, and Joe watched Bev move to grab his plate and lower it before him, then pad to a nearby booth to wait on a trucker who'd just ambled in. Good.

Even now, after all this time, he tried to keep his contact with Bev short and to the point. He knew she worked hard, and she did her best to be a good mom to Carissa—but hell, she *still* greeted him with that same come-hither expression every time he walked into the Waffle House. She was still flirting, still hoping. One ill-fated night together and she'd never moved on.

Just then, she lifted her gaze toward the door, her eyes lighting. "Well, hey, look who it is."

He knew from her tone even before glancing up, but turned to see Carissa dragging her grandfather by the wrist through the plate-glass door. "Grandpa wanted waffles before we start working," she announced.

"Hey, Care Bear," Joe said easily.

"Hey, Joe. What's up?" She hopped onto the stool next to him in denim shorts and a fitted T-shirt that reminded him she was starting to look like a girl. He tried not to let that worry him.

"Just grabbing a little breakfast before I drive a car up to Brookville. What are you and your gramps up to today?"

She rolled big brown eyes. "Yard work."

He cast a playfully scolding look. "You'll survive."

"Darn right she will," Beverly's dad, Willie, replied, landing a hand on her shoulder. "Little hard work never hurt anybody. Just ask Joe here—he knows all about it."

Joe and Willie had always gotten along—Willie was one of the few who knew about Carissa's paternity, and Joe realized the man respected him for helping out where he didn't have to. As for how a decent guy like Willie had raised a girl like Bev, Joe didn't know the whole story—only that her mom had never been around and Willie had worked a whole lot back then, too. "Your grandpa's right, Care Bear. Working builds character."

The statement earned him another eye roll. "Yeah, it's real hard driving some fancy car around. I feel *so* sorry for you. What is it? A Porsche? A Jaguar?"

"Porsche," he acknowledged with a soft grin. "A special-edition Boxster." He didn't usually work on weekends *or* deliver cars back to their owners. But this particular customer's wife was battling cancer, so when Joe had sensed that finding time to pick up the car was an issue, he'd offered to make the drive and enlisted Kenny to follow and drive him back.

"Must be nice," Carissa said, eyebrows lifted.

"Yeah, I live a charmed life," he assured her.

"Waffle for you, Care?" Beverly asked.

She nodded as Willie said, "Me, too," and they started talking with Beverly until Joe zoned out, concentrating on his eggs, his sausage . . . and Trish. Damn, he still couldn't believe she'd just waltzed into the Last Chance out of nowhere. He was usually too tired on Friday nights to socialize, but he'd wandered in knowing Kenny and Debbie would be there, his main purpose reminding Kenny about today. He'd never imagined that before the night was through he'd be holding Trish in his arms again.

Just then, Kenny walked in and took the stool on the other side of him, exchanging greetings all around but looking a little worse for wear. "Hangover?" Joe asked once Carissa and her grandpa were back out of the conversation.

Kenny sighed. "You could say that. And by the way, it was pretty damn cheap to challenge me at pool when you knew I was drunk."

Joe gave his usual easy shrug. "I saw an opportunity."

"Made you cocky," Kenny said, then switched his focus to Bev, who was looking his way, order pad in hand. "Just a couple of scrambled eggs and toast." Then he drew his gaze back down to Joe and lowered his voice. "That's the only reason I can figure for you putting the moves on Trish so hard. I mean, all things considered. Like that you hadn't seen her in a thousand years. And the last time you did you were an asshole. What were you thinking, man?"

Joe thoughtfully chewed a bite of sausage, then shoveled some hash browns into his mouth. "Yeah, that didn't go real well, did it?"

Kenny lowered his chin. "Unless you consider it a big success to send her stomping out of a bar in a huff."

He didn't, but he couldn't help taking a little masculine pride in recalling just how *long* it had taken her to reach the stomping part, and how *close* she'd come to giving in to what they'd both wanted.

Joe didn't answer, but his best friend knew him well enough to read his face. "Man, you kill me. You *do* think it was a success."

Joe chuckled softly, although without much amusement. "No. But there for a few minutes . . ." He sighed, letting the memory of her soft body moving against his stay private before moving on to how things had ended. "I went too far too fast, but hell—I was just following my urges."

Kenny cocked his head derisively. "Following urges has been known to get you into trouble a time or two."

Joe couldn't deny that. A mere glance at his waitress served as a grim reminder. But he'd meant what he'd said to Trish—he hadn't planned it, it had just happened. She'd looked damn good, all grown up. And she'd felt even better. Somehow his body had taken over—it had remembered the pattern of him and her, together, and he'd fallen instinctively back into an old, familiar rhythm. "A little warning might have helped," he pointed out to Kenny.

"I forgot."

Joe raised his eyebrows. "You *forgot* my old girlfriend was about to walk into the bar *I'd* just walked into?"

"I was drunk, remember?"

Joe shrugged in understanding, then found himself reliving the moment he'd first seen her, the liquid heat that had rushed through his body, the quick flash of memory and regret and yearning.

"So what now?" Kenny asked.

Joe glanced toward his buddy. "What do you mean?"

"Don't think I didn't hear you last night." Kenny gave his head a rakish tilt and spoke in a deep, hokey voice. "'This isn't gonna go away. We both want each other.'"

Joe rolled his eyes in reply.

"What's your plan, dude?"

Last night, his general plan had been hot pursuit—he'd quickly realized he wanted her just as much now as he ever had. But this morning, well . . . he'd screwed up, and in the light of day he figured the best thing to do was leave her alone. "Nothing."

Kenny blinked and drew back as if Joe had just spouted something crazy. "Nothing?"

Joe forked the last bite of eggs into his mouth. "Maybe I'll . . . give her a call or something, apologize for last night." But even that seemed worthless, considering that he'd just apologized to her for his *last* mistake—right before making the next one. "Other than that, I'm gonna let it go." He wiped his mouth on a napkin.

Kenny's eyes narrowed in doubt and surprise. "Really?"

And Joe understood why. He wasn't the kind of guy who usually shied away from what he wanted. But he lowered his voice again to say, "Even if things were good for a little while, that was just about lust."

Kenny tipped his head back, eyeing Joe warily. "Since when are you against lust?"

"Never. But after last night . . . well, if she didn't hate me *before*, she probably hates me *now.*"

As Beverly lowered Kenny's plate to the counter with a "Here you go," Kenny grimaced at the eggs, still looking sick.

"Hate's a strong word," Kenny said. "But in this case . . . you might be right."

Trish sat in a red vinyl booth in her parents' diner, combing over contract changes. And nibbling on a chunk of chocolate fudge she'd picked up at Sweetie Pie's candy and ice cream shop three doors down on impulse. Damn impulses.

She'd needed to get out of her motel room—where she was staying because her Aunt Alma was currently bunking in her old bedroom at home, recovering from emergency bypass surgery. There was still room for Trish if she'd wanted to stay at her parents' house, but she couldn't help imagining them all tripping over one another and waiting in line for the bathroom—so she'd opted for the Red Roof Inn in town until Aunt Alma headed home in a few days.

She'd told her mom and dad she'd stop by the diner, take a look around, maybe start cleaning and breaking things down—so she'd simply come early and brought the contract with her. But now things felt bleak.

The place she'd known all her life as a busy, bustling restaurant seemed almost dead with quiet. The last daily special, OPEN FACED ROAST BEEF AND MASHED POTATOES, was still spelled out in little plastic letters on the sign behind the cash register, the laminated menus still lay stacked on one end of the counter, and chrome napkin dispensers still graced every Formica table, but seeing the place closed for business made her sad in a way she hadn't anticipated.

And that wasn't the only trouble. No way were these contract changes going to fly. Clearly, the buyer thought her parents were a couple of desperate suckers. The woman had demanded a number of repairs and overhauls, and in a couple of cases even new equipment, all of which would cost thousands of dollars and greatly reduce her parents' profits—which they simply couldn't afford retiring on a fixed income. On Monday she'd have to call Lois Faulkner, her parents' real estate agent, to place a counteroffer—but she wasn't willing to give much. All of this stuff should have been addressed during the initial bidding, not now, weeks later, in the contract.

The contract problems had personal ramifications, too. She'd planned to come here, close this deal for her parents, spend a few more days with them, then hightail it back to Indy. How big of a crimp would this put in her plans?

And sure, she could head back anyway and return to Eden once the deal was worked out, but one quick look around the diner had made something clear. Her parents weren't as young as they used to be. Which she'd known, but . . . she'd quickly realized equipment her dad had claimed was clean actually was not—not clean enough, anyway. Things didn't look as good around here as they could. Her counteroffer was going to include a thorough scouring of the place that might make some of the older equipment appear a lot more promising. And she had a feeling she was going to be needed—if not to do the cleaning herself, then at least to supervise. She sighed, a sadness settling in her bones. Her parents were aging; life was changing.

And all of this meant two big things: She'd be gone from work—and her shot at partner—for longer than planned. And she'd be here—closer to Joe, and his hands, and his mouth—for longer, too. She scarcely knew which worried her more.

No, wait, yes she did. Joe.

She *should* be paralyzed at the thought of being an absentee attorney at the firm where she was trying to build her future, but the real terror coursing through her veins was combined with a hot dose of lust.

Last night had been . . . overwhelming. Nearly. She *had* gotten hold of herself eventually, of course—but just barely. And the truth was, given how the juncture of her thighs tingled even now, just remembering everything about him—the broad shoulders, the captivating eyes, the bulge in his jeans—she wasn't sure she could turn him down a second time.

Of course, she could just stay away from him. Just like if you stayed away from fudge—you weren't tempted if you kept your distance. She licked a bit of melty chocolate off her thumb and realized that Eden held all *kinds* of temptations she hadn't expected.

But she had a feeling staying away from Joe was going to be harder than staying away from fudge—and she hadn't even done very well at *that* so far. After the things he'd said last night, she fully expected him to track her down and attempt to seduce her before she left town. Couple that heated threat with how weak and hot he got her and this was a problem—a big one.

She *refused* to let herself be seduced by him. And yet, what chance did she have of escaping his heat a second time if put in a similar position? She'd always thought of herself as a strong, capable woman, yet last night she'd felt helpless with the same temptation still flooding her right now.

*Sex. With Joe.* The very thought made her heartbeat pound in her ears. *Skin. Sweat. Hunger. Bodies interlocked, moving as one.* She bit her lip. *His hands, touching her. His muscular arms and thighs wrapped around her. That weirdly sensual snake mesmerizing her with its every sexy ripple.*

*Let me show you what you missed.*

Nope, she sincerely doubted she had the strength to turn him down again.

*That boy's trouble. Pure trouble.*

She'd just reached for another bite of fudge when she spotted Debbie peering in the window, her face stuck between the words PIE and BURGERS painted on the glass. Seeing her inside, Deb waved and Trish motioned her in.

"I saw your car," Debbie said, then looked around the diner. "Wow, this is weird. It's so . . . empty."

Trish nodded. "I know. I guess it's no different than being here after hours, but . . . it still *is* in some way, isn't it?"

Debbie tossed her purse in the seat across from Trish and sat down, then spied the fudge. "Oooh, Sweetie Pie's!"

Trish shoved the fudge toward her. "Here, eat it. Get it away from me. I don't want it."

Debbie didn't argue, diving right in to pinch off a bite-sized chunk and plop it in her mouth. "Mmm," she sighed in sugar-filled ecstasy, but then she focused tightly on Trish. "So . . . about last night."

Trish narrowed her gaze on her friend. "I really *should* kill you."

Deb flashed an oh-come-on-now smile. "Why? You looked like you were having fun."

"Before I made a spectacle of myself by storming out, you mean?"

Debbie shrugged. "This town needs some spectacle every now and then."

And Trish sighed. "So glad I could provide the entertainment."

Debbie leaned over the table, looking conspiratorial. "So . . . spill."

"It's pretty simple." She tapped the end of the ink pen in her hand on the table. "He tried to seduce me and I said no. Eventually."

Debbie nodded, seeming to understand—until she said, "Why?"

"*Why?*"

"You're two consenting adults, right?"

Trish blinked. "*No.* Because I don't consent."

Deb gave her head a knowing tilt. "Oh, come on—I saw consent written all over your face in big, bold neon letters."

Trish flashed a pointed look. "What's written on my face now? Annoyance, I hope."

"Among other things. But I think I still see consent, too."

"You're very wrong about that. Lust, maybe." She stopped, snatched up a bite of fudge. "But consent, no way. No way can I let him seduce me. It would be too much like . . . he finally wins or something."

Debbie scrunched up her nose. "Is this a game?"

That's when it hit Trish. Maybe it was. In a way. She'd never in her life thought of sex as a competition, but maybe if she did . . . it would solve all her problems. Or at least one of them. The Joe problem.

"Here's the thing. After what happened when we were young, if I let him seduce me *now*, especially now that I've just turned him down rather profusely . . . well, it *will* be like he wins, like he wore me down, like I'm just another conquest, another bedpost notch. And I couldn't *stand* that, Deb. It would reduce me to . . . well, to the girl I was back then."

"I *liked* that girl. I'm pretty sure you're still her."

"In ways," Trish admitted. "But I'm also a mature, confident chick who does *not* let herself be any guy's conquest. And I intend to stay that way."

"Your loss then, I guess." In the sex department, she knew Debbie meant.

Unless . . . "Maybe not."

Debbie drew back slightly. "Huh?"

Trish took a deep breath, then spit out the idea that had slowly bubbled up inside her over the last few minutes. "I'm going to seduce him."

Debbie flinched. "What? I'm confused. I thought you said you couldn't—"

"No. *I'm* going to seduce *him*. Which is completely different than letting *him* seduce *me*. See?"

"Not really."

"Then you're not paying attention. If I'm the seducer, then I win."

Debbie pursed her lips, looking slightly confused. "And he loses?"

"No. We *both* win. But *I* don't lose. As long as it's very clear that I'm the one doing the seducing, making it happen—as long as it's clear that he hasn't persuaded me. Do you get it yet?"

Debbie nodded, although it was clear she still didn't understand. "Only . . . if you're so dead set on not being seduced, wouldn't it just be easier to keep on saying no? Or better yet, just keep your distance from him?"

Trish raised a finger emphatically in the air. "Easier said than done. The fact is, I'm not that good at saying no anymore. And I'm afraid that if I'd been there with him much longer, or if we'd been alone, I'd have given in. He's too hot. I can't defend myself against that. So I figure if I seduce him first, if it's my decision and not his—I won't feel so much like a flimsy little pushover. If I'm going to have sex with him, I want to be the one to call the shots." The truth was—now that she was forming a plan, having sex with Joe was back to sounding pretty darn good again.

"And when you're done seducing him?" Debbie asked.

Trish hadn't exactly thought through this part yet, but . . . "I leave."

"You what?"

Yeah, that sounded good. "I leave. I just get up and go. I make sure he doesn't think it means anything to me. I don't give him a chance to patronize me in any way. I stay in control of this whole situation."

Across from her, Deb's eyebrows knit. Damn it—here she was, getting a good plan in mind, and Debbie still looked doubtful. "You sound kind of manic," her friend said.

Trish gasped. "I am *so* not manic. I'm just aggressively solving a problem. And how I acted with him last night—all smitten and nervous—I didn't like it. I want him to know that I'm an aggressive, capable woman."

"That I get. But . . ."

"Yeah?"

"Just getting up and leaving afterwards . . . that sounds kind of mean."

Trish blinked and stared at Debbie in disbelief. "*Mean*? Oh, like he'll care. I mean, his apology was one thing—I didn't particularly want to hear it, yet I could respect it. But trying to get me into bed two minutes later? That had conquest written all over it. It screamed selfishness. And like I said, I don't think I can say no to him if we end up close again. And if anyone's going to have a conquest and be selfish here, it's me."

Still, Debbie sighed, looking way too worried for Trish's peace of mind. She leaned slightly nearer over the table. "Dare I suggest that this sounds sort of like revenge?"

Trish's mouth dropped open. "*What?* How could seducing him possibly equate to revenge? It's more like . . . a gift or something." She widened her eyes for emphasis. "Like I said, we both win."

"It's not the seducing I was thinking of so much as the leaving afterward. It sort of sounds like you just want to show him . . . what it's like to be hurt."

The accusation stung. Trish was a lot of things, but vindictive wasn't one of them. She softened her voice slightly. "Again, Deb, I don't think I *can* hurt him. We haven't seen each other for nearly fifteen years. Last night on the dance floor, that was sex.

And tonight, me going to his place, that will be sex, too. Just sex, no feelings. I'm just beating him to the punch to save myself the embarrassment of being used."

Debbie's eyes flew open wider. "*Tonight?* You're doing this *tonight?*"

Apparently she was. Now that she had a plan. "No time like the present."

It would be just like the fudge. Now that she'd had some, she no longer wanted any more. Tonight she'd have Joe Ramsey once and for all, and then she could forget he'd ever reentered her life and get back to normal.

At dusk that night, Trish sat down to a home-cooked meal with her mom and dad and her sweet, gray-haired Aunt Alma, who felt well enough to come to the table. It was meat loaf and mashed potatoes and cornbread all around, and Trish served and cleared and dished up the apple pie her mother had made for dessert. There was something undeniably comforting about it—the familiarity of the home where she'd grown up, the aromas of her mother's home cooking, the very concept of slowing down a bit, not being in a mad rush to do something or get somewhere.

By the time darkness fell, though, dinner and homey comforts were a distant memory—because she now stood in front of the mirror in her motel room looking like sex on a stick. She'd never *looked* like sex on a stick before, so it was hard to get used to. This afternoon, she'd driven over to the outlet mall less than an hour west in Columbus to procure a "seduction suit" and—yikes—she couldn't believe the woman staring back from those heavily made-up eyes was her. She didn't look like little Trish Henderson from Eden, and she no longer resembled Patricia Henderson, attorney-at-law, either. The chick in the mirror was . . . Trish the Vixen or something. And she had a feeling Trish the Vixen might be related to that inner biker chick she'd just found out about last night.

But this Trish wasn't out for a day on a Harley. Nope, this Trish was all about the night.

She wore a low-cut black corset dress that hugged every curve, showed lots of cleavage, and stopped high on her thigh. Underneath, she'd kept it mostly basic, but also very hot—a dark purple demi bra with black lace trim, a matching thong, and a garter belt attached to lace-top stockings. On her feet she wore pointy black stiletto pumps with ankle straps.

She'd taken a thick curling iron to her usually casual hair, creating flirtatious curls around her face. And speaking of her face—she looked like she'd attended the French Whore's School of Makeup Application. But in a good way, she thought.

She'd never known she could look so sexy.

Or feel so sexy.

Sex nearly hummed through her body like electricity. She wanted it. Needed it.

And she was going to have it.

Of course, she'd never actually seduced anyone before.

But as she got in the car—okay, she sort of *snuck* to the car, scampering like a squirrel in case anyone noticed her leaving— she decided she could do this.

Debbie's last words from earlier still rang in her mind. *This is a bad idea*. But Trish thought it was the best idea she'd had in awhile. Everything else in her life suddenly felt a bit in disarray. She was worried now about her parents' retirement and worried about when she'd get back to her job. Everything felt unsettled. Settle *this* and it would be one less issue clouding her mind.

And as she drove toward the small white clapboard house Joe

had grown up in—which she knew from Debbie he'd bought when his dad had remarried—everything about this felt *right*. *Hot. Wickedly alluring.* From the snug, uplifting bra to the lace straps of the garter belt stretching tight across her thighs, she felt like a completely sensuous animal. For tonight and tonight only, she would make herself a part of Joe Ramsey's sexual world—and she would relish it.

At first, she'd seen this simply as a defense mechanism. But now she had to admit, she really *wanted* it. She hadn't dated anyone seriously in—dear God—nearly a year, which meant she also hadn't had sex in that long! This was the first time she'd actually stopped to count the months, but now she figured her dry spell had surely added to her response last night. And if she was going to have meaningless sex for the first time in her life, it made sense to do it with a guy as totally hot as Joe.

Although she wasn't really thinking of him as Joe. Not *her* Joe, the Joe she'd once known and loved. No, she thought of him only as New, Hot, Smooth-Talking, Smooth-Moving Joe—Man of Great Sexual Prowess. She was about to put her own prowess up against his, and she expected it to be a completely heated and pleasurable little battle.

Of course, her stomach rippled with a sudden onslaught of nerves when she rounded a bend and Joe's house came into view, a porch light bathing the home in a soft glow. She hadn't been here since that last summer before college. For some reason, her mind flashed on the day he'd shown her the kittens the Ramsey family cat had just given birth to. She'd immediately gravitated to the little orange one, the runt mewing its head off because its brothers and sisters had been hogging all the milking spots at the mama cat's belly. Joe had brought the kitten over to her a few weeks later.

*Crap. Quit thinking about the past.*

*In fact, just quit* thinking *and concentrate on* doing. Seducing.

Too bad pulling in the driveway felt a little like suicide. *But push that down. You can do this. Moreover, you want to do this. You are a sexual vixen. Go show him.*

Then it hit her—it was Saturday night. What if he wasn't home? What if he was out taking her advice from last night—getting it someplace else? But that's when she realized there were lights on inside and a vehicle in the driveway in front of her—her headlights shone on the tailgate of a big pickup with . . . oh my God, chrome women on the mudflaps!

She gasped. That truck had been *his?* What a Neanderthal he-man!

But it provided even more assurance that this would be nothing more than sex—and clear proof that he indeed wasn't the guy she'd once known. Nope—the man in this house was just a hot, sexy guy whose bones she was going to jump, and then it would be out of her system, just like a nasty flu bug.

She killed the lights, then the engine. Took a deep breath. Realized the suicide feeling still lingered as Debbie's words—*This is a bad idea*—were joined with her own—*Dear God, what are you doing?*

But she ignored it all. She had to. She'd come too far to turn back—hell, she'd invested a small fortune in seduction-wear. And even amid the little bits of panic now assaulting her, desire still lingered. Actually, it did more than linger. It pounded through her veins like fast-moving blood. It urged her to be the strong, sexy, confident seductress she'd come here to be. She was going to have Joe, once and for all.

Getting out of the car, she slammed the door, looked to the house, and thought—*this is it.* And she was so ready for this, so suddenly, that it almost scared her because she felt like someone else. Vixen Biker Babe Trish. She drew in her breath and let it slowly back out, growing aware of the pulsing sensation in her panties.

Her heels clicked up the thin concrete walk as her body vibrated with heat. The sounds of tree frogs and crickets perforated the air as a hot breeze lifted the hair from the nape of her neck. She stepped boldly up onto his covered porch and, without allowing herself to hesitate, rang the bell.

Of course, she briefly considered running, leaping in the bushes to hide, but she forced herself to stay put.

When the door swung open, Joe stood before her wearing only a pair of blue jeans. A smattering of dark curls dusted his chest—just as broad and muscular as she'd suspected—and narrowed to a tidy, sexy little line leading right down to his zipper. His hair was messy, his chin covered with stubble. And his blue eyes shone dark and fiery as they narrowed on her. Oh my.

She waited for him to speak, but he seemed too busy taking it all in. She watched various forms of confusion and shock pass through his gaze until finally it filled with exactly what she'd hoped for: hard core need. He slowly perused her body, from head to toe and back again, his look as potent as if he were touching her.

After a long, still, heated moment, she finally concluded that he wasn't going to say anything. Fair enough, she supposed—the ball was in her court. "I changed my mind," she said.

His eyes rose from her chest to her face. "About?"

She thought it was pretty obvious, but indulged him anyway. "Coming home with you. Here I am."

**Reversal:** the act of a court setting aside the decision of a lower court; <u>or</u> the state of acting in a manner that is opposite or contrary to the usual.

# Three

He gave his head a light shake as if to clear it. "Am I dreaming?"

"What if you are?" she asked smoothly. The very sight of him, it turned out, had transformed any doubt or nervousness into pure heat.

His gaze seemed to bore into her, then he spoke slowly, as if thinking through his answer aloud. "If I were dreaming, then . . . I wouldn't ask you what the hell you're doing here. I wouldn't waste any time on how damn shocked I am."

"What *would* you do?"

He lowered his unshaven chin. "I'd just take you."

"Then take me."

*But no, stop.* As much as she wanted to be thoroughly ravished by Joe this very second, as silkily as the plea had left her lips, she had to remain the one in control. So she revised her instructions. "Better yet, let *me* take *you*." As he stood there devouring her with his eyes, she pressed one palm flat to his chest and pushed her way past him into the room.

She moved with graceful purpose, rather liking the sound of her heels clicking across his hardwood, along with the feel of his gaze on her back. Walking to the coffee table, she snatched up the remote and turned off whatever old Tom Hanks movie he was watching, the action leaving the room illuminated by only the overhead in the kitchen, filtering in across the counter that separated the two rooms. Finally, she looked back up at Joe—whoa, it was easy to forget how hot he was until his eyes were glimmering on her—and curled one red-painted fingernail toward her, beckoning him.

As he shoved the front door closed, then padded across the floor in bare feet, everything inside her boiled with want and need. This seduction business was coming far easier than she'd expected—which only proved it was the right thing to do, meant to be.

She and Joe were worlds apart now, their lives separated by far more than a mere two-hour drive to Indianapolis—there could never be anything real between them again. In fact, she suspected Joe *seldom* had anything real with women these days—it just didn't seem like a part of the grown-up him. *Sex*, however—*that* was clearly a *big* part of the grown-up Joe, the most obvious part, something he couldn't even begin to conceal. And sex with him she could have. *Would* have. Right now.

"Sit down," she said when he reached the sofa, and she helped by giving his chest another push, watching as he plopped backwards.

She instantly liked the fact that he looked up at her now, that she stood over him. She liked his eyes. Etched with experience, a past, they sported just a hint of those little crinkles at the edges that made a man look as if he'd lived, as if he knew things.

Easy to get lost in them, those eyes. It always *had* been.

And right now, they were melting her, owning her.

But that couldn't happen. *You have to do the owning here. You have to be the one calling the shots.*

So she didn't squander another second. And like everything else so far, it came shockingly easy to skim her hands up her body to the top hooks of the dress, between her breasts. It came easy to flick them open, feel the snug fabric parting, exposing more of the cleavage her tight bra created. Her breasts ached beneath his gaze, and she remembered the last time he'd seen them—that night at the lake.

*But no, don't think about that. This is now. And this is like sex with a stranger—because he's not the guy you knew then.*

"Don't stop there, cupcake."

His voice moved through her as powerful as a kiss—she felt it at her very core, his low rasp fueling her, letting her know he was edging back from shock into the lust she required from him. She undid the next few hooks, letting the dress open further.

She liked hearing his breath catch. Liked the heat climbing her thighs, spreading through her like warm fingers.

"Keep going," he prodded in a low voice, and she did, revealing her body to him bit by bit. Another few hooks and her lacy bra was on display, her stomach bared. Soon the dress opened completely, and Trish shrugged free of it, letting it fall to the floor behind her.

She stood before him feeling like erotica personified in her lingerie, stockings, and heels. His eyes burned on her like blue flames, and her entire body began to sizzle with an almost animal need.

Suddenly, she suffered a want that surpassed last night, or even a few minutes ago.

She suffered a want that burned feral and reckless.

A want that knew no thought or decision—only impulse.

And that impulse led her to drop to her knees between his parted legs. To reach out, deftly undoing the button at his waistband with a flick of her wrist. To smoothly ease the zipper down over that bulge.

Oh God. Yes. He was so hard . . . and she'd never . . . back then, they'd never . . . she'd only once touched him through his jeans, but it had felt too brazen, too raw, and she'd drawn her hand away and resumed letting *him* touch *her.*

But now she was finally ready to do some touching. Brazen or not.

Using both hands, she spread the denim wide, then lifted the white cotton of his underwear over the column contained within. She let out a tiny gasp when she saw him—full, erect, magnificent. She didn't mean to, but he was too incredible like this.

"Aw, God," he breathed, his gaze dripping with arousal.

Normally, she would never be this intimate with a man she didn't know well, with someone who was practically a stranger to her now. But like *all* of this—it felt right, natural. So easy to skim her fingertips down his length, smooth as satin, hard as steel. Easy to bend over him, licking a path from base to tip.

She absorbed his sweet shudder, heard his low moan. She wanted this so much, more than she'd even realized until this moment, and she'd long since ceased thinking about control, or who was getting, or giving, or who would win. The encounter had escalated into something far more powerful than that.

Lifting her gaze, she found his face wrenched with desperation, passion, disbelief.

And with her eyes still locked on his, she lowered a tiny kiss to the tip of his erection, making them *both* shudder this time—just before she took him in her mouth.

As she let him fill her, she experienced the overwhelming bliss of delivering ultimate pleasure, and even as his sighs and moans echoed above, sounding almost like pain, she knew his response was actually the deepest sort of ecstasy.

But when she least expected it, he raised her head between his palms and gazed into her eyes. "No more."

"What?" The words paralyzed her.

"I don't want to come yet."

"Oh." Paralysis over. Pleasure to be continued. Thank God.

Biting her lower lip, she met his eyes again, then moved smoothly up onto the couch to straddle him. When she lowered her palms to his bare shoulders, the simple contact radiated through her, along with his very *nearness*, their faces close now. It was one kind of intimacy to be near a man's penis, but another to be eye to eye, mouths only a few inches apart. Every part of her ached for him—urgently.

Brushing her lace-covered breasts teasingly across his chest, she angled a kiss across his lush mouth, tasting a hint of pizza—she'd noticed an empty box on the coffee table—and drinking in the fresh, clean scent of soap on his skin. Oh God, to kiss him again nearly took her breath away. One kiss turned into another, and another, until she sank heavy against him, lost in the passion, their tongues mingling in wild abandon. They'd learned to kiss together all those years ago, and she realized only now that no other man's kisses had ever meshed so well with her mouth, ever made her feel so complete.

But soon there was more than just kissing—his hands roamed her back, bottom, sides, and then her breasts. *Mmm, yes.* He rained more hot kisses to the curve of her neck as he firmly kneaded her through her bra, his skilled touch sending spasms soaring down her spine to ricochet to other key points of her body. And when he stroked his thumbs over her nipples—oh!—she heard herself pant with the hot pleasure of it.

When his fingers slid smoothly between her legs from behind, she arched instinctively. *Oh God, yes. He's touching me there again. Really touching me there.* Not under her panties, not yet—but the pleasure was almost as intense.

Which was when all rational thought departed, leaving only action and instinct.

While he peeled her bra straps down, they kissed more—wild, rough, slaking kisses made all the more amazing by the fact that his hardness pressed naked between them, nestled against the lace of her panties.

He whispered her name between kissing her lips, cheeks, neck, shoulders. He whispered it hotter just before he yanked the lace down from her breasts, allowing him to draw one taut nipple into his mouth.

"Oh . . ." she moaned, the intense pull echoing all the way to the juncture of her thighs. His eyes fell shut as he suckled her deeply, deeply—and she arched her chest, letting him know she wanted more.

"I need inside you, Trish," he growled.

And their gazes met. Their bodies went still.

It was like being wrapped in the eye of a hurricane—the strange, brisk calm of their eyes locking, of recognizing the storm they'd just been through, and the bigger one they were about to experience together.

She recalled the times he'd dared to say those words when they were teenagers. It had seemed like the ultimate dirty talk then—so blunt about the geography of it, making her think about the sizes and shapes made to fit that way. And she thought about all the naughty responses she could give him in this ultimate moment of fruition, but it seemed the best, most natural, most fitting reply was simply to . . . rise up on her knees, reach down and pull the lace aside, and lower herself smoothly onto him until he was sheathed warm and tight inside her.

"Unh . . ." she moaned, overwhelmed by the sensation, the fullness, the . . . *reality*.

*Oh God. No.*

*No, no, no.*

She knew instantly it was the biggest mistake of her life. Because nothing had ever felt more physically or emotionally perfect than finally having him inside her, connecting their bodies so profoundly. They both sat breathless and trembling and holding each other tight.

She'd been so stupid—this *wasn't* just sex. This was exactly what he'd promised her—*what she'd missed*. Every sweet, stirring emotion of her youth swirled with the rush of deep physical pleasure and fulfillment. Not even moving. Just being like that, him in her. Pure rapture.

She kissed his neck, then raked her teeth across her earlobe, loving him—oh God, *loving* him—but desperately avoiding his eyes. Because if she looked into those blue depths now, it would be all over; he'd see every pang of passion, romance, hurt, agony, and love currently assaulting her.

*Make this sex again. Just sex. Just pleasure.* That was what she had to do.

She had seduced him and now she had to see it through to the end. She had to remain the lusty vixen. She could not let herself care.

And so she began to move on him—not a hard thing to do, the natural inclination, in fact—but she had to think sexually, not emotionally.

She bit her lip as the heat of the movements grabbed hold of her. And she kept her eyes shut tight. *He could be anyone, any guy in the world. He's not your Joe. He's not the guy you fell in love with.* But emotions still mingled with sensation, adding to both her deep pleasure and her addled dismay.

"Trish. Oh God, Trish." He was doing it again, whispering her name. Closer to moaning it, actually. The sound of his wrenched voice only added another layer of depth and history to the connection.

She moved in slow, tight, sexy circles. Kept her eyes closed still. *Don't see him. Don't feel him. Just feel your body being pleasured.* But it wasn't working very well. His hands clutched at her bottom, his fingers reaching, massaging, somehow seeming to open her to him more. His tongue laved her nipples hotly. She hissed at each added sensation as the most violent part of the storm began to build inside her, growing, amassing, getting more colossal with each heartbeat.

She gyrated on him more fervently, her breasts grown heavy, her soul lost to the pursuit of the pure ecstasy bearing down on her, getting nearer with each stroke, with each time he filled her, each time her body collided so tight and hot with his.

Finally, she whispered his name, too, heard it leave her lips, just before the tidal wave of pleasure crashed. "Joe. Oh, Joe." And then the wave fell, crushing her, tossing her wildly, and her whispers expanded into heated cries as the climax ripped through her with more intensity than any storm surge. "Ah, Joe. Oh God! Oh God, Joe! *Oh God.*"

She clung to him after. She didn't mean to—it just happened.

He held her just as tight, sprinkling kisses on her shoulder. Their bodies had never been this close—never. Until now.

And then he was lifting her, shifting her, until she lay on her back on the couch. "I know this is selfish," he breathed, their faces no more than an inch apart, "but I want you under me."

And she wrapped her legs around his back as he moved in her, harder with each thrust, and she met his eyes because they were so beautiful filled with such heat, and because she knew this was her one chance to live that, to soak that in, to love him like this.

*This is how it would have been back then. You beneath him, peering up, feeling that bond for the first time, together.* She hugged him even tighter, gave herself over to him even more completely.

And when he came, emptying inside her, rocking her body with the power of his deep plunges, it was with a huge groan that left him collapsing atop her, his head on her chest, his hands firmly gripping her hips. "Aw, Jesus," he breathed. "You're so beautiful, Trishy."

*Trishy.* The very most childish form of her name—what she'd been called in elementary school. She'd known him for that long, since the first grade, even though they'd not been close until much later. It was as if he were dipping back into their lives, deep. As if their entire existences had led up to this one moment.

But she said nothing. Because she was reading too much into it. And she was playing the role of the mad seductress here, after all—not a foolish teenager in love.

Even though she knew now—since the moment he'd entered her body—she *was* in love with him. Still, or always. And she never should have done this, never should have been so stupid to believe she could have sex with him and have it mean nothing. Because even if she was the seductress and he the conquest, it was still going to hurt now. It was going to hurt much worse than she could have imagined.

This was the part where she was supposed to get up and leave.

A shame she hadn't really thought that out better.

She kind of hadn't expected him to be lying on top of her, still inside her. She kind of hadn't calculated how a girl was supposed to make a quick escape with her underwear askew and her dress discarded on the far side of the room. And she was fairly sure she'd had keys when she walked in here, but she harbored no recollection of what she might have done with them.

She also—stupidly—hadn't expected lying with him afterward to feel so darn wonderful. Warm. Cuddly. *Yeesh.*

*That boy's trouble. Pure trouble.*

But her job from this point forward was not to let him see all the emotion pummeling her, not to let him suspect she felt anything at all. Because nothing had changed, really. He was still the town stud—and she knew why now; even just responding to her lead, he was the best lover she'd ever had—and he was still the guy who'd found it more convenient to have sex with Beverly Rainey than wait for her. And *she* was still the girl who'd been made tough that way—and who would *continue* to be tough that way. She was still the girl who couldn't wait to get the hell out of this town as soon as she closed the sale on the damn diner next week.

Joe kissed the ridge of her exposed breast and slowly rose on one elbow to peer down at her. The kiss shuddered through her, almost enough to get her hot all over again. "So," he said, "you gonna explain this to me now?" He fingered the lace of her bra where it rested below her breasts.

She bit her lip. Weighed her options. Answered quietly. "No."

Above her, he sighed, but didn't look upset. "All right, cupcake—have it your way."

She sucked in her breath a bit. He'd first called her by the pet name in the fifth grade, teasing her because her mother sent cupcakes to school for every conceivable occasion and holiday. She still remembered the very first time. *I'm gonna start callin' you cupcake—'cause every time I see you, you're carryin' a big tray o' cupcakes down the hall.*

She'd been embarrassed, affronted, not sure how to take it. *You don't have to eat 'em if you don't like 'em.*

*I like your cupcakes just fine—cupcake.*

"Is it my imagination," he said, sliding his palm to cup one of her breasts, "or . . . have these grown?" She tensed inside from the pleasure, still not used to being touched by him so intimately again.

"Bodies change," she said, realizing his observation was true. "I suppose they grew when I started taking birth control pills, too."

He gave a slow, thoughtful nod. "Taking them now?"

She nodded in return.

"Good. Since I . . . didn't exactly have time for a condom."

*Oh no! What a terrible seductress she was!* She hadn't even *thought* about protection! "Are you . . . I mean . . ." She drew in her breath, not quite knowing how to phrase it.

"No worries, cupcake. I'm usually good about that sort of thing. Just wasn't expecting what I got when I opened the door."

"Understandable," she said, feeling sheepish now and not quite able to meet his eyes. *This is why you should have had a better leaving plan.* Postcoital small talk hadn't been part of the equation here.

"Damn, Trish, I never dreamed you could be this . . . this . . ."

Dear God, what was he getting at? "This what?"

"*Hot.* But . . . way more than hot." He glanced down at her disheveled underwear. "The lace, the shoes, the dress. That dress blew me away, honey."

She hardly knew what to say. *This isn't actually me. I've never seduced a man before. And this is the first time I've worn a dress that could double for lingerie.* But confiding in him would be a mistake. Even the birth-control-breast-growth issue had felt too . . . honest, or personal, the moment she'd said it. So instead, she settled on, "I'm glad you liked it."

"I liked it *all*," he said, nuzzling her, then dipping to rake his tongue over one still-beaded nipple. She hissed in her breath at the flurry of sensation. "But now," he went on, sliding his arms behind her to handily unhook her bra, "I want to take it all off you."

She blinked up at him. "Why?"

His voice came slow, serious. "Because I want you naked."

"Why?" she asked again.

"It's been a long time I've waited for this," he rasped. "And your body is beautiful."

Oh boy. She knew he hadn't *really* been waiting for her all this time—but the sentiment got to her just the same. Being told she was beautiful didn't hurt, either. Well, as long as she didn't count her peace of mind. Since this would soon be over and she'd probably spend years recovering.

But as it was, she didn't quite have the strength to respond, so she simply lay there, letting him remove her bra, then her shoes, before he carefully undid the garters and rolled the stockings painstakingly down her legs. She bit her lip, watching him, trying not to moan or sigh or do anything to let him know how much she felt it—every touch, every whisper across her skin. He reached behind her to unsnap the garter belt and she tried to ignore the little pinch that came with understanding this wasn't his first time with such an apparatus. Finally, he peeled her sexy panties down and off, tossing them over the back of the couch.

When she was completely naked, he skimmed one hand slowly across her skin from breast to knee, then dragged it lingeringly back up between her thighs. "Damn, Trish," he breathed. "I can't believe you're lying here with me."

"Neither can I," she said, melting in a whole new kind of intimacy—having him study her in the dim lighting, knowing he'd never seen her like this before.

*Stupid, stupid, stupid.* Why had she thought this would be easy, meaningless? Why had she thought it would be like sex with any other man?

Suddenly, she suffered the urge to wrap herself around him, press her body against his—so she followed it, twining her arms around his neck, soaking up his masculine warmth, and pulling him close enough that he wouldn't be able to see the tear she feared was about to roll down her cheek.

He held her, too, just as tight. "Still like pancakes?" he whispered warm in her ear.

God, somehow he made even *that* sound sexual. And the question whisked her back in time, made her remember being at her house, or his, when she would suddenly decide she wanted pancakes—maybe on a Saturday afternoon, or while doing homework on a school night—and they'd stop everything and make them together, exchanging kisses over a bowl of batter.

"Mmm-hmm," she said against his neck, a small lump in her throat.

"Tomorrow morning," he murmured, "we'll make pancakes. And you'll tell me about your life, cupcake. I want to know you again."

His warmth, all around her, his voice in her ear—it was like being back in that Trans Am by the lake. But this time he wasn't asking for sex. He was simply asking to know her, just know her. It made her heart beat faster than she could understand. "All right," she whispered back softly.

When Trish awoke, she was aware only of the scent and feel of his body draped heavy about her. As she remembered where she was and the insanity of it all, her eyes took in other things: the shadows of trees outside the windows; family pictures hanging on a wall by the front door, their shiny frames gleaming in the dim lighting . . . the shape and feel and texture of his home.

It was comfortable. Warm. The furniture slightly worn but cozy.

He wasn't a bad person. Maybe she'd hoped deep down that he was. It would have made this a hell of a lot easier. But then, if she'd really believed he was a jerk, she probably wouldn't have felt so attracted to him last night, and sleeping with him wouldn't even have become an issue.

She reviewed the facts. He wasn't a bad person. She'd finally had sex with him. And she'd let herself believe, during and right after the act, that she was *still in love with him.*

Temporary insanity. Had to be. Because as she kept reminding herself, she didn't even know him anymore. You couldn't love a guy you didn't know. So what she'd felt during their heated coupling had been only a resurrection of old memories, old feelings, nothing more.

And as for his offer of pancakes and knowing her . . . well, he'd clearly been in a sex-induced haze, so she couldn't buy into that, either. She couldn't stay anyway. That hadn't been part of the plan. If she didn't get up and walk out of here right now, the whole dynamic would flip—she'd lose the sense of control she'd been hanging onto by a mere thread and end up feeling conquered again. Staying could only lead to hurt.

Part of her couldn't deny the urge to reach between them and touch him—*there*. She yearned to make him hard again. To feel him inside her again. Any other lover in the same situation and that was what she'd do right now. But she'd come here to seduce him, then leave. It hadn't gone exactly as planned—she'd stayed too long and felt too much—but it was time to get things back on track.

*Stay one more minute and you could end up more emotionally involved than you already are, which could only lead to another dose of humiliating heartache.* And Trish had stopped doing humiliating heartache a long time ago. *Get out now and maybe you can forget this and move on with your life.*

She very gingerly lifted his arm from her waist and placed it carefully along his side. Then she slowly slid off the couch.

If last night in the bar with him had felt surreal . . . yeesh—it wasn't even in the same ballpark as this: standing naked in Joe Ramsey's living room in the middle of the night wondering where she'd find her corset dress and dominatrix shoes.

She took a deep breath and crept to the end of the couch where she located her stockings—she'd take them with her, but certainly saw no need to waste time putting them back on. She tripped over a shoe and nearly plunged to the floor before catching herself on the wide, soft arm of the couch. Damn it, that was close—but at least she'd found her pumps.

When her bare foot met with a soft pile of fabric, she knew she'd located her dress. She put it on and quickly did up the hooks, then located her panties a few feet away behind the sofa, deciding that putting them on could wait, too. Gathering shoes and lingerie in a heap in her arms, she spotted—thank you, God!—her keys on a table by the door. She padded to quietly snatch them up, then paused to look back at her lover. But only for a second, *because this was only sex, this didn't matter.* Yeah, right. *That ship has sailed, sister, so you might as well give it up.*

She felt like a criminal scurrying to her car under the glow of the moon—and the same porch light that had helped her make her way to the door an hour or two ago. And something caught in her throat as she started the engine—some kind of guilt, just like Debbie had implied she would feel. *Sneaking* was worse than just leaving, of course. But she'd *had* to—she'd had to get the hell out of there before she let herself start thinking she loved the guy again. She shivered at the very thought—but felt that shiver rush all through her, through the breasts he'd recently kissed and the place between her thighs where he'd recently . . . been.

She released a heavy breath, then backed out of the drive-way, her heart pumping nearly as hard as when she'd arrived. Debbie's words from earlier came back to mind—*Dare I suggest this sounds like revenge?* If this *was* revenge, it wasn't very sweet.

Well, maybe in a way—but not in a boy-I-showed-him way. More in an oh-God-that-was-heaven way. Which was not at all what she'd had in mind.

Just sex—it was supposed to have been just good, hot sex. Maybe if she kept telling herself that long enough, she'd make herself believe it was true.

\* \* \*

Morning sun shone through the living room window, stirring Joe awake. He'd slept like a log. But why was he on the couch?

Then he remembered. The impossible had happened.

Trish had come to him. And they'd . . .

*Oh yeah, had they ever.*

He opened his eyes, ready for more.

But his chest constricted when he realized he was alone.

He considered calling for her but didn't waste his breath. He knew instinctively she wasn't in the bathroom or the kitchen. Letting out a sigh, he sat up, scanned the living room. Not a trace of her remained—except for a lacy purple bra he'd managed to toss onto a lampshade.

*Shit.*

It shouldn't matter. Two people have sex, sometimes one of them gets up and goes home—it wasn't a crime. He wasn't usually real big on "spending the night" himself. So she'd been completely within her rights to leave. But to wake up without her after how unbelievably good it had felt to finally, *finally* be inside her warm, sweet body—hell, it stung.

She'd been . . . amazing. A fantasy come to life. It hadn't been *his* fantasy of Trish—he'd had no idea she could be a bad girl. But he'd liked finding out. He'd been confused from the word go, but when a woman you once loved shows up at your door in something tight and black, you don't ask questions.

Being with her, at long last, had been better than in his imagination. It hadn't been tender, it hadn't been sweet—but it didn't matter what tone the sex had taken. It was the best he'd ever had.

He still didn't get it. Not any of it.

Not that he knew her anymore. Hell, maybe she was into casual sex, no chitchat required.

But the hot chick who'd seduced him last night had seemed like a different girl than the one he'd met up with at the Last Chance. *That* had been Trish. More grown-up, confident, every bit a woman—but he'd still sensed the girl he'd once known hiding inside.

Of course, when they'd gotten to the actual sex, maybe *then* he'd seen hints of Trish, too. When she'd called his name. When she'd held onto him like there was no tomorrow.

But the wild woman in black, and the woman who'd snuck off in the night . . . He shook his head. What the hell was she doing? What was she trying to prove?

Pushing up from the couch, he zipped his pants and let out a low growl of frustration. Any other woman on the planet and he wouldn't have cared. But with Trish . . . damn, he cared. He knew he'd behaved like a jerk the other night, and he knew he'd completely fucked up their relationship the night before she'd left for college, but hell, when he remembered how close they'd once been—even if it *was* nearly a lifetime ago—sneaking out in the middle of the night was shitty.

Well, one thing was for damn sure. Just like he'd told her at the Last Chance, this wasn't over. He might have decided yesterday to let it go—but last night changed that. It might have been over then, but it *definitely* wasn't over now.

**Grievance:** *a complaint filed against an attorney or judge; or resentment against an unjust or unfair act or treatment.*

# *Four*

"Well, I guess this means she doesn't hate you."

Joe turned on Kenny with a dry look. They sat in Kenny's Toyota pickup eating lunch at the local drive-in, the Burger Barn, which—other than the occasional new coat of red paint—hadn't changed much in their lifetime. "Sneaking out in the middle of the night doesn't exactly say 'I like you,' either."

Kenny shrugged, maneuvering his foot-long hot dog for a bite.

"I still can't believe it," Joe muttered under his breath. Hell, if he hadn't found her bra, he might have gone back to thinking it was a dream.

"I can," Kenny said, wiping at his mouth with a napkin, the footlong stretched carefully across his lap.

Joe eyed his best friend. "You can?"

"I knew."

Joe leaned forward slightly in disbelief. "You what?"

"I knew she was coming."

Jesus. "And I guess you were too busy to pick up the phone."

"Well, I probably only found out around the time she was get-ting there. I was feeding the chickens and cows 'til dark, then I took a shower, and *then* Deb told me."

Joe only sighed, still irritated. "And if you already knew, why the hell did you sit here and let me tell you the whole miserable story?"

Kenny grinned. "It didn't exactly sound miserable, dude."

No, he guessed not. But he hadn't gone on about how her departure had left him feeling so burned—and he didn't in-tend to.

He also hadn't gone into the details of exactly what had hap-pened, either—like the way her luscious mouth had sunk down on him, or how she'd eased herself so warmly onto his erection. Unlike Trish, he didn't go broadcasting *everything*. "Tell Debbie I said thanks for the warning, too. I hope she won't miss those free oil changes."

Kenny shrugged again. "You know she's loyal to Trish."

"Well, for Deb's sake, I hope Trish is good with cars." He didn't mean it, but it pissed him off to know Trish had run her little plan past Debbie. Everything *about* this was beginning to piss him off. When Trish had shown up, he'd thought it had been about him and her and hot, hard need—now he felt like the whole damn world had been in on it. "Debbie probably knows more about this than *I* do, so why *did* Trish leave?"

When Kenny shrugged yet one more time, Joe wanted to slug him, but he ate a French fry instead and tried to keep his cool. "According to Deb, Trish just wanted to have sex with you— nothing else."

For the first time in his life, Joe felt like a cheap, tawdry one-night stand. Which was odd, since he'd had his fair share of cheap, tawdry one-night stands, and they'd never made him feel cheap or tawdry before. "So she was just using me. For sex."

"Something like that." Kenny looked preoccupied with his footlong again.

Joe raised his eyebrows. "Does she do that often?"

Kenny shook his head as he managed to wrangle another bite. "As far as I know, only with you. Deb thought it was like revenge, like she was trying to hurt you or something."

Joe didn't answer, didn't mention he'd had a similar thought, until finally Kenny glanced up from his food, looking a little more serious now. "Did she?"

Joe pressed his lips into a grim, straight line. Kenny knew good and well that Trish had been the one and only heartbreak of his life. But he hadn't liked talking about it then—and he still didn't want to talk about it now. "Just would've been nice of her to say good-bye, that's all."

"Doesn't sound like too much to ask," Kenny agreed. "Unless . . . you think back to the past."

Joe arched one eyebrow in Kenny's direction. "She said she was over that. If she wasn't, she should have thrown a drink in my face or called me a son of a bitch—not come to my house looking to get laid and then go sneaking off after I fell asleep."

Kenny squared his gaze on Joe. "You know, a lotta guys would see this as the perfect fantasy come true. Chick comes to your door, does the dirty with you, then disappears so you can go right on like it never happened."

Joe couldn't deny that, but didn't answer this time, either. Even so, Kenny's expression said he knew exactly what Joe wasn't saying. Back in high school, they'd both planned to marry their girlfriends and live long, happy lives here in Eden. For Kenny, it had worked out, and for a guy with a fairly shitty job and not much money or opportunity coming his way, Kenny was about the happiest guy Joe knew. Joe hadn't spent the last fourteen years pining over Trish, but no way could she ever be just a chick, a one-night stand.

"Is she staying at her mom and dad's place?" he asked.

"Nope." Kenny shook his head. "So happens she's taken up residence at the Red Roof Inn—room 117 to be exact. I saw it on a note on the fridge under a Spiderman magnet," Kenny concluded with a wink.

"Good to know," Joe said. And a hell of a lot more convenient than her parents' house.

"What are you gonna do?"

"She forgot her bra when she slipped out. Figure the least I can do is return it."

Beverly stood behind the counter at the Waffle House, looking out on the blistering hot kind of August day that made you smell the blacktop in the parking lot when people opened the door to come inside. The lunch rush had passed, every orange booth and stool was empty, the whole place still, and Patsy Cline crooned something mournful on the jukebox that managed to echo Beverly's emotions today.

She'd worked here so long that she felt as much like a fixture as the griddle or the rows of waffle makers. Her feet were tired, her back sore. She felt pathetically older than her thirty-four years.

She should be someplace else. And she didn't indulge *unreasonable* fantasies—she wasn't standing here wishing for the Greek Isles or the French Riviera or palatial mansions or sandy beaches with cabana boys. She just wanted a nice little home where she and Carissa could spend more time together. She wanted to be sitting on a porch swing right now, petting a dog and watching the occasional car pass by, or working in a flower bed, maybe with her daughter by her side. She wanted a husband who would be home soon, kissing her hello, maybe offering to take them out to supper and a ride afterward.

Up the two-lane highway out the front plate-glass windows, she spied a big hulking red semi hurtling westward, coming this way. The yellow and orange flames painted on the sides, fanning back from the chrome grill, told her it was Butch—a trucker from over near Aurora who took this route across to Interstate 65 once or twice a week.

The soft reaction between her thighs made her anxious, wondering if he'd stop. He didn't always. But when he did, and if she had time for a break or it was near the end of her shift, she usually ended up in his extended sleeper cab, where they could make each other feel good for awhile.

She didn't know much about him—he was a long-haul trucker, owned his own rig, and hauled retail products like canned food or lawn mowers or whatever else needed to be moved from one place to another. He was at least forty, wore flannel in the winter, faded T-shirts in the summer, and a Mack Truck cap that squashed down his blond hair. He was starting to gain some weight the last few months. She didn't know his marital status and didn't want to. She just needed a little secret pleasure in her life, and Butch seemed to be the only guy providing it the last couple of years.

The truck's horn sounded—a musical little *beepity-beep-beep* as it went sailing by the Waffle House without ever slowing down. It meant, *Can't stop today, baby, but on the way back through.* Beverly wasn't sure whether she was let down or relieved. Her body suffered a twinge of disappointment, but she decided it was just as well.

When she'd first started sleeping with Butch, maybe she'd thought he was the man who was going to give her what she yearned for—that porch swing, that family ride out for some chicken or burgers on a Sunday evening. He wasn't rich, she knew, but he drove a top-of-the-line truck, and he'd once told her he owned some acreage behind the house he'd built—enough hints that he made a healthy living. And he might not be the snazziest guy around, but he wasn't bad-looking—and he knew how to give her an orgasm, which was nothing to sneeze at.

But sometime during the last six months she'd begun to accept that some sex in the back of his truck wasn't adding up to a future. She almost laughed at herself now to realize—*Hell, Bev, it only took you a freaking year and a half to figure it out.*

All she really wanted in life was to be loved and to provide a good home for her daughter, and she wasn't sure she'd succeeded with either yet. God, Carissa was thirteen. Beverly didn't have much longer before her girl would be grown and gone and probably filled with unhappy memories of the shabby little apartment they rented over Sophie's Hair and Nails, and how many hours she spent alone or with her grandpa because her downtrodden mother worked weekends and sometimes nights, too.

Bev let out a sigh. Why couldn't *Joe* just fall in love with her? She could make him happy, she knew it. And she knew he wanted to be more of a father to Carissa than he was being— just because the DNA hadn't been quite *right*, quite *his*. He was a good man, good enough to care for a girl who didn't carry his genes just because the timing had been close. And he was a hell of a *sexy* man, too. He'd been a cute-as-hell boy, but the *man* he'd grown into—damn, she could almost come just thinking about him.

"Christ," she muttered. Talk about slow to realize something. She'd been pining and hungering and lusting for Joe her entire adult life, always hoping for some miraculous shift in his feelings. Each and every time she saw him, she hoped for it, she waited for it, trying to believe in the power of positive thinking. And she occasionally earned a gorgeous smile that, for a second, made her think, *Yes, yes, finally, he's beginning to soften, to care, not just for Carissa, but for me, too*—yet it never lasted, was never real.

And now Trish Henderson was back in town? And Joe had seen her, maybe had sex with her? She felt sick to her stomach just thinking about it. She'd always thought Trish was too prissy for Joe—she remembered the night she and Joe had done it in her dad's ancient Impala, handy because it had a huge backseat, when she'd convinced him he shouldn't keep waiting for a girl who must not love him since she was leaving, and who would probably never really come back no matter what she'd promised. She'd thought he was better off without someone who felt the need to look beyond him for fulfillment.

Bev had spent all these years knowing that no matter who Joe slept with, Trish was the only girl who'd ever really meant something to him—and maybe that should have depressed her, but it'd had just the opposite effect instead. Because as long as Trish was gone, off somewhere a world away living some entirely different life, there had remained that little bit of hope that he would finally decide to settle down, and that he'd make Beverly the one.

Only now that Trish was back—hell, Bev had no idea what this even meant. Was Trish here to stay? Or just to tease and torment Joe some more? Either way, it meant the chances of Joe ever loving *her*, making a family with her and Carissa, were even slimmer than before.

Hell. What was a woman to do when her only hope was stolen?

Just then another toot of an air horn drew her gaze from where it had dropped to a bin of dirty plates below her. A red eighteen-wheeler with flames burning along the fenders angled its way into the truck parking area situated alongside the regular lot. Her heartbeat kicked up a notch as Alan Jackson began to sing "Where I Come From" on the jukebox.

Out of habit, Bev smoothed back her hair and hefted up her bra a little. Butch wasn't going to marry her—or even love her—but she still wanted him to like what he saw. And who knew, maybe she was wrong. Maybe he *would* fall for her. He'd come back, hadn't he? He'd gotten up the road and decided to turn that big rig around just for a few minutes with her.

When the door opened, he wore a gray tee with the sleeves cut out—and maybe he'd lost a couple of pounds since she'd last seen him. His eyes—blue like Joe's and one of his best features—glimmered with flirtation. "What's shakin', darlin'?"

"Thought you must be too busy for me today, Butchy," she said, trying to look interested yet offended, and glad Floyd was in the breakroom, leaving her to behave however she wished without having to lower her voice.

"I thought I was, too. Runnin' hellaciously late if I want to get any miles behind me tonight. But . . ."

"But?"

His grin held just a hint of lechery. "But it's a hot day, and it's gonna be a long week on the road. Headed all the way to Phoenix, baby. I decided I couldn't make it without stoppin' to see you first." He jerked his head slightly in the direction of the truck lot. "Head outside with me a while?"

She might be better off without it, but her body was glad he'd come back—she needed some release and knew Butch would give it to her. He wasn't the only one who suffered through hot days and long, lonely nights. Lowering her lashes seductively, she reached up to undo the top button on the front of her striped uniform blouse, opening it just far enough to show some cleavage—a promise. "Let me tell Floyd I'm going on break."

After finishing lunch in Kenny's truck, Joe got back in his own and headed home, thinking about returning Trish's sexy bra. From there, he wasn't sure what would happen, but he'd figure it out as he went.

Pulling into the driveway, he walked around back. To the right sat a small metal barn he'd erected for the Cobra, with work space for any other projects he wanted to tackle at home now that the car's restoration was done. To the left stood the same old slanted shed that had always been there, housing the lawn mower and gardening tools. Sunshine, a stray cat who'd stuck around when he'd taken pity and started feeding her about five years back, was about to drop a litter of kittens, and the last time that'd happened, she'd parked them in a hollow spot under one side of the shed. Through Debbie, he'd lucked into a connection with a Brownie troop of little girls who'd all wanted cats. This time, he doubted he'd be so lucky.

His saggy-jowled old dog, Elvis, came ambling around the corner of the house to greet him. His little sister had come up with the name because their mom had loved Elvis and because he wasn't "nothin' but a hound dog"—a beagle/basset mix. "Hey, bud," he said, bending to give the dog an easy scratch behind the ears. "I haven't seen you since yesterday morning." He eyed Elvis with suspicion. "You been out puttin' the moves on that little blond collie over at Mrs. Crowley's?" Elvis usually stuck close to home, where he led a wild life of naps on the front porch and the occasional stroll around the yard. So when Joe didn't see him for a day or two, he figured Elvis was out looking for love.

"Guess I've been doing the same thing," he told the dog absently, adding, "sort of. But your girl probably likes you better than mine likes me."

Scanning the backyard, Joe narrowed in on the shed, moving closer. Sure enough, Sunshine lay stretched out on her side with four kittens busily nursing, so tiny their eyes weren't yet open. Two were the same yellowy-orange as their mother, one solid black, and the last fluffy and gray. "Looks like you did good, girl."

After watching them for a minute, he pulled the drooping limbs of a gangly forsythia bush next to the shed over one side of the hollow spot—just to provide a little protection. "But looks like I need to find some more Brownies," he muttered as he headed in the back door.

No sooner had he shut it behind him than the doorbell rang—and his first thought was Trish. Had she come to apologize? Or at least explain? Despite himself, his heart beat a little faster as he strode through the house to answer.

He opened the door to find—damn, just Jana. Not that he minded seeing his sister. But, as usual lately, she looked . . . too made-up, especially for a Sunday afternoon. She wore a sparkly halter top and black miniskirt that seemed more suitable for a big city dance club—high-heeled shoes with lots of straps on them, too. Her tanned skin contrasted with lips of neon pink.

"Hey!" she said, throwing her arms around his neck, and he

couldn't help the ironic thought that this was the second time in twenty-four hours a scantily clad woman had shown up on his doorstep. If old Mrs. Crowley—who owned the only other house in sight on the country road—was paying attention, she probably thought things were getting pretty wild down here at the Ramsey house. And after last night, she wouldn't exactly be wrong.

"What's up?" He probably didn't sound overly glad to see Jana, which should maybe make him feel bad but didn't. He'd been pissed ever since she'd gone running off to Ohio with some older guy he'd never met. All he knew was that the guy owned the bar where she worked and his name was Vinnie Balducci. She'd been wearing sparkly tops ever since.

"I brought your car back." She hiked a thumb over her shoulder and he glanced out to see the old Trans Am—the same he'd driven in high school. It was far past its prime, but he kept it as a spare, and since Jana had needed a car when she moved, he'd let her use it. Behind it in the driveway sat a shiny black Lincoln Town Car with tinted windows. He wondered if his sister had joined the mob.

"Your boyfriend in that?"

She nodded, then pushed past him into the house, obviously trying to draw his attention elsewhere.

Joe spoke pointedly. "Why doesn't he come in? I want to meet him."

She shrugged. "He needs to make some calls while you and I visit. Business stuff."

Ordering hits, Joe guessed. He flashed a look that let her know exactly what he thought of Vinnie. "The guy couldn't even come in?"

"He's *really* busy, Joe. Running the club is, like, *more* than a full-time job."

He narrowed his gaze on her. "And what kind of club is it again exactly?"

She blinked. "You know. A club. Where people drink."

He eyed her with suspicion. "Is there dancing?"

She hesitated for only a second. "Yeah."

*Mmm-hmm. I just bet there is* His jaw tightened. But self preservation prevented him from taking the thought further, so for his own sanity, he changed the subject. "You don't need the car anymore, huh?"

She shook her platinum blond head and he found himself missing the old *brunette* her. Some women looked great as blondes—Trish, for instance—but on his sister it looked fake. "Vinnie leased me an Infiniti."

*Huh.* So the guy had plenty of money. Joe guessed the mob paid well. "Nice," he said dryly, then decided to change the subject *again.* "Want a kitten?"

Jana's eyes went girlishly wide. "A kitten? We have kittens?"

"Four of 'em, under the shed. I need to get rid of 'em."

"God, I'd love a kitty. But . . ." A slight grimace reshaped her normally pretty face. "I don't know. We're not home a lot. And I don't know if Vinnie would want a pet in the condo."

*Yeah, and the whole fucking world revolves around Vinnie.* "Figures," he muttered under his breath.

"What did you say?"

"Nothing." He raised his gaze, tried to push his irritation aside. But he didn't like the idea of some guy he didn't know controlling his sister's life. He let out a sigh and knew he still sounded gruff when he said, "Want to at least see 'em?"

She nodded enthusiastically and they both started toward the back door, his sister's heels making little clicks across the floor—until she pulled up short. "But first . . . uh, Joe?"

He stopped and glanced back at her. "Yeah?"

"There's a purple bra hanging on your lampshade."

She pointed across the room and Joe turned to see. He hadn't bothered taking it down yet. "You don't think it looks good there?" he asked almost without missing a beat.

She laughed, and he found himself glad to ease the tension between them, glad the bra was bringing *somebody* some laughter. "What I don't get," she said, "is how did it take me this long to notice it?"

Despite himself, he quirked a small grin in her direction. "You probably missed the collection in the kitchen, too. They're chained together over the window as curtains."

She laughed again, then met his gaze, her look earnest— more like the Jana he used to know before she'd moved away six months ago. "So, this bra, does it belong to anyone special? Or just a one-night fling?"

Joe practically snorted at the irony—the answer to both questions was yes. "It's Trish's," he said simply.

His sister's jaw dropped nearly to the floor as shock reshaped her expression. Jana had only been a kid when he'd dated Trish, but Trish had spent a lot of time at their house and Jana knew how important she'd been to him. "Oh my God, Joe—tell me everything."

"Nothing to tell." He wasn't going into the details of his sex life with his little sister, no matter how grown up she suddenly wanted to be.

She rolled her eyes. "Come on."

But he just shrugged. "She's in town for a week. We spent a little time together. End of story. Now do you want to see the damn cats or not?"

Jana grimaced at his tone but walked toward the door.

Ten minutes later, it was clear to Joe from all the oohing and ahhing his glittery sister had done that she'd fallen for "the twins," as she kept calling the two yellow newborns.

"Tell you what," he said as they strolled around the corner of the house to the driveway. "I'll walk you to the car and you can ask Vinnie about the cats. And I can finally meet the guy." He tried to keep the rancor from his voice.

But Jana looked uncomfortable at the very suggestion. "I told you, he's making business calls. If I interrupt him, he'll be ticked."

"Sounds like a great guy you've got there, sis," he said through slightly clenched teeth. No hiding the rancor this time—he didn't even try. He glanced again at the big black ride in his driveway, still peeved by the tinted windows.

"He *is* a great guy, Joe, I promise."

"Then why the hell haven't I met him? Why can't I even meet him when he's sitting in my fucking driveway?"

She snapped her gaze to him, since his anger was coming through loud and clear now and he no longer cared if Jana or Mr. Tinted Windows knew it. "What's your problem, Joe? I just wanted to bring your car back, not get the third degree."

Joe took a deep breath and reminded himself she was an adult who could do what she wanted. But she was also the only family he really had left, and he was the same to her. He lowered his voice. "Maybe I worry about you, okay? Maybe I don't think it's too much to ask that I meet the guy you're living with."

She looked guilty—not his goal exactly, but if it got him introduced to Vinnie Balducci, possible mob boss, okay. "I'm sorry Vinnie's not . . . all that social. He's just . . . kind of shy sometimes."

*But he runs a bar?* He kept his doubt to himself and instead said, "I don't bite."

She lowered her chin. "From the look on your face right now, I'd guess otherwise."

Another deep, calming breath was required at this point to keep Joe from stalking to the car and yanking Vinnie out of it.

"Listen," Jana said, reaching to touch his arm, "I promise you'll meet him soon. Really. He's just not in the greatest mood today." When he gave her a scolding look, she quickly added, "You've been known to get in a bad mood or two yourself sometimes, so give him a break. We all get in bad moods. I'm pretty sure *you're* in one right now. But soon, Joe, I swear. And you'll like him—really."

A minute later, Joe was hugging his sparkly sister good-bye while, unbeknownst to her, over her shoulder, he snarled slightly toward the Lincoln's tinted windshield.

After watching them drive away, he calmed down and immersed himself in normal Sunday stuff. He mowed the lawn, paid some bills and wrote Beverly a check for the stuff Carissa needed, then did a load of work clothes and another of towels. He tried his damnedest not to think about Trish—about her hot seduction, about how amazing it had been when their bodies had finally connected, about the sharp sting of waking up alone afterward. And it worked. Mostly.

Before he knew it, the sun was dipping low, ending the day and bringing on another hot summer night in Eden. The weekend had sufficiently worn him out—he felt ready to veg in front of the TV and mentally prepare for the work week ahead. Tomorrow was Monday, and he had a Lamborghini that needed a tune-up, which was going to take all his attention. He decided he should go to bed early and get a good, restful night's sleep.

But when he exited the shower, stepping into underwear and

a pair of jeans, he found himself glancing across the living room at his lampshade . . . and knew a restful night would be impossible. Because like it or not, he *was* still thinking about Trish—all the good parts . . . and the bad.

And he still had a purple bra to deal with.

Trish sat on the bed in her motel room, laptop humming on the flowered bedspread before her. Tomorrow she would call Lois Faulkner and hopefully get the diner contract's issues hammered out, taking her one big step closer to heading home and away from Joe Ramsey. But in the meantime, she needed to keep up with her real life, so she was going through her e-mail.

Skimming the inbox, she stopped on one from Kent Delacorte, associate, partner in her firm, and potential romantic interest. *Potential* because nothing had happened yet, but Kent had just broken up with a long-time girlfriend two months ago. Trish and Kent had always gotten along well, seen eye to eye on most things, and been frequent lunch partners, but lately, she'd sensed new bits of flirtation in their relationship. And she'd liked it—since Kent was pretty much everything she could want in a man.

Okay, so there was no snake tattoo.

Or searing blue eyes.

But before a couple of days ago, she never would have missed such things, so she couldn't let them be part of the equation. And now that she'd *had* the snake tattoo and blue eyes, it was time to focus on guys who were actually *suitable* for her, actual *possibilities* in her life. She'd had sex with Joe—and now it was over.

It still felt surreal to know she'd truly gone to his house and seduced him. It was her first one-night stand ever. She tried to ignore the irony that it had happened with the only guy she'd ever wanted to marry.

Kent's message was mostly social, jovial, full of inside jokes.

> You should have seen Stinson's tie the other day. He's going to start scaring clients away with those things. He forced me to go to Burrito Bob's on Wednesday, by the way. I couldn't get out of it because he knew my usual Wednesday lunch date—that's you—was out. Bob's wasn't as bad as you and I suspected, so my treat when you get back.

She smiled softly. Now, having sex with *Kent* would make sense. She tried to envision it—then sighed. Because when she imagined being naked with Kent, he had a snake on his arm. And broader, more muscular shoulders. And, actually, an entirely different face. Which belonged to Joe.

Okay, so this was apparently not the right moment to visualize sex with Kent. No problem—there'd be plenty of time to get to that later. After she got Joe out of her system. She tried not to remember that *having sex* with Joe had been intended to get him out of her system. Now she had to get the sex part out of her system, too, she supposed.

The next e-mail was from her associate Elaine, second chair on a big case going to trial soon—the Richie Melbourne rape case. Trish scanned the message to learn that her favorite DNA expert was currently examining evidence, including some plastic cups found at the scene of the crime, as well as the victim's underwear.

Given everything she'd learned so far, she knew a girl had indeed been raped leaving a college party after having ingested the date-rape drug—but for Trish's money, all fingers *should* be pointing to Dane Eldridge, a hulking Purdue jock who'd been accused of rape before, yet had gotten off, because of his parents' money and political connections. Another young woman had recently taken out a restraining order against him, too.

Trish's client, Richie, also played sports at Purdue, and while she doubted he was an angel, she believed in his innocence. She'd interviewed him extensively, and he'd struck her as an upstanding kid with a bright future. She'd liked him immensely, and God knew it helped to defend someone you truly thought free of wrongdoing. On the other hand, it also added pressure—pressure to make sure an innocent client didn't go to jail. But Trish considered it a *welcome* pressure, one that fueled her enthusiasm for the case.

According to Richie, both guys had been flirting with the girl—Jessica—hanging with her at a party just off campus. Richie had asked Jessica out and she'd turned him down, but it had remained a friendly exchange. The three had happened to leave the party at the same time, but Dane had offered to walk Jessica to her car, so Richie had headed in the opposite direction toward his dorm. The next day, he'd found himself charged with rape.

Jessica had woken up on the back lawn of a frat house with no clear memory of the event, and then, as so many girls made the mistake of doing, she'd panicked and raced home to shower. Only late the next morning had her roommates talked her into calling the police. And because she and several witnesses had last remembered Richie giving her a drink at the party, he was going on trial.

But when Richie's DNA didn't show up on any of those cups or the panties, it would provide exactly what Trish needed to get justice for Richie. She could only hope it might finally get some fingers pointed at Dane Eldridge, too.

Just then, the phone rang and she wondered if it was the pizza guy, calling to tell her he'd be late bringing her dinner. Having just sent a quick note of thanks to Elaine for the Richie update, she reached for the receiver. "Hello?"

"Well?" Debbie. She should have figured. She'd spent most of the day at her parents' house, and she'd purposely left her cell phone behind in the room.

"Well what?" Trish plopped her head back onto a pillow, sighing.

Debbie practically screeched on the other end. "Don't you 'well what?' me, young lady. Out with it."

Trish stiffened. Despite all that had happened, she'd decided to commit a mortal best friend sin and not tell Debbie the whole truth. Like the there-for-a-minute-I-thought-I-was-still-in-love-with-him part of the truth. That had been history talking, and it would be less painful to just do what she'd planned in the first place—keep the emotions out of it. "Well, I went to his door, his eyes nearly popped out of his head, I took off my dress, and we had wild sex." She added a quick afterthought. "Oh, and then he fell asleep and I left."

The phone stayed silent.

"Deb? You there?"

"Yeah. Just sort of stunned."

"Why? You knew the plan."

"I didn't really think you'd be able to do it that coolly, that unemotionally. After all, the girl I know should be *gushing* as she tells me this story, giving me every ridiculous detail from what he was wearing to what he was having on his pizza."

All right—wait just a minute here. "*Pizza?* How did you know he was having *pizza?*"

Debbie hissed in her breath, caught. "Oops. Sort of let the cat out of the bag there, didn't I?"

"And I guess this cat's name would be Kenny?"

"They had lunch together today. In the course of the conversation, I guess Joe mentioned he'd had pizza before you arrived. But to get to the point—"

"Yes, please do."

Debbie let out a sigh. "Kenny said he seemed kind of . . . upset about the whole thing. So I wanted to hear your version."

It was difficult to imagine the Joe she'd encountered the last two nights getting upset about sex, so Trish was skeptical. "Upset how?"

"Well, maybe upset isn't quite right. But he was definitely mad at me for not warning him. And he was pretty mad at you, too, for leaving."

*Oh, mad, was he? Well, too bad.* She knew going there had been a mistake, that she *wasn't* the cool, unemotional woman she'd just tricked Debbie into believing she was, but her regrets had nothing to do with *Joe's* feelings—she had, quite honestly, been thinking only of herself, what *she* needed, what *she* wanted. It hadn't even occurred to her that Joe would *have* feelings on the subject—other than the satisfaction of getting laid.

So what was his problem? Was he miffed because he hadn't gotten to call the shots, make the moves, decide the precise moment when their little soiree drew to a close?

The *nerve* of him being mad!

So she'd gotten up and left. Big deal. Next to nothing compared to what *he'd* done to *her* all those years ago.

She held in her sudden gasp and shot to an upright position on the bed.

Oh God—was it true? Could she really still be angry with him over something that had happened fourteen long years ago? Could sex with Joe possibly have been what Debbie had accused her of—revenge?

*Bleck.* She rolled her eyes and hoped to God not. She didn't want to be that kind of petty, live-in-the-past woman—she *so* didn't see herself that way.

"Trish, you there?"

"Uh, yeah." Her stomach churned. At the moment, she wished she'd never come home, wished she'd never bumped into Joe at all.

Well, except for the fact that the sex had been mind-blowing and that finally having him inside her had surpassed her wildest expectations. But she was supposed to be getting that out of her system.

"Are you okay?" Debbie asked.

Numb with emotion, she was trying to formulate an answer when a brisk knock came on the door. The pizza guy. Which, it suddenly hit her, was probably some ridiculous subliminal choice caused by his kisses having tasted like pizza last night. "Deb, I'm fine, but my dinner's here. Let me call you back after I eat."

"All right," Debbie sighed. "But make it snappy. I'm not done grilling you about this."

"Swell," Trish said, then hung up.

Suspecting her hair pointed in all directions, she quickly gathered it in a clip behind her head, grabbed the twenty she'd laid out on the dresser, and whipped open the door.

Joe leaned against the doorjamb wearing jeans and a white

button-up shirt, her missing bra dangling from one outstretched finger.

She drew in her breath. Shocked that he wasn't the pizza guy. And breathless at how darn good he looked.

His gaze dropped quickly to the money in her hand, then rose back to her eyes. "I know I'm good, but I wasn't expecting you to pay me."

Oh my. She wished she had a comeback, but the only one she could think of had to do with him *not* being good, and claiming *that* would just be silly. Thus she stood statue-still, mouth open.

"And if I *had* been planning to charge you, afraid twenty bucks wouldn't cover it."

No, she supposed not. If he were a gigolo, he'd be the high-priced kind. But she sure as hell couldn't tell him *that*, either. Which left her utterly speechless, still. She wasn't ready for this, him, right now.

"You forgot this," he went on, unfazed, motioning to the bra. "Or was it supposed to be a souvenir?"

She still couldn't talk, but she pulled herself together enough to scowl and snatch the bra from his fingertip.

"Good," he said, the corners of his mouth turning up in only the slightest superior smile. "The last thing I need is another souvenir. Already have plenty."

Joe tilted his head and peered into those gaping green eyes. If she wanted to make their sex just sex, two could play at that game. Besides, he'd be damned if he was going to tell her how disappointed he'd been to wake up and find her gone, and how much it bothered him even now—just seeing her.

Although she looked a hell of a lot different than she had last night. She'd traded in her black dress and stockings for a pair of gray drawstring running shorts and a pale green T-shirt that hugged her breasts nicely. Her hair was twisted up on top of her head and she wore no makeup. Her feet were bare. He was still damn pissed at her—but as the moment stretched on, he also became painfully aware that he wanted to kiss her. And not gently.

He'd spent the last couple of hours trying to think of her as just another woman, another roll in the hay, or on the couch—and he'd tried to convince himself that it truly meant nothing to her, either.

Problem was—he wasn't buying. He kept remembering the way she'd looked at him when he'd been inside her, her gaze brimming with passion, but also something more. Something that ran wild and deep.

He knew he was acting like an asshole, but maybe if he was enough of a jerk, she'd admit the truth. "So was it good for you? Did I satisfy you? Or do you want to put on another tight little outfit and prance around in it for me again?"

Her eyes narrowed tightly just before she drew back her hand and slapped him. Hard.

He'd seen it coming, but hadn't moved. And his cheek burned with some combination of shame and gratification, but he wasn't done yet because he still hadn't gotten what he wanted—an explanation. "Does the truth hurt, cupcake?"

She still said nothing and he was tired of standing outside, so he walked through the door and shut it, forcing her to take a step back.

"Get out," she snapped, and he couldn't help enjoying the fresh fury raging in her eyes.

"Not 'til I get what I came for."

"Which is?"

"I want you to tell me what the hell happened last night."

She raised her eyebrows, cool sarcasm invading her voice. "Weren't you paying attention?"

Hmm, suddenly she was in rare form. "Refresh my memory. Start with what exactly you wanted from me and end with why you went sneaking out in the middle of the night."

She hesitated, but only for a second. "I came because I wanted sex. And I left because I'd gotten it."

The words caught him off guard. He hadn't really thought she'd confirm Debbie's story. But she'd said it with such conviction, so much that he almost believed it, and an invisible fist squeezed his heart.

When a knock came on the door, they both flinched. He looked at her as if to ask who was out there, at the same time telling her with his eyes that they weren't anywhere near being done with this yet.

"I ordered pizza," she said.

He yanked the twenty from her hand and flung open the door to find a bored-looking kid chewing gum and holding a pizza box. "Medium sausage and mushroom?"

Joe whisked it from his arms and thrust the twenty at him. "Keep the change." He shut the door and strode briskly across the room, just past where she stood, to toss the pizza on the dresser.

And realized that the move had brought him way too close to her—only a few scant inches separated them.

And she hadn't stepped away.

He could almost feel the heat emanating from her body, and a quick glance downward revealed her nipples puckering to life beneath her bra. It wasn't a lengthy moment, just a too-long hesitation on her part—but when she did finally shift to put some distance between them, he realized he couldn't let her go. Not that easily.

Instinct took over—he grabbed her hips and pulled her to him, tight. Her lush curves molded against him and his body went taut with the thick, consuming hunger he'd been trying not to feel.

"Aw, damn it, Trish," he muttered. He buried his gaze deep in hers, trying to see what hid inside her. And when a long second passed and he still couldn't tell, his body urged him to give up on her eyes and move to other areas.

He brought his mouth harshly down on hers and sank into the hot, glorious struggle of having her kiss him back just as hard. Anger and longing still battled inside him until more words spilled out. "If it's sex you want, Trish, I've got plenty."

He heard her labored breath as he rained brisk kisses on her neck, then moved back to punish her mouth—her lovely, delicate mouth. He'd not have believed such soft lips could kiss him with such feral power.

He leaned her back into the dresser, sliding one hand firmly to her ass to lift her onto it. Her legs spread for him naturally and he moved in, pushing hard against her. Coils of heat spiraled outward from where they connected.

They exchanged short, frantic kisses then, Joe getting lost in the friction as their bodies moved together. Damn, he wanted her—like he'd never wanted anything before. "Jesus," he muttered as the sensations threatened to swallow him. He lifted his hand to the lush fullness of her breast, the move gruffer than intended, but her sharp intake of breath filled him with masculine satisfaction.

Trish feared she might faint—the pleasure was too swift, too hard.

But—*oh God, oh no*—she couldn't do this! Not again.

She'd made a tragic error last night—but at least it had been *her* idea, *her* in control. This was something different entirely— the tables had turned. She *couldn't* let him seduce her now. She already hurt too much as it was.

"Stop," she said.

Both their bodies went painfully still and she felt for a moment as if they had transformed into some human sculpture of entwined lovers, forever frozen on the brink of ecstasy. Finally, he pulled back slightly, his hand still on her breast, to peer heatedly into her eyes. "Really?"

He sounded shocked, as if the demand was unfathomable. Her mind and body still reeled, with pleasure and yearning, and with the ugly lie she'd told him about it being only sex when it had quickly become so much more. Why had he come here? And why did he have to be so angry? She'd done nothing wrong— after all, two nights ago he'd invited her home for sex with no expectations or promises. Why was it so terrible that she'd done to him what he'd tried to do to her—have a one night stand? People did it all the time; it wasn't a highly unusual concept. Yet he'd somehow managed to make her feel like a criminal.

And now, here she was, back in his arms—and he was trying to turn her plan of one night into something even more confusing than she'd already created.

Their eyes locked, his filled with a passion that seemed almost brutal. "Answer me, damn it. Yes or no." He spoke softer then. "If you say no, Trish, I'll walk out that door and not look back—because whatever game you're playing, I don't like it. But if you say yes . . . I promise—I'll make you feel things you've never felt before."

Oh boy. Just like when he'd issued such assurances at the bar, she didn't doubt him a bit, and heavy spasms of desire rippled relentlessly through her body in response. No man had ever said such things to her. And given that he'd already achieved that goal last night, wondering what deep pleasures awaited her if she allowed this to happen now, again, created a rock-hard temptation inside her.

But she had to say no. No, no, no. Her sanity depended upon it. If she slept with him again, she'd be lost to a man who had injected the worst hurt of her life straight into her heart, lost to a man who—when it came down to it—she had no reason to trust.

Even if his hands on her were like rough velvet. Even if his kisses made her entire body pulse. Even if his flesh pressing so heatedly against hers begged her for surrender. She had to say no.

"Yes or no, Trish," he said gruffly. "Answer me."

*Say no. Just say it. That one tiny word.*

"Yes." Uh-oh—wrong tiny word.

**Ready:** prepared to start the trial or begin oral argument. Usually said by an attorney or party in response to a judge calling the list of scheduled cases; _or_ in such a condition to be imminent, likely at any moment.

# Five

He groaned at her answer and she let her eyes fall shut.

Dear God, she'd just given in.

And she couldn't have been more relieved that she hadn't let him walk away.

"Do things to me," she whispered.

His breath came hot on her ear. "I'm gonna do *everything* to you, baby."

The words sent a hot rush of sensation scurrying from the base of her neck all the way down her spine. His kisses returned then, and he massaged her breasts through her top, slowly, so slowly. Moaning at the exquisite pleasure, she couldn't deny that it was significantly heightened by the hard bulge in his jeans pressing hotly to the sensitive spot between her legs. She pushed back—against his hand, against that bulge—and, oh God, she wanted him, exactly the way she'd had him last night. "I want you in me."

"Soon." His breath came labored.

"No, now."

"*Soon*," he insisted again.

He reached to pull down her shorts, and she lifted for him automatically, everything below her waist aching with maddened desire. He took her cotton panties, too, and when the clothes hit the floor, she bit her lip and parted her legs for him farther.

His gaze dropped there, raw animal heat taking over his expression. The same reckless need surged moistly at her core, and she yearned for him to open his jeans and fill her.

But instead . . . he dropped to his knees.

Oh.

Oh my.

His breath warmed her inner thighs, making her lips tremble. And just as she'd never pleasured him with her mouth in their youth, they'd never done this before, either. She sucked in her breath and watched him lean closer.

The first kiss to her most sensitive flesh made her shiver. The second made her sob. And then his tongue sliced so deeply into her that she heard her own hot whimper as she drowned in the wondrous sensation.

"Joe." She hadn't meant to whisper his name, but there it was. Her body arched toward him, unplanned. "Oh God, Joe."

Lord knew the man had good hands, but the way he used his mouth was pretty fabulous, too. His lips, suckling slowly, his tongue, tasting deeply. Put them together and it was like a symphony, like she was the instrument and he was playing her.

Those skilled hands, too, rose to join in—one stroking her, then parting her wider so that he could slip the fingers of the other inside. She gasped, trembled, thrust involuntarily, swept away from the reality of anything but him and her and raw, consuming heat.

He pushed her higher, higher, making her cry out. She cried his name. She cried words like "Yes!" and "Oh!" Once she murmured, "So close"—and then her body shattered to leave her writhing uncontrollably as moan after moan rocked her. *Yes, oh yes.*

Until finally she came back to herself, back to the motel room, and back to Joe, who gazed heatedly up at her.

She wanted to say a million things, but most of them had to do with love, so she let silence prevail. Which was all right, because their eyes said more right now than words ever could—things about passion and sex and emotions that hid deep in the heart, about sharing something powerful and soul-stirring.

He pushed to his feet, stepping close enough that she could smell the manly, musky scent of him again—and then he reached for her hand, pressing it flat against the erection shrouded in his jeans. Oh—so hard. It stole her breath.

"Unzip me," he said, their gazes locked hotly.

She undid the top button, pulled down the zipper. Reached into his briefs to wrap her fist full around his length. He shuddered and she bit her lip at the pleasure, then they both pushed his jeans past his hips.

His voice came deep, raspy. "Do you want me to wear a condom this time?"

She didn't even consider it. "No. I want to feel you completely. Nothing between us." He made her so reckless.

He growled in reply, a sound that moved through her like

thunder, and they both watched as he entered her. The blatant sight combined with being so smoothly, deeply filled left her weak. Her eyes fell shut.

"No," he said softly. "Look at me."

She forced them back open and met his gaze, fiery and possessive, as he moved inside her. She clung to his shoulders and he wrapped his arms around her waist. She continued peering at him through each powerful stroke, until finally she had to kiss him. Had to. No choice. Just compulsion.

One kiss became two, then more—long, sweet, tongue kisses that matched the rhythm of their sex, the connection of their mouths as deep as the connection below.

"So good, Trishy," he breathed.

"Mmm . . . yes." Things had somehow turned slower now, each thrust long, raw, and real. Trish had never felt so very captured by a man—in a good way. An *incredible* way. This was so far beyond "just physical" that the force of it nearly broke her in two.

*I love you still.* She held in the words. Because as astounding as this was, as deeply as he possessed her in this moment—nothing had changed. Her heart still hurt. She *couldn't* love him still. Yet she drank up each precious kiss, found herself living for this sacred connection of their bodies, and savored every second of it.

When his hands closed tight over her rear, he pushed in even deeper—which, dear God, she hadn't known was even possible. "Oh!" The slight shift changed *everything*, and she knew she'd have another orgasm. Soon. *Really* soon.

She clutched madly at his shoulders, holding on for dear life, and moved against him harder, faster, the pleasure inside her rising, fast, so fast—until she was toppling into ecstasy, deep, wild moans being torn from her throat.

"Aw, God," he said suddenly. "Aw, God, baby, you're making me come."

She still clung to him as he drove wildly, groaning his release in her ear, and taking him there brought her such profound feminine satisfaction that she didn't care if *she* ever had another orgasm again.

A tear rolled ticklishly down her cheek, but she wiped it quickly away on his shirt, thankful he hadn't seen. She'd never been so sated in her life—but she'd also never felt more lonely, because the truth in her heart hadn't changed.

Somehow  she wasn't sure when—he'd lifted her up off the dresser to support her weight completely, and now they collapsed in each other's arms on the bed. They lay silent for a few seconds, both frozen in the moment, a mess with tangled clothes and wetness, but neither made a move.

They faced each other, so it was impossible not to peer into those searching blue eyes. He lifted one hand to her cheek to brush back a lock of hair that had fallen free from her clip. "I didn't plan this," he said. "I only came here for answers."

Trish's mind was a blur. "Answers?"

"Whatever last night was about, Trish," he began, voice soft, "just tell me."

His words hung in the air like the dark ash that drifts slowly down after fireworks, and she realized that she, too, was tired of this lie. Especially after what they'd just shared. Besides, she'd be going back to Indianapolis soon anyway. And as much as she hated to say anything to him that would imply she still cared, she couldn't keep being so stupidly dishonest. "I . . . wanted you. But I . . . didn't want it to mean anything, because . . . I guess the truth is," she whispered, "I just haven't really forgiven you."

Although something in his eyes looked a bit wounded, he gave a solitary nod. "Last night was shocking as hell, cupcake, but to finally be with you . . . it *did* mean something. At least to me."

*Me, too.* But she refused to take her honesty that far. Refused to put herself out there, at risk. So she stayed quiet.

His expression shifted then, into something more gruff than sad. "You said you'd stay. I thought you were giving me a chance to make up for the past."

She didn't quite know how to answer, so her voice came small. "I guess I shouldn't have agreed to pancakes. It was just . . . easier, I guess."

"Than?"

"The truth."

His gaze burned on her and his voice was frank. "It was pretty shitty to leave in the middle of the night."

Fresh anger sparked inside her, making her sit up in bed. Suddenly feeling naked, she reached to pull the skirt of the bedspread up over her waist as she stared down at him in disbelief. "What about what *you* did to *me?* That wasn't shitty?" She didn't mean to go back there, but she couldn't help it.

He sat up next to her, bringing their faces close again. "Of course it was—it was the biggest fucking mistake I've ever made. But I never got to tell you that because you didn't want anything to do with me. And now we're grown-ups, Trish, not kids—and just because I handled things rotten *then* doesn't mean you should keep handling them rotten *now*. It seems like . . . trying to get even with me." He shook his head lightly. "Is that what you wanted? To try to hurt me?"

Trish took a deep breath. She honestly didn't know the answer to his question, so she couldn't answer. Instead, something deeper boiled to the surface. "You should have come after me," she blurted.

He blinked. "What?"

"When I left for college, you should have come after me."

"But you said—"

"Who cares what I said—you should have ignored it! You should have made a grand gesture! If you loved me, you should have made me *see* it, you should have found some way to *prove* it, some way to make things *right*. I might have slammed my dorm room door in your face for all I know, but no matter what I might have done, you should have gotten in your car and come after me."

She hadn't even known she'd wanted that until this moment. Or at least she'd never admitted it to herself. But maybe back then, she'd waited, hoped—just in the back of her mind—that he'd come, that he'd beg her forgiveness. And he never had.

He released a heavy breath, ran his hands back through his hair. He sat with his head slumped over, but finally looked up. "You think I didn't consider that? Because I did. Probably a hundred times."

"But you didn't do it."

His gaze narrowed. "It seemed awful easy for you to leave, Trish."

She gasped, utterly shocked, and almost wanted to slap him again. "How dare you!" she snapped. "You have no idea . . ." *How much I hurt. How long it took to quit feeling the pain. How it changed me inside.* But she still didn't want him to know all that. A hint of self-preservation.

"No, I guess I don't," he said, sounding surprisingly contrite for a second. "But you were gone, off having a new life, and for all I knew, our breakup worked out good for you."

*Well, it didn't.* Another thing she hadn't the bravery to tell him. Because this would all be over soon, and she wanted him to remember her as she was *now*—a strong, bold, confident woman. Not as she'd been then, after the breakup—a broken, devastated girl who'd feared she'd never recover from losing him.

"Believe it or not," he went on, his voice lower, "you're not the only one who was hurting. What happened was my fault, but it changed my life, too. In a lot of ways."

"You have . . . a daughter," she said, the very words pinching in her stomach. She knew about Beverly's child, knew from Debbie that there were questions surrounding the paternity, but that Joe had taken at least some role in the girl's life. She supposed she'd chosen not to let herself think about that since coming back home, but now that they were putting certain truths on the table, she could no longer ignore it.

He looked up. "It's complicated."

"So I hear." Even Debbie wasn't sure if Joe was really the father.

"But that's a story for another time. Right now what I want to know is . . ." He lifted those blue eyes back to hers, looking earnest and sexy and so tempting that she could taste it. "Couldn't we start fresh? Couldn't we move past what happened then, and what's happened the last couple of days and just . . . start over?"

Trish blinked, trying to understand. She was pretty sure he was suggesting . . . a relationship. A grown-up romance. Being lovers.

Her chest tightened. First with hope—and a strange tinge of happiness. But then with the utter impossibility of it. "Joe," she began, too softly.

His eyes still met hers, yet she knew her tone said it all—she saw it in his eyes, in the flat, straight line his mouth made, stretching across his handsome face.

She tried again. "Joe, I don't live here anymore. I have a different life now—so completely different. But more than that . . ." *You could hurt me again—so, so badly—if I let you.* Already she knew that. She didn't know if she was really, truly, still in love with him—but dear God, there was *something* there, something big, more than sex.

"More than that, I . . . don't know if I can forget the past. I've moved on, obviously, but seeing you, being with you . . . it's dredged up some old memories. Some good. But some pretty awful."

He sighed, yet never broke their gaze. "I get all that, Trish. Every bit of it. But I'm asking you to try to forgive me. Just try."

She drew in her breath, sat up a little straighter, attempting to steel herself. "I'm not trying *not* to forgive you. I don't like that I haven't, believe me. I don't think of myself as someone who holds a grudge. But I can't help how I feel. And the fact is," she went on, "soon I'll be leaving and you'll probably never see me again, so whether or not I forgive you doesn't matter in the big scheme of things."

He let out a breath. "Maybe it matters in *my* big scheme of things."

She plopped back on the bed, only to feel the sharp edges of her hair clip bite into her head, so she yanked it out and tossed it to the floor. She stared at the ceiling because she couldn't bear to look at him any longer. He was too beautiful. "What I mean is . . . it won't change anything. Our lives will still go on as they have all these years."

"So making love with me didn't change anything for you?"

*Making love?* Whoa. She'd never been with a man who'd called it that, and Joe was the last guy she'd have expected it from.

And she couldn't help remembering how frantic their coupling had been, both times. She glanced up at him. "Would you call it that? Making love? We were . . . like animals."

"Lots of different ways to make love, cupcake."

She looked back to the ceiling. His blue eyes shone on her too intently.

But when he reached under the bedspread still covering her to graze his palm up her bare thigh, hip—oh boy—desire flared again.

"I don't think I could ever get enough of you if we did this every day and night forever," he said, and the startling notion sent a great warmth rushing through her womb.

Yikes. She needed to put a stop to the temptation that kept erupting inside her. She needed to get to the *end* of this hot encounter.

In fact, she needed to quit being *real* Trish and instead act like Patricia Henderson, attorney at law, take-charge woman who didn't pull any punches.

"That's too bad, Joe, because it can't happen again."

Damn, that was good. She'd sounded utterly sure, completely in control.

He hesitated, probably because her voice had just changed— yet his gaze continued to burn through her even as she kept her eyes focused on the plain white ceiling. "So you think if I come back here again," he asked, "you'll be able to send me away? I gave you the chance to say no, Trish. And you couldn't. You wanted it as much as I did."

True. But Lawyer Trish knew how to dodge an answer and change the topic. "If you come back, I won't be here. I'm leaving tomorrow."

"Back to Indy?" He sounded disappointed.

If only it were that simple. "No," she confessed, "just to my mom and dad's."

Even in her peripheral vision, she saw relief flood his expression—but she resolved to ignore it. She *could* resist him, and she was getting stronger inside with each passing second. It was just like being in a courtroom, putting on a grand show, pretending she believed in something she didn't, as defense at torneys so often had to do.

"And," she went on, "I don't think it's a good idea for us to see each other again."

But—oops—apparently she'd taken her little act too far, because in an instant, every ounce of cocky confidence returned to his gaze. "I dare you to look me in the eye and tell me it was just sex, Trish. Last night or right now."

She could have. She was in full attorney mode now. But she saw no point, since she'd already surrendered that truth. "It *wasn't* just sex," she admitted, and she met his eyes to say it, since it would drive her point home. "But that doesn't mean it wasn't a mistake." She gently forced out the next, vital words. "You should go now."

He sat there for a long, painful moment—then finally rose from the bed, making it feel big and empty, to calmly zip up his jeans, his back turned. God, even from that view, he looked incredible—the denim hugging his butt beneath the tail of that white shirt, his shoulders stretching the fabric out so broad.

*Stop staring, damn it. Be strong.*

As he walked slowly to the sink outside the bathroom, she listened as he washed his hands, maybe his face. She took the opportunity to reach for her shorts—which had fallen near the bed—and scurry into them, but then she lay back down, wanting to appear nonchalant about his departure. She realized for the first time that the heavy scent of pizza permeated the air.

*He's going to leave now. Then you can eat. And sleep. And take care of business tomorrow. And put all this behind you, once and for all.*

He crossed the room and she thought he was headed to the door—but instead he rounded the bed and dropped to his knees, leaning toward her. "I'll go, but I'll need a kiss good-bye."

*Oh my.*

With that, he skimmed one palm up onto her cheek and lowered his mouth to hers. He pressed his tongue between her lips and—damn it—she responded. Hell, her whole *body* responded, perking to life from head to toe as she kissed him back, drank him in, even found herself threading her fingers through his soft, thick hair.

It would be so easy to forget everything she'd just said and pull him back down onto the bed with her, open those jeans back up, and let him fill her again. So, so easy. And so, so good.

He stretched it out, letting one kiss turn into another—each as warm and fevered as the ones shared in that Trans Am so long ago—and she got lost in them, at once loving the simple, sweet melding of their mouths but also yearning again for more, for their bodies to be interlocking.

Oh God, could she do this? Let herself have him again?

Maybe. Maybe it would be all right. Just one more time.

Which was when he finally pulled away, ending the kisses, pushing to his feet.

He gazed down on her, his eyes knowing. "Still want me to go?"

*No. God, no.*

"Yes," she whispered.

Right little word this time.

Or at least she thought it was.

Joe spent much of the next day under the hood of a Lamborghini Gallardo, which no one was allowed to touch but him. Even though the guys in his employ were good mechanics, he wasn't sure he trusted anyone but himself with a $150,000 car that belonged to one of his wealthiest customers. And besides, getting to put his hands inside a car like that was one of Joe's pure joys and he was too selfish to share it. Working on this car wasn't work at all—it was something he sank into, each turn of the wrench made lovingly, each task in the tune-up completed with the utmost respect and care. The service—which involved removing the engine, adjusting the valves, replacing the timing belts, and changing all the fluids, filters, and spark plugs—would take him the better part of a week, but he didn't mind, especially since it came with a tidy chunk of income. Guys who owned Lamborghinis didn't scrimp on service.

"Hey, Joe."

Even before looking up, he knew it was Carissa. "Just . . . one . . . minute, Care Bear," he said, tightening a bolt. Then he rose up, reached for the rag in his back pocket, and wiped his hands as he turned to face her.

"What the heck kind of car is *that*?" she asked, wide-eyed.

"That, Miss Care Bear, is an Italian Lamborghini."

"Cool."

Joe didn't personally love the look of this particular model— he was more of a roadster man—but there was no denying the car was a fast, well-tuned machine. "Yeah," he said. "Cool."

"You should quit calling me Care Bear, though."

He blinked. "Why?" He feared he wouldn't like what was coming.

"I'm *thirteen*," she said as if she were thirty. "I'm going into the *eighth grade*."

Joe sighed. Over the summer, Carissa had started acting more like a teenager than the tomboyish little girl she'd been up to now, but he'd been trying to ignore that. Tomboys he knew how to relate to—teenage girls, not so much. "Tell you what. I'll keep it quiet, just call you that when it's only me and you." He winked, then shouted over to the garage's other three bays, "Nobody heard me call her Care Bear, did they?"

"Not me," his buddy Carl's voice echoed from beneath a Mustang.

"Me neither," called Johnny Rogers, a young mechanic who'd only been with him a year or so.

"I guess you think you're funny or somethin'," she said with an exaggerated eye roll.

And he felt the urge to ruffle her hair, but resisted since she'd probably have a fit. She looked kind of dressed up, wearing flare-legged jeans and a tight little top that showed off her shape. Hell, when had she gotten a *shape?* Of course, he'd noticed it just the other day at the Waffle House, too, but that didn't mean he was *used* to it.

"What?" she said, narrowing her gaze on him.

Aw, crap—she'd clearly caught the troubled look in his eye. But he answered honestly. "You're growing up. I'm not sure I like it."

The truth earned him another eye roll. "Then you're *really* gonna hate *this*."

"This what?"

"What I came to talk to you about."

He raised his eyebrows, as if to say, *Go on*.

"Justin Vance asked me to the Fall Fling."

"The Fall what?"

"Fling. It's a dance."

Oh. A dance. Okay. He usually associated the word *fling* with sex, or at least fooling around. But then again, he knew what happened at dances. He'd taken Trish to dances. They'd made out like maniacs in the dark. "This dance, what's it like? Will there be . . . chaperones?"

She shrugged. "I guess." Then gave him a sarcastic look. "Relax, dude—it's a middle school dance, not an orgy."

*Christ*, how did she know what an *orgy* was?

"Why do you look weird?" she asked.

*Because I'm freaking out*. He had no idea what Carissa knew about sex or about waiting 'til you found someone special, no idea what Beverly might or might not have taught her—especially given *Bev's* past in that area. "Just tell me about this boy," he said, probably too gruffly. "What's his story? What does he do? What kind of grades does he make?"

*What kind of grades does he make?* Aw, crap—he really *was* acting like a dad.

But one of the things he loved about Carissa was that she never let his brusqueness intimidate her. "I haven't checked his report card," she offered, crossing her arms indignantly, "but he's in the gifted math class. He's good at video games, and he's into skateboarding."

Sounded like an average enough kid, so Joe couldn't complain. And the closest *he'd* ever come to any "gifted" classes had been when he'd walked Trish to hers. So he boiled it down to the heart of the matter, lowering his voice. "You like the guy, Care Bear?"

She nodded, a coquettish little smile stealing over her face, but what really answered the question was the red stain climbing her cheeks. He tilted his head, remembering first crushes and girls so pretty he'd thought they'd never look at him—but they had. *She* had. He'd had a crush on Trish since the fifth grade. "And would *I* like the guy, Care Bear?"

"Why? You want to go to the Fall Fling with him?"

"See, I was trying to be nice, not mess up your hair like I used to—but now you're just asking for it."

Her smile widened, and she looked more like little-girl Carissa than teenager Carissa as she took a playful step backward, just in case he made good on the threat.

"This dance," he said instead, "is it dressy?"

Another nod from her. "Not formal, but the girls all wear fancy dresses."

"Do you have something?"

As usual, when topics like this came up, she went a little sheepish, rocking from one foot to the other, letting her eyes drop to her beaded flip-flops. "I have a dress from last year," she said, trying to sound cheerful about it. "I might go with my friend Taylor and her mom over to Columbus and see if I can find something on sale."

"Got any money?"

She kept rocking. "Grandpa gave me twenty dollars for the yard work Saturday, and I made twelve babysitting Sophie's little boy last week."

Wiping his hands on the rag again, Joe eased his arms out of his coveralls and reached into the back pocket of his work jeans for his wallet. He'd just been to the bank this morning, so he had ample cash on him at the moment, and he slid a fifty into her hand. She took it but looked reluctant. "Joe, you don't have to give me money."

"I know that. Must mean I want to."

"Well, at least let me work for it or something."

They'd been through this before; he guessed Carissa had developed a healthy understanding that money didn't grow on trees. He tried to think of something for her to do and remembered a stack of paid invoices sitting on the corner of his desk. In fact, the whole damn office had been pretty messy lately. "You've filed invoices for me before, right?"

"Yeah." She nodded.

He motioned toward the door just beyond the Lamborghini. "There's a pile on my desk marked paid. You know what to do with 'em."

She smiled, then scurried toward the office. The job wouldn't take her half an hour, but that was all right—he didn't want her to waste her whole afternoon at the garage.

She paused, hand on the doorknob, to look back at him. "And Joe?"

"Yeah."

"When I'm done . . . you think we could talk for a few minutes? About Justin and the dance, I mean . . ." She blushed prettily and lowered her voice, probably in case the other guys were still listening. "Maybe you could tell me what to say, what kind of stuff he'll want to talk about."

He met her gaze. "Sure, Care Bear."

She smiled, eyes sparkling, then disappeared behind the gray office door.

Whether or not it made any sense, he was glad she was in his life, glad he'd decided to take part in hers. He knew some people gossiped about him shirking his responsibility—they assumed he wouldn't be in her life at all if he wasn't her father, so they thought he should have claimed her. And he knew others just wondered what the hell the deal was. Even Debbie didn't know for sure, because he'd sworn Kenny to secrecy all those years ago, and as far as he knew, Kenny had followed through. Mainly because everyone—including Kenny—knew that telling Debbie a secret was like taking out an ad in the *Eden Gazette.*

He didn't much care what anyone thought—he was just glad that maybe he gave Carissa something she needed. Money—but something else, too. They'd never talked about what his connection to her might be, yet they'd always shared a comfortable bond.

Although what the hell he was going to tell her to help with her "date" he didn't know. Zipping up his coveralls, he picked up his wrench and stared into the inner workings of the Lamborghini as if all the wires and tubes and hoses might spell out an answer. He'd never actually had those awkward adolescent dates. He'd known Trish their whole lives, so by the time he'd actually asked her out, it had been pretty easy. They'd been in some of the same classes, had hung with the same friends.

The very thought of Trish made him shake his head, and anyone watching him would have figured the Lamborghini's motor had him stumped, when in fact what had him befuddled was Trish Henderson.

The events of the weekend had shown him two things. The first was that, damn, he *really* wanted something with her again. He didn't know her like he used to, of course, but he *wanted* to—and the past they shared meant they'd always have at least *that* in common. And the passion between them hadn't faded one iota. If anything, it had grown. That passion had nearly knocked the wind out of him the moment he'd seen her. And Jesus Christ—had he really told her they were *making love?* Why did he even *know* that phrase? God knew he'd never used it before—but there it had been, popping out of his mouth like something he said every damn day.

The second thing he'd found out was that Trish *didn't* want something with *him*. Or at least her *mouth* said no—until he started kissing it.

At least he'd gotten her to admit it *wasn't* just sex between them. But for crying out loud, what the hell had she been thinking? Had she seriously thought that two people who were once madly in love could have sex without it meaning something? He knew Trish had been a smart girl and he felt certain she was an intelligent woman, but she'd missed the mark on that one.

The question was, what was he gonna do about all this?

Respect her wishes and consider this over?

Or screw that and do what he *really* wanted to do, which was convince her they could have something damn good together again?

Common sense said to leave this alone. Let her go back to her life in Indy if she was so dead set on it—hell, let her see if she could find any other guy who made her whimper and moan like that. He didn't think so. Because he didn't think any other guy could make her feel the way he did—not only in her body but in her heart, too.

So . . . common sense said to leave this alone. But it wouldn't be the first time he'd refused to listen to common sense.

**Continuance:** the adjournment or postponement of a court case to another day; <u>or</u> the act of remaining in the same place or condition.

## Six

Everything about this trip was a disaster. Joe was a disaster. Now the whole diner sale was a disaster. Because suddenly there *was* no diner sale.

By ten-thirty Monday morning, Trish had spoken not only to Lois Faulkner but also to the buyer's agent and the buyer herself. She'd refused to budge on the unreasonable terms she'd slid into the contract, declaring that the deal was off if Trish's parents wouldn't cough up the money for improvements. Trish explained that her parents were retiring, living on a very fixed income, that there simply *was* no money to cough up. And that was that. No deal.

Then she'd packed her suitcases, checked out of the Red Roof Inn, and moved back into her old room since Aunt Alma had departed yesterday.

Of course, her mom and dad took the failed sale better than she had. Because they were in denial—that was the only conclusion she could reach.

They hadn't even seemed alarmed. "There, there, dear," her mother kept saying, patting her hand—since clearly *she* was the one who needed to be comforted, because all of her simple, well-laid plans for this trip were going haywire. "Another buyer will come along."

*Ha*, Trish had wanted to say.

The fact that no one in Eden wanted to recognize was that Main Street was slowly . . . well, not *dying* exactly, but definitely molding itself into something new. Taking the place of the drugstore, bank, market, and five-and-dime Trish had frequented growing up were quaint establishments like an antiques shop and a vintage toy store. And a lot of empty storefronts. Business remained on Main Street, but the place wasn't bustling with townsfolk conducting their daily affairs, and she just wasn't sure the diner *fit* anymore. She'd felt beyond lucky that they'd found a buyer so quickly, and now that this one was gone, she had no idea how long it might take to find another.

She'd kept her *ha* to herself, though, not *wanting* to alarm her parents. Really, one alarmed person here was enough.

*This will all work out*, she told herself now as she drove toward town.

It was late afternoon and she was headed back to the diner for a more serious assessment. They'd gotten an appraisal before putting it on the market, but she needed to study the place closer, for herself. Maybe there were *cheap* things that could be done to increase the property's appeal and attract another quick sale.

Of course, the diner wasn't the only thing on her mind. Which was probably why she found herself driving right past it—right past the whole Main Street business district, another mile or so to the outskirts of town, past the new grocery store and a car dealership, past the new middle school and a pizza place that hadn't been here when she was a kid . . . and then past Shermer's Garage—which she hardly recognized.

A big, new brick façade fronted the building that now sported an attractive gable above the office area. Bold, appealing signage told her the establishment had become Ramsey's Auto Repair. The garage possessed two more work bays than the original two Mr. Shermer had operated. And fortunately, Joe's business sat far enough off the road that she felt safe driving past slowly, taking in all the details.

The only thing about the place that looked remotely familiar was the peeling wooden sign hanging from a front awning, announcing in an old-fashioned 1950s sort of script, *We Fix Anything on Wheels*. She had to smile, remembering the sign, and suspecting it remained as an homage to old Mr. Shermer.

Joe and his dad hadn't been overly close. Mr. Ramsey had been pleasant enough to *her*, but often grumbly to Joe for no reason she could figure out. Joe had always acted cool about it, but she knew it had embarrassed him; probably hurt him, too. And he'd never said so, but she'd also known in high school that Mr. Shermer had grown special to Joe because he'd treated him with respect and kindness.

As for why she was driving past the place—and now turning around in the new bank lot across the street . . . she had no idea.

All she knew was that her skin tingled whenever she thought about him.

And Lord, just remembering the intensity of having him inside her, of looking deep into his eyes while he moved in her—yikes, it sent a shiver down her spine even now.

*Yeah, sex with him really got him right out of your system. Good call on that one, Trish.*

Of course, some hedonistic part of her—likely that damn biker chick—wanted to pull into his lot, walk into his garage, back him into some dark room or closet, and have her way with him again. Turned out it was hard to get enough of Joe.

But she knew she couldn't do it. Only madness that way lay. It didn't matter how much sex they had—she'd still be going home to Indianapolis once this whole diner fiasco was somewhat settled, and more importantly, she still wasn't even remotely ready to deal with the barrage of emotions he brought tumbling down on her.

What she'd told him was true. She didn't forgive him.

She wanted to be bigger than that, more mature—but in her heart, she remained hurt by what he'd done all those years ago. How could she have something—*anything*—with a man she didn't completely trust? And having more sex would just create more emotions. It was a no-win situation.

Well, unless you counted orgasms into the equation.

Which was easy enough to do—because he gave her *earth-shattering* orgasms. When she'd been giving *him* an orgasm, she'd told herself she didn't care about her own, but really, she did.

Yet orgasms, unfortunately, only lasted a few blissful seconds. Emotions lingered.

As she exited the bank lot back out onto the two-lane highway with a sigh, she was thankful Joe didn't know her car, since driving past his garage demonstrated all the maturity of a sixteen-year-old. But she supposed she'd just wanted to see his place, see what he'd made for himself.

Now she had. And was duly impressed. *And that's the last ridiculous move you're going to make that has anything to do with Joe.* She hoped.

Letting out a sigh, she headed back to Main Street, remembering she really had far bigger problems now. Her parents might not think this failed sale was a big deal, but she had to think, plan—and worry. They were going to be in serious financial trouble if the restaurant didn't sell, and it was up to her to make that happen.

Pulling to the curb outside the Henderson Family Diner, Trish went inside, without bothering to lock up this time. Debbie was right—no one stole things from cars in Eden.

Heading to the back room, she found some all-purpose cleaner and set to wiping down tables and booths, windows and doors, counters and cook surfaces. The place had sat empty for a few weeks now, and a *shiny* diner was an *appealing* diner. Glad she'd worn old jeans and a tee, she soon realized she was wiping down the diner so vigorously that it was almost as if she thought she could somehow wipe away her memories of the weekend just past, as if the hard work would purge all the emotions still ravaging her. Because no matter what she did, he was still on her mind. And not just a little—more like with every breath she took.

She suddenly stopped scrubbing one of the booths, struck with a memory: stolen kisses over milkshakes and hamburgers.

For heaven's sake, everywhere she went, another recollection waited to leap out at her.

But then, maybe it was unrealistic to expect herself not to think about him. After all, her whole perception of the world had changed—she'd finally had sex with Joe. And not just sex. Hot, ravenous, blood-curdling, spine-tingling, moaning, practically *screaming* sex. Way better than fudge.

She lowered herself onto the booth's vinyl seat and replayed in her mind the moment when he'd left her last night—after he'd delivered those lush, melting kisses good-bye. She'd watched him walk to the door, feeling awkward and empty, and thinking—*This is it, the only thing I'll ever have with him, and it's ending, over.*

But then he'd shocked her by stopping, looking back over his shoulder—and a strange arrow of hope had pierced her heart. *He's going to find some miraculous way to change things, some magic sentiment that will make me trust him and forgive him and make me* really, truly *believe something good can happen here.* Yet instead he'd only said two little words. "Bye, Trish."

She sighed heavily. Ill-fated love sucked.

Life was easier without love of any kind than love gone wrong.

'Twas *not* better to have loved and lost than never to have loved at all.

"Time to get back to work," she muttered. It had been a long time since she'd sat around wallowing in despair fourteen years to be exact—and this was no time to start.

She refocused her energies on her cleaning and by the time she finished, she felt even *more* discouraged. The Henderson Family Diner, with its aqua booths and white Formica tables and the ancient jukebox that hadn't played any new songs since 1980, might be considered stylishly retro in a big city or even a bustling suburb—but here, in small-town America, it just seemed old and outdated.

If she really wanted a quick sale, maybe the place would benefit from a light makeover. Just as houses sold easier if one took the time to hang some new curtains and paint a few walls, so might the diner. She wasn't sure what she could do to update the booths and tables, but a little painting couldn't hurt. And besides making the place more marketable, it would also be a good diversion, a good way to banish thoughts of Joe Ramsey from her mind until she could get the hell out of Dodge—or Eden—once and for all.

Just then, the bell on the front door jingled and she flinched, immediately wondering if Joe had come to ravish her again. Unfortunately, the lightning-quick thought appealed—because the diner possessed a number of dark rooms and closets and would be just as good as the little fantasy she'd been indulging about the garage a couple of hours ago.

So it came as a bit of a blow to look up and see Marjorie Wilmers, who ran the flower shop next door.

"Trish Henderson, is that you?" She splayed her fingers across her chest. "Why, as I live and breathe, it *is* you! Little Trishy, all grown up! My word—come here and give me a hug!"

With someone as enthusiastic as Marjorie, there was little to do besides give her the hug. Marjorie was around the same age as her parents, and it was as shocking for Trish to see the older version of Marjorie as it was for Marjorie to see the adult her. Marjorie's dark curls, always cut close to her head, had gone gray, but she looked just as energetic as Trish remembered, her eyes shining through stylish mauve-framed glasses.

"I heard you were in town, helping your folks with the diner, but—my *goodness*, it's good to see you, hon."

Trish said, "It's good to see you, too, Marjorie," and she meant it. Sometimes she forgot about all the people she had known and genuinely cared for in Eden. Just like her relationship with Joe, that part of her existence seemed a lifetime ago.

So Trish put on a pot of coffee and sat down with Marjorie in the same booth where she used to kiss Joe, and they spent some time catching up—on Marjorie's kids and husband, and the fact that her shop had lost a little business over the years but she was still making a living. "Guess people still get married, get sick, and then die," Marjorie said, matter-of-factly accounting for the bulk of her orders. "When are *you* ever gonna get married?" she asked in the way only someone with no idea of the romantic turmoil in your life could.

"Me?" Trish knew it was a hypothetical question, but she felt as if someone had just shone a spotlight on her. "Probably never." She laughed, trying to play it off.

Marjorie waved her hand down through the air. "Oh, pshaw. But when you do"—she sounded slightly dejected now—"you'll probably have some big-city wedding and won't even let me do the flowers."

Trish tilted her head and gave Marjorie a sincere smile. "I'll make you a promise. When or if I ever get married, wherever it happens, you're my florist. Okay?"

Marjorie nodded, appeased. "I still want to kill that Debbie for eloping the way she did. I know it was a long time ago, but when she got engaged to Kenny, I got this vision in my head—yellow roses with lots of baby's breath and sprigs of white alyssum—and it never saw the light of day."

Trish, for one, had thanked her lucky stars when Debbie and Kenny had eloped to Gatlinburg, Tennessee, since it had meant she didn't have to walk up an aisle with Joe two short years after she'd left home. Now, though, she couldn't resist asking, "What do you see for *me*? In wedding flowers?"

"Pink," Marjorie said without missing a beat. "Very dark pink tulips—a warm, dramatic shade." Then she waved her palm through the air. "Nothing else. For you, just simple and elegant. A small bouquet—only the tulips, short-stemmed, tied with a thin ribbon the same color."

Trish tilted her head to one side. She'd never—at least in her adulthood—thought of herself as a woman anyone would associate with pink, but to her surprise, she liked the idea.

"That sounds nice," she said. Then thought—what the *hell?* She was about as close to getting married as she was to leaping off a bridge. Time to make that perfectly clear. "But I won't be saying 'I do' anytime in the near future. As soon as I get the diner situation under control, I'll be headed back to Indy and concentrating on making partner in my firm. That'll mean even more work than I already have, so dating will have to take a back burner."

Marjorie rolled her eyes. "You know what they say about too much work."

Trish shrugged. "If I become a dull girl, so be it. I love what I do."

Marjorie tilted her head, looking speculative. "You know, maybe you could help me with a problem I'm having."

Trish knew that head tilt—she got it from friends and acquaintances all the time. "A legal issue? Shoot."

"Well, I have this sweet little dog, Jeremiah. He's a brown highland terrier-mutt mix, cutest little guy you ever did see. And John Munk, my next-door neighbor, has a mean old German shepherd who he doesn't keep chained half the time. Well, it was one thing when that dog was just pooping in my yard or barking his fool head off at Jeremiah. But a couple months ago, Munk's dog barreled into my yard and attacked him!"

Trish gasped. As she'd told Joe, she didn't have pets due to time constraints, but having grown up on a farm, she still loved animals.

"By the grace of God, Jeremiah survived, and he's getting back to his normal spunky self now. But it was touch-and-go there for a while, and his vet bills were over seven hundred dollars. I gave Munk the bill, but he refused to pay. So then I took him to small-claims court, but the judge only awarded me fifty bucks."

Trish narrowed her gaze. This sounded very wrong. "By what reasoning?"

Marjorie's eyes widened. "Well, are you ready for this? The judge said fifty dollars was the *replacement cost of my dog.*"

Aghast, Trish felt her *own* eyes fly wide. *"What?"*

"That's right. Judge Hanley said the vet bills were unreasonable and that Munk only had to pay me what it would cost me to get a new dog. And since Jeremiah is part mutt, that didn't amount to much."

Trish's jaw dropped. She'd never heard of anything so ludicrous in all her years in law. "My God, Marjorie—that's a travesty."

"You're tellin' me. You got any advice for me—any way I can get my money out of that rat next door?"

Trish turned it over in her head. She'd originally planned on going home around the end of this week. But if she was seriously going to work on painting the diner and looking for other ways she might spruce it up on her own, that time line was impractical. Staying an additional week made it all sound more feasible. Which made her wonder . . . "How long did it take to get on the docket in small claims after you filed?"

"A couple of weeks, I guess. Why?"

"And how long has it been since the judgment?"

Marjorie tilted her head. "About three weeks."

Trish certainly hadn't come here planning to take on anyone's legal matters, but how could she not help Marjorie? On principle if nothing else. "I'm not sure how long I'll be in town, but . . . we could file an appeal. You have thirty days after a judgment to file, so we're good on the timing. I could represent you. We'd win, I promise."

A surprised smile unfurled on Marjorie's slightly wrinkled face. "You'd do that for me, Trish? But . . ." She winced. "I have to admit, I don't know how much you big-city lawyers charge—or if I could afford it."

Trish just shook her head. This wasn't about money. "This one's on me. When we win, send me some flowers or something. If you can bring me whatever paperwork you have on the case, I'll call the courthouse tomorrow and see how soon we can get this scheduled." If she was lucky, she could apply a bit of pressure and get on the docket next week.

It was only after Marjorie had departed and Trish sat busily scribbling ideas about wall colors and other décor changes, planning a trip to the new Home Depot outside town, that she stopped and thought—*Wait a minute.* How had all this happened? She'd come home to read a contract, visit with her parents, get some papers signed, and head home. Now she was remodeling the diner and appealing a small-claims case? Oh, and she'd had a wild weekend of sex with her first—and if she was honest with herself, only—love.

There for a brief while this afternoon, she'd fooled herself into thinking she was actually getting some things accomplished.

But what it boiled down to was—this trip was still a total disaster.

Washing up his few dinner dishes at the kitchen sink, Joe flashed a wicked grin no one else could see. Did Trish think he was blind? He hoped she was a little slicker in court than she'd been concerning some aspects of their "relationship" so far. Not that he minded her lack of slickness. He'd liked it just fine when he'd spotted her tan Lexus creeping past the garage this afternoon, her eyes turned his way. Debbie had once mentioned in passing that Trish had bought a Lexus, and for a guy who lived and breathed cars, it hadn't been hard to spot. Nor had her blond hair or searching gaze, even hidden within the confines of the car.

*You still want me, too, cupcake. Now I just have to show you how much.*

When the phone trilled, he wiped his hands on a dish towel, but knew better than to hope it was Trish. She might have gone driving past his garage when she'd thought he wouldn't see, yet getting her trust back wasn't gonna be easy.

"Hello?" He shoved the receiver between his ear and shoulder, turning back to the sink to scour the skillet he'd fried up a hamburger in.

"Hey, it's me." Jana.

"Well, lucky me. First a visit, now a phone call." He didn't mean to sound so sarcastic, but he didn't think he'd heard from his sister two days in a row since she'd moved away.

He could practically feel her smirk through the phone before she resumed her merry attitude and said, "I have some great news, Joe! The best news of my life, actually."

Uh-oh. This couldn't be good. "What is it?"

She paused, clearly for dramatic effect, then announced, "I'm getting married!"

Aw, Christ. Screw the skillet—he released it into the dishwater and dropped into a chair at the small kitchen table.

"Did you hear me? I'm tying the knot! Saying 'I do'!"

"To Vinnie, I guess."

She let out an irritated sigh. "Of course to Vinnie. Who else?"

About anyone he could think of would be better. "Of course," he said, sounding morose.

"Aren't you going to congratulate me?"

He took a deep breath and forced out the word. "Congratulations."

"It's next weekend," she twittered.

"What is?"

"The wedding!"

Joe about slid off the chair.

"It's quick, but Vinnie knows a lot of people who can pull a lot of strings."

"I bet he does."

She let that go—or was too caught up in bridal fever to hear it. "We've rented this great place with a gazebo and lots of wildflowers, and it's just outside a big hall where we're having the reception."

"So this isn't . . . a *small* thing."

"Oh, God no. I wouldn't stand for a small wedding. Vinnie suggested just going to Vegas, you know"—where there are still mob connections, Joe thought—"but when I told him I wanted a big wedding, he said nothing but the best for me."

Joe's mind spun. "Jana . . ." Hell, he had to ask. "Are you pregnant?"

She gasped. "Good heavens, Joe—of course not!" Spoken like a chaste Catholic schoolgirl—as opposed to a woman who became more glitter-laden and sparsely dressed every time he saw her.

"Then why does this have to happen so fast?" He was trying not to raise his voice, but damn, she made it hard lately.

"We just don't want to wait, you know? When it's right, it's right. And with Vinnie and me, it's right." Without pausing for even a breath, she rambled on about the place and the time, adding, "But you'll get an invitation in the mail in a few days. We're doing invitations all night tonight. Believe it or not, the rushing is kind of fun. Everybody's pitching in to help. Brittany, my maid of honor, has the prettiest handwriting, so she's doing all the envelopes. She took a calligraphy class."

Brittany? He'd never even *heard* of his sister's maid of honor. And who was "everybody"? "Have you called Dad?"

He almost felt her eager nod through the phone. "He's coming up—bringing Marna, too." Their stepmom, a raspy-voiced chain-smoker who was barely cordial on the rare occasions they saw her. Their dad's initial departure from their lives, just after their mom's death, had only heaped more pain on them—yet his subsequent marriage and escape to Florida a few years later had actually been a relief to Joe. "He's walking me down the aisle, of course."

*Yeah, that makes sense. The guy deserts you when you're a kid, but he's walking you down the aisle.* Yet Joe shoved that from his mind—it wasn't any of his business. "Did he have any . . . worries? About never having met the guy?"

"I guess not. I just heard him tell Marna to pack a suitcase 'cause they were heading home to see his little girl get married."

This served as confirmation—although not shocking—that Joe was indeed the only sane Ramsey left. A thought that reminded him his sister would soon be Jana Balducci. Mob moll.

When they hung up a few minutes later, Joe went outside, just to clear his head. Some things never changed. His family had always possessed a certain manic quality and everyone knew it.

As a kid, he'd heard the disparaging tone in people's voices when they'd mentioned "the Ramseys," not knowing he was within hearing distance, or maybe just not caring. His parents did things most people in Eden didn't. Drank. Smoked. Swore. Fought. It had taken a hell of a lot of work to get the smoky smell out of the walls after his parents were gone and his father had agreed to sell him the place. He'd thought of it as a sort of exorcism—purging the house of all the arguments and ugly times.

Of course, it hadn't been like that *all* the time—in some ways, they'd been a totally normal family with plenty of good, regular days and nights together. Trish had been over to his house a lot in high school and had only once or twice witnessed anyone yelling. But he heard the yelling inside him sometimes. And at moments he thought it was weird that he'd even *wanted* the house and the surrounding acres that had come with it. Yet it was his home, for his whole life, and maybe making it *truly* his had seemed like a chance to make it a . . . calmer, *saner* place.

Letting out a sigh, he whistled for Elvis—but the dog didn't come. "Probably gettin' laid again," he muttered. He should be so lucky.

About to turn back toward the house, his gaze dropped accidentally to Sunshine and her kittens, still tucked in their cubbyhole next to the shed, nursing—and for some reason it stuck there. He wasn't the kind of guy who went all soft on a bunch of furry little kittens, but hell—in that moment, he found the sight of them oddly . . . peaceful. It made sense. It was *sane*.

He supposed Trish had provided that same kind of sanity in his life once upon a time. Maybe that was part of why he'd fallen for her. She'd been smart and pretty, but also undeniably . . . steady, reliable. Her parents were the same way, and everything at the Henderson home had been comfortable . . . in its place . . . calm and inviting.

And now Sunshine was giving him that same feeling on a quiet August evening while the horizon turned a hazy shade of purple.

Just then, Elvis came trotting around the house, long ears bouncing and belly hanging low. Joe jerked his gaze to the dog. "About time," he snapped, then looked toward the garage where he kept the Cobra. He suddenly felt the need to tinker around under the hood a little. "Come on," he said to the dog. Made a damn sight more sense than cooing over kittens.

On Tuesday morning, Trish exited her parents' house to find that the weather had changed radically overnight. Whereas Monday had been another balmy August day, Monday night a cold front had shifted down from the Great Lakes to bring a bizarrely early frost. She stood on the porch, looking out as the sun began to melt off the strangely early nip of winter covering "God's country" with a thin sheen of icy crystals that shimmered in the fog. The very air smelled so different in the country, and weather changes were so much more . . . apparent, dramatic, spreading across the land in a way you couldn't avoid seeing.

For Trish's father, the first frost triggered the last hay cutting of the season since it locked the sugar inside. So on his suggestion—"Wouldn't want to help your old man out with the hay today, would you?"—she'd changed her plans and stayed home. She could have said no—he'd applied no pressure—but her parents had had her later in life, and her dad was getting on in years. And she'd thought—*How often am I here? How often do I get a chance to help out with family things anymore?*

Although cutting and baling hay didn't really require a

crowd, so it was more a matter of Trish's going along for the ride, putting on a sweatshirt and sitting behind her father on the tractor like she had as a little girl. She watched the big blades mow it all down, then the tractor passed back over it all a second time with the old hay rake attached. Changing equipment again, they drove the fields once more, sucking up the loose hay in the baling machine to see it emerge a few moments later in neat rectangular cubes that sprinkled the field. She'd found herself peering out over it all, soaking in the sights and scents of her youth on a day that felt more like November than August.

On Wednesday, the weather was a lot closer to normal—not blistering hot, but the cold front had moved on and the air grew warm again. She used the day to do everything she'd planned on doing Tuesday, getting out bright and early.

Heading to the diner, she parked herself in the back office to make some phone calls. She succeeded in getting Marjorie and Jeremiah's appeal scheduled in small-claims court a week from Thursday. Then she contacted a few local realtors to sing the praises of the diner and let them know it was "undergoing renovations." After that, she measured the windows for curtains, then hit the road, ready to shop for supplies.

Although she hadn't mentioned her "sprucing up" project to her mom and dad, not wanting them to think there was anything wrong with the way they'd left the place. And there wasn't— this was just a combination time-filler and sales booster.

Her first stop, at The Home Depot, was actually fun. All her life the diner walls had been painted off-white, and she decided it was time for something cheerier. She picked a number of fun colors, buying only small cans of each, in case they all clashed too horribly with the aqua booths. But on her way out she learned from a sales clerk that you could spray-paint vinyl, which she thought might be another way to bring in a new look.

From there, she headed out of Eden, knowing she'd have more selection on curtains in Columbus. She also stopped at a restaurant supplies wholesaler where her mom and dad had always done business. There, she stumbled upon a bunch of cute even if mismatched café tables and chairs that the guy was willing to bundle together cheap.

Since it would mean a *whole* new look for the diner that went way beyond fresh colors on the wall—which seemed a bit drastic, especially without her parents' blessing—she told him she'd think about it. But the idea appealed more and more as she made the return journey to Eden.

Turning into the driveway late that afternoon, she came in to find her dad lying in his reclining chair, clearly in pain, with a bottle of ibuprofen at his side. "What happened?" she asked.

"Back went out," he said on a soft groan. "First thing this morning when I was putting out some new salt licks for the herd."

Trish grimaced. She thought of her father as an infinitely stout, strong man, so it was difficult to see him hurting.

"Wouldn't matter so much except for that," he added, lifting a finger toward the TV.

Trish looked up to see a big weather map of the eastern half of the United States. A rotund weatherman was talking about a sizable hurricane currently pummeling the lower East Coast. For God's sake, when had *that* started? Trish gave her head a light shake—only more proof that her brain wasn't functioning like normal if she didn't even know about major news events.

"She's already started to dissipate after coming ashore this morning," the weatherman said of the hurricane, "but here in the Midwest, we're gonna see some torrential rains as early as tomorrow evening."

Trish and her dad both let out audible sighs. "The hay," she said, dejected. Normally, it was best to leave hay out to dry a few days before loading it into the barn, but if it wasn't brought in before the storm, it would rot completely.

Never a dull moment, it seemed. And here she'd thought Eden was boring.

She studied her dad's worried expression, also noting the heating pad peeking out from behind his lower back. Little did he know that the hay was only *one* small worry—he hadn't yet figured out that the sale of the diner was a much bigger one.

And one *more* thing Trish *hadn't* come home to do was load hay bales into the barn—but she couldn't see any other solution. "I'll get up early tomorrow and start getting the hay in," she volunteered.

He frowned, deepening the lines in his face. "Honey, you can't. It's too much for one person."

Maybe so, but one person was all they had. Given that her mother had developed arthritis in her shoulders and hands over the past few years, everyday tasks were more than enough for her. And Trish knew without asking that all the other local farmers were in the same boat and would be lucky to get their *own* hay in. "*You* do it by yourself, every cutting, every year," she pointed out.

"But I can usually take breaks, spend all the time I want on it," he reminded her. "This is different. We got a lotta hay needs to get in the barn before that storm hits."

Trish's stomach churned. She had no idea how much she could conceivably move by herself in less than a day, but she hid her worries. "Well, I'll at least try. And at least it's baled."

"Maybe I'll feel better by morning," he said, but she didn't think that was going to happen, which meant he had no choice but to accept her offer.

And really, it was the least she could do. As she'd realized a few days ago, she hardly ever came home, and she *never* helped out with the farm. So this would be her chance to contribute at least a *little* something.

A couple of hours later, Trish had napped and showered and now sat watching more TV with her dad before heading over to Debbie and Kenny's for dinner. She wasn't usually a napping kind of girl, but she hadn't gotten a lot of sleep last night upon returning to her old bedroom. She'd stayed there a number of times since leaving home, but *this* time, only *this* time, something about the room—still decked out in the daisy theme of her girlhood—reminded her of Joe.

They'd made out in that bed more than once. It had been a big deal because it had been the only place they could really lie down together. The first time she'd let him take her top off had been there, in the same bed, atop the same yellow daisy-covered quilt, on a day when her parents had gone to sell cattle at the stockyards and hadn't been due back until late. Crazy how fond the memory was. And how intense.

Now more than one man had kissed her breasts. Hell, Joe himself had kissed them just the other night—another memory that made her shiver while she sat pretending to be utterly absorbed in watching someone on *Wheel of Fortune* buy a vowel. Yet there was just something warm and fuzzy and passionate about recalling the first time, that first intimacy. Joe hadn't been tentative. He'd kissed her nipples like he was kissing her mouth—tongue and full lips and a slow, leisurely rhythm that had nearly made her come undone.

"I forgot to tell you, Debbie called while you were in the shower," her mother relayed, drying her hands on a dish towel as she entered the room. "She said Kenny's overtime will put him home around eight, but you can come earlier if you like."

Trish looked up. "Maybe I'll go on over."

"She also said . . ." Her mother stopped, eyeing her peculiarly, and Trish thought—*dear God, what else did my bigmouth best friend say?*

"What?" Trish asked.

Her mother shook her head. "You know Debbie—she was rambling a bit. But something about wanting to know if Joe came to see you the other night after what happened?"

Oh, boy. The fun just never ended around here, did it? One great thing about living in the city—the place wasn't a fishbowl where everyone was aware of your every freaking move. One of these days, Trish *was* going to kill Debbie, once and for all.

Trish's dad jerked his gaze from the TV to her. "Joe Ramsey? You've seen Joe Ramsey?" Despite the *pure trouble* declaration, her dad had tolerated Joe when they'd been a couple—but she knew he'd never forgiven Joe, either, for how things had ended. And Trish had had a big argument with him over it all on the day she'd left for college. While she'd been trying to deal with her freshly broken heart, her father had yelled about how right he'd been and how if she'd only listened she'd have been so much better off. Even now, her father still took his vehicles to Stan Mobley's garage instead of Joe's even though, according to Debbie, everyone knew Joe's place was a lot more dependable.

"That would be the Joe in question," Trish replied tightly. "And yes, we bumped into each other when I was out with Debbie Friday night." She conveniently left out the sex they'd had on *Saturday* and *Sunday* nights and hoped her lingerie and corset dress were well enough tucked away in her bedroom to keep anyone from stumbling onto them. She knew she was a thirty-two-year-old woman, but she also knew that held no sway with her father.

There was no denying he looked upset, deep creases growing between his eyes. "Is there anything going on I should know about?"

*Besides a couple of wild sexual encounters?* She swallowed nervously, feeling as if she were seventeen and about to be caught in a lie. "Not really. We just . . . caught up a bit on each other's lives." *Then got naked. And I walked out on him. And then we got naked again—from the waist down, anyway. And had a big fight afterward.*

"I didn't know you'd seen him."

She gave her head a short shake. "It wasn't important enough to mention." *Unless you consider ravenous sex important. Or the fact that I momentarily feared I was still in love with him and haven't been able to quit thinking about him since.*

Her father looked uncertain, but finally just nodded and she assumed that meant—for the first time ever—her lies had actually worked. She attributed her success to the pretenses involved in constantly defending guilty people.

"Well," she announced, rising to grab her purse from the table next to the front door, "I'm headed to Debbie's." *To commit premeditated murder.* "I might be late."

"Trish," her dad said, his voice slow, thoughtful, "I'm sure you're a smart enough girl to know Joe's still the same kinda trouble he was years ago. He's made something of himself, sure, but he's got a reputation. I'd hope you wouldn't let him smooth-talk his way back into your life, 'cause as far as I'm concerned, you still can't trust him."

In one way, the words grated, making her want to grind her

teeth. She already knew good and well how her dad felt on the topic, and she resented that he was still shoving it down her throat all these years later.

But in another way, she couldn't be *too* angry—because she agreed.

"Don't worry, Dad," she promised. "I know all of that." *And I don't trust him, either. Because I trusted him with my whole heart once and look what that got me.*

"Okay," Trish said as she stood tossing a salad at Debbie's kitchen counter, "tonight, dinner with you guys. Tomorrow, I put up hay. Then on Friday I get back to work in the diner."

Debbie stared at her, blank-faced. "I thought this trip was supposed to be sort of like a vacation."

"*Wrong.* Vacations include drinks with little umbrellas in them and a nice tan."

Debbie shrugged. "Wear a bathing suit in the hay tomorrow and you'll be halfway there. And hey, sometimes vacations include *sex*, and you've certainly gotten some of that." She raised her eyebrows as if to say *woo-woo.*

Trish only cast her driest look in return. "Thank you ever so much, by the by, for mentioning 'what happened with Joe' to my *mother*, for God's sake."

Deb winced as she mashed a big pot of potatoes the old-fashioned way. "Yeah, that kind of just popped out. Sorry." Then her eyes grew hopeful. "But you never did tell me if he came to see you after he talked to Kenny."

Trish let her brow knit. She *really* didn't want to talk about this, and God knew it was smarter not to tell chatterbox Debbie every detail. Although she was surprised the news hadn't made its way here via Kenny already, so what the hell. "Yeah, he came," she said, not bothering to hide her irritation. "And we did it on the dresser in my motel room. Happy?"

As usual when given such news, Debbie's eyes nearly bugged out of her head. "Holy crap, Trish. On the *dresser?*"

She spread her hands before her, helpless. "It's not like I said, 'Hey, let's try out the dresser.' It's just where we were when things happened."

"And then what?"

"What do you mean?"

"What do you *think* I mean? Did you make up? Are you seeing him again? Where do things stand?"

Trish put her hands up in a "stop" motion. "Whoa there, girl-friend. No, I'm not seeing him again. Because . . . well . . ." She sighed. Felt that little stab of sadness all over again and tried to push it back. *Just spit it out.* "Over the course of having sex with him twice, I figured something out. I don't like it, but it's true. And it's that I just haven't ever really forgiven him for breaking my heart   and I don't think I can. So I told him that was the end of things."

"And then you drove past his garage."

Trish blinked. For crying out loud. "How do you know that?"

Debbie tilted her head in sympathy, having momentarily abandoned the mashed potatoes. "He saw you. It came up when Kenny asked him about you."

Trish closed her eyes, trying to absorb the horror. "Okay, first of all, just shoot me. Just put me out of my misery, will you please? I *cannot* believe he saw me." Coming home to Eden really *was* like being thrust back to age seventeen—in more ways than one. "And second—he told Kenny he saw me, but he *didn't* tell Kenny we did it on the dresser?"

Debbie sighed, thinking it through. "Well, maybe he did,

but sometimes Kenny doesn't tell me stuff because some people think I don't keep secrets very well."

"Who are these people? I want to join their club and run for president."

"These people are Joe."

"Oh. Never mind." Figured. She refocused on the salad.

"For what it's worth, by the way, I'd help you with the hay if I could, but with school just back in . . ." Debbie did administrative work at the elementary school.

And Trish felt bad for being mean. "I know you would, Deb, but it's okay. I'll be fine."

Just then, the front door opened and Kenny walked in, looking weary from work but smiling when he saw Trish. "Hey there, stranger." Then his voice took on a certain playful lilt. "So, how're . . . *things?*"

The change in his tone forced her to meet his eyes. They twinkled knowingly. Yeah, he knew about the dresser. "Things are fine," she said, trying not to blush. After all, they'd been friends forever, and she certainly knew about things *he'd* done in bed, given his wife's propensity for telling all.

Just then, Debbie's two boys came barreling around the corner making fast-car noises as they slid into Kenny's arms. Kenny pulled them close but kept his gaze on Trish. "I thought about inviting Joe to dinner, but figured you'd hate me."

"Excellent call."

"Although when I heard you drove out past the garage, I thought maybe you wanted to see him and were just too shy to stop."

"Ha!" she said. "Nope, no shyness involved, I'm afraid. I was merely curious to see the place, that's all. That's where my interest ends." A claim that was kind of hard to pull off given that Kenny knew about the dresser, but she had to insist anyway.

At the sound of the oven door, Trish turned, thankful for a distraction, to see Debbie hauling out a meat loaf the size of Indiana. "Yeesh, Deb, there are only five of us."

"Kenny and the boys like to make sandwiches out of it for a couple days after. And you'll be happy to know," she said, lowering the meat loaf to the table on a potholder already placed there, "I've given the boys strict instructions on potato-hurling so you'll have a new experience to take back to Indy with you when your trip is over. Just in case nothing else interesting happens to you while you're here."

*They lay in the reclined seat of his Trans Am next to the lake, just holding each other, feeling each other's nearness, and her whole soul was filling up . . . with him. They weren't having sex—he wasn't even kissing her—but it felt just as good in a different way. She couldn't tell if it was now or then, if his shoulders had yet broadened, if there was yet a snake on his arm—they seemed ageless, like time didn't exist.*

*"I love you, Trishy. Always have, always will."*

*She nuzzled closer to him, understanding for the first time in her life that thing people said about not knowing where one person ended and the other began. She'd always thought that sounded silly—how could you not know where you began? But she didn't now—she knew nothing but sweet summer scents drifting in the window, and pure joy from being intertwined with Joe.*

"Trish, breakfast!"

She jolted awake in bed, warmth permeating her whole body. She'd been dreaming of him—a really *wonderful* dream. And even if they *hadn't* been having sex, the crux of her thighs tingled. Oh my. Yum. What a way to wake up.

*"Trish, did you hear me?"* Her mother's voice echoed up the stairs and through the old farmhouse, jarring her.

"Yes!" she yelled back, "I hear you. I'm coming." *Although why I can't sleep in even one day here, I have no idea.* Despite herself, she wished she could have finished the dream. Just in case they did have sex. And she was wondering about the snake—if it was there yet. Much as she wished she could deny it, she definitely had a thing for the snake.

She was tempted to march down the stairs and remind her mom that she was kind of on vacation, as Debbie had pointed out—but then she remembered. She really *did* have to get up early today. She had to be Farmer Trish and get the hay in. And despite Debbie's advice, she couldn't wear a bikini—because hay scratched. As for an umbrella drink, she didn't hold out much hope given that the Last Chance didn't even have wine.

Trish dragged herself out of bed, not bothering with a robe since it was only her and her mom—Dad probably *was* sleeping in, poor guy. Descending the stairs in a lime green cami and bright, striped drawstring pants, she drank in the aroma of fresh, greasy bacon and let it soothe her frustrations a bit.

Yet before reaching the bottom of the stairs, she stopped, halted in place by hushed tones below. "Now, Jasper," her mother was saying, "you just keep your thoughts to yourself. Besides, Trish'll only be here a little while and then she'll be off to the city again."

"You just mark my words, woman," her father said in a harsh whisper anyway, "guys like that never change."

"Let it lie," her mother commanded, brusque but low. "As far as we know, nothing's going on between them. So just let it lie."

Swell. This Joe thing seemed to be taking on a life of its own. She took a deep breath, then made quite a show of clomping down the rest of the steps to make sure they heard her and quit talking about her behind her back. She knew her dad was concerned for her, but she was suffering enough confusion over Joe already without any more input from him. "Good morning," she said, pasting a not-very-sincere smile on her face.

Her mother started slightly. "Morning, dear. Come get some bacon and eggs before they get cold."

Her father rose from his recliner in the living room but let out a painful-sounding yelp and ended up back in the chair. Trish winced, sorry he was hurting, but at the same time she wasn't sorry she didn't have to face him over breakfast under the circumstances. She didn't want to think about Joe anymore—or that crazy dream. It had seemed all nice and cozy there for a minute, but it wasn't real. Besides, she had other things to worry about. Like would she remember how to drive the tractor? Or how to stack the hay efficiently? How long would it take by herself? Baling hay might be a one-person job, but getting it in the barn with any ease usually required a whole team. Even if her father *did* choose to do it alone, it was a task done much easier with help.

And she also didn't want to argue with her father. She loved her dad, and she knew they were on the same side, yet Joe still remained a sore subject and probably always would be. It took her back to the fight they'd had when Joe had cheated on her, something that had caused a serious rift in their relationship. The truth was, they'd never been as close afterward as they'd been before. Mostly because it had coincided with Trish leaving home—but the fact remained that the argument had gone unmended and had changed things between them.

She was just sitting down at the table when a knock came on the front door.

"Who on earth?" her mother murmured, echoing Trish's

thoughts. People didn't come casually knocking on doors this far out in the country at eight in the morning.

"I'll get it—you've got your hands full," Trish said, looking to where her mother stood with a bowl of scrambled eggs in one hand and a pitcher of orange juice in the other.

She padded on bare feet to the entryway, feeling only slightly sheepish about being in her cami—anyone who came by this early would just have to deal with it.

Of course, when she opened the door, she didn't expect to find Joe standing on the other side. Speak of the devil.

He wore faded jeans and a white tee with the sleeves cut out, and leaned casually against a porch column, one thumb hooked through a belt loop. A slow smile spread across his face beneath a straw cowboy hat, pushed low. "Morning, cupcake."

**Appeal:** a request made after a trial by a party that has lost on one or more issues that a higher court review the decision to determine if it was correct; _or_ the power or ability to attract, interest, or stimulate.

# Seven

She'd never been much of a cowboy hat person before—but then, she'd never been much of a tattoo girl before, either. And all she could think at the moment was, *Ride 'em, cowgirl.* She stood utterly tongue-tied by the sexy sight of him but finally managed to spit out, "What are you doing here?"

"Came to help you get your hay in."

She sighed. Debbie? Kenny? It didn't even matter. Traitors. They probably thought they were helping her in some way when, in fact, she suddenly felt doomed. Because he'd said he'd come to help her get her hay in, but his tone had implied getting something more than hay. "Um, don't you have a garage to run?"

"I have enough guys working for me that I can take a day off," he informed her, then gave his head a speculative tilt. "I saw you drive by the other day."

God help her. *Please let me sound casual and convincing.* "I was in the neighborhood. And . . . curious. Just to see the place. It's been awhile."

His gaze, intense and seductive, said he wasn't buying a word of it, and she was pretty sure her nipples were poking through her cami now, damn it. It wasn't enough to wake up aroused— no, no—the object of her desire had to show up at the door two minutes later.

"Joe," she said softly, thinking that if she were really lucky maybe she could get rid of him before her dad even realized he was here, "this is . . . nice of you, but you don't need to do it. There's not much hay," she lied. "It won't take me long. So there's no need for you to be here."

Any hint of amusement in his expression faded as he spoke matter-of-factly. "I know how much hay there is, cupcake. You need my help and you're going to take it."

"*Joe,*" she began again, irritated by his presumptuousness.

But he interrupted her, his voice softer this time. "Trish, just let me do this for you. Okay?" He lowered his chin so that she could barely see those unwavering blue eyes under the brim of his hat as she absorbed the determination in his words. Helping with the hay could never atone for the past, yet she understood that he at least had to try in some small way.

"Who's out there?" her dad boomed behind her suddenly, since he couldn't see the door from his chair.

Trish flinched, then sighed. Why couldn't she just be in a nice, tense courtroom right now, where she knew exactly what to do and how to handle things? "It's Joe," she said rigidly.

Her father's voice lowered an octave, taking on an unpleasant edge. "Joe Ramsey? Why does he keep bothering you?"

Trish's gaze locked on Joe with mortification since her dad had just made it sound as if she'd been saying bad things about him. She mouthed her defense silently—*He doesn't know*—and gave her head a short shake. Which meant she'd just reminded him they'd had wild sex together very recently. Which made her nipples even harder since she was standing there staring into those alluring eyes and remembering.

Joe shrugged it off and spoke in a hushed tone. "Guess I forgot how much he hates me." But she could see the seriousness behind the easy gesture—and it changed things. It reminded her that she was a grown woman and had control here. She could do what she wanted. And she didn't want a relationship with a guy she couldn't forgive—but maybe she *did* want his help today.

She turned from the door to face her father, who was now leaning around to peek from his place in the recliner. "It's okay, Dad. He's come to help with the hay, and I could use it. So be quiet." Then she turned back to Joe. "Come in and sit down. I'll get dressed and we can get to work."

His hesitation was so short that anyone else might not have caught it. But Trish supposed that even cool, confident Joe might feel a bit uncomfortable coming into her house for the first time in fourteen years, especially since her father had just made him feel unwelcome. Still, he stepped in and shut the door behind him. Only to have her father glare at him. "Sit down," she told him again, nudging him toward the couch. Then she looked to her dad. "And try not to kill each other while I'm gone."

Joe watched her scurry to the stairs in her cute little pajamas, then darted his glance back to Trish's dad, hoping the older man hadn't noticed him taking in the view. Unbelievable that he couldn't control his urges at a moment like this, but ever since he'd seen the all-grown-up version of Trish, it had been this way. He couldn't *not* feel heated up when he was around her.

"Hi, Joe," Trish's mom said, entering the room carrying a breakfast tray heaped with bacon, eggs, and biscuits. She lowered it carefully in front of Trish's dad as Joe settled on the sofa. Unlike her husband, she'd softened toward him over the years and he suspected she no longer held the past against him, that maybe she understood he'd just been a stupid kid who'd screwed up the one good thing in his life.

He smiled. "Hi, Mrs. Henderson. It's nice to see you." And strange to remember all the time he'd once spent here, all the meals he'd eaten at their table.

"It was good of you to come like this."

"Probably should have called first," he said, but he'd known Trish wouldn't accept his help if he didn't force it on her. "Sorry if I interrupted your breakfast."

She waved a hand down through the air as if he were being silly. "Would you like some? There's plenty."

"Thanks, but I already ate." A quick egg sandwich he'd grabbed from the Waffle House on the way.

"You've got a lot of work ahead of you today." She gestured to the table on the opposite side of the foyer, sprinkled with plates and bowls. "And you're more than welcome. Isn't he, Jasper?"

They both glanced tentatively at Trish's father, but he only grunted from his recliner.

"Maybe I'll, uh . . . have a little," Joe said.

Mrs. Henderson clasped her hands together and smiled. "Good. I'll get an extra plate."

Which left him alone with Trish's dad—and he knew what he needed to do. Clear the air. Or at least try. He spoke in a low, even voice. "I know you have good reason not to like me much."

Jasper Henderson shoveled a forkful of eggs into his mouth without meeting Joe's eyes. "I don't trust you—especially around my daughter."

Joe nodded knowingly. "I get that. But I can't change the past. And I've grown up a lot since you last knew me."

Now Henderson turned to glare at him some more. "You run around with a lot of women."

*They don't matter to me.* But how good did *that* sound? Not very. Since he couldn't deny it, he said nothing.

Henderson's gaze narrowed on him. "Don't hurt her again, boy, do you hear me?"

Joe was six-foot-two and thirty-two years old, and it had been a long time since anyone had called him a boy. He didn't like it—but instead of reacting, making things worse, he quietly curled his hands into fists at his sides and swallowed back his anger. "Don't worry," he said. "There's nothing like that going on." Which was a lie, he guessed, considering their sex. But it wasn't so much a lie when he considered Trish's feelings on the subject.

"See that you keep it that way," Henderson demanded.

And Joe bristled further. He figured he still didn't stand a chance with Trish, but if he got an opportunity to get closer to her, more than just physically, he'd be taking it. And for today, anyway, his motives were pure; he'd come to help her get the hay in and that was all. "Don't worry," he said again, his voice tight.

"Come and fix yourself a plate, Joe," Trish's mom called from the table, and he pushed to his feet. He'd hardly made peace with Trish's dad, but at least he'd been man enough to try.

As Joe settled at the table, Trish came down the stairs wearing a faded pair of blue jeans with rips at the knees and another cute little T-shirt—this one buttery yellow—that sweetly hugged her breasts. She'd pulled her long hair back in a ponytail and couldn't have looked more different than the woman he'd met at the Last Chance on Friday night. Warmth spread through him at the sight of her, at realizing he got to spend the whole damn day with her, even if it did mean some hard work.

But wait. He'd come to get the hay in. That was all.

*Yeah, you just keep telling yourself that, buddy.*

The scent of hay filled Trish's senses as the sun grew hot on her back. They'd taken her dad's old farm truck down the dirt road that led to the barn, where they'd exchanged it for the tractor and wagon. Now they meandered through the bumpy field, stopping every hundred yards or so to gather the surrounding bales, one by one, wearing heavy gloves to protect their hands from the baling twine and sharp, prickly hay.

She'd let Joe handle driving the tractor and she rode on the wagon behind. It was easier that way, because if there were only a few bales in any particular spot, he could jump down, toss them up to her, and she could stack it, making for quicker work. And it was also easier because it put some distance between them.

Thank God the job was laborious and tiring, she thought as she rode bumping along behind him. And thank God the sound of the tractor's old motor made it hard to exchange much conversation. Now, if only the work weren't so darn time consuming. She wished they could just finish it up, thus ending the torture of watching his muscular torso on the tractor ahead, his broad, tan shoulders glistening with perspiration, the snake on his arm twisting and slithering with each bale of hay he tossed up onto the wagon.

Okay, was that torture—or pleasure? She hissed in her breath, glad he was facing away and couldn't see her reaction to him simply driving a tractor. Oh boy, this was sad.

*Think of Kent. You like him, remember? You might go home and start dating him. You'll be extremely well suited. Life will be pleasant.*

Only . . . Kent would never look like this on a tractor.

Hell, he'd probably never *seen* a tractor.

Which wasn't his fault; he'd been raised in the suburbs.

But *damn*, Joe looked good on a tractor.

And this job was going to take all day? How would she ever survive?

Just then, though, a vastly conflicting thought hit her. As slow as the work was with just the two of them, how had her father managed it by himself all these years? A fresh wave of guilt for not being here more often assaulted her. After all, Indy wasn't *that* far. And a little hard work never hurt anybody. And maybe all this farm stuff was actually sort of nice—soaking up the fresh air and the scent of newly mown hay, really feeling the earth beneath her feet again.

Much to her surprise, the thought of selling the diner and returning to her loft in the city left her feeling oddly wistful. As complicated as her encounters with Joe had made her homecoming, in another sense, it remained strangely peaceful to only check e-mail once a day or make the occasional business call. It was sort of like . . . being a girl again.

*But all this touchy-feely-earthy mumbo jumbo is probably just because you're so stupidly wrapped up in* him *right now.* She focused again on Joe's strong shoulders, the tips of his dark hair growing wet around the edges under the back brim of his hat.

And as soon as she left she would become *un*wrapped, because life would be busy and normal and stressful again, and men in tailored suits would become attractive to her again, and her heart would return to the even keel where she was comfortable having it.

And where she intended to keep it from now on—as soon as she was able to get away from him.

Joe took off his hat and lay back on the blanket they'd spread on the wagon, letting his gaze focus on the blue-white sky. It had seemed the smart move to make before Trish realized he was gaping at her breasts, something he'd had a hellacious time stopping today. But when she worked, her top stretched over them so nice and tight, giving him no choice but to recall having them in his hands, his mouth . . . he wanted to groan at the memory, but held it in.

Because he was here to help her with the hay, that was all.

They'd taken a few wagonloads to the barn and filled the rafters with it. And now they'd stopped for lunch—Trish's mom had packed sandwiches, chips, fruit, and a small cooler with water and soft drinks.

"Thank you," Trish said softly when he least expected it. The only other sound was a bird singing in a tree somewhere at the field's edge. "I doubt I could get this done without your help."

He sat up and met her green eyes—they sparkled beneath the sun and tightened his chest. "You're welcome," he replied, trying not to look like a wolf on the prowl.

"You . . ." She looked tentative as she unwrapped a ham and

cheese sandwich, dropping her gaze. "You've done really well for yourself, Joe."

He didn't know what she was getting at. He lowered his chin, tilted his head. "I guess."

She raised her eyes back to his. "I just meant . . . the garage. I'm . . . glad for you. And proud of you, I guess. Although I'm not sure I've been in your life enough to have the *right* to say I'm proud."

She lowered her gaze again, but he reached out to gently lift her chin with one bent finger. "If you want to be proud of me, I'll take it."

"The garage is impressive. And Debbie's told me what a good mechanic you are."

He just shrugged. He liked her praise, but he had to give credit where it was due. "Old Mr. Shermer had a lot to do with *all* of that. Guy looked out for me in a big way."

She nodded. "Yeah, I knew even then that you were fond of him."

"It's more than that, though. Besides teaching me a hell of a lot about cars and getting me interested in foreign makes, he gave me the courage to believe I could run the place on my own when he was ready to retire. It was a big investment and I was young, but he had so much confidence in me that I started having confidence in *myself*." He stopped, paused, remembering. "And besides all *that* . . . he gave me the Cobra."

Maybe he'd made that last part sound overly dramatic, but the car had changed his life in a way. It had been the first time he'd so totally applied himself to a project, partly for himself— and partly for Shermer.

"So this car," she said, looking less sheepish now and smiling softly as she popped the top on a can of Coke, "you like it well enough to have a symbol of it tattooed on your arm."

"It's . . . more than a car to me, cupcake."

She lowered her chin, looking curious. "But it's pretty valuable, too, right? One of the partners in my firm had one, and I think it was worth around sixty thousand bucks. Which I guess isn't outrageous for a sports car, but still . . ."

He smiled indulgently. Most people who saw his Cobra thought it was a hell of a cool little roadster, worth about fifty or sixty K, but they didn't realize they were actually looking at a true automobile classic, a *real* Shelby Cobra. "Most Cobras you see on the road are kit cars—and yeah, they can price out at anywhere from thirty to sixty. But mine's an original."

Her eyebrows knit slightly. "What does that mean?"

"Kit cars are just replicas of the real thing. A guy buys a Cobra kit and builds it himself. But mine is an authentic 1967 Shelby Cobra. Very rare. It's been appraised at half a mil."

Her mouth dropped open. "*Dollars?* Half a million *dollars?*"

He gave a single nod.

"Whoa." She blinked, then gave her pretty blond head a light shake. "That must be a hell of a car. And . . . no offense to Mr. Shermer, but . . . dare I ask how a mild-mannered old guy like him ended up with a car worth that much money?"

Joe loved telling this story. "Found it, believe it or not. When he retired, he bought an old farm about an hour south of here in an estate sale. The old lady who'd owned it had died and had no surviving relatives, and it hadn't been a hot property—only a couple of people even showed up for the auction.

"He found an old fallen-down barn way back on the property, and the Cobra was just sitting inside. God knows how long it had been there—the woman obviously didn't know what she had on her hands. It had been neglected, but Shermer still knew exactly what *he* had on his hands.

"Carroll Shelby was a race car driver who had to quit for health reasons, so he started *building* cars instead. He had a vision, wanted to make a race car from a lightweight European chassis with an American V-8 engine under the hood. He even dreamed the name one night the Cobra. When the first one was made in 1962, it was the fastest car on the planet and, in my opinion, the Cobra was the greatest sports car ever designed. And like I said, there are all kinds of replicas out there, but mine's an original 427, one of the last Cobras built, in 1967. It's a classic."

Trish titled her head, looking duly awed as she ate a bite of her sandwich. "So Mr. Shermer just *gave* you this car?"

Hell, he'd gotten so wrapped up in talking about the car itself that he'd left out the most important part. "Yeah, he did." But he had to swallow a small lump in his throat then. "He found out he was dying. Lung cancer, too far progressed for much hope. He gave me the car because he knew I would love it as much as he did. And he asked me to restore it, even though he knew it would take a long time and he wouldn't be around to see it." He glanced away, remembering the sadness that had consumed him at the old man's passing, then returned his gaze to Trish. "I would have restored it anyway—I loved that car the second I saw it, and I knew its value, too. But maybe I wouldn't have restored it with . . . quite the same care . . . if I didn't feel like . . ." He stopped, dropped his gaze. He didn't usually tell anyone *this* part—it had just started coming out. "This sounds hokey, but maybe I felt like he might be watching from somewhere, and like maybe each turn of the wrench was a way of giving him a little something back."

Shit. What the hell was he doing, spilling crap like that? At the very least, he'd created an awkward moment since Trish probably hadn't expected him to announce he thought his old boss was watching him from the big repair shop in the sky. He closed his eyes briefly, wishing he'd shut up a few seconds earlier.

So when he opened them back up, the last thing he anticipated was to see her face filled with awe, as she offered a soft little "Wow" that echoed all through him. "That's . . . pretty incredible, Joe."

It was? Damn.

And thank God.

"He was a good guy," was all he said in reply.

But then he reached for a potato chip from the bag between them, and since she'd just grabbed for one, too, their hands touched—and he felt it in his groin. And he got bold, more like his usual self. "Maybe you'll, uh . . . let me take you for a ride sometime."

Their eyes met and he realized what he'd said.

"In the car," he added with a grin that—no doubt about it—had come out wolfish.

But she only laughed, even as her cheeks pinkened lightly. She glanced away yet still smiled as she said, "Maybe."

*No maybe about it*, he thought, her blushing answer killing any doubt. He was definitely going to take his cupcake on a nice, long ride—very soon.

"By the way," he said, "sorry I pissed off your dad this morning."

She shook her head. "It's *his* problem. And no matter how he feels about you, he should have been more appreciative."

He shrugged. "Still, the guy's nursing a back injury, so he's probably irritable. And it's only 'cause he cares for you."

Trish rolled her eyes. "I know that, but I'm all grown-up now, Joe."

*Oh yeah, you definitely are.* "Even so . . ." He focused his gaze on her, just enjoying the fact that he was with her, they were *talking*, and this was really Trish—*his* Trish—a fact that he maybe hadn't really quite adjusted to yet. "It's good, the way they watch out for you. Look at this—a picnic lunch and your dad still worried about who you're with. In my family . . . well, it wasn't like that."

She pursed her lips lightly and he realized the sun was starting to turn her nose red. "It wasn't?" she asked, hesitant.

He removed the hat from his head, settling it onto hers. "Face is getting pink," he said softly. "And, uh, no." He narrowed his eyes just a bit. Even now, after being apart from her for half his life, he was finding there were still things he could say to her that he couldn't say to anyone else. "Come on, Trish, you knew my family."

"Yeah. And?"

He spoke quietly. "I know how people thought of us. If there'd been railroad tracks running through Eden, we'd have been on the wrong side of 'em. It's not a secret."

She looked troubled—like maybe she didn't want to admit what they both knew.

"It's okay," Joe promised her. "It's not news to me."

"Maybe I *liked* your family," she said. "Maybe I liked being around people who were so different from *my* family."

He raised his eyebrows in question, not quite believing her.

"Like, remember how spontaneous your mom was? Remember the time we wanted to make cookies, but she didn't have the right ingredients, so she tried to improvise? We figured they'd be inedible, but they actually weren't half bad. Remember how the three of us and Jana laughed the whole time she was mixing them up and telling us she could invent her own cookie recipe and it was going to make her famous?"

Joe hadn't thought about that in . . . damn, a very long time. Maybe since the summer night it had happened, a warm breeze blowing through the windows, along with the steady chirp of crickets. Hell, he'd probably been way more concerned with finding a minute to get Trish alone so they could make out than interested in cookies—but she was right, it was a good thing to look back on. On her good days, his mom had been fun and energetic, her mood infectious. "I'd forgotten that," he said slowly.

"And remember the time your dad souped up the riding lawn mower and we were all buzzing around the yard on it?"

Joe laughed at another rekindled memory. "That was dangerous as hell—we're lucky somebody didn't get hurt."

She shrugged in agreement. "But I'm just saying . . . I had a good time with your family back in those days. So . . . maybe you sold them a little short."

*Aw, honey, you don't know everything. You don't know about the drinking. Or the yelling. Or the night Mom died.*

But he wasn't going to dump that on her. Not when they were just getting to be friends again. "Maybe so," he said simply instead.

Crushing a soda can in her hand like some bruiser, Trish said, "We should probably get back to work. If we want to get this finished sometime before midnight."

"You're right," he said. *And I'd like to be doing far different things with you, cupcake, by the time midnight rolls around.*

Then he cringed, hoping she didn't see the lust on his face. *Buddy, you've gotta get your animal impulses under control. You're here to help her with hay—that's all*. Still, he couldn't resist saying, "But working together like this isn't *so* horrible, is it?"

She actually slanted him a grin, then teased him. "Well, no, not *so* horrible, just . . ."

"Just *kind of* horrible," he supplied for her.

"Right," she said, laughing.

And his natural instinct was to playfully tackle her, push her back into the stack of hay bales piled behind her, and kiss her senseless. But instead he just threw his wadded napkin at her—and she said, "Hey, watch it."

"Or what? You'll fire me?"

They both laughed as she pushed away a wisp of hair that had escaped her ponytail, and things were suddenly so easy and comfortable that, unlike her, Joe didn't want the day to end.

Conversation faded quickly enough, however, when they got back to work, loading the wagon and getting the bales into the barn. By midafternoon, the bright hot day was fading into something more warm, humid, and gray. Clouds rolled in from the south, and Joe yelled to Trish over the sound of the tractor, "We'd better step on it if we're gonna beat the rain."

"I thought we'd have the whole day," she shouted back.

"Must have moved quicker than they expected." *Kind of like him*, with *her*, he thought.

Judging from the sky, which soon grew darker with every minute, he didn't think there was any way they'd make it—another couple of loads of hay still lay in the fields. But he'd grown up on a farm—they'd had cattle when he was young and had harvested the hay for winter feed—and he'd been in this position at least twenty times before. You almost always thought you weren't gonna make it, but a lot of times, you did. This just meant it was time to kick it into gear.

Each time he stopped, Trish jumped off the wagon and they both rushed to tote the bales. They didn't take the time to stack them as neatly as before, which meant they didn't get as much per load, but speed seemed more important knowing the skies could open any minute.

As they worked feverishly, side by side, Joe concentrated on his task, but also on Trish—the shift of her hips, breasts, as she hefted bales up on the wagon, the dew of perspiration lighting her cheekbones and spanning the long line of her neck. It took a rare woman to make this kind of work fun. And he could no longer deny that it had been hard as hell not touching her all day. Being alone with her, in the heat, had slowly stirred his desire to near bursting, and occasional accidental contact had fueled the fire. Now his adrenaline was building as they hurried to collect what he was pretty sure would be their last load.

Sure enough, as the tractor and wagon lumbered through an open gate onto a dirt lane that led to the barn, drops of rain began to pelt his arms. Ah, it felt great at first, cooling his skin after the heat of the day—until a thunderclap sounded, signaling a dense downpour.

Joe actually laughed as he turned to Trish amid the drenching deluge. She sat atop the bales stacked behind him. "We just made it, cupcake!"

She was laughing, too, but his own mirth became stilted, forced, when he caught one glimpse of her in the rain.

Strands of hair that had come free from her ponytail plastered her cheeks and her T-shirt stuck to her skin, too—he could see through it and even through the lace of her bra to take in the dark color of clearly beaded nipples. He went instantly hard, despite the rain, despite everything. Jesus.

Turning back around, partly to make sure he didn't wreck the damn tractor and partly to quit gaping at her, he maneuvered the load into the barn, killed the engine, and hopped down to the earthen floor.

Taking the few steps to the wagon, he met Trish as she was climbing down and instinctively reached up, planted both palms at her slender waist, and lowered her to the ground with him.

Of course, he didn't want to let her go now that he had his hands on her.

But he did.

Even if she looked slightly unsettled by having been in his arms. Even if releasing her felt like a huge sacrifice. Even if his cock strained behind his zipper, begging him to pull her into a crushing embrace.

"You know what?" she said as she found her footing. "I'm exhausted. Let's not worry about getting any of this in the loft. It'll be fine for now."

Normally, Joe would have protested—he was a guy who liked finishing what he started. But in this case, it was actually a good idea. "Top layer of hay is wet anyway—it's best we leave it like this to dry instead of burying it between other bales." And besides, his thoughts had turned to an entirely different subject now—namely Trish. Wet.

He turned still harder just looking at her—the droplets running down her face, the cotton T-shirt drenched against her curves. The steady cadence of the rain on the barn's old tin roof seemed to cocoon them.

"Ready to make a run for it?" she asked with a smile, motioning to the faded red truck outside the barn. She clearly had no idea how she looked right now—or what it was doing to him.

Trying again to push back his desire, he replied with a nod and they both dashed out into the downpour toward her dad's old Ford pickup. His workboot slipped in the mud and she got ahead of him, but when she reached the passenger door and gave it a yank, she couldn't get it open.

He automatically ran to her side of the truck and reached around her, closing his hand over hers on the handle to help.

He pulled hard, but the damn thing was stuck tight—he couldn't get it open, either.

Which was when he realized he was touching more than just her hand.

The front of his wet body pressed fully against the back of hers.

He honestly hadn't meant to do it. He'd just been trying to help her get in.

But suddenly rain didn't matter.

And getting in didn't matter.

Both of them went still.

He could have sworn the rain sizzled on his skin, the way he was burning up inside. He'd had hot, urgent sex before—hell, he'd had it with Trish in her motel room—but *this, this* was new, different. His need had been building all day, and now, suddenly, it was ready to burst.

Yet he couldn't move.

Because he didn't know how she would react, and because— holy God—he didn't want to blow this, this good but surely fragile connection they'd built today.

*And* because it felt pretty damn good just to press his erection against her ass, feel that hot, raw connection, even if they *were* both getting soaked.

Everything changed, though, when she looked over her shoulder, biting her lip, rain running down her face. Her eyes shone on him like liquid heat, and he knew. He knew.

There was no thought then, only action. He slid one hand around her hip to cup the denim between her thighs and listened to her hot intake of breath. The other he shifted from the door to her wet, pliable breast, so soft and seeming made to fit his palm. "Damn it, Trish, I tried not to do this, I swear," he growled hot in her ear. "But God help me, I want you. And I can't stop."

"I want you, too." Her voice came thready, weak. Beautiful. "I want you so much."

"Right here?" he whispered.

"Right here," she said. "Right now."

**Discovery:** a formal request by one party in a lawsuit to disclose information or facts known by other parties or witnesses; _or_ the act of finding something that had previously existed, but hitherto been unknown; new knowledge, or a new insight.

# Eight

Trish trembled with the reality of what she'd just set in motion, of what they were about to do. She'd been trying her damnedest to avoid this, and now she was giving in to it. Practically begging for it.

Okay, she hadn't begged _yet_, but she probably would if she had to. Yeesh.

This was bad.

Or _good_, depending upon your perspective.

Oh hell, when it came to Joe, all the lines were blurred.

But when his hand began to move back and forth between her thighs, his fingers stroking through the denim to her very core, his palm pressing firm to the front of her mound, she quivered in heated delight. _Yes, yes, feel me._

With his other hand, he caressed her breast with the skill of a master, the touch somehow both gentle and rough at the same time. People always said artists were good with their hands. Those people had apparently never been touched by a mechanic.

This made no sense—not in the big picture of her life, not in the promises she'd made to herself these last few days. But even through their jeans, she could feel how hard he was. And after spending the entire day watching him work in the hot sun, looking into those deep blue eyes whenever chance had allowed—oh God, there was no resisting him.

Then both his hands were reaching to the front of her jeans, deftly unbuttoning, unzipping. Then under her shirt, at her hips, pulling down the wet, heavy denim, baring more of her skin to the rain as he lowered her jeans to her thighs.

They were a mile away from anything—the house, the road—shadowed only by the large old locust trees that grew to one side of the barn behind them. Beyond the truck and the gated fence lay an open meadow, freshly cut. She'd never felt at once so exposed to the elements yet so very sheltered—by the rain that seemed to wrap around them somehow, and by Joe's very maleness, the sweet scent of his sweat, the roughness of his fingertips as they moved over her wet bottom. The rain, she thought, made her feel everything more—every nuance, every sensation. Each tree, the hay, the aged wood of the barn—everything around her possessed its own earthy scent and feel that mixed with Joe's, and when she put it all together, it smelled like . . . home.

But in a whole new, unimaginable way. She'd never have dreamed home could be so . . . hot. Or make her so needful, hungry. "Please." She heard herself murmur the word. She wasn't even sure where it had come from or what it meant. Only that the begging had commenced and she didn't even care.

But when his erection pressed bare and wet against her rear, and she arched for him involuntarily, and his hard fullness came rushing into her—rough, strong, commanding—she knew *exactly* what "please" had meant. It had meant, *Hurry, I need you like I need to breathe.* And now she had him, buried in her warmth, his strokes coming as hard and tumultuous as the pouring rain.

She'd never experienced anything so feral, wild, as Joe's powerful thrusts pummeling her as she braced herself against the truck, palms pressed flat against the wet steel of the door. Each deep plunge echoed out through her fingertips, down through her thighs. She'd never done anything like this, yet somehow it seemed natural, not even shocking, and she instantly wanted to relish it, luxuriate in each heated bit of hedonistic pleasure. She leaned her head back to feel the cool rain on her face as she drank in his deep plunges below, emitting a low moan at each. She stopped thinking—and simply *felt*. All of it. All of *him*.

Behind her, he groaned his own pleasure, and even without being able to see his face as they moved together, she stayed acutely aware that it was Joe inside her—Joe, the boy she'd loved with all that she was; Joe, whom she'd wanted to marry with her whole heart; Joe, who had been her whole world once upon a time.

He murmured heated words in her ear—"So hot," "So wet inside," "So good, baby"—and she let them roll down through her like thick, warm honey.

And when his hand slid from her hip over her thigh to dip into the cleft between her legs, the sensation was so overwhelming that she sobbed. "Joe! Oh God, Joe!" *I love you.*

Damn it, she'd almost said that—almost screamed it out in the rain.

But she couldn't worry over that right now, because he was touching her, in just the right way, sweeping away her sanity, lifting her to an entirely different plane.

She moved against his fingers, fingers that stroked in perfect rhythm, and she heard her heartbeat in her ears, muting the static of the downpour.

"I want to make you come," Joe said low in her ear.

She bit her lip at the intense pleasure his mere words sent shooting through her as a gripping heat gathered low in her belly, and the moment was so wild and perfect that she didn't want it to end, not ever.

But her body hurtled forward anyway, so quick, no warning—*oh God, oh God*—until she was crashing into stunning bursts of hot, hard ecstasy that made her cry out and whimper and shudder like a baby in his arms. *Yes, yes, yes. I love you, Joe. I love you.*

She held it in again, thank God. And this time didn't even bother berating herself for it, instead just pushing it aside for now, in lieu of bliss.

He held her tight as the waves settled and reality returned—rain and the scent of it in the trees still mixing with the pungent smell of the hay, and him. Her lover. Her . . . love? She'd cared for other men and she'd been in their beds, but she couldn't deny the startling revelation that next to him all men paled, all sex paled, even all . . . love paled.

Behind her, his breath came heavy and he whispered in her ear hot, sweet words about how he loved making her come. And she was timid enough when not wearing Spandex that she normally wouldn't have responded to such a declaration, but without even thinking, for it was so natural, she looked over her shoulder at his rain-soaked face and said, "I want to make you come, too."

His body jolted as if she'd just delivered an electrical shock, and she reveled in the feminine sexual power flowing through her. His eyes went dark and his mouth slack, as if she'd just drained all his strength with that one sentence. "Aw, Trishy," he murmured in the rain. His eyes fell shut as he released a heavy groan, then punished her body with strokes so wonderfully hard that, again, she felt them in the tips of her fingers and toes until he spilled himself deep within her.

When he went still, he nearly collapsed against her body, pinning her to the cab of the truck, arms wrapped tight around her waist.

Seconds passed that way, rain still falling as they both recovered in silence.

Trish watched the patterns the raindrops made on the truck's window, trickling down, realizing for the first time how ridiculously wet they both were, and thinking also how ridiculously *good* this had been.

Except for one thing. That damn *I love you* that kept drifting through her mind. And *drifting* was a generous understatement. She'd nearly shrieked it.

Finally, he loosened his grip on her, then slowly turned her in his arms to face him. She was struck fresh with what a beautiful man he was, his blue eyes shimmering, wet hair dripping around his face, his chin dusted with dark, rough stubble that drew her hand up impulsively, her fingertips trailing down his jaw. Like their passion, the deluge had softened now into only a heavy drizzle, and he gazed long and hard into her eyes with such warmth that it began to melt her all over again.

And then he was kissing her—deep, paralyzing tongue

kisses—his embrace warm and almost magnetic as their wet bodies clung together. It was minutes later before the kisses faded to gentleness, to tiny, heated touches of mouths, tongues. And when finally they stopped and stood staring at each other in the light rain, he tilted his head slightly to say, "Are you okay?"

When she started to speak, she grew aware of how deliciously swollen his kisses had left her lips, so only nodded instead.

Joe gazed down on her, utterly amazed. Sex with her before had been incredible—but what they'd just shared defied description. He lifted his hands to her face. "Do you have any idea how beautiful you are?"

She dropped her gaze briefly, looking strangely bashful considering what they'd just done. "Maybe you should tell me."

He grazed his thumb over her lips, continuing to cup her cheeks in his hands, just to feel her skin, the shape of her face, the delicate bones. "You are—I promise. You were a pretty girl, Trish. But you grew up into a very beautiful woman."

She bit her lip, blushing slightly, and slid her hands up over his wet arms to say, "You grew up pretty good yourself."

He laughed softly, loving the mere fact that she was in his arms and they'd just had hot, urgent sex out in a field, in the rain. Ever since she'd come home, Trish had fulfilled any and every sexual fantasy a guy could have—plus, she was Trish, *his* Trish. He couldn't help thinking the whole thing would be pretty damn perfect . . . if only she would forgive him.

"Maybe," he said, letting his lips curve ever so slightly, "we should get out of the rain?"

She laughed, then rolled her eyes, almost as if maybe she'd forgotten they were *in* the rain—easy enough to do given all the other things there'd been to feel.

He pulled his jeans together as she maneuvered hers back up, too, and then he reached for the truck door—only to discover it was still stuck. "Damn thing," he muttered, but he really didn't mind since, if not for that truck door, he wouldn't have experienced such pure, reckless pleasure with her just now. "Other side," he said, taking her hand and leading her there.

When they climbed up into the truck, Joe slamming the driver's side door behind him, he didn't hesitate to pull her wet body right back into his arms and kiss her again. This kiss was more slow, lingering, than what they'd shared outside—but hell, if he didn't watch it, he'd be taking her in the truck before long.

When the kiss ended, her legs stretched across his lap and he held her in a loose embrace. "So . . ." he said, looking down at her.

"So . . ."

He didn't want to ask her again—but he had to. "Are you okay? About this?"

She looked a little troubled—just what he'd been afraid of, but just what he'd been expecting, too. "I . . . don't know." She avoided his eyes.

"I swear I didn't plan it this way. I just wanted to help you with the hay. But seems like whenever I'm around you, I want you—bad. And by the way, your T-shirt is way too tight, especially when you get rained on."

She laughed softly, yet all went quiet but for the sound of the rain on the truck's roof. Then she lifted her eyes—emerald eyes that had suddenly gone deadly serious. "Tell me about . . . that night."

Joe's stomach dropped. He hadn't seen this coming. And he didn't have to ask which night she was talking about. Hell. He lowered his chin slightly, peering at her from under the brim of the soaked hat she'd plopped back on his head at some point. "Do we really have to go there, Trish?"

She looked resolute, like he imagined she must look when she was cross-examining some witness in court. "I think we do. If you really want me to understand."

Joe rubbed his lips together uncertainly, finally saying, "I don't expect you to *ever* understand. I don't have . . . a good explanation."

"I still need to hear it," she said without missing a beat. "I just need to know what happened, Joe. I need you to tell me. Because sometimes, I think the pictures in my head are maybe worse than the truth. Even if the truth is bad, then at least I know, and I can . . . process it."

Joe took a deep breath, surprised to find he couldn't quite look at her when he tried to speak—so instead he focused on the hood of the old truck stretching out in front of him beyond the rain-spattered windshield. He couldn't see the good in this—he feared it would only stir up the hurt, maybe make her hate him all over again. But if this was what she asked of him, he wouldn't deny her.

"Do you remember," he began, "how things were that night? You were leaving, and I . . . hell, Trish, I wanted you. You know that. I wanted you just like I still want you now. But then . . ." His voice softened, unplanned. "Then . . . shit, honey, it was hard as hell. I know girls don't quite get this, and I also know it sounds lame, but it's brutal when you're a teenage boy whose dick is going crazy."

She flinched, and he said, "Sorry, but that's how it was. And even though that doesn't exactly sound . . . romantic, you know I loved you, cupcake." He *did* focus on her then, needing her to hear this part more than the rest. "You know that, right? You know I loved you. You know you were pretty much *everything* to me back then, don't you?"

Her voice came out small, delicate. "I *thought* I was. But later, I didn't really believe it anymore."

He pressed his lips together, sighing, his chest tightening at her words. "I loved you more than anything, Trish. Maybe . . . hell, maybe I loved you too much."

She blinked. "How can you love someone too much?"

He looked at her long and hard. Forced himself to remember all the feelings roiling through him that fateful night. It wasn't easy. He'd never been good with feelings of . . . inadequacy. Not with his dad. And not with Trish.

But he swallowed and forced out the words. "Maybe if I hadn't loved you so much, I wouldn't have been so fucking scared."

Her pretty eyes widened on him. "Scared? *You?* Of what?"

He knew most people didn't think much of anything scared Joe Ramsey. The Ramseys were tough, mean, the kind of people who'd kick your ass if you looked at them the wrong way. And Joe could only remember a couple of times in his life when he'd ever felt truly afraid. The night his mom had crashed her car into that tree. And before that, the summer after graduation, when he knew Trish was leaving him. "I was afraid you'd never come home."

She drew back slightly. "I was supposed to come home in two weeks."

"I don't mean that. I mean I was afraid you'd never come home for *good*, like we planned. I was afraid you'd never really come home to *me*."

She blinked again, looking stunned. "Why?"

And Joe sighed. Wasn't it obvious? It had felt *plenty* obvious to *him*, but he'd been too cool, too Ramsey tough, to ever tell her. "Trish, you had dreams. You wanted to be something, you wanted to see other places. We had this plan of getting married, keeping things the same, but when you talked about college, about the city—your eyes lit. In a way they never lit up for *me*. You wanted more than me and Eden, and I knew it."

He saw her draw in her breath, her legs still angled across his lap—he saw the memories well in her eyes. The wisps of hair around her face were starting to dry, to draw into loose, tiny blond curls. "I did want to see new places, Joe, I'd *always* wanted that, ever since I was a little girl. And college was going to be my time for that—my time to do new things. But when I made my plans to leave, coming back was the *main* thing in my mind. By the time I was set to go, I didn't even really want to anymore."

He let out a breath, trying to see her, really see her heart. Who was she? The farm girl with the ponytail who'd put up hay with him today? Or the confident, worldly lawyer he'd met at the Last Chance almost a week ago? "Are you sure, Trish?" he asked slowly. "Are you sure those new things might not have changed what you wanted? Are you sure that meeting new people, new guys, wouldn't have made it so that Eden and me seemed kind of . . . same old, same old?"

He appreciated the fact that she didn't just rush to say she was sure—her eyes saddened softly as she thought about it. "I guess I can't *really* be sure of anything, Joe—given the way things happened, I guess we'll never know for certain. But I can tell you that I loved you completely, and on the night before I left, all I really wanted was to come home in four years and marry you."

"I guess I thought," he went on, "that if we had sex before you left that it would be more like . . . we were real, solid. More like you were really gonna stay mine."

She leaned back against the seat next to him, looking tired, her gaze on her knees. "You have no idea, Joe, how much I wanted to be with you that way. There was just a part of me that wasn't ready." She raised her eyes back to his then. "Which leads me back to that night. I need to know what happened after you left me."

He let out a heavy breath. He didn't like remembering that part, but looked like he didn't have a choice. "Hell, Trish, what can I say? I was eighteen and horny as hell. Frustrated, too. And I guess I was hurt that you'd said no again, when you were leaving, and when I'd really thought . . ."

"That was my fault, I know. I'd promised you."

He sighed. "I was heading home when a car blinked its lights at me. I pulled over, thinking it was Kenny—but it was Bev."

She stiffened in his lap but said, "Go on."

"She had beer and I drank it. We talked about the usual crap. And then . . . we talked about you. I was getting drunk fast and I guess I told her you were leaving and that I was bummed about it." He stopped, remembering. Some parts he recalled only vaguely, through the haze of alcohol, but other moments were all too vivid. "Well, Bev was never one to miss an opportunity, so she said if *she* were my girlfriend that she wouldn't be going away, that she'd be staying here with me."

Trish cringed slightly, but he tried not to feel it, tried to keep going, so he could get through this.

"I wasn't used to drinking much, so I guess the beer made me feel sorry for myself. And I guess . . . hell, I guess it was nice to hear someone make it sound like that was good enough—just me, just this town." He paused. He was getting to the hard part, the part he'd rather forget, the mistake that had screwed up his future. At the moment, it all felt too recent, like yesterday.

"I got in her car at some point. And she started kissing me. And I knew it was wrong, Trish, but right then . . ." He considered sugarcoating this part but didn't. She wanted honesty from him—she was going to get it. "Right then, I didn't care. I was drunk, and it was . . . too easy to let her."

"What then?"

He balked, staring at her. Was she serious? "You know what then."

Yet she shook her head. "No, I don't. How many times? Who was on top? Was there foreplay? Did she have an orgasm?"

He just gaped at her. Then swiped his hand slowly down his face as he let out the heaviest sigh yet. "And we have to go through these details why?" Was she trying to torture him?

But she looked earnest when she answered, like there wasn't a bit of malice intended. "Because I need to know, Joe. I just need to know."

Joe glanced down, focusing on the worn steering wheel, the same faded red as the dashboard. "Okay. It was only once, I was on top, there wasn't much foreplay, and I have no idea if she came, because to tell you the truth, at that moment, it was all about me."

Next to him, she let out a soft breath. "And so, how . . . was it?"

He made himself look at her again. "It . . . filled a certain need, I guess—satisfied my curiosity. But it left me empty inside—because I knew it should have been you. And because I knew I'd made the biggest mistake of my life. It was over before I even knew what was happening and I couldn't take it back." He suffered the hurt, felt it washing over them both, all over again—and he wanted this awful talk to be done. "Is there anything else? Anything more you want to know?"

Slowly, she nodded—and shit, he sensed something else big coming.

"Tell me about your daughter."

Joe shot his gaze to her. "She's not my daughter."

She flinched, so he knew he must have said it too brusquely, but he couldn't help it. The words had just come out that way, and despite having the power to dispel the rumors if he wanted, maybe he was tired of everyone in town *assuming* Carissa was his.

"What do you mean? I thought . . ."

"She's not mine, Trish. I had a DNA test done after she was born."

Yet Trish still looked completely confused, and he supposed he could understand why. "But Debbie told me you . . . spend time with her, sort of helped raise her. Why would you do that if she's not yours?"

Maybe that was part of the reason he'd let so few people know the truth. Maybe it was easier to let people think he was a shithead for not officially claiming Carissa than it was to explain why he'd been there for someone he really had no connection to.

"It's hard to explain," he began. "The whole time Bev was pregnant, I thought the baby was mine. I knew she slept around, but I didn't figure she'd slept with somebody else right at the same time she'd slept with me. I was pretty freaked out, but I was planning to do the right thing, take on the responsibility."

Trish nodded, and Joe thought back to those strange days that had altered his life so drastically. That whole year had changed . . . everything. "When Carissa was first born, I saw a lot of her. I changed diapers, gave her bottles, all that. I had no idea what I was doing, but I was trying.

"Then I ordered a DNA test. My mom's idea. She watched a lot of TV, knew about stuff like that. I did it just to be sure. And Bev was pissed. But then it came back negative—I wasn't Carissa's father.

"Thing is, though, by that time, I felt like I was." He shrugged and let his voice soften. "I'd never been much of a baby guy before, but she was pretty damn cute—little brown eyes, little blip of a nose. And when Bev told me the only other guy who could be Carissa's dad had been passing through town to join the Marines and that she didn't even know his last name—well, it bothered me to think of Carissa never having a dad.

"And right then . . ." Joe drew his gaze away as his chest tightened, along with his throat. "My mom died. And things were bad. Really bad. My dad left, and—"

"Your dad left? Left you and Jana?"

The interruption drew his gaze to Trish's; he'd forgotten she didn't know that. "Yeah."

Shock repainted her face. "And Jana was . . . how old? Eleven or twelve?"

His voice went a little lower, remembering. "Yeah."

"Why? Why on earth did he walk out on you?"

Joe could only sigh. He wasn't going into *these* details, too, no way—all this was hard enough to talk about as it was. So he kept it simple. "Mom's death was . . . hard on *all* of us. In different ways. But the upshot is . . . you see your little sister suddenly left without a mom or a dad and . . . you kinda don't want *anybody* to be stuck that way. So even though I wasn't Carissa's father, I just . . . kept coming around.

"Not as much as before, and I never pretended to be her dad or asked her to call me that—I was just . . . this guy in her life. And I still am. I don't see her as much as I used to—she usually stops by the garage once a week to hang out a while—but that's only because I don't have a clue how to entertain a thirteen-year-old girl. I'm just kinda . . . there for her when she needs me. That's all."

Trish's expression bordered somewhere between puzzled and amazed. "So she doesn't know why you're in her life?"

He shook his head. "We've never talked about it, so I don't know *what* she thinks. But she probably thinks I *am* her dad."

Trish leaned slightly forward. "Is that why . . . you've kept it a secret all this time?"

"That's part of it. Hell, I don't know if she wants me to be her dad or *not*—but if she does, I don't want to break her heart by letting it get around that I'm not. As far as telling her the truth goes, I feel damned if I do, damned if I don't. I didn't think through this well enough when I was a kid—I was just doing what felt right at the time. But I figure she'd probably rather have me than nobody—know what I mean?"

She nodded, yet he went on. "The fact is—it's a pretty screwed up situation. Part of that's my fault. And part of it is Bev's, for not being clearer on it, too. I think Bev has always wished . . ."

"What?"

"That there was . . . more between me and her. But there's not." He looked her in the eye. "Never has been, Trish—nothing but that one night, I swear. I just think maybe she's never told Carissa the whole truth because she hoped someday I'd want to make a family with the two of them or something."

"God," Trish finally breathed.

"I know," he told her. "Pretty fucking ridiculous mess, isn't it?"

She shook her head. "Well, actually, that's not what I was thinking."

He looked up. "No?"

"I was thinking that . . . you're kind of amazing."

He flinched, taken aback. "I am?"

"To try to be a father to her even when you're not obligated to. And to let people think you aren't owning up to your full responsibility just to keep her thinking she *does* have a dad. That's pretty generous, Joe."

Joe couldn't have been more shocked. He almost started to argue with her, to insist that he'd handled things wrong, but instead, he just turned it back on Carissa. "Well, she's a cool kid—it's easy to want to do right by her."

"Thanks," she said, "for telling me that. I know even Debbie doesn't know, or she'd have told me."

He managed a smile. "Exactly why Debbie doesn't know. She'd have told the whole damn world."

When they went silent, listening again to the gentle sound of the rain, he finally said, "Anything else, Trish?"

*Please say no. I'm fucking exhausted here.*

She looked sheepish but said, "One more thing."

He took a deep breath. "What?"

"Tell me about the women. All the women I've heard about."

*Christ.* If she *wasn't* trying to torture him, she was doing a damn good imitation. He'd never even realized until her dad had brought up the same thing this morning that he was considered such a playboy. He suspected he had good old Debbie to thank. "I'm a normal guy, cupcake, not a priest. Yeah, there have been some women. That's all I can say."

"Have you been in love with any of them?"

His throat clogged again. He didn't want to tell her the truth. But he wasn't gonna start lying now. "Only one," he said. "You."

"Oh." She sounded slightly surprised as their eyes met. But there it was, out on the table—now she knew.

"You?" he asked. He figured after this, he had the right to know.

"Are you asking about sex? Or love?"

"Both."

She swallowed again, looking nervous. And damn, his stomach was churning like a schoolboy's waiting for her answer. "I've been serious with a couple of guys since you. And I've slept with . . . a number of men, some who were important, some less so."

"How many?"

She blinked, looking slightly perturbed now—but hell, she'd started it. "How many for you?"

He shrugged sharply. "You'd have to ask Debbie. She's probably kept a closer count than me."

"Six," she said softly. "Counting you now."

Six. Counting him. Not that many. Despite instantly hating the other five, it still felt like a weight lifted from his chest.

"A hell of a lot less than you, I'm betting."

That was for sure. "But you were the best," he said, not gauging the words, just telling it like it was. Their eyes met, and he leaned toward her, coming closer, until their foreheads touched beneath the brim of his hat.

"You . . . don't have to say that, Joe."

"I don't lie, Trish. I don't just say things. That's how it is." Then he added something he'd been needing to tell her for fourteen years now. "I'm sorry. For the whole damn thing." Then he shook his head. "You're the last person in the world I ever wanted to hurt."

He sighed, tired of all this sad shit, and God knew he'd suffered for it back then; he didn't want to keep suffering now. So instead he pressed his mouth back to hers, firm but gentle. The energy of the kiss flowed through his veins, filling him up, giving him what he needed. He wasn't gonna have her forever, he knew that, but he had her now, in this moment—and he needed to feel her, drink her in, as much as he could.

When the kiss ended, she looked breathless—but then raked one delicate hand back through her wet hair to say, "We should . . . probably go. It's been raining awhile now—Mom and Dad will be worried."

He nodded gently and didn't protest as she slid off his lap and waited as he started the truck.

The moment was over, the sweet closeness gone.

His heart sunk a little, but hell—what was he expecting? He supposed he should just be thankful for what they'd shared. Both the sex *and* the talking. The talking had been hard, but at the same time he felt like a criminal who'd finally gotten to confess, so maybe he understood now why she'd needed to hear it. Maybe he'd needed to say it, too.

They stayed silent as they traveled the now muddy path out of the valley and across the ridge where the Henderson house sat, and when he parked the truck next to the big red barn near the farmhouse and killed the engine, he thought—*what now?*

And then he *knew* what now.

Hell, if he was going down, he'd go down swinging.

She was starting to move across the seat away from him, to exit through the stuck door, but he grabbed onto her wrist.

She looked up, their eyes locking.

"Let me see you again, Trish."

He had to ask, even though he knew he was wasting his breath. Now he waited to see exactly how she'd word her refusal. *No, Joe—it's not that I don't want you, it's that I don't trust you. It's that I can't forgive you. It's that you've slept with every woman in town. It's that we've got different lives and I don't even live here and I'm leaving soon, blah blah blah.*

"Okay," she said instead.

His jaw dropped. "What did you just say?"

For the first time in awhile, her eyes truly softened. "I said okay."

*Okay?* She'd said *okay?*

The next day, a week since she'd first stumbled headlong into her first passionate encounter with Joe, she found herself back at the diner, working vigorously, probably trying to get yesterday out of her system.

Not the sex in the rain part, though.

And not really the talking in the truck part, either.

Mainly the *okay* part.

What had she been thinking?

Probably that she wanted more sex and talking. But now, she couldn't help worrying. Did this mean she . . . trusted him suddenly? Did it mean she was diving into a *relationship* with him?

No, and no, she decided, stomping her foot on the old tile floor. She'd just kind of decided, when he'd told her about Carissa, maybe he was a better person than she'd realized up to now. And that maybe it wouldn't be awful to let herself spend some time with him.

*Keep a cool head. You just said you'd see him, not have his babies.*

She wasn't even sure she *wanted* babies anyway. Did *Joe* want babies? After all, he already had Carissa—sort of. Wow, how weird to think of Joe changing diapers, cooing over some tiny baby, feeling warmly toward it.

*Yikes*—what was she doing thinking about *babies?*

What she *needed* to be thinking about was whipping this place into shape, once and for all. And hey, if she saw Joe another time or two over the next week while she worked on her remodeling project, no big deal. It was . . . an affair. Yes, an affair. That sounded very mature and cosmopolitan—and it had nothing to do with babies, either.

She looked at the plethora of paint cans around her. She'd been back to The Home Depot amid the morning drizzle. There were also painting tarps, and tape, and rollers and brushes.

*And* tables and chairs. She'd bitten the bullet and called the wholesale guy, and he'd delivered them less than two hours later! So there was no turning back now.

She feared her parents might have a heart attack when they found out what she was doing to the place, but she felt bizarrely energized by the project before her. She'd never really done any decorating—she'd even hired her loft out to an interior design team—but she had the wild feeling that she was onto something potentially spectacular here, something at once sophisticated yet small town, funky yet quaint. Before long, she'd have buyers *begging* her to sell them the place.

The cans of paint sat heaped one atop the other. To the colors she'd bought the other day, she'd now added shades of peach, mint, and lemon for the walls. Bolder shades of purple, red, fuchsia, and tangerine sat nearby, too—for the new tables and chairs, which would make much better use of the big floor area between the two rows of booths than the *nothing* that had always occupied it before. Some of the chairs had curlycue backs and she planned to paint each curling piece of wood a different color. She wondered if she was artistic enough to pull off simple designs on the tabletops—maybe a sun here, a moon there, or just some shapes. If worse came to worst, Home Depot had stencils. She'd also bought some spray paint that should work on the booths.

Of course, the possibility existed that this was a rash decision. Brought about by what had happened with Joe. When real life got challenging, Trish traditionally focused on her work—and right now, this was her work. So was she planning to turn the diner into a Crayola-colored beatnik coffeehouse just to distract herself from how close she'd felt to Joe yesterday afternoon?

When she'd made him tell her what had happened with Beverly, she'd sensed the agony just dripping from him. And she'd seen him toughing it out for her. And she'd felt herself falling, falling . . . a little deeper in love with him with each passing moment.

And sure, she could keep telling herself she *didn't* love him, that it was all sex-induced crazy talk in her mind—but she really feared she did now. Love him. She let out a heavy, whooshing breath. Whoa. That was big.

And now she had eight café tables and twenty-four chairs to paint. Not to mention ten booths. And a lot of walls. Boy, she hoped she knew what she was doing. With the diner, and with Joe, too. Both felt pretty iffy right now. Life was easier when it came with pointy-toed pumps, power suits, and legal briefs.

*"What the hell is this?"*

Trish spun to find Debbie standing in the doorway in a bright pink rain jacket, the bell above her head tinkling beneath her brash greeting.

Trish tried to act cool, as if she hadn't gone totally overboard. "Some paint. And a few tables and chairs."

Debbie's eyes narrowed. "Are you moving in?"

"I told you I was sprucing things up, making things more modern. Some buyer is going to love it, trust me."

Debbie's shocked gaze dropped to the numerous cans of paint, all of which had their sample swatch taped to the side for easy recognition. "I hope they're color blind."

Trish grimaced. "I thought you had a job this time of year. Why aren't you at it?"

"Lunch break," Deb announced, her tone shifting instantly into "cheerful." She handed Trish a greasy bag. "Burger Barn."

And as usual, Debbie's thoughtfulness totally overrode Trish's irritation at her—at least for the moment, since she was hungry. "Thanks, Deb."

But as her best friend slid into an aqua booth, she scowled slightly again, still looking around. "I thought you said this place was hot property *already*. Why on earth would you invest money just to sell it?"

Trish sat down across from her. "This was all less than a thousand bucks—the tables and chairs were a steal. And it *is* hot property—I just want to make it even hotter."

To her surprise, Debbie replied with an impish little smile. "Speaking of hot . . . aren't you gonna tell me you had help with the hay yesterday?"

*Yeesh*—Trish kept forgetting that she and Joe had *no* privacy given that they shared mutual best friends. "So I have *you* to thank. I wasn't sure if it was buttinsky you or your buttinsky husband."

Debbie lowered her chin to cast a wicked look. "Sticks and stones, but we all know you can't resist him."

Trish let her eyes go wide. "That's the problem!" Then she took a big bite of her hamburger. "I can't resist him, yet you keep shoving him in my face."

Debbie pushed up her glasses with her index finger, just as she used to do in high school. "For your info, this is actually the first time I shoved him at you. Last Friday night, we accidentally ran into him. The next night, you decided to go have sex with him. The night after that, he decided to bring your bra back. I was responsible for none of that."

Trish's face dropped, along with her stomach. "Crap. You're right. I guess it just *felt* like you were butting in."

"All *I* did was get you some help with your stupid hay, and I'm betting you needed it."

"I did," she admitted quietly. Then lifted her eyes to her friend. "Why didn't you ever tell me his dad left him and Jana?"

"I tried. But those were the days when——"

"Oh yeah." The days when the topic of Joe had been strictly off limits, and anytime Debbie had brought him up on the phone, Trish had stopped her cold with something like, *"I don't want to hear about Joe. He's not in my life anymore. Got it?"* The only time Debbie had persisted was when Joe's mom had died. "But God, Deb, that's huge. I can't believe you didn't tell me anyway."

Debbie sighed. "I recall trying to tell you, like, five or six different times, but each time you shut me down."

"Oh." Fair enough. Trish had eventually eased up on hearing about Joe, yet all that bad stuff had happened to him less than a year after their breakup, when he'd still remained a very sore subject. Trish let out a huge breath. "I can't believe he had to raise Jana from the age of twelve. And he was still dealing with his mom's death and finding out about Bev's baby——" She almost said *not being his*, but caught herself, remembering Debbie didn't know and that Joe meant to keep it that way. Yeesh, that was close!

"You guys must have had *some* talk," Debbie said, eyes wide.

"Yeah. It was, um, intense."

"So, did you do him on the hay wagon? Or maybe it was the tractor."

Trish responded with an exaggerated eye roll. "My God, Debbie, of course not! Why do you always assume something like that?"

"Where then?"

Trish sighed. Oh, hell. "Outside the barn, in the rain."

Debbie's eyebrows rose about a foot. "Ouch, girlfriend!" Then she grinned. "Although I'm betting it didn't exactly hurt."

"Not at all. Except a little, in the good way."

"There's a good way for it to hurt?" Debbie's expression twisted. "God, what have I missed by being married my whole adult life?"

Trish laughed and ate a slightly limp French fry. "I just meant that he's, you know . . . kind of big. And that can be a tight fit—but a lot more good than bad."

"Oh. My." Debbie actually flushed.

Figuring she might as well get to the part Debbie would eventually drag out of her anyway, Trish went on. "We talked afterward. And I . . . sort of agreed to see him again."

Debbie's face lit up. "Trish, that's fantastic!"

But she just shook her head. "No, that's bad. And weird. And confusing."

Debbie's voice went wry. "Why?"

"Because I told him before that I couldn't keep having sex with him if it didn't mean anything, and that it *couldn't* mean anything because I'd never forgiven him. So if I've agreed to see him—which kind of equals having sex with him, since I can't seem to see him and *not* have sex with him—isn't that sort of like saying the sex means something and that I've forgiven him?"

Debbie slapped her palms down on the table, making Trish jerk. "Stop the madness!"

"What?"

She leaned across the table and lowered her voice. "Listen to me. This is simple, and you're making it complicated."

"This is *so* not simple, Deb."

"I disagree. It's like this. Joe is a hunka hunka burnin' love. You *like* his burnin' love. So just go with the flow while you're here, Trish. Just fuck his brains out."

Trish went a bit cross-eyed for a minute but then shook free of it, scrunching her nose. "Since when do you say things like that?" Neither of them ever had.

Debbie held up her hands. "Sometimes it's easier to just say it, flat out."

Trish sighed. "Fair enough. But . . . what if I have feelings for him when I'm doing this? What's going to happen when it's over, when I'm done working on the diner and I head home? What then?"

"There's the beauty of it, Trish," Debbie said as if Trish were thick-headed. "*You* get to decide. It's all up to you. But for now, you just have fun. You just hang out with him and do what feels good and worry about the rest later."

Trish blinked, a bit dumbfounded. "Is that the advice you're going to give your boys when they grow up?"

"*No.*" Deb rolled her eyes. "But you're different from them. You *need* to have some fun, let yourself go."

"And I haven't been doing that with Joe already?"

"Yes, and keep it up. But nix the overanalyzing. In fact, stop analyzing it at all. He's a hot guy. You want him. He wants you. For once in your life, Trish, just go for it and stop worrying."

★　　★　　★

Two hours later, Trish was painting a yellow squiggly line around the edge of a table she'd transformed from gray to purple that morning. She smiled, realizing that painting was actually relaxing her. She'd never done a lot of painting before, so it came as a surprise.

And maybe Debbie was right. Trish had *gone for* plenty of things in life, but she seldom *stopped worrying*. She was a lawyer—it was her *job* to worry. And maybe it spilled over into her personal life—just a tad. So perhaps that was an area she could stand to do some work on.

Could she really do what Debbie said? Go for it? Without worrying about the consequences?

She drew in a deep breath, worrying—as usual.

But then she finished her squiggle with a flourish and tried to relax again. *Go with the flow. Go with the flow.*

When her cell phone rang a few minutes later, she set her brush aside and retreated to the booth where she'd left her purse. She didn't recognize the number, but flipped it open and answered. "Hello?"

"Hey."

Joe. Warmth moved all through her, just from his voice. "Hey."

"Debbie gave me your number."

Trish couldn't help laughing. "*Of course* she did."

She could almost feel his smile. "I know it can be hellaciously annoying, but it comes in handy sometimes, too."

"Very true," she agreed of her best friend, and realized she could hear the sound of something banging in the background. He must be calling from the garage.

"So about the Cobra . . ." Something in his voice sounded determined—and slightly wicked.

It curled her toes, along with other key body parts. "What about it?"

"Wanna go for a ride, little girl?"

Yeesh. Why was that sexy as hell? "Yeah," she said, "sure," trying to sound completely casual and not as if this had been the absolute best sixty seconds of her day so far.

"How about tonight? Rain's supposed to clear by then."

Her stomach churned. Tonight? Already? She was supposed to give up worrying that fast? "Sounds good," she heard herself say. She firmly suspected it had been her *body* answering—but if she worked really hard, maybe she could get her mind to go along with it.

He sounded surprised. "Damn, *that* was easy. I expected a fight."

"I don't want to fight anymore," she said, her voice coming soft. *I don't want to keep fighting my attraction to you.*

She could tell it stunned him. "Me neither, honey."

But the whole point of not fighting anything anymore was to lighten things up, right? So she said, "Besides, how can I pass up a chance to see the famous Cobra?"

"I'll take you on a ride you won't forget, cupcake."

*Mmm*, she didn't doubt it.

"Seven o'clock? We'll get dinner while we're out."

"Okay," she said. Miss Agreeable, suddenly.

Looked like she really *was* going for it.

**Rest:** to be finished presenting the evidence in a case, as in "the plaintiff rests"; *or* relief or freedom from anything that wearies, troubles, or disturbs; to quit fighting something.

## *Nine*

Trish dressed in a long peasant skirt and beaded tank top, thankful she tended to overpack for any trip she went on. And between a day of painting and pep talks, she was ready. She *could* have a casual albeit sizzling affair with Joe—in fact, she was *going* to.

She peered in the white wicker-framed mirror in her old bedroom as she slid a long necklace over her head—small beads sprinkled with chunkier wooden ones—then hooked her delicate cat bracelet around her wrist.

*No more I-love-yous, though, even in your head.* That was the only way to play this, the only way to *enjoy* it. *And if you were right earlier, if you really do love the big lug . . . well, deal with the fallout later, like Debbie said.* Of course, Debbie didn't know the L word was bouncing around in Trish's mind. But still, the same theories applied—have fun, then move on with your life.

Upon descending the stairs, she found her mother washing up dinner dishes. Although her mother didn't complain often, over the last few days Trish had noticed the way she slowly flexed her hands between tasks and knew her mom's arthritis was flaring up. Funny the things she couldn't see over the phone, yet maybe they were going on all the time. "Let me finish those for you, Mom," she said, coming up behind her.

Just then, her mother pulled the stopper from the sink, sending the water down the drain. "Too late," she said, turning to Trish with a smile. "I'm done. And I wouldn't have let you do it anyway. You're going out and I'm sure your nails are done up pretty."

Trish forced a smile and curled her hands into fists. Her nails were far from pretty right now, given her work at the diner, but she couldn't let her mom know that. Trish had finally told her parents she was putting up some new curtains and doing a thorough cleaning, but that was all.

"You look nice," her mom said as she dried her hands with a dish towel, then added with a wink, "Joe'll think so, too."

"Speaking of Joe . . ." She glanced toward the living room where her father remained laid up in his recliner. "Does Dad know where I'm going tonight?"

Her mom shook her head. "I just said you had plans, that's all."

Trish nodded, then made her way into the living room. "How's the back?"

Her dad shrugged. "Getting a little better, I think." He looked more relaxed than he had in days, which relaxed her, too.

Until she heard a car pull into the driveway and decided it was her cue to leave. "Okay then, I'm off. See you later."

"Going out with Debbie again?" he asked.

She knew she could lie, but upon suddenly feeling backed into a corner, Trish refused to let her dad keep making her feel like a teenager. "No," she said calmly, grabbing up her purse and opening the front door. "Joe."

"Joe?"

"Bye, Dad," she said, then rushed out onto the front porch and down the walk before he could stop her.

She looked up to find the hottest man she'd ever seen leaning up against the hottest car she'd ever seen. Wow. Joe wore dark jeans and a fitted black tee tucked behind his belt buckle, but loose around his hips—his arms were crossed, and the coiled part of the cobra edged his sleeve. His thick hair could have used a trim, but she liked it that way, and he hadn't shaved, but she liked that, too. Behind him, a dark pearl red convertible roadster glistened in the rays of the setting sun. Taking in the car's sexy curves and flawless gleam, she could almost feel Joe's years of painstaking work.

"Hey, cupcake," he said in his deep, seductive voice.

Her heartbeat sped up. "Hey."

He gave her a slight, playful grin. "I was gonna come to the door, you know. I'm not afraid of the big, bad wolf."

She glanced back toward the house. "I just thought I'd save us the trouble." Then she switched her focus to the Cobra. "It's beautiful, Joe." Getting closer, she spied soft black leather seats and lots of little round gauges on the flat dashboard.

Joe looked lovingly on the car. "She's my baby," he admitted, gently running his hand along the fender in a way that made Trish suspect he didn't even realize he was doing it. "Aren't you, girl?"

She raised her eyebrows at him, amused.

And a soft laugh rose from his throat. "Hey, some guys name their penises. I occasionally talk to my car."

She smiled, thinking that when he put it like that, it sounded perfectly reasonable.

When he opened the door for her, she got in to find a familiar cowboy hat in the passenger seat.

"I brought you a hat. My sister says you have to have a hat in a convertible if you have long hair or it beats you to death in the wind and gets tangled."

Trish grinned at his thoughtfulness. She'd had the same thought, so had stuffed a ponytail holder in her purse, but she liked wearing Joe's hat better, even if it was a little big on her. She pushed it down on her head and checked her look in the side mirror as he walked around the car.

Backing out of her parents' driveway with Joe in the most perfect little red sports car ever created felt kind of like seeing him that first time a week ago—surreal. But tonight, it was surreal in a good way, a *dreamy* way. Trish didn't often feel dreamy, but . . . well, Joe affected her like no other man.

The Cobra hugged the winding country roads lined with tall green grasses, summer thick trees, and miles of fencing. Tim McGraw's voice echoed from the radio, declaring that he may be a real bad boy but that he was also a real good man. And Trish felt happier inside than she had in a very long time. Maybe coming home to Eden hadn't been such a horrible thing, after all.

Joe had offered to take her anywhere she wanted, but she'd chosen the Burger Barn. Not that Eden had any five-star restaurants, and not that he'd know what to order in one, anyway—so her choice was fine with him. Even though she told him as they drove that she'd just had a burger from the barn for lunch that day.

"And you want another one?"

She'd just smiled. "I think I forgot how much I like greasy food."

The truth was, Joe had never eaten in the Cobra before—nor had he let anyone else eat in it, either. But for Trish—hell, she could do anything she wanted in his car.

They ran into Kenny and Debbie, on their way for pool night at the Last Chance—they'd pulled over when they'd seen Joe parking the Cobra in a back corner of the drive-in's lot. Kenny totally blew Joe's cool, nonchalant attitude when he said, "You must rate, Trish. He doesn't let people eat in the Cobra."

She covered her pretty mouth in horror, swallowing the bite of burger she'd just taken. "I'm sorry, Joe. I had no idea."

"That rule only applies to some people," he assured her, glaring at Kenny. "You're neater than him. Eat up."

"You guys coming to pool night?" Debbie asked, clutching Kenny's arm at Trish's side of the car.

Joe exchanged looks with his date. He had zero interest in pool night given the alternative, but if Trish wanted to hang at the Last Chance, he'd be agreeable. He couldn't read her expression, so replied, "Who knows. Could be we'll end up there."

"I'd prefer you didn't," Kenny said dryly. "I need to regain the respect of my pool buddies."

Joe leaned back slightly, offering a smug grin. "Oh yeah, that's right—I kicked your ass last week. Tell you what—I'll stay clear of the Last Chance for now. Until the next time I think you need your ass kicked, that is."

The two of them traded jabs and bragging for a few minutes while the girls just rolled their eyes, and Joe couldn't help thinking—*Man, this is nice. This is how I always imagined it, how it was supposed to be.*

But he guessed it was pretty damn early to start feeling that confident or comfortable with Trish. She'd be going home soon. And sure, he was glad they'd finally cleared the air about their breakup, but he knew this wasn't going anywhere. Despite how Trish waffled between being the country girl he remembered and the city woman she'd grown into, he knew that city woman was only on vacation right now, and that what was happening between them might be *real*, but it was also *temporary*.

And maybe, realistically, that was for the best. It had been a hell of a long time since he'd thought beyond the next day or week, and when he did, it was work-related—not about a woman. It wasn't that he didn't want her—God knew he did. Just yesterday, he'd been hellbent on getting closer to her. But . . . he'd learned some stuff about himself since he'd known Trish, stuff that made him think that . . . well, despite what Beverly might believe, he wouldn't exactly be a great catch for *anyone* when it came to seriously sharing a life, being in a real relationship.

He didn't let himself think about that part of his existence much, didn't allow his brain to go there, since it was something he couldn't fix and had to live with, but he could only guess that contemplating serious life changes—even ones that weren't gonna happen—brought that kind of stuff to the surface, like it or not. He didn't want to let it cloud his thoughts right now, though—no way. So he pushed it aside and concentrated on the blonde in the seat next to him. Things were too good here, and he didn't want to squander even one second with her.

After their friends departed, Kenny promising they'd meet again over pool cues real soon, Joe found himself watching Trish eat, shoving fries into her dainty mouth and taking heaping bites of the burger—and he couldn't help smiling. He'd known for years about Trish being a big-city lawyer, and he'd figured she'd changed completely. Until a few days ago, he couldn't have pictured her still being down-to-earth enough to eat greasy French fries in a car, even a car as nice as his.

"What?" she asked, catching his look.

"Nothing. Just watching you eat."

She blinked. "Why? Is there ketchup on my face or something?"

He laughed lightly. "No, cupcake—all clear on the ketchup. Guess I was just thinking how different this must be than what you're used to."

She tilted her head, looking damn cute in his hat. "What do you mean?"

"In the city," he explained. "I just don't imagine you wearing cowboy hats and eating fast food every day."

She looked at once sheepish but defiant. "I can be flexible."

"In more ways than one," he assured her, enjoying the slight blush that climbed her cheeks. "I like you this way. I like finding out you're still a country girl at heart."

She turned to stare at him. "I wouldn't go *that* far."

He lowered his chin, teasing her. "Aw, come on. I saw you stack that hay like a pro—like you never left Eden."

She shrugged. "I like to think I'm multifaceted. But the fact is, I'm a city girl now, Joe. This is just . . . a break."

Yeah, just as he'd thought. And as he'd just concluded, that was okay—wasn't it? Because this was temporary. *Get that through your head, buddy.* "You're happy then," he asked, "living in Indy, being a lawyer?"

She nodded, popping two more thin fries into her mouth. "I'm very good at what I do."

"I don't doubt it." Trish had always done well at anything she tried. But he couldn't help wondering, just from something in her tone, if she really *enjoyed* her job. "So when you're a defense attorney, are most of the people guilty—or innocent?"

"Some of both." Yet her voice softened as she admitted, "Mostly guilty, though. I work at a prestigious firm with a good track record, and we're known for getting people off whose cases seemed hopeless. I guess we draw a lot of guilty people who figure we're their only chance."

"That sounds hard, defending criminals day in and day out."

"It's just about winning," she replied. "That's how you have to look at it. You have to be a competitive person, that's all." She spoke with full confidence, but he couldn't help noticing what was missing—the little light that shone in her eyes when she was excited about something.

"And *sometimes* you get innocent clients," she added, and there it was—the light came back and those green eyes sparkled. "And if you can get someone off who didn't do it, that makes it all worthwhile. Like right now, I've got this college kid accused of rape. But he says he's innocent and I believe him, and I'm pretty sure I can point the evidence toward the guy who *really* did it. My guy's got his whole life ahead of him, a bright future, so when I win his case—well, it'll be worth any . . . discontent I may feel over defending people who should be going to jail."

Discontent, huh? "I thought there *wasn't* any discontent. I thought it was just about winning."

She smiled. "*Touché*. And objection. Argumentative."

"Overruled," he said without missing a beat, making her laugh. Then he tilted his head and peered into her eyes. "You know, it's kinda hard to picture you raking some hard-ass criminal over the coals on the witness stand." When she'd left here, she'd had no plans to study law and it had come as a big surprise when he'd heard about it.

"You'd be surprised how tough I can be." She smiled, no spite in her expression, but he wondered if he'd had some unwitting hand in toughening her up. Then his brain shot to the image of her coming to his house and shoving him back onto his couch and riding him to heaven. Definitely bolder now, his Trishy. In a lot of ways.

When they finished eating, Joe shoved all their empty containers in the Burger Barn bag and walked them to the nearest trash can. Friday night, and it was getting dark, the lot beginning to fill with teenagers, and as he strode back toward the Cobra and saw Trish sitting in the passenger seat, he no longer wanted to be here. He wanted to get her alone.

"Want to go for a drive, cupcake?" It was a perfect night for a convertible—late August and warm, but the humidity hadn't returned after the frost. That and the rain had combined to make the air feel fresh, brand new.

When she nodded, he asked, "Anyplace special you want to go?"

She simply shrugged, her gaze sexy, inviting. "Surprise me."

And as her look spiraled straight to his groin, he knew *exactly* where he was taking her.

"Um, what are we doing *here?*"

Joe glanced over at her as he eased the Cobra along the narrow road that led to Crescent Lake. "Guess you legal types would say returning to the scene of the crime."

Her sheepish grin reminded him of the way she'd looked as a girl. Or maybe it was just the setting, the dark foliage dipping heavy on both sides of the car, the chirps of crickets in the trees surrounding them. "Except we never . . . you know," she reminded him. "So what would be the crime?"

"We did a lot of *other* good stuff here that felt pretty damn naughty at the time."

"Yes, we did," she nearly purred, and her sensuous tone said she was remembering exactly the same things *he* was—hot nights, his hands, her body, those very first discoveries. And the sexy timbre of her voice reminded him of something else, too. Yeah, he liked seeing the old Trish in her, but this new, grown-up Trish—she was *hot*. She knew what she liked. She wasn't afraid of it. And he grew harder behind his zipper with each passing second *because* of it.

"And besides," he added, "it's never too late."

A trill of laughter echoed through the dark. "You think we're going to have sex *here*, surrounded by a bunch of high-schoolers out on hot dates—and in a convertible, no less?"

He flashed a knowing look, letting just a small grin leak through. "No more high-schoolers making out at the lake. When too many girls started turning up pregnant, the cops cracked down a few years ago and ran everybody away. Nobody comes here anymore." With that, he eased the Cobra off the road into a flat, grassy area where the water, shimmering beneath the light of the moon, came into view through tall pine trees. He killed the engine, leaving no noise but the softly playing radio and the night sounds beyond the car. It was the exact spot where they'd parked years ago. "Which means we're alone."

Even in the dark, he could see her expression—tempted yet skeptical. "You *think* we're alone. You can't know for sure."

He tilted his head. "Take a chance, cupcake." *Let me take you for a whole different kind of ride, honey.*

Next to him, Trish gave her lower lip a sensual little bite, and he suddenly regretted that the Cobra's center console was so damn thick—wider than in most cars. But he reached for her anyway, sliding one palm onto her thigh through her thin skirt and skimming smoothly upward.

She instantly shifted toward him, parting her legs slightly. He swallowed hard but had no time to absorb the simple pleasure of her move before she reached down, covered her hand with his, and guided his touch swiftly higher, between her legs. He groaned and she sighed, and he thought he'd burst the zipper on his jeans—and oh *yeah*, he liked grown-up Trish *a lot*.

She peered over at him in the darkness, her eyes glimmering with a readiness he could only have dreamed of as a kid. "Come to me, baby," he said, reaching out to help her climb smoothly over the console until she was straddling him tight in the Cobra's driver's seat.

He'd never felt anything warmer than the way that softest part of her hugged his erection. "You feel *so* damn good," he whispered, drinking in the scent of her flowery perfume as he bracketed her hips with his hands. He let his palms glide up, up, slowly, until he framed her breasts with his thumbs and forefingers.

She hissed in a hot breath of pleasure that stiffened him further still. "You feel good, too," she assured him in that same low, sexy purr as she began to move, rubbing against him below. "So hard."

His own breath grew thready as he closed his hands fully over those lovely breasts and began to knead her. So soft, so round, so . . . Trish.

"Ah . . ." she moaned, her head falling back as she arched further into his grasp.

*Oh yeah, baby. Give yourself to me.* He massaged deeply, lifted his pelvis to meet her hot grind, found himself tweaking her beaded nipples between thumb and finger through her top and bra. He was being consumed by her, by all that she was, by every pleasure she delivered merely by letting him hold her, touch her.

"I need this off you," he said, pulling at the hem of her top. As many times as they'd been together now, he'd only seen her breasts on that first occasion, when he'd been almost too shocked to fully enjoy them. This time he planned to drink his fill.

She hesitated, looking resistant—but he continued pushing the ribbed fabric up, revealing her smooth stomach and a hint of a pastel bra, until she finally said, "Oh, what the hell," and ripped the shirt off over her head to fling it to the other seat.

He growled at the sight of her sumptuous curves arching from smooth pink cups, and immediately went for her bra straps, drawing them down—he wanted her out of the damn thing. He didn't see a clasp in front, so reached around back, deftly unhooking it and watching it loosen around her. He used both hands to pull it away, off her arms, leaving the heavy beads around her neck to fall between her beautifully bared breasts in the moonlight.

"Jesus," he sighed at the view.

Above him, her laugh held an ounce of trepidation. "You'd better be sure about no one coming here."

The truth was, at this moment, as he ran his hands over her ass through the skirt, so sweet and firm, he no longer cared if anyone came here or not. His mind was too fully wrapped around *her* to think of anything else. "The worst that would happen is a cop will tell us we have to leave."

"And see me like this!"

He cast a wicked grin. "It'll be the highlight of his night, honey, I promise." Was she wearing a thong? He didn't feel any panties.

But he forgot that quickly enough when he lifted his touch back to her breasts, so perfect and round, her dark nipples taut and pointed for him. He pinched them slowly, sensually, just enough to make her purr some more, as he rhythmically massaged the soft flesh around them. "I've missed these, baby," he said, peering up at her and hoping like hell that wasn't the wrong thing to say, the wrong moment to remind her of the time and distance that had split them.

"They've missed you, too."

Aw, God, *yes*. He let his eyes fall shut—but only for a minute, because he had to see her, had to soak her up.

Leaning in, he let his tongue flick gently across one dusky nipple, then listened to her lovely little whimper of delight. He licked her again, and again, his hands back on her ass now, pulling her down to meet his body, tight, tight, so damn good. Then he closed his mouth over her breast, suckling, gentle and soft, and needing more of her so bad that he feared he'd begin to tremble.

"You taste so good, Trishy," he whispered against her flesh.

"I want you inside me."

*Jesus God—thank you.*

"Want to know a secret?" she asked.

Joe lifted his gaze to hers, practically drunk on her, and nodded.

Her eyes took on a whole new sultry, wicked gleam that reminded him of the night she'd come to his house and seduced him. "You bring out my inner biker chick."

A groan left him as that image shot down through his body, all the way to his cock. "*Aw, baby.* That's *so* hot."

"Remember my tight black dress? That was her."

He nodded some more, lost in her eyes, her body. "I *liked* her. A lot."

Now her voice came lower, breathy, sexy as hell. "You make me . . . want to do things. You make me want to be bad for you."

Another hard moan left him in response as need roared through him like a locomotive. He began to gather the fabric of her skirt in large fistfuls, working his way underneath, and when he got there, he indeed found nothing but a tiny strip of fabric stretching down the center of her ass. He could barely speak through his labored breath. "How much do you like these panties?"

"Huh?" She was breathless now, too.

"I'm gonna rip them unless you tell me not to. 'Cause I need them off you, *now.*"

"*Rip them,*" she said. No hesitation any longer, not a hint of doubt.

He found the narrowest part, where they made a T in back, and used both hands to tear until they snapped and fell away from her. She gasped slightly as he slid his fingertips down the valley of her ass, passing over the tight little fissure there until his fingers sank into her warm, welcoming moisture below. "Ohhh," she moaned.

"Wet," he whispered.

"All day," she breathed. "From thinking about you."

He let out a rough groan, slipping two fingers inside her as she hotly met his gaze.

"Move on them," he told her.

"Unh," she replied, and rocked against his straining hardness in front and his fingers in back. He watched her, feeling her sensual rhythm echo through him, knowing he was getting her hotter and hotter—and he was starting to wonder if she was about to come when she suddenly fell into hard, heated convulsions, writhing against him, drenching his hand still more, crying out, "Oh God, Joe! Oh God! Oh God!"

*Oh baby.* He watched her beautifully hypnotic dance, entranced by her and whispering, "That's right, baby, come for me, ride it out, that's so good," until finally she sank against his body, her arms closing warm around his neck. She almost seemed to wilt. He, on the other hand, felt supercharged.

"Are you okay?" he asked low, near her ear.

He felt her nod, said no more, let her rest—and tried not to freaking explode in his pants.

Finally, after a few deep breaths, trying to relax, he whispered in her ear again. "Was it good, honey?"

She lifted her head from his shoulder to face him. "Mmm."

Damn, he liked that—his Trishy sated in his arms, too pleasured for words. "And I'm not even inside you yet."

The reminder seemed to break her free from her post-climactic lethargy—thank God. Because he liked her sated, but he was still on the edge himself. He tried to be a patient man, yet with Trish he'd not been very successful so far, and right now his cock physically hurt.

He watched as she sat up, cast the most predatory look he'd ever seen on her face, then leaned back on him and began to undo his belt buckle. His erection strained behind, anxious and ready, as she used both hands, one after the other, to pull the length of his belt from the loops. When it was free, she tossed it out of the car, into the grass!

"*Hey,*" he said, shocked.

She spoke low, sexy, controlling. "You'll get it later."

"Yeah, I'll get it later," he murmured, glancing down to where she was reaching into his jeans now, wrapping her fist full around him, and freeing him from his underwear. *Aw, yeah.* She instantly caressed him, stroked him, squeezing firmly, making him grit his teeth in heated delight. "Oh God, baby."

She'd touched him like this the first time they'd had sex, too—but now he felt it more, because he wasn't trapped in stunned confusion this time, and because she seemed so much more to him like Trish now, *his* Trish—as if the girl he'd loved had just gone away for a while, taken a long vacation from him, but now she was back and even more perfect than she'd been before.

She pumped him lightly, again, again, and he thought he'd die from the pleasure—but that was nothing compared to when she scooted back, right up against the steering wheel, so that she could bend down to lick a sizzling hot trail around the tip of his erection.

Another deep groan escaped him through clenched teeth, and then she was sinking down, down, and his hands were in her hair, massaging her scalp, and he almost couldn't breathe, couldn't think. There was nothing but sensation, profound bliss, and it was Trish giving it to him, and it was a miracle that didn't seem real.

But the bliss escalated, hotter, hotter, and when finally she rose off him, her lips appeared slightly swollen, and he immediately needed them beneath his. So he pulled her into a hard kiss, pressing his tongue between, drinking her up in yet another way, letting his hands roam her sweet breasts, her round ass under the skirt she still wore, the hot moisture between her thighs. "Ride me," he forced out between hot kisses to her mouth, her throat. "I need in you."

He heard her suck in her breath, then felt her lift—and sheathe him. "Oh!" she cried, sinking down.

He groaned. She was so wet, so warm, so tight, encasing him in thick velvet. He'd had sex with a lot of women, and he'd had it several times now with Trish—but he'd still never felt anything more amazing than this moment.

Then, somehow, things slowed.

Her breasts swayed softly with her movements.

He looked up into her eyes. *So long I've wanted you, Trishy—so, so long.*

Through the car speakers, Josh Turner sang "Your Man," a song of slow lovemaking, and he felt her tune into it as well, letting her rhythm match the music.

He heard himself whisper to her—he told her she was beautiful, perfect, his perfect lover, and he sensed her circular motions somehow deepening, tightening, still slow but more heated.

"Kiss my breasts," she pleaded, and he gave her what she needed, kissing, licking, suckling. "Harder—*please*," she whispered, making his chest constrict, so he pulled more firmly with his mouth, dug his fingers into her ass, thrust higher into her.

And then she shattered again, screaming his name, and God's, until Joe realized he *was* damn thankful no one else was around, because she was beautifully loud.

And it pushed him over the edge—everything about her, her soft moves mingling with her rougher needs, her hesitation coupled with her enthusiasm, and now her orgasm, echoing through the night. He couldn't hold back and didn't try, coming deep inside her—hard, hard, hard—the mind-numbing ecstasy owning him for a few long, idyllic moments when he vaguely heard himself muttering, "Oh God," and "Trish," then felt her collapse into his arms.

They stayed quiet and still for a few minutes after. He could have stayed that way all night, could have easily fallen asleep, but fought it.

Finally, her voice cut gently through the music still playing. "Wow—amazing."

Still in a post-orgasmic haze, he shifted, peering down to where she nuzzled at his shoulder. "Huh?"

She gazed up, her eyes bigger, more luminous, than usual. "I don't usually . . . uh . . . come twice."

He raised his eyebrows slightly, the declaration waking him up. "You do with me," he pointed out. "I made you come twice in your hotel room, too."

She bit her lip, looking well pleasured as she remembered. "Oh yeah, you're right. I guess I did. I guess this means it's sort of . . . getting to be a habit."

Joe couldn't help enjoying just a pinch of masculine arrogance as he cast a playful grin. "I bet you're starting to wish you hadn't waited so long to come home."

Her pretty laughter filled the night as she slapped playfully at his chest. Then her expression edged into something slightly coquettish and all the way sexy. "Next time, though," she said, "not in the car."

He lowered his chin at a scolding, teasing angle. "Hey, don't disrespect the car. What's wrong with the car?"

She sat up slightly. "The car's *great* for riding in. But a smidge cramped. Next time, Joe, a bed. We need a bed. I want to stretch out with you. I want to take my time."

His stomach hollowed. "Well, cupcake, when you put it that way—okay, next time, a bed."

After Joe pulled the Cobra into the garage and locked it up tight, he found Elvis curled up by the front door in his usual spot. It was late but still warm out, so Joe eased down onto the top porch step as the dog slowly rose to greet him. "Hey, bud— takin' it easy?"

Elvis settled back into a big ball of hound dog at Joe's side, so Joe scratched behind his ear and tried not to think about Trish. "I'd be smarter," he said to the dog, "if I just handled my sex life like you do. A quick roll in the hay, some nose-rubbing, then you're gone, right?"

Of course, he *had* handled his sex life that way up to now, minus the nose-rubbing part. Generally, Joe slept with a woman a time or two and that was it—he wasn't interested in more. It wasn't some macho thing, just usually an honest loss of interest that had left more than one woman hating him.

But with Trish, each time he was with her he wanted more of her. Each time it was over, he wanted it again, and again. He didn't even know what to do with a need like that—he'd never felt it before.

"She's going home soon, El." He peered down at the dog's sleepy eyes. "So what would you do if you were me? Try to stop this, try to leave her alone—or get as much of her as you could while you've got the chance?"

Looking bored, Elvis yawned and let his dark eyes fall shut.

Joe just shook his head. "I think you and me have different priorities, buddy."

But he already knew the answer, with or without Elvis's help. It would be smarter to back off, cool things down, just a little.

Because tonight . . . tonight something had changed.

Up to now, he'd been taking this one hot encounter at a time. He'd wanted her body, and he'd wanted to apologize, make amends. But he hadn't seriously thought of the future—of a *real* future, with *her*. He hadn't imagined something like that was even possible.

Now, he had no idea where they stood. But hell, the way she'd looked at him tonight, he was beginning to wonder, think, feel—maybe . . . God, maybe he actually had a chance for more, something real, something like they'd shared a long time ago.

He sighed. That *should* make him happy.

If only it were that easy.

He peered upward to the black sky sprinkled with bits of light and a white crescent moon, old memories creeping into his brain unbidden.

What would Trish think if she knew how his mom had died? Would she still look at him the same way? Or would she look at him with shock, or maybe pity?

Aw, hell—maybe the answer didn't even matter. Either way, she'd understand that people were right about the Ramseys and that he'd lived up to his name.

Sure, he'd built a business, tried to do right by Carissa, went through his days content enough. But when he thought about the past, especially about his mom, he felt like that adrift eighteen-year-old kid all over again. That kid who'd lost the girl he loved, then his mom, and then even his dad. That kid who'd suddenly found himself trying to raise his little sister and care for a baby that wasn't his. It had been the darkest, strangest time in his life, and he seldom let himself go back there in his head, but Trish was *taking* him back. Making him remember. Making him feel responsible for his mom's death all over again, even though she couldn't possibly know it. All *he* knew was that he'd never be able to forgive himself.

Just like Trish couldn't forgive him for Bev.

He didn't mess up in life often, but man, when he did, he messed up *bad*.

He looked down at Elvis. "Know what I like about you? You're easy. As long as I fill your bowl with Gravy Train and give you a scratch or two behind the ears, you're happy."

In fact, Joe usually looked at life the same way Elvis did. He didn't normally over-worry things. He mostly left his mistakes in the past, where they belonged, and didn't think about them—until just lately, with Trish's arrival back in his life. And maybe that was a damn good way to live, now that he thought about it.

"Enough of this crap," he muttered, pushing to his feet. "I'm going to bed."

As for Trish, he supposed it was simple. As long as she was here and letting him, he'd be getting as much of her as he could. He could tell himself it was a choice, but it wasn't—it was just how things were.

And as for the future, hell . . . it wasn't like she was going to stay. No matter what he'd thought he'd seen in her eyes tonight. And yeah, when she left, he was going to miss her, a lot. But he'd throw himself into his work, into Carissa, into all the other things that made him feel good and enjoy life. And he'd quit thinking about all the shit that had happened the year he was eighteen—he'd be able to push it to the back of his mind, again.

And that would be the one and only good thing about Trish heading back to Indy and leaving him behind.

Trish was driving. To the diner. To work.

It was Saturday, so she could have given herself a day off during her "vacation" without feeling any guilt, but the place wasn't going to paint itself.

As she found herself reaching down to tune in a country station on her car radio, she couldn't help sucking in her breath, remembering the very intensity of their sex last night. It seemed, with Joe, that it was *always* intense, that it never turned softer or average in any way. The sex was never just good—it was always *spectacular.*

They'd not talked on the way home, just listened to the radio—the Eagles harmonizing on the old song, "Seven Bridges Road"—and they'd held hands on the center console as a warm breeze had washed over them.

At her door, he'd kissed her and whispered in her ear, low and raspy, "Thanks for letting me take you for a ride."

She'd grinned at his double entendre, then said, "It was . . . a good ride, cowboy," reaching up to plunk his hat from her head onto his.

*It was a good ride, cowboy?* She cringed slightly now, remembering the words. Since when did she talk like a woman who hung out in honky-tonks? And yet, it had earned her one of Joe's sexy little smiles, and another kiss before he'd left her on the big wraparound porch, nearly reeling from the night just past.

God. Men had taken her to the ballet, to French restaurants, to hear orchestras play. She'd worn velvet on dates, the occasional satin gloves, and one time even floor-length lace. But *this*—takeout at the Burger Barn and sex by the lake—had been the best date she'd ever had.

As she came up over the rise that led onto Main Street, it pleased her to see the older part of town bustling a bit this morning, a few people strolling up the street, and Marjorie standing outside her shop talking with another woman who'd just bought flowers, judging by the fresh bouquet in her hand.

She beeped, and Marjorie waved, and Trish realized she'd just driven right past the diner. She hadn't exactly planned it, but she knew where she was headed. She'd be back painting cheerful colors on the walls and tables soon enough. Her heart kicked up a bit—although it had little to do with paint.

*You're happy then, living in Indy, being a lawyer?* Joe's words came back to her. She'd answered automatically, saying the things she *always* said, the things she'd always thought she *felt*. Only they'd seemed a bit wooden to her—for the first time ever—and she had no idea why.

Probably just too caught up in *him*.

She couldn't resist smiling when she pulled in at the garage, seeing his truck with the racy mudflaps parked to one side of the lot. None of her friends in Indianapolis would ever believe she was sleeping with a guy who owned those mudflaps—and she could barely believe it herself.

Except for when she remembered it was Joe.

He'd mentioned last night that he'd be here today finishing up a special job on a Lamborghini since the truck it had been shipped to the garage in was coming to pick it up that evening.

Three of the four bays were occupied by cars and guys working on them, and even though she'd never seen a Lamborghini before, it wasn't hard to spot it in the first bay, nor was it hard to recognize Joe's butt in well-worn jeans bending over it. No one had noticed her yet—all busy with their tools—and she didn't want to startle Joe in case he was in the middle of some critical adjustment, so she stood back, just watching. From a speaker somewhere, Travis Tritt declared that it was a great day to be alive, and she couldn't disagree. Something about standing here watching Joe work felt undeniably simple and right.

As he moved around the open hood of the car, she witnessed the concentration etched on his face, the narrowing of his blue eyes as he focused more closely on some part of the engine. When he twisted the wrench in his hand, the snake on his arm flexed slightly, making the crux of her thighs ripple in domino effect. The precision and care of each move somehow drew her in, reminding her exactly how good he was with his hands.

Just then, he rose up and gently let the hood drop shut with a solid little *poomf.* Drawing a red rag from his back pocket, he wiped away a handprint on the hood and another on the fender, finishing with a small stroke of the cloth just above the headlight that struck her as almost . . . loving, as if he were bidding the car farewell.

By the time he looked up, she was standing slack-jawed, that slight ripple from before spreading outward now, through her whole body.

His gaze swept admiringly over her, even though she was dressed the same as him—T-shirt and jeans. "Hey." He didn't quite smile, but looked glad to see her.

She pointed. "So that's the famous Lamborghini."

He gave a short nod. "Yep, all freshly serviced and ready to be shipped back to his owner in Louisville."

She cocked a grin. *"His?"*

He simply shrugged, the corners of his mouth quirking slightly.

"How do you tell if they're boys or girls?"

He didn't miss a beat. "By the size of the tailpipe."

She slapped a hand over her mouth to stifle a laugh but still drew a glance from a mechanic working in the next bay.

"Come here," he said, stepping closer for a short kiss, his hands closing softly at her waist. The thought that they might be greasy flitted through her mind for a fraction of a second, but who cared? Being touched by Joe made grease sound a lot more appealing than usual. "What are you up to today?"

"Just heading to the diner to keep painting." She'd told him about some of the changes she was making there and why.

"Need help? I'm almost done here."

"Tempting," she said. Not only to make the work go faster but because she suspected having Joe there would make it more fun, too. She could only imagine the trouble they could get into with some cans of paint and a restaurant full of nooks and crannies not visible from the windows. "Except . . . there's something about this project that makes me want to do it all myself. Just to see if I like the finished product, if I can make it what I want it to be on my own. Does that make any sense?" Even as she spoke the words, though, she couldn't believe she was turning down time with him.

"*Perfect* sense," he said in a way that told her he really got what she was saying, and that maybe it had something to do with when he'd restored the Cobra.

"Before I get to work, though, I wanted to . . . invite you over. For dinner. And a game of Monopoly. Tonight." She and her mom had cooked up the idea this morning over breakfast and she'd planned to call him later—until she'd found herself driving here.

Yet Joe looked less than thrilled. "Uh, yeah, that sounds like a real fun Saturday night. Monopoly with the cutthroat Henderson family while your dad glares at me the whole game. Hell, I'll be afraid to buy any property, and God help me if he's the banker."

She couldn't hold in her grin. While she harbored fond memories of Monopoly games with Joe all those years ago, she'd sort of forgotten how they'd always turned out. He'd frequently accused her family of being too competitive and ganging up on him. Which was mostly true, she supposed. She'd gotten her competitive nature from her parents—even her mom, who was perfectly mild-mannered until you put her in a game or contest of some kind.

"I was just thinking," Trish explained, "that if you spend a little time with him, he'll realize you're not the devil incarnate and won't give me such a hard time about seeing you while I'm here." But then she sighed. Now that she really thought about it . . . "On the other hand, though, I don't blame you if you don't want to come. If it sounds like a total drag, I understand."

To her surprise, however, Joe's eyes softened on her. "Cupcake, nowhere you are could possibly be a drag. I'll be there. What time?"

**Precedent:** a legal decision serving as an authoritative rule or pattern in future similar cases; _or_ any act or decision that serves as a guide for a later situation.

# *Ten*

Trish mashed potatoes—the old-fashioned way, just like Debbie, because her mother insisted—while her mom stood at the stove frying chicken. The sweet, greasy scent filled her senses with childhood memories—she cooked a little, but she'd never fried a chicken. And the last time she'd used the masher to mash potatoes was before she'd left home.

"This would be a lot easier with the mixer, you know."

"And wouldn't taste nearly as good," her mother shot back at her knowingly.

"But it might get the lumps out. I was never any good at this." She looked down at the pot, feeling doomed.

"Nothing wrong with a lump or two. Just says they're homemade."

Trish considered debating that using a mixer didn't negate

their being homemade, but she knew she'd never win, lawyer or not, so let it drop—and moved on to something else. "Mom, do you think I'm stupid? For letting this thing with Joe . . . get started?" Of course, it had far more than *started*, but she couldn't think of how else to say it.

Her mom wielded a pair of tongs, turning a chicken leg over in the sizzling, popping grease, and Trish wondered how she avoided getting burns. "I trust your judgment. What happened was a long time ago and I don't like to hold grudges."

"Unlike Dad," Trish said, still mashing.

Her mom looked up, eyes inquisitive. "Does this mean it's serious? Because I expected you to balk when I suggested dinner and game night. But you didn't at all. And this is the first time you've brought a man around us since . . . well, since you went away to college."

*Oh, dear God.* Her mom was right! She'd never, *ever* brought a guy to meet them—since high school, since Joe. And other than the occasional "Are we going to meet this young man?" question when she was dating someone, she'd never truly even thought about it. Despite having had a few relevant relationships over the years, no one had ever really been important enough.

Of course, maybe Joe's previous presence in the house made it easier to bring him back. Plus, he was already here—there was no travel involved, so it was less of a big deal.

"No," she said, "not serious. We're just, you know, enjoying each other's company." *And going at it like rabbits.*

"Oh." Her mom almost sounded disappointed. "I've always liked Joe—discounting what happened when you were young, of course. I remember he always enjoyed my fried chicken."

Trish smiled—she'd forgotten that. "Yeah, he did." But then she cleared her throat and mashed some more, thinking she'd sounded a bit too dreamy there for a second. And there was nothing dreamy—or serious—about this. She was having a wild affair with Joe that would soon be over. And some chicken and Monopoly would just make things easier in the meantime. "By the way, how did Dad take it when you told him Joe was coming to dinner?"

Turning another piece of floured chicken in the skillet, her mother pursed her lips. "That part's a little tricky. He's been out tending the cattle all day—and I kind of didn't tell him before he went."

Trish felt her face drop. "Oh, Mom." It was *so* unlike her mother to let them get into a sticky situation. It was much more like Trish. Lately, anyway.

Just then, the back door opened and her dad stepped inside. As the doorbell rang.

Her dad took off his cap, which sported the likeness of a wide-mouth bass on front. "Well, doesn't this smell good?" Then he looked toward the foyer. "Who could that be?"

Trish and her mother exchanged panicky glances, frozen in place for a moment—until her mother set her tongs down, sang out, "I'll get it," then scurried for the door like some twenty-first-century Edith Bunker.

"What's going on?" her dad asked, looking confused. "Are we expecting somebody?"

Trish peeked up, continuing to ram the potato masher into the stainless steel pot. "Um, kind of."

He leaned forward, widening his eyes expectantly. "Who?"

She took a deep breath, then tried to speak matter-of-factly. "Joe. Joe's here for dinner. And games."

Her father's face went rigid. "Joe? Again? *Why?*"

Somewhere in the front of the house, she sensed her mother

going about the business of opening the door *very slowly*. "Because I invited him. Because it's a nice way to thank him for his help with the hay. And because he and I are sort of . . . seeing each other while I'm here." She forged ahead quickly. "But it's nothing serious, so there's no need to get worked up about it. I'm not home that often, as you know, and all I ask is that we have a pleasant dinner. Then you can beat him at Monopoly and it'll make you feel better. Okay?"

He still looked inflexible—mouth grim, hands fisted—but gradually his expression began to soften.

In the distance, she heard her mother saying, "Hi, Joe—it's nice to see you again. Come on in. I hope you still like fried chicken."

Trish could practically *hear* his smile. "You made chicken? Aw, it smells great."

And when he walked into the dining room adjoining the kitchen and Trish turned to face him—*oh yum*. He wore his usual—jeans and a tee, this one with a Mercedes logo on the chest—but it was the *way* he wore it, the way it fit him. Just slightly snug, enough to show off muscles—and a telltale bulge rose slightly behind his zipper. Most of his cobra coiled below one sleeve. His dark hair lay smoother than usual—he'd clearly worked to tame it for the evening—but a wayward lock still dipped recklessly over his forehead. His eyes shone on her, blue as ever, melting her enough that she nearly let the pot of now well mashed potatoes crash to the floor.

"Trish," he said with a light nod. But his eyes said, *cupcake.*

"Hey," she replied, then realized he carried flowers, a small bouquet of mixed tulips—yellows, reds, pinks—which he held out to her. It took her breath away.

She shoved her pot toward the counter and moved toward

him. She assumed she'd actually *made* the counter, since no crash resulted. "Thank you," she said, taking the flowers. "You didn't have to . . ."

But then she trailed off, because this was starting to feel like such a *moment*, and because she needed to play it down. And because one of the tulips in her fist was that warm pink color she thought Marjorie had been talking about for her nonexistent wedding. *Yeesh*. Yeah, she *definitely* needed to play this *way* down. "They're pretty," she said brightly, then whisked them off toward a cabinet where her mother kept vases.

"Mr. Henderson," she heard Joe say grudgingly behind her.

Oh boy. This should be interesting. She tried to watch from her peripheral vision as she ran water in an old-fashioned porcelain vase.

"Joe." Her dad sounded equally unhappy.

Both men looked as if they would draw six-shooters at any moment—but then Joe said, "Thanks for having me."

And her father gave a slow, short nod. "Glad to."

Of course, no one sounded anywhere remotely close to glad, but maybe this at least meant there wouldn't be a showdown in the kitchen.

"Jasper, why don't you get washed up," Trish's mom stepped in to say. "Joe, you take a seat, and Trish and I'll get dinner served."

Trish's mom took the vase of flowers from her, parking them right in the middle of the table as Trish risked her life taking up chicken from the hot grease.

It was only as they all settled at the table laden with chicken, potatoes, green beans, corn on the cob, and fresh rolls that Trish thought—*Holy mother of God, what was I thinking?* This was going to be a disaster of epic proportions. If it wasn't bad enough to feel her father and Joe silently squaring off against each other, she had that dark pink tulip staring her in the face, making her suffer weird, indecipherable yearnings about home, and her heart, and what she wanted out of life. *Bleck*. But she couldn't deal with any of that right now—she needed to try to make some sort of safe, pleasant conversation.

"Joe was working on a Lamborghini today," she came up with. Her father was mildly interested in fast cars, a holdover from his youth.

" 'Sthat right?" her dad said, and she thought—*Bingo!* He suddenly sounded more curious than mad.

Joe swallowed a bite of chicken, the drumstick still between his fingers. "An '04 Gallardo up from Louisville. It's a fine piece of machinery."

"I imagine so," her father said, then proceeded to ask some mechanical question that totally escaped her.

Joe's answer went on at length—which suited her fine, all the better to get through the meal. She heard something about an Audi-inspired V-8 and an aluminum space frame, whatever the hell *that* meant. "Now, my Cobra has a tube frame and an aluminum chassis," he went on, "but the Gallardo's tube frame is more intricate and modern, loaded for tension and torsion."

Her father was nodding, so apparently *he* knew what Joe was talking about. "I've heard about that Cobra of yours—boys up at the feed store have mentioned it from time to time. Hear it's a beauty."

Joe hiked a thumb over his shoulder. "It's in your driveway right now. If you want to take a look at it later."

Her father leaned forward, clearly delighted but trying not to let it show. "You don't say. Well, maybe I'll just do that after we eat."

From there, new conversation bloomed. They talked about Joe's business and the Hendersons' retirement from the diner. Her mother thanked Joe for his help getting the hay in and, even if stodgily, her father added his appreciation, too. No one asked Trish about her work—her *real* job—and she was just as glad. It seemed so . . . out of place with everything here, in her parents' home—in all of Eden, really.

"You still play Monopoly?" her father asked Joe when the meal was almost done. Joe had just taken the last roll because Trish's mother had kept nudging him to eat it.

Joe shrugged, smearing margarine across the top. "Haven't in a while, but I could be persuaded. You still *cheat* at it?"

Trish's entire body tightened, but then she realized her father was actually holding in a grin. It had been a running joke back in the day—in addition to Joe's claims that they'd all banded together to make sure he lost, he'd insisted that her father was the instigator.

"There's cheating and then there's strategy. *You* could never recognize the difference. But I'll be willing to whip your butt in it, fair and square, as soon as you show me this car of yours."

Both men were up and nearly out the door, quick as that, with Trish's mother calling, "Hurry back—I made apple pie!" behind them.

And Trish simply sat staring after them, stunned. She'd spent the whole meal on pins and needles, willing it to be over, but now that it was—she realized she'd actually kind of enjoyed it. "Well, *that* went well," she said to her mother.

"Your father's not a complicated man. An appreciation for cars and Monopoly can do a lot to sway him."

Apparently so. And how convenient that Joe was a man with an appreciation for cars and at least a *willingness* to play Monopoly.

Would Kent play Monopoly? Would he have even the faintest interest in cars? She knew he drove a Camry simply because all the reports said it was dependable and safe. And would he even have a clue how to win her father over?

Of course, it didn't matter. When she returned to Indy, life would change—back to normal. Her dating life would no longer intersect with her family life. Which had always suited her fine—until right now.

Rising up to help gather dishes, she glanced again toward the vase of tulips, her eye drawn by the warm pink one. Then she picked up some dirty plates, but instead of taking them to the kitchen, she instead found herself walking to the front window, peering out to spot Joe pointing at something on the Cobra's dashboard as he talked with her dad.

And—oh my God, was she seeing things or was her father really getting *into* the car, behind the wheel? Was he—dear Lord—actually starting the engine? Joe was actually letting him *drive* the Cobra? She nearly dropped her plates.

And then, for one single, solitary moment, she allowed herself to feel it: *Leaving was going to be harder than she'd expected.* For lots of reasons.

Her dad. Her mom. Debbie. *Joe.*

The way things just somehow *fit* here. Naturally and inexplicably. Even her dad and Joe now—amazingly—finding common ground.

But then she banished the thought—because it was useless, and therefore impractical. She'd been doing pretty good with Debbie's advice, to just enjoy Joe and their hot, steamy affair without any worries. So she was going to keep doing that.

And when she set the tulips aside on the rolltop desk a few minutes later, clearing the table for the Monopoly board, she turned the vase so that the pink one was in the back where she couldn't see it anymore.

It was like stepping back in time for Joe to watch Trish's dad collect most of the best property, but he held his own, capturing the green group on the fourth side of the board, along with Boardwalk and eventually Park Place. Of course, in the usual Henderson way, Trish's dad had discouraged his wife from bargaining with Joe for the blue property, but he'd convinced her with big cash and utilities. Trish seemed in her own happy little world, with hotels spanning the first quarter of the board, a self-declared slumlord. Joe had also picked up one railroad to Jasper's two, and hell if he'd sell it to him, no matter what he offered—Jasper was already raking in enough dough from the properties surrounding the No Parking space.

Not that it mattered if he lost. He'd come here *knowing* he would lose—he doubted anyone *ever* played Monopoly with the Hendersons and came out alive. What mattered was that Trish's dad didn't seem to hate him anymore. And even though he'd thought he'd accepted this invitation just to please Trish, as the night wore on, he began to realize he wanted to change Jasper Henderson's low opinion of him.

Not because he cared what people thought of him—he was used to some people having a low opinion of him—but because . . . hell, because he wanted to be welcome in the Henderson home, and welcome in Trish's life.

And not just now. Not just next week. He wanted to be *in her life.*

Damn, he hated recognizing that. Hated the way it had been bearing down on him the last day or so.

This had snuck up on him fast. One minute it had been about some weird combination of lust and apology. The next it had become . . . something he hadn't planned on. An attachment. A need.

Three long hours after the game had started, her father won. It had been inevitable, so Joe wasn't too broken up over it, but he let Trish's father gloat and pretended he'd cared. "Dice were against me from the start," Joe said as they rose from the table. "You skated past my property almost every time."

Jasper laughed good-naturedly. "The fourth side of the board isn't enough to win on. Too much going to jail and advancing to Go and taking a ride on the Reading. Players reach that side of the board a whole lot less than the others."

Hell, Joe had never thought about that before. *I'll be damned.*

"Now, me," Jasper went on, "I like the orange and red properties. Prime location. And the railroads. You can get rich on the railroads alone when the dice are rolling right."

When the game was packed away, Joe casually grabbed Trish's wrist to glance at her watch—nearly midnight. He couldn't believe the evening had passed so peaceably.

"Got late on us," Trish's dad said, standing up from his chair and stretching into a yawn, then scrunching his face into a grimace that showed his back was still bothering him.

Joe supposed that was his cue to go. But he didn't want to.

The way he saw it, he'd done his time at the Monopoly board, now he wanted a reward.

He lifted his gaze to Trish, looking for a sign, an invitation for more—but salvation came from her mom instead. "I think it's time for us to head up to bed, Jasper. Let these two have some private time."

Of course, Jasper's eyes narrowed in tight on Joe at the mention of "private time," but he just turned to Trish with a shaking finger. "Don't you stay up down here all night."

She pasted on a small, calming smile. "Don't worry, Dad."

And when goodnights had been said and her parents had disappeared slowly up the stairs, Trish turned to Joe and grinned. "He still thinks I'm sixteen."

Joe cast a lecherous grin. "Maybe he's right to worry. Because all I can think is—alone at last." He slid his arms around her, pulling her close, just soaking up the scent and feel of her. She wore another long, gauzy skirt—this one with a fitted little tee that had been tempting him all night. "You feel good," he whispered down to her.

"Come on, lover boy," she said, taking his hand and leading him through to the back of the house. "Let's go out on the porch before you get yourself into trouble in here."

Joe's desire spread warm through his body—it *was* like they were sixteen again. The screened-in porch was a place where they'd escaped her parents' watchful eyes to share lots of kisses in those days. Now they stepped onto it to see everything outside gleaming wetly—a soft drizzle turned the night green and lush as a light cadence pattered the porch's tin roof. The woods edging the large backyard glistened beneath the pale moonlight fighting its way past rain clouds.

They settled on a cushioned wicker sofa, the same he recalled from all those years ago, and he wrapped a firm arm around her, drinking in her soft warmth.

"I'm glad I came tonight," he told her as she cuddled against him.

"Me, too." She lifted a tender kiss to his lips, tightening his groin. Then a suspicious glint lit her emerald eyes. "I'm guessing you don't let a lot of people drive that car."

"Nobody," he confirmed simply. "Nobody but me. Ever."

"Then why did you let my dad, of all people?"

He didn't quite meet her gaze. "Guess I want the guy to like me," he murmured, then glanced her way. "For you. To make your life easier."

"While I'm here," she clarified quickly.

A soft fist gently squeezed his heart. "Right. While you're here. And I'm glad your dad won at Monopoly. The evening might have taken an ugly turn otherwise."

She smiled, then lifted her head to peer accusingly into his eyes. "You didn't *let* him win, did you?"

"No, cupcake—I don't let anybody get the best of me if I can help it." Their smiles faded, however, when their gazes caught and held. "But I'd be lying if I said I didn't spend the whole damn game thinking how much I'd rather be kissing you." And as a whole day's worth of pent-up desire flowed hot through his veins, he couldn't wait another minute. He lowered his mouth to hers, anxious for a sweet taste. Their tongues met, mingled, and he lifted his hands to her face.

The rain had cooled the late summer air, but the longer they kissed, the less Joe could think of anything cool. His body went taut as he leaned her back on the couch and slid his hand to her breast, listening to her breath turn ragged. "I want you so damn much," he breathed warm in her ear, kneading her soft flesh. Her nipple jutted into his palm through her top and bra.

But she pulled back, sat halfway up, surprising him.

He drew back to meet her look—a silent *What's wrong?*

"You know we can't do it *here*."

Aw, hell. They were on her parents' back porch—a detail he'd managed to forget the second he'd started kissing her. God, this whole night kept taking him back in time, and now he was stuck in an old, familiar fog of frustration, forced to remember all the *other* nights they'd gotten too heated up on this sofa, knowing her parents could walk out at any time.

"I bet they're asleep," he said with raised eyebrows, offering a wicked grin.

"Oh-h-ho no. No way," she replied, giggling lightly.

"We could be quiet."

"I highly doubt that."

Actually, he did, too—she was the noisy type. But he said, "Come on, honey," anyway. Half teasing. Also half serious. "Let's play just a little dangerously."

He raked his thumb slowly over the peak of her breast and leaned in close, letting his voice go thick, raspy. "Let me kiss you. *Here*." He delicately pinched the taut nipple between thumb and forefinger, sending a visible shudder through her.

She sucked in her breath in reply and gave him a sexy look that he was pretty sure meant just one thing—she couldn't resist.

His kisses were slow and hot—on her neck, then grazing downward until he was kissing her breasts through her top. He slid his hands under her shirt and up the incredibly silky skin of her midriff, just to hear her warn him. "Joe."

"Just one kiss, cupcake. One perfect little taste." His voice was a hot whisper as he took possession of both breasts, massaging their weight in his hands. Beneath him, she bit her lip, sighed her pleasure—and gave in.

He pushed her top up to reveal a simple white lace bra, then kissed the tender skin swelling provocatively above the fabric, listening as she let out the softest moan he'd ever heard.

He wanted to . . . say things. Make her promises. Promises he would keep this time.

But no. He was lucky just to be here edging his way back into her world. The sex part had turned out to be amazingly easy, something he never could have predicted with Trish. But the rest of it *wasn't* as simple, so he pushed it from his mind and got back to the easy part.

He dropped warm, little kisses over her breasts through her bra, finally biting tenderly through the lace to capture one beaded nipple between his teeth. She whimpered, trembled. He hoped like hell she wouldn't notice he was trembling now, too.

Reaching under her top to her shoulder, he gently lowered one bra strap enough that he could run his fingertips all the way down into the cup, freeing her breast. "Aw, Trish," he whispered.

He raked his tongue over the sweet, hard pink tip, watching her eyes close in ecstasy. Then he did it again, and again, until she was panting, and until he was suckling her, and the sensation was spreading like wildfire through his body, and her breath was coming faster and faster and his hand went between her legs, under her skirt, rubbing her through her panties. Her breath took on the rhythm of a slow-moving train, yet gaining speed, and all that mattered right now was touching her, taking her to heaven.

But more—he needed to give her more. So he shifted, sinking his fingers under the cotton between her thighs. She gasped when his fingertips found wetness, and he kissed her neck, cheek, lips. He took the peak of her perfect round breast into his mouth again, suckling in the same rhythm she'd found moving against his hand, stopping only to whisper, "I want to make you come, baby. I want to make you come *so* hard."

And then she did. He felt it in the wild contractions around his fingers. He saw it in the tense quivering of her lips. He heard it in the low, sudden sob that escaped her as she drew his body tight against hers. And he absorbed it in the frantic beating of her heart near where his cheek rested. He simply lay there absorbing the joy of having taken her there, smiling at how powerful it felt to give her such pleasure.

When she relaxed in his arms, he raised to peer into her eyes—and her expression was easy enough to read. *I've come back down to earth now and I can't believe I let you get me to do this on my back porch.*

"Mad at me?" he asked.

She let out a breath. "Well, it would be hard to be mad. But . . ."

He gave his head a playfully scolding tilt. "Come on now. You wouldn't have liked it if I stopped in the middle, would you?"

She slapped playfully at his chest and didn't reply, but he knew the answer.

"I have just one question, though," he said. "What happened to 'Next time, a bed'?"

She laughed softly, pulling her bra back into place, her top back down. "This isn't quite next time. And besides, this reminds me of . . . you know, back then. Kissing out here."

He liked knowing she was being whisked back in time, too. So he sank his mouth back to hers, kissing slow, deep—but soon realized that wasn't going to take care of the hard-on currently torturing him.

"Kissing you out here *is* really nice, cupcake," he whispered, "but . . . you want to come over to my place tomorrow night?" Then he winked. "I have a bed."

While most of the residents of God's country were at church praying, Trish was painting. And thinking about Joe's bed.

And his tulips, too, oddly enough. Why had they struck her so dramatically? Other men had given her flowers before, after all. But . . . well, Joe had never been a flower guy back in high school. And from the way Debbie talked about his love life, she suspected he wasn't really a flower guy now, either. Except he had been for *her*, last night.

Letting out a sigh, she dipped her roller in a tray of lilac-shaded paint and began rolling it onto the wall in the "W method" she'd seen on HGTV. Not that she watched a lot of HGTV. She was just thankful she'd somehow caught that helpful hint.

She'd already finished most of the tables and chairs and had now moved on to tackling the walls before she advanced to the potentially disastrous painting of the booths. And while there were moments when she began to fear she'd used too many colors in too many places, the more she worked, the more she actually began to think she might just be a genius at interior design—at least in diners.

She didn't know if anyone else would agree, but each time she stood back and looked around, she couldn't help thinking it was all coming together beautifully. It felt strange—like a whole new place, yet also still the same restaurant where she'd practically grown up.

She'd never thought she had any sentimental attachment to the diner, but as she poured more and more of herself into the place, she was forced to realize that maybe she did—that maybe even leaving *it* behind was going to be difficult when the time came. And it *would* come. Soon. Another week, tops.

When the bell above the door jingled, she looked up to find Marjorie—and in her arms, the most adorable little brown dog Trish had ever seen. Her heart nearly melted on the spot.

"Oh my goodness, this must be our little plaintiff," she cooed, setting down her roller to greet them.

But Marjorie seemed more interested in the diner at the moment. "Glory be, Trish—this is . . . something."

Hmm. Trish pursed her lips. "Would that be a good something or a bad something?"

Marjorie looked around. "A good something," she finally declared.

"Are you sure?" It had taken a while for her to answer.

In reply, Marjorie gave a slow yet emphatic nod. "Yes, absolutely. Now, it's a lot to get used to when a person is accustomed to it being a little old diner, but it definitely looks like . . . the future of Eden."

Trish smiled, thinking she liked that. "That's my hope. That it's modern, but still quaint enough to fit here."

Marjorie continued scanning the room—and nodding some more. "Yes, yes—I think you've nailed that exactly." Then she smiled and Trish decided to believe her.

"So this is the famous Jeremiah," Trish said, reaching up both hands to scratch the little dog behind his ears. "He's adorable, Marjorie."

And when Trish thought of some big, mean, nasty dog hurting him, and of a judge who thought he was replaceable, her blood began to boil all over again. She shook his paw and heard herself speak in a silly cartoon voice she probably hadn't summoned since the *last* time she'd talked to a cat or dog—about half her lifetime ago. *"We're going to get you justice, Jeremiah, do you hear me? Yes, we are—we're going to make that mean man and his mean dog pay through the nose."*

Then she looked up at Marjorie, slightly embarrassed. "Don't worry—I'll talk like a grown-up when we're actually in court."

*     *     *

"Do you have a wife, Butch?"

There, she'd said it—just come right out with it.

Beverly lay in Butch's extended cab with him on Sunday afternoon—he'd waited 'til her shift ended. Gretchen Wilson's "Redneck Woman" blared from the radio up front while the AC drifted back to keep them cool as Butch unbuttoned the top of her uniform blouse and popped the front clasp on her bra.

He rolled toward her, their clothes in a tangle, to kiss her neck, murmuring, "Why you have to go all serious on me, Bev? Since when do you like to talk when we're doing it?"

"Maybe since now. And I want to know. Are you married?"

He ignored her, skimming his free hand up under her black work skirt.

"Are you?" But shit—the words came out too soft this time. Because his hands felt good. She lifted to let him pull her underwear down.

"Why does it matter?" He sounded annoyed with her even as he settled between her parted legs.

And hell, maybe it didn't. She wasn't sure it would stop her. And she supposed his refusal to answer *was* an answer, even if she didn't want to hear it. He still gave her what she needed, a man's touch, the knowledge of being desired, the excitement of sex right here in the middle of the day.

Still, even as he kissed her some more, her thoughts drifted to the best sex she'd ever had—with Carissa's father, Charley. Which was all she knew about him—his first name and how to spell it. He'd said, "Charley with an e-y, not an i-e," when she'd asked his name. Sex with Joe had been a close second, but there had just been something *about* Charley—something almost magical.

She'd been working at the Dairy Queen which still stood across the road from them right now, serving up cones and banana splits. He'd ordered a sundae and asked for extra whipped cream.

"That'll cost ya," she'd said, flirting instantaneously, because he was so cute, in a tall, lean, clean-cut sort of way. Older, she'd thought. Twenty-one, at least. She'd been nineteen, but back then, two years was enough difference to seem older.

"What'll it cost?" he'd asked.

She'd smiled her best smile and said, "How about you share it with me when I take my break in five minutes."

He'd grinned. "Better hurry or it'll melt."

Well, that wasn't the only thing that had melted—he'd melted her Dairy Queen uniform right off her, late that night, in the backseat of her father's Impala. She'd known it was crazy to have sex with a stranger, someone she'd never see again, but that had been the beauty of it, too. People all over town had been mad at her for breaking up Joe and Trish—and with Charley . . . well, no one would ever know. And she'd never seen what was so awful about a girl letting a guy make her feel good.

She'd never dreamed she'd get pregnant. The fact was, she'd been embarrassingly stupid about birth control in those days. She'd had sex with plenty of boys already, letting lots of them do it without a rubber, and nothing had happened. She'd never had regular periods and had thought that meant she couldn't get in trouble.

Not that she could regret it exactly. She could never regret Carissa.

As Butch finally stopped kissing and reached for a condom, she realized how sidetracked she'd become, that she was almost bored. She wished this felt more like usual, even like it had five minutes ago. She shouldn't have thought about Charley. He'd had slower hands, firmer lips. He'd kissed her in a way that had made her know he wanted her to feel as good as he did. He'd told her he was joining the Marines and that meeting her was a mighty nice send-off.

She considered telling Butch she'd like more with him than just sex in his truck—she considered asking him if anything more would ever come of it, of them.

But she couldn't bring herself to do it.

If nothing else, Butch was a nice way to distract herself from her troubles. And if she didn't have that, hell, what *would* she have to bring her any pleasure? Carissa, of course, but that was a different kind of pleasure.

Of course, Butch wasn't the only trucker to grace the counter of the Waffle House, and Beverly knew more than one of them would be perfectly happy to fool around with her. But the truth was, she liked Butch. Better than the rest anyway.

If this was as good as it got, then she supposed it was better than nothing.

When Joe heard a car in the driveway Sunday evening, he yelled around the house from where he knelt in the backyard near the shed, an old slab of plywood in his grasp. "I'm around back, cupcake."

A moment later, he glanced up to see Trish looking summertime pretty in capri pants and a flowy, flowery top sporting only tiny straps on her shoulders. It was the same outfit she'd worn the first time he'd seen her, at the Last Chance. Damn, they'd come a long way. "Hey," he said with a small smile.

She drew closer, then said, "Kittens!" just the same as the girl he'd once known.

Their eyes were open now, and their mewing was about to drive Joe crazy. Sunshine lay in her usual hollowed-out spot under the shed, where two kittens nursed and another lay discovering he could bat at his sibling's pointed tail with his paw. The little gray one took tentative steps through the grass that came up to its shoulders.

"Oh my God, Joe, they're totally adorable." She held out her hand to hold one. "Can I? It's been forever since I've held a baby kitty."

Balancing the plywood against his shoulder, he reached for the gray, passing the cat to her.

"Boy or girl?" she asked.

He shrugged, noncommittal, remembering their first discussion at the bar—about Pumpkin. With kittens, you just couldn't tell for a while.

He watched Trish preen and coo over the cat, stroking its thick fur, until she said, "I have the perfect name for him or her. Pepper."

He refocused on his task with the plywood. "I'll pass that along to whoever adopts it."

She gasped, pulling back. "You're getting rid of this one?"

Clearly the gray was already her favorite, even though she hadn't yet checked out the others. She'd always been like that with kittens or puppies—she got attached to the first one she got a look at.

"Well, I'm not gonna toss him out on the street or anything, but yeah, I'll be looking to find him another home." He explained about Debbie's introduction to the Brownie troop last time. "You know what happens when you keep a lot of cats around, cupcake. They multiply."

Kneeling next to him in the grass, Trish pursed her lips. "You should at least keep *one*," she argued, still holding the gray, although his paws moved now, as if trying to walk on air. "Don't separate the mama from *all* her children. And this should be the one."

He lowered his chin, amused. "Why's that?"

She looked at him as if he'd lost his mind. "Because he's incredibly cute, of course!"

He nodded indulgently. "Of course."

That's when she started in with baby talk to the kitten. "*Yes you are. Say 'I'm the cutest little kitten ever.'* " She held him up in front of her face, lifting one of his tiny paws to wave it at Joe. " '*Please don't give me away, Joe. I like it here. I promise I'll catch lots of mice. And . . . I'll turn out to be a boy, so I won't go out and get pregnant like my mom did.'* "

Joe couldn't help laughing, and finally concluded with, "We'll see." Then thought—*We'll see?* Like she was going to be in his life by the time the kittens were weaned? He shook his head clear of the thought, then took "Pepper" from Trish and lowered the cat back to the cubbyhole as he balanced one edge of the plywood against the shed, having slid the other firmly between the branches of the forsythia.

"What are you doing, making them a little pen?"

He didn't glance up. "Something like that. Never know when a mean dog or tomcat's gonna come along." Not that he really *cared* about the cats, but he figured his sister—and now Trish—would kill him if something happened to them. "And now that that's done, I need to check on dinner."

She looked slightly stunned as he helped her to her feet. "You cooked?"

"Damn straight." Not that he'd had a clue what he was doing.

He'd called Debbie for a lasagna recipe, then spent most of the afternoon constructing the damned thing.

So it was gratifying to reach the house, smell the spicy Italian scents wafting from the oven, and have Trish say, "Yum, that smells great," as he held the door for her.

"So I guess you probably cook all the time, huh?" he asked.

It surprised him when she shook her head. "Occasionally, a little. But I never got in the habit—too busy. Being at home, eating my mom's meals, has been pretty wonderful."

Checking his bubbling masterpiece of sauce, meat, cheese, and noodles, Joe thought it looked like it had a while to go. Trish agreed, but they went about getting out plates, putting a loaf of frozen garlic bread on a tray to bake—and then Trish reached in an overhead cabinet for two glasses.

And—damn. Joe caught sight of her tummy—just a smooth, silky little hint of it when she lifted her arm—and started getting hard, just from that. And hell if he could resist moving in behind her, wrapping his arms around her, and lowering a kiss to her neck.

"Mmm," she purred coquettishly. "Is that a loaf of garlic bread in your pocket or are you just happy to see me?"

He threw his head back in a laugh, then leaned near her ear and spoke throatily. "I'm *definitely* happy to see you, baby." After which he turned her in his arms and lifted her ass onto the kitchen counter in one smooth move. Sliding splayed hands up her thighs, he listened to her sigh, then met her pretty green gaze. "I was gonna wait until after we ate to lay a finger on you—but there's a problem with that."

Her look was sexy as hell as her arms looped around his neck. "What's that?"

"I'm about to self-combust. I've been suffering since last night—remember?"

She bit her lip, appearing at once sympathetic and seductive. "I promise I'll make it all better."

He practically growled in response, his cock stiffening further as he bent in to lower an open-mouthed kiss to the center of her lush cleavage. She shuddered, then let out a breathy sigh. Mmm, God, yeah. He wanted more, and he knew his cupcake did, too.

His next gentle kiss skimmed the inner curve of one sumptuous breast and made her legs curl around his body, drawing his growing erection to the soft crux of her thighs. Heat enveloped him as he sank his next kiss over the fabric concealing her chest, over the beautifully hard little bud now poking through. Pressing against her below, he began to feel lost to her, to the moment.

That's when her voice came in his ear, breathless. "Wait. Not here."

He looked up. "No?"

She bracketed his face with her hands, her eyes hot and needful. "The bed, Joe, I need the bed. Now."

**Venue:** the geographic area in which a court has jurisdiction; _or_ the scene or locale of any action or event.

# *Eleven*

Trish wasn't usually so demanding when it came to sex. But something about Joe made it so that she *could* be.

Maybe it was that first night, the way she'd taken charge.

Or maybe it was just *Joe*. The heat in his eyes. The innate sense that he was wild about her, *all* of her, and that she could be whoever or whatever she wanted to be with him.

"Wrap around me," he said, so she locked her legs more firmly around his hips and her arms tight around his neck. He picked her up, hands planted on her rear, and carried her to the bedroom.

They fell across the bed together in steamy kisses that ran through her like lightning on a hot summer night. As his hands roamed her curves, she took in bits of the room—sage green walls, pale curtains, and the quilt beneath her. She remembered the blanket—done in soft browns and greens and made by his grandmother, it had covered Joe's bed as a boy. But that was all she could grasp of the space before her focus turned solely on him. His mouth, taking possession of hers. His skilled hands massaging her breasts, then reaching downward, for her zipper.

She yanked her gauzy cami off over her head, then pushed his T-shirt up his chest. "I never get to see you naked," she heard herself breathe. "I want you naked."

"Aw, baby," he growled, tearing the T-shirt off and flinging it away. "You want me naked, you'll *have* me naked."

*Mmm, Joe naked. Could life get any better?* Sucking in her breath, she decided to help him, working at his belt and zipper even as she lifted to let him pull off her pants and undies. She shoved his jeans past his hips and watched his sturdy erection burst free, sighing at the sight of it.

Lifting her gaze, she caught his wicked grin. Which fueled her even more. In response, she bit her lip, cast her best come-hither look, then wrapped her hand around him below, relishing the hard heat that filled her fist. "In me," she said.

Without ever taking those piercing blue eyes from hers, he reached down both hands to part her legs wide. And then—oh God—the rough, hot entry, the beautifully filling intrusion. She cried out, then reached for his hips, digging her fingernails in, pulling him tighter, deeper, and listened with joy to his moan. "You fill me," she said.

"I'm gonna give you all you can handle, baby."

After that, thoughts faded—only heat and hard thrusts and core-deep pleasure overflowed her senses. She heard her cries of mindless ecstasy, seeming to echo through the small house—at some point she reached over her head to grip two of the wooden dowels on his headboard. His hands closed rough over her breasts through the strapless bra they hadn't gotten around to taking off, until finally he shoved it down and molded his palms warm over her achy flesh, tenderly pinching the nipples between his fingers with each rhythmic caress.

And then Joe was groaning, hot words slipping out between, as his thrusts grew deeper, harder, more punishing. "Aw, God, baby, God. I'm gonna come in you, Trishy, I'm gonna come *now.*"

She braced herself against the headboard and drank in each stroke as he plunged his orgasm into her, each powerful drive spreading through her body like an earthquake, echoing out from the epicenter between her legs. She absorbed each thrust, cherishing the heat, all because it came from him.

As he collapsed gently atop her, he whispered against her bare shoulder. "Aw, damn."

"What?"

He turned his eyes on hers, their faces close. "I didn't make you come."

She hid her smile. "I don't care, Joe. It's not always about that."

He narrowed his gaze on her. "What's it about then?"

*Crap.* That had almost been like saying it was about . . . caring, about much more than she wanted to let him believe she felt. She'd managed to stop with the mindless *I love yous* inside her lately, and she'd thought maybe she was really succeeding in her have-a-wild-affair quest, but this was definitely a bad sign.

So she made up an easier answer. "It's about just . . . feeling how big you are inside me."

Yeah, that was good. He liked that—she could tell by the flash of masculine arrogance darkening his expression. And it wasn't a lie—she *loved* how big he was inside her.

But she couldn't deny—at least not to herself—that she also

*cared.* She couldn't deny there were also still some very deep, complicated emotions swirling around inside her. And maybe that *I love you* had been closer than she'd thought, because now, as she lay looking into his eyes, sprawled on the bed with him naked, she couldn't deny the warmth in her belly, stretching even deeper, maybe all the way to her soul. It was much more than just physical. Oh God—she *wanted* to love him, *wanted* to trust him. But . . . she just didn't know if she could.

She knew he was a different person in ways now—a man, not a boy.

And yet . . . hell, *this* was why it was so much easier to think of it as just an affair. Because turning off the emotions meant turning off the memory of that old pain, too. And being with him these last few days, without that pain in the mix, had been pretty darn nice.

Time to turn off the emotions again. *Make it for good this time, Trish. Get back to the fun stuff, the sex, the way he makes your body feel.*

"Aw, *damn*," he said again, this time looking truly alarmed.

"What now?"

"I think my damn lasagna is burning."

She gasped, because that's when she smelled it, too, the acrid scent of something that had been in the oven too long. Joe jumped to his feet and rushed from the room, giving her the first real view of his butt she'd ever seen—and *mmm*, it was just as nice and round and tight as she'd suspected from viewing it through jeans.

A moment later, after some muttered curses from the kitchen, he appeared in the doorway, wearing nothing but two oven mitts and holding a tray of slightly charred lasagna. "Look at this," he

said, clearly incensed that all his hard work had been for nothing. "It's ruined."

She held back her smile, since he was upset—but she couldn't
help thinking it was about the cutest sight she'd ever beheld. Or
maybe—actually—the sexiest. Since he was still fairly erect. "I'm
sorry, Joe. I shouldn't have dragged you into the bedroom."

But he shook his head. "You didn't drag. I carried. And I'm
the one who started this, so you're off the hook."

She sat up, taking a closer look at the tray, which he held
down to show her. "Maybe we could . . . dig down underneath
the burned part?"

"No, I'm not feeding you burned food," he said on a sigh.
Then he disappeared, returning a moment later sans mitts and
tray. "How would you feel about pizza? There's a place in town
that delivers."

"Pizza would be great. Except for one thing. One of us would
have to go to the door to get it. And I'd like to stay naked with
you."

His gaze swept over her in a way she felt from head to toe.
"Here's the plan. I'll put on pants to get the door. Then I'll take
them back off. Then we'll eat. Then I'll make you scream. All.
Night. Long."

Trish swallowed at the promise and eked out, "Good plan."

They'd stripped the quilt from the bed to lounge across tou-
sled beige sheets, naked, with an open pizza box between them.
Given that Trish didn't lay around openly naked a lot, even with
guys she'd had sex with, it felt amazingly . . . easy. And right.
"I've never eaten pizza in bed before," she mused.

He cocked a playful grin. "Hang with me, baby, and I'll give
you all *sorts* of new experiences."

Yep, she couldn't deny *that*. Like sex on a dresser. And in the rain.

But Joe's amusement quickly faded to something more inquisitive. "I bet you probably eat in fancy restaurants all the time—huh, cupcake?"

She shrugged. "Sometimes."

"And so *I* take you to the Burger Barn and order pizza."

He didn't sound self-deprecating—but as if the contrast had just hit him. And somehow, it gave her the urge to reach across the pizza box and touch his face, rake her fingertips over the stubble on his jaw. "That doesn't matter. The time you and I have spent together—eating, or talking, or . . . touching—it's been . . ." *Amazing. Phenomenal. Perfect.* "It's been *good*, Joe. *Really good*."

Those other words would have held too much drama, too much of the *caring* she didn't want to open up between them. Even if her eyes probably said it all anyway, at least "good" wasn't a terribly incriminating way to describe sex—or time spent together.

"Well, in that case . . . I can serve dessert."

She let a smile unfurl across her face, thinking him adorably cute for a guy who could be so rough and masculine most of the time. "Dessert, huh?"

"Nothing fancy," he warned, getting to his feet and clearing the pizza box from the bed. "But at least I didn't burn it."

Trish watched him stroll to the kitchen, so clearly comfortable with his body, his nudity, that she began to feel tingly again. She wanted his dessert, but she also wanted an entirely *different* kind of dessert when they were done.

He returned with a large plastic container, lowering it to the bed next to her. Loosening one corner, he drew back the lid to reveal . . . cupcakes. Simple, chocolate icing from a can, and if she remembered Joe's taste, they would be from a yellow cake mix. But nothing could have delighted her more.

"Like I said, nothing fancy."

She smiled up at him as he joined her back on the bed. "Joe, you have no idea how long it's been since I've had a cupcake."

He flashed a devilish grin. "Myself, I had one just about an hour ago, right here." He motioned to the sheets they lay on.

"You're bad," she teased, her blood sizzling.

"Says the woman who showed up here a little over a week ago looking like she was going to break out whips and chains."

She lowered her chin, feeling a bit sheepish. That hadn't really been her, and she supposed they both knew it. "It was the most expedient way to accomplish my plan."

"The 'have sex and move on' plan," he clarified.

She nodded softly. "I realize now it wasn't . . . very well thought out."

He tipped his head back. "Maybe not—but it worked out okay in the end." Then he pointed toward the container. "Have a cupcake, cupcake."

Peeling down one side of a pastel paper cup to take a big bite of yellow cake, Trish sighed. "Mmm, yum." It took her back to her youth—just like everything else in this town.

She didn't know why Joe's eyes had gone dark or why he was leaning swiftly in toward her—until he licked a glob of icing from the corner of her mouth. "Mmm, yum," he repeated, and the juncture of her thighs rippled.

On impulse, she held out her cupcake for him to take a bite, which left remnants of chocolate on his upper lip, so now *she* licked *him* clean. He sighed, and this time when she said, "Mmm, yum," it came out throatier than intended.

Without hesitation, Joe swiped his finger through the top of what remained of her cupcake, then dabbed the icing on her nipple. *"Oh,"* she said on a light gasp. Their gazes met, and her whole body heated as she set the cupcake in the container and leaned back on a pile of pillows.

Pushing the plastic aside, Joe eased his way up her body, barely grazing her flesh with his—although the flesh between his legs, growing rapidly, did a little more than graze. Dipping sensually toward her breast, he licked at the blob of icing, suckling her clean, the ministrations reaching deep enough to make the small of her back tingle.

*"Mmm,"* he moaned, lifting his hands to caress her breasts, tweak both nipples. "Yummy, baby."

After that, there were no more cupcakes—there was only being tangled up in one another. Joe sank hot kisses between her parted legs, then used his tongue, proving he was good with more than just his hands. Trish got lost in it all, aware of nothing but heat and light and her fingers clawing at the sheet at both sides of her. *I love you. I love you.*

Ah, damn, the *I love you*s were back.

*Stop it. Just feel this. His mouth on you. Nothing else.*

*Feel this.*

*Feel this.*

And fortunately, Joe made that part pretty darn easy.

When it was long after dark, moonlight spilling through the window above Joe's bed, they were still kissing, their hands gliding, touching each other everywhere. Trish had lost track of time, and of how long they'd been having sex—she only knew Joe had incredible staying power when he tried. She only knew he was making good on his promise of all night long and that she'd been right about the bed and lying down with him and stretching out beside him.

Now she kissed her way across the snake on his arm, then down his chest to the taut muscles of his stomach, and then further, further, until she was taking him into her mouth. She'd never been such a big fan of this particular activity . . . until now. Him.

And then he was back inside her again—deep, hard, filling. And there were no thoughts, because she'd banished the *I love you*s hours ago, relegated herself to pushing all the emotion aside, at least as much as possible—yet she clung to him tight and needful.

More time passed, more touching, more feeling, until she found herself atop him, the full moon casting a bright glow over their bodies. She rode him, and he thrust up inside her until they both came together, moaning and writhing like animals, finally collapsing together on the bed.

She lay on her back next to him, recovering, lost in the afterglow, when his voice broke through the silence, low, quieter than he usually spoke. "Want another cupcake?"

Despite utter exhaustion, she cast a half smile. "Do you mean a *real* cupcake? Or were you talking about sex?" Ever since he'd used the icing as foreplay a few hours earlier, it had become confusing.

She glanced over to catch his soft grin. "I meant a cupcake. But I guess this can be our new code. If we're around other people and I want you, I'll just ask if you want a cupcake?"

"And I'll say, 'Maybe later, I'm not hungry right now.' "

"No, you'll say, 'Oh yeah, baby, let's go eat some sweet, tasty cupcakes.' "

They laughed softly and Trish turned on her side, letting

her arm rest atop his, her hand curving over his shoulder. They smiled at each other with their eyes.

Yet then his expression went serious, along with his voice. "Can I ask you a question?"

*Say no.* Because this seriousness couldn't be a good direction for a girl who was trying to keep things light and sexy here. "Okay."

He never broke their gaze. "Do you still not trust me, Trish? Do you still not forgive me?"

The words stole her breath as she lay next to him, numb, scrambling for an answer. "I . . . don't know. I haven't been thinking about trust. I've just been thinking about . . . *this*." She motioned vaguely to them, the bed. Then she rolled to her back, planting her gaze someplace safe—the ceiling. "It doesn't really matter, though. It would only matter if this was . . . a long-term situation. And I'll be leaving soon."

His voice came uncharacteristically tender. "I'll be sorry to see you go."

*Maybe I will, too.* But despite the feelings she still harbored for him, leaving Eden, and Joe, *soon*, was vital to her well-being.

And maybe he couldn't understand why, because she'd held so much back from him, worked so hard to hide her feelings whenever she could. So in the heat of the moment, she made a rash decision—to tell him what she'd *never* planned to tell him, ever. Because even as it might expose her vulnerabilities, it would finally make it clear why this could go no further.

"Joe, I need to tell you something." She turned back on her side, toward him, and he faced her now, too.

"I'm listening." Clearly, he knew something big was coming.

She took a deep breath. "I need to tell you that when I went away to college, I . . . cried myself to sleep every night for two whole years." She shook her head at the intensity of the memory, at how mourning their love had become as big a part of her life for awhile as their love itself had once been. And already, it was hard to keep going, hard to admit how deeply his betrayal had gouged into her, but she knew she had to.

"I . . . couldn't stop feeling it. I wanted to, believe me. But somehow I just couldn't quit being devastated by what you'd done. I just kept experiencing the hurt over and over again, every day. It was strange—as if I would think through it all somehow expecting a different outcome at the end of the story, but the outcome was always the same. And it never quit feeling fresh, new. It was like falling down and skinning the same knee time and again.

"I learned to hide my feelings around other people—I focused on my classes, I made friends, I went on with everyday life. I even started dating again. But at night I cried and just kept asking *why, why, why*. There were times I feared I'd *never* get over you, that what you'd done would haunt me forever.

"I know that sounds pathetic—maybe it *was* pathetic—but I was young, and it was first love, and I'd thought it was going to be *forever* love, so it ran deep." She stopped then, stuck for how to finish, shocked at the breadth of her own honesty. "So, there it is—now you know."

Somehow her gaze had drifted from his face to his snake, to the fine details she'd never studied before—the small horizontal ridges inside the cobra's open hood, the intricate pattern on its body. When she gathered the courage to raise her gaze back to Joe's, she found his eyes glassy, his expression wrenched with sadness.

He lifted a warm hand to her cheek. "I'm so damn sorry, honey. If there was any way I could have taken it back, I would have, I promise." He stopped, let out a heavy breath. "I *hate* what I did to you, I *hate* that I hurt you."

Her throat clogged at the strain in his voice—she'd never heard him sound so full of pain. She lingered about an inch away from weepiness herself—and God knew she didn't want to go *there*. So she sat up in bed, just to distance herself from him a bit. His face had loomed so near, the musky scent of him permeating her senses. She'd told him the yucky truth about the long-lasting effects of their breakup—and now it was time to toughen back up into the sturdier woman she'd become.

Without examining why, she pulled the sheet up to cover herself and said, "But I did get over it, Joe, eventually. And that's why . . . why I needed to leave the night I came to seduce you. And it's why, even though we've been having a good time together, I don't think I can ever let myself go there with you again, to that deeper place. Can you understand that?"

Only then did she turn to look down at where he still lay.

Slowly, he nodded against the pillow. "Yeah, I can understand." She hated how sad he still sounded—so she was pleased when his voice lightened then, just a bit. "Come back down here with me. I need to ask you something else."

Oh boy. What now? And of course she didn't *have* to lie back down with him—but she did anyway.

Which brought their faces close again, made their arms touch.

"My sister's getting married on Saturday. Will you go with me?"

Whoa—she hadn't seen *that* coming.

Before she could even respond, however, he went on. "Thing is, this guy she's marrying seems pretty shady. He owns the bar where she works, which is a whole *other* worry I won't even get into—but the point is, this wedding is gonna be about as much fun as a funeral. And . . . I could use a friend there."

She tilted her head against the pillow. "You could take Kenny."

He blinked, drew in his breath. "I could really use . . . *you* there."

Trish swallowed. Going to a family wedding seemed like a bad idea. It was the kind of thing a "girlfriend" did. And he'd just told her he *needed* her there. *Her*—not anyone else.

So she was just going to say no. Plain and simple.

Of course, she'd say *more* than that one little word  she'd explain, she'd be nice about it. *Joe, I'm sorry, but I think it's a bad idea. Ask Kenny. It'll be better that way.*

Which was when she heard herself utter a light, airy-sounding, "Okay."

*Crap*. Like once before with Joe, wrong little word.

In the following days, Trish fell into a comfortable routine. Working in the diner through the day and seeing Joe at night. And there was fun, and there was sex, but there was no more serious talk, for which Trish was thankful.

On Monday, they had an impromptu dinner at Debbie and Kenny's, where Joe regaled their friends with tales of burned lasagna, glossing over—of course—what exactly had distracted him from keeping an eye on the oven. But he provided the rest of his cupcakes for dessert and Debbie's boys went wild. It also gave him the opportunity to repeatedly ask Trish if *she* wanted a cupcake, and finally she admitted she did, and they left. For old times' sake, they'd driven Joe's Trans Am that night, and they found themselves "having cupcakes" in the same car where they'd shared so much passion in high school.

On Tuesday, she rented a movie and took it to his place. More cupcakes afterward—both kinds.

On Wednesday, another dinner at her parents' house, sans Monopoly—instead, Joe let Trish's father show him a new fishing pole, which led the two men out to the little pond behind the barn for a bit of just-before-dark fishing. Joe caught a small blue gill and Trish's dad tried not to act miffed, stating that it was clearly the reel and his hand-tied lure that had made it happen. No cupcakes that night, either kind.

In between diner detail and passion with Joe, she kept up with e-mail from her office and read over some discovery relating to the Richie Melbourne case—the police report and the grand jury testimony. The trial was only a few weeks away and she needed to keep fresh on the facts. There was no word yet from their DNA expert, except that he was backed up with work, so she continued basing her strategy on what she strongly suspected: Richie's DNA wouldn't show up on those cups but a third party's would—likely Dane Eldridge—and Richie would be a big step closer to freedom.

Although she couldn't deny the sudden strangeness of preparing for a trial, thrusting herself back into high-powered-attorney mode, at least in her mind. She feared it would seem almost odd to suddenly find herself back in her loft, putting on her panty hose and suits, going into the office, and to court.

She would have liked to look forward to it—that was often how she felt as a vacation drew to a close, as if the change of pace had been nice but that getting back to work would be energizing. Now she stood in her old bedroom putting on the casual tan linen suit she'd brought home just in case she was called back to Indy on some legal emergency—it was Thursday, and she was ready to meet Marjorie and Jeremiah for their day in court. And she *was* energized by the task, ready to very tactfully but decisively show this farce of a judge the error of his ways. Yet at the same time, the suit felt oddly binding, her panty hose stifling, and the thought of going back to her *real* job made her feel . . . ugh, a little sick.

It was about Joe.

She hated admitting that to herself, but it would just be silly to deny it.

She might have sworn up and down to him—and herself—that she was keeping this light and uncomplicated. She might have insisted to herself that a bunch of crazy, silent professions of love meant nothing. But she knew now exactly what she'd known the first moment she'd impaled herself on his powerful erection: She loved the guy.

She sighed, then sat down on the bed, feeling light-headed.

Yeesh. She loved the guy? Really?

*Yep, really.*

But she still couldn't *tell* the guy, or *stay with* the guy.

Because she had a life in Indy, a whole world, an existence she'd worked hard for. And also because what she'd told him the other night was true—love aside, she just didn't think she could risk her heart to him again.

Of course, maybe the fact that she loved him pretty much meant she was way past risk. Leaving him was going to be . . . hard. More than hard. Quite possibly misery-inducing.

And yet she couldn't help thinking that if you didn't trust someone, they couldn't hurt you. And if she left willingly, it meant *he* could never leave *her*. She'd gone to his house that first night to take control—and she supposed she'd sort of *lost* control soon after, in a big way. But she retained a bit of it still. And as long as she *kept* that bit of control and made the right decisions . . . well, leaving him might be horrible, but at least it would be *her* decision and he could never wound her again.

Checking the little clock next to the bed, she saw she had a few minutes to spare, so she booted up her laptop on the old wooden desk where she'd once done homework and written long, passionate notes to Joe telling him how much she adored him. Her e-mail contained several messages from coworkers asking for her input or advice on case-related issues. She scanned them quickly but would have to wait until later to answer.

And then—*blip*—another new message appeared that very instant, from Kent. She clicked to open it.

> Hey stranger—word on the street is that the partner announcement will be made sooner rather than later, and I'm betting on you, kid. I know you thought your leave of absence might hurt your chances, but I think the opposite is happening. Everywhere I go, I hear your name—people miss your expertise around here. And of course, some of us just plain miss you. Any ETA? I have discovered that Burrito Bob's has a surprisingly tasty margarita, so happy hour is on me your first day back. I promise not to get you drunk and take advantage of you—maybe.

Trish just sat staring at the screen, stunned. She barely knew which part to absorb first. The partner part—or the sexual innuendo part. She and Kent hadn't quite worked *up* to sexual innuendo yet. Until now, suddenly. When she wasn't particularly in the mood to think about sex with anyone but Joe.

She blew out a big whoosh of breath and tried to think how to answer.

Under normal circumstances, she'd have been happy. About the partner part. *And* the sexual innuendo part. But she felt so disconnected from her life at the firm right now that the partner part felt . . . weirdly distant, like it was news meant for someone else—for that woman who lived in her loft and wore expensive pumps and five-hundred-dollar suits. And now that she was sleeping with Joe almost every night, flirtation with Kent didn't seem as easy.

But that was crazy. It wasn't like this Joe thing was gonna last. She'd made that perfectly clear—to both of them. She'd be going back to the city as soon as she finished her diner spruce-up project. Wouldn't she?

Of course she would.

*Of course she would.*

But she wasn't going to think about that anymore right now. No, right now she was going to go save a little dog from a big one.

Joe had been under the hood of a 2001 Mercedes E320 for an hour and had finally found the problem—one of the six coils was bad. An easy fix now that he knew what was wrong. He'd just wiped off his hands and dropped the hood, then headed to the office to order the part for next-day delivery, when the phone on his desk rang. "Ramsey's Auto Repair. This is Joe."

"Hey, it's me."

Carissa. He let his voice soften. "What's up, Care Bear?"

He waited for her to scold him for the nickname, but instead she said, "I bought my dress for the dance." She sounded giddy and nervous, and he still couldn't help wondering when he'd blinked and missed her turning into a teenager.

Still, he was pleased that she'd called to tell him. "Find one you like?"

"Uh-huh. In fact . . ."

"Yeah?"

"Well, I'm over at the Waffle House—my friend Taylor's mom dropped me off. And I have the dress with me 'cause I forgot and left it in Taylor's car last night after her mom took us shopping, so I was thinking . . . maybe you could give me a ride home, 'cause Mom is working 'til eight and I don't feel like sticking around. But I could maybe . . . show you the dress first . . . if you wanted to see it."

Damn, she wanted to show him her dress. It twisted his heart up a little.

He glanced toward the digital clock on the corner of the messy desk, finding he had to lift a stray invoice just to read it. Four-thirty. Earlier than he liked to knock off, especially given the way paperwork was building up around here lately, but . . . "Give me twenty minutes. I need to order a part and do a few other things, but then I'll head over. Hell, I'll even buy you dinner while we're there."

When he walked through the door shortly before five, half the booths were filled and the counter was busy. That suited him fine, since it meant he got off with only a quick wave toward Bev before settling into a booth across from Carissa, where she sat bent over a math book. "Homework, huh?"

She looked up. "Algebra sucks."

"Yeah, that's how I remember it."

But then she smiled, clearly recalling why he was there. "I'll go put on my dress." Most girls might not feel comfortable changing in a restaurant bathroom or doing a fashion show in front of everyone eating their waffles and eggs and hamburgers, but Carissa had practically grown up in the place, so she merrily grabbed up the plastic sack from the seat beside her and scurried off to the restroom just a few steps away.

Just then, Bev appeared beside him. "Something to drink?"

"Coke," he said, barely glancing up.

"Thanks—about the dress. It meant the world to her to get to go shopping with her girlfriend. They drove over to Columbus after school yesterday."

He nodded shortly. "You know I'm glad to help out."

She looked like she was about to say more, but fortunately that's when Floyd called, "Order up!" and drew her away.

A few minutes later, the ladies' room door opened and Carissa strolled out looking like—oh hell—a much older girl. The slinky red dress sported a deep-cut halter neck and a too-short hem. He didn't think he'd ever heard her sound happier than when she said, "What do you think?"

Joe couldn't help feeling a little sick to his stomach—but he knew he had to be careful here. So he kept it simple. "You look . . . great, honey." *Too* great.

"You took too long to answer," she pointed out. Quick on the draw, his Care Bear.

He let out a heavy breath. "Guess I'm just . . . surprised."

"By?"

"Uh . . . how much older you look."

Her eyes lit up. "Really?"

Shit. He'd totally forgotten that thirteen-year-old girls *wanted* to look older. "Yeah, really."

Her face dropped slightly. "You don't like it."

Aw, damn. "Sit down a minute, honey." *And quit giving the truckers at the counter an eyeful.*

Her eyes drooped softly as she plopped into the booth.

"I'm not lying about you looking good in the dress, Care. Any guy would be tripping over himself to get next to you in that dress."

She widened her eyes expectantly. "Well, isn't that what I want? To make boys trip over themselves?"

He wasn't sure how to answer, so he still kept it simple—but real. "I just want you to be careful. This is your first dance, your first date. What it comes down to is . . ." He sighed, ran a hand back through his hair. "This dress makes me nervous."

Her arms were crossed and her gaze had dropped to his chest. "So you don't want me to wear it."

"It's not my decision," he replied, then tried to speak more gently. "But . . . if you wanted to look at some other dresses, I'd even take you shopping. When's this dance of yours?"

"Saturday night."

Today was Thursday. Hell. "I thought it was the Fall Fling—it's still August."

Her eyes widened. "Look, I didn't schedule it—I'm just trying to survive my first date without freaking out."

So she was freaking out—and he'd picked on her dress. Smooth, Ramsey, real smooth. Still, something in his gut told him he couldn't let her wear that. "What are you doing after school tomorrow?"

She raised her eyes. "Shopping for a dress, I'm guessing."

"Good guess."

"Here ya go," Bev said, lowering two plates of food in front of Joe and Carissa. Her heart beat too fast, though, because Butch sat in a booth at the far end of the counter. He'd never before happened in when Carissa was here and it made Bev nervous. She didn't like to think of those two parts of her life—the purest and, well . . . the least pure—rubbing up against each other.

"Joe's taking me shopping tomorrow after school, so I won't be home," her daughter said.

Bev drew back slightly. Joe hung out with Carissa here and at the garage, and he'd taken her places when she was younger—but never shopping. "What for?"

Carissa glanced at Joe, then back to her, and spoke quietly. "He thinks I should get a different dress."

"Why?" Carissa was still wearing the red one and looked incredible in it. Beverly had almost envied her daughter when she'd seen it a little while ago—she'd never gone to any big-deal dances in school except one prom, and then she'd worn a hand-me-down dress from a cousin that she'd not gotten to choose.

Joe spoke up, drawing her attention. "I just thought this one might be . . . a little too mature."

Beverly caught the pointed look in Joe's eyes, then glanced back to the halter dress—and her mind reeled.

Oh God, she was a horrible mother! *Of course* that dress was too showy for Carissa! She was only thirteen.

Although at thirteen Beverly had been making out with boys, close to losing her virginity already. She'd never been popular or had many friends, and she'd been lonely—both at school and home. But boys had liked her because she had boobs and a butt, and she'd loved the way it felt—being liked.

Yet Carissa was totally different—Beverly would be shocked to find out her daughter had even been kissed. Carissa had lots of girlfriends, but she was far more nervous around boys than Bev had ever been—and maybe that was a good thing.

So why hadn't she seen how inappropriate that dress was?

Hell, maybe *she* wanted to be going to *her* first dance, looking pretty, attracting boys. But she didn't want Carissa to attract the same kind of boys she had—boys who invited you into their backseats instead of out on dates.

"Maybe Joe's right about that, honey."

Carissa just nodded, looking irritated, and Beverly felt bad—

but she'd have to thank Joe later for seeing what she hadn't. He was so very good to her daughter, and even as she said, "Gotta get back to work," and walked away, she felt that old, familiar tug to make a perfect little family with him, and she couldn't help seething at the thought of holier-than-thou Trish Henderson back in his arms. She knew they'd been seen around town together, cruising in the Cobra. And she also knew Trish would never give Joe what he needed—a family, a wife, something solid and lasting. *Oh Joe, why can't you see how good we'd be together?*

Picking up the coffee pot, she strode down to Butch to freshen his cup. The early dinner crowd was thinning, and she hoped Joe and Carissa would leave soon now that they'd finished eating— but Carissa hadn't even changed out of that dress yet, and she'd seen Joe eyeing the pie case.

Butch wore a lazy smile, seduction teeming in his eyes. "Head out to the truck with me, darlin'?"

Her body wanted to—no matter how he treated her, her body still desired him. He wasn't Joe, of course, but then, nobody was. She'd always been very aware that a girl had to take what she could get in this world.

And yet . . . having him here, in the same room as Carissa, made her a little nauseous for reasons she couldn't explain. Maybe it was easier to sleep with men she didn't know very well when she was focusing only on herself. It was harder with her daughter just a few feet away—even now, she heard Carissa laugh and felt glad her mood was lightening. Maybe Bev was suddenly wondering what Carissa's future held and hoping it was something better than hers had. She'd have died if Carissa ever knew she slept with truckers passing through town, so desperate to be held that even a stranger would do.

"I can't, Butch," she said finally. "My kid's here."

"Yeah?" He started to lean around her, to glance toward Carissa, but Beverly found herself stepping over to block his view. To keep those parts of her life from touching any more than they already had. He leaned back in the booth, his interest in her daughter clearly a passing thing, and lifted his small, flirtatious grin back in her direction. "I can wait."

"I don't think it's a good idea. Not today." Besides Carissa's presence, it was the middle of the dinner hour—not Butch's usual time. It was one thing to climb up into his truck on a quiet afternoon or in the dark of night, but somehow, the dinner hour felt more seamy.

"Come on now, sugar, don't tease. I've had a hankering for you all the way since Illinois. And you know you can't say no to me."

Something in Beverly's chest burned. She was no more than a hankering to him, merely sex in the back of his truck—while he probably had some unsuspecting wife at home who Bev had been trying like hell to pretend didn't exist all this time. And if that wasn't bad enough, he was so smug that he thought she couldn't resist. "You know what, Butch?" she said.

"What's that, darlin'?"

She bent closer over his table. "The truth is, I don't think this thing between us is working out for me anymore. It never did, really—it was just a way to pass the time. So you're welcome to come in for a waffle or some coffee, *darlin'*, but afraid all you're gonna get after you eat from now on is the check."

With that, she ripped his bill off her pad, lowered it to the table, then turned and walked back to Carissa and Joe, to see if they wanted some pie. And in the short time it took to travel the length of the counter, she suddenly felt better, stronger, than she had in a very long time. Who knew—if she worked real hard, maybe she'd learn to be somebody her daughter could look up to.

*   *   *

Late Thursday night, Trish lay naked in Joe's bed. A cool front had urged him to turn off the AC and open the windows, so a soft breeze wafted over them, lifting the sheer curtains to flutter overhead.

"And then what?" he asked. She lay cuddled against his chest, his arm anchored gently around her.

"And then Marjorie burst into tears of joy and Jeremiah barked, and everyone in the courtroom laughed—except for her scumbag neighbor, but I guess I can't blame the guy because he's about to be nine hundred dollars poorer, and he also either has to fence his yard or keep his scumbag dog on a chain." Joe smiled down at her, and she realized she was actually giggling against his chest, remembering the outcome in court.

"This made you happy, helping out Marjorie, huh?"

She nodded. "I guess it just felt good to do something nice for someone with my law degree that didn't involve days or weeks of heated debates, or wondering who was guilty and who was innocent—even though I try not to focus on that when I can help it. It was nice just to get a little justice for someone I like."

"I'm sure Marjorie appreciated it."

She raised her head slightly, perching her chin on her hands to peer inquisitively down at him. "When you brought me those tulips last week, did you get them from Marjorie's shop?"

He nodded easily. "Why?"

She'd been meaning to ask ever since, because she'd wondered . . . "Did she help you pick them out?"

To her surprise, he shook his head, looking only slightly affronted. "No, I can pick out flowers by myself."

She drew in her breath. "Why'd you pick tulips?"

He shrugged against his pillow. "Saw them in the cooler and

thought they were pretty—that's all." Then he added, "I was gonna get all pink—that color drew me for some reason—but she only had one left, so she mixed up other colors for me."

Trish's stomach hollowed. Joe had picked the one flower Marjorie had suggested for Trish's wedding? Whoa.

Not that it mattered. It was a flower in a cooler, for heaven's sake.

Still, what a . . . romantic coincidence. In fact, it nearly took her breath away.

"You okay?" he asked. "You look a little weird."

She came back to herself. "Thanks. You look a little weird, too." Then she playfully smacked his stomach and rolled to her back next to him with a laugh.

"So, think you can stand not seeing me tomorrow?" He eased up on his side, propping on one elbow to grin down at her. "I have a feeling this dress thing is gonna take all damn night. We'll probably be there 'til the stores close."

She cast a placating smile. "I'll try to survive." When he'd told her about Carissa's dress, she'd almost offered to go with them, sensing his worry over the task. But she'd decided that would only immerse her *too* deeply in his world, right when she needed to start—somehow—backing away a bit.

The fact was, she was putting the finishing touches on the diner. And when she was done, she had to go back to Indianapolis. It wasn't just about her sanity, but also about her job, her responsibilities. She'd ended up staying in Eden—and Joe's bed—a lot longer than she'd ever planned, but checking her e-mail today had reminded her that she *was* up for partner, that Richie Melbourne's case *was* pending, and that other people in the office counted on her. She hadn't told Joe yet—and she wasn't going to right now, not until after his sister's wedding on

Saturday. But she needed to start mentally disentangling herself from him—in her head, and also in her heart.

"I hope Beverly realizes how lucky she is to have you in her daughter's life."

"I think she does. She thanks me a lot. But . . ."

"But what?"

He pinned her in place with his gaze, looking deadly serious. "I talk to her as little as possible, Trish."

She tilted her head against the pillow, confused. "Okay."

"I mean . . . I just want you to know she's not in my life other than when we discuss Carissa. And I keep that short. Like I told you after we put up the hay, there was only that one night with her—nothing else. I stop in and eat at the Waffle House once a week or so, just to check on Carissa, but that's the only place I ever see her."

Trish let all that sift quietly down through her.

The truth was that she didn't want to care about what he'd just told her—but she did. She didn't want to feel relief over it, but she did. She'd not thought a lot about Beverly Rainey—in the present, in his life—since coming home. But maybe something *had* nagged at her deep down—the connection they shared over a child, even if the child wasn't technically his. She'd never let herself even recognize it until this moment.

So she considered playing it cool, tough, and telling him it was none of her concern because she'd be leaving soon. But instead she simply said, "Thanks for telling me, Joe."

Then she kissed him.

And thought—*Oh boy, this is bad, feeling so close to him.*

And it was only then that it hit her. She'd never had *this much* sex with a guy before.

Over time, maybe, but she'd never had a boyfriend or lover

who she couldn't get enough of no matter how many times they did it, who she saw every night and couldn't resist.

And now, now . . . somewhere along the way, it had become not just sex, but sex and *talking. Laughing. Sharing.*

*Put the wall up, Trish. Keep your priorities straight. Remember your responsibilities. And remember to guard your heart. Don't let anyone ever hurt you that badly again.*

"Stay the night?" he asked.

She hadn't so far, claiming it had to do with not getting her dad in an uproar. This was no time to start. In fact, it was a good time to leave. "No, I'm gonna take off." She rose to look for her panties, which she found at the foot of the bed.

"Don't know what you're missin'," he teased her. "I'd snuggle up to you all night long."

She couldn't even smile—the promise sounded too tempting. But she had to *stop* being tempted by Joe Ramsey, once and for all. "Sorry, Joe—I'm leaving."

He sat up behind her. "I want to watch the sun rise with you, Trish."

Stepping into her underwear, she stopped, looked over her shoulder. "Huh?"

"Let's go outside," he said. "Let's sit in the backyard and talk. I bet we don't run out of things to say before dawn."

**Stay:** temporarily stopping a judicial proceeding; _or_ to remain; to not leave.

# Twelve

The truth was, it had surprised him when she agreed. But he'd been just as surprised when he'd asked. He hadn't planned it, had simply heard the words leaving him as the idea entered his head. Maybe it was his way of saying he didn't have to be naked with her or even _looking forward_ to getting naked with her to want to _be_ with her.

So they'd gotten up, put on clothes, and made pancakes in the middle of the night—both for old times' sake and because they'd worked up an appetite. After plopping them on plates with some butter and syrup, they'd grabbed forks and headed out to the two big Adirondack chairs in Joe's backyard. He planned to build a deck onto the house one of these days, but for now, the chairs sat under a sprawling maple that he'd climbed as a boy and watched turn orange every fall.

They'd sat soaking in the scents and sounds of a late summer night—she'd tossed on one of his sweatshirts to ward off the cool air—and they had, just as he'd promised, talked all night long.

They talked about her parents, her concerns for their future as they aged. And she caught him off guard by telling him that her dad's new contentment concerning Joe had somehow silently mended a long rift between them, something that had seemed to hang over them ever since Trish had left for college.

She told him how much she'd enjoyed renovating the diner, and admitted that her attachment to the place had grown as she'd put so much work into it, so much color and creativity that she hadn't quite realized lurked inside her.

She confided in him about her job, both the good parts and the bad—the success and the heartache, the sense of achievement versus the long hours. She even admitted she was tempted to adopt one of his kittens, because she could use the company—but she feared the cat would end up lonely.

"Never know," Joe told her. "Maybe it's like having a kid. Maybe you'll *make* the time when you have to, because you'll know little Pepper is depending on you."

She flashed a suspicious smile in reply. "You're just trying to unload a cat."

He shrugged and grinned, caught in the act—but then *he* proceeded to tell *her* lots of stuff, too.

He talked about Carissa—about how seeing her in that dress had made him realize, all in one moment, that she was growing up, and that he couldn't protect her forever. He talked about Jana and this wedding, this guy he didn't know. He told her he wasn't looking forward to seeing his dad on Saturday, even though it had been almost three years since the last time. And hell, he *almost* told her about the night his mom died. But then he shut up, because he had no idea where the hell all this was coming from anyway—he'd never dredged up so much honesty for anyone in his life. And as for his mom, he just didn't want to go there.

No, he just wanted to hold Trish's hand, their arms stretched out between the white chairs, and enjoy the night with her. At some point, she left her chair and cuddled into his lap, twining her arms around his neck and resting her head on his shoulder as he told her about the only other time he'd stayed up all night talking with somebody—old Mr. Shermer, on the night they'd made the deal on the garage.

"It was sorta like this," he said. "Late summer, pretty night, and just shootin' the breeze so easy we forgot about the time."

Before Joe knew it, a pinkish glow rimmed the horizon to the east, and it started to spread, the sky growing paler, lighter, and he said, "Look, cupcake. Sun's rising."

She peered out toward the dimly lit dawn. "I haven't seen a sunrise in forever."

"Guess it's just not a thing you do in the city," he mused.

She shook her head. "Not that I did it much in the country, either," she laughed, "but *never* in the city."

And they stayed quiet as the sky transformed, and Joe felt the newness, that passage into a fresh day, felt as if he knew what it was to sit and feel the world spin with her, like the two of them were the only people on the planet watching the morning begin.

"You're going to have a long, long day," she told him.

He nodded, somber, quiet. "It's okay."

Watching the world change into something new with her was worth it.

★   ★   ★

Carissa held out a flesh-colored dress that looked like it would hug every inch of her adolescent body. Joe narrowed his brow, shook his head no.

She tried again with something black, and so short it looked more like a top than a dress. Another head shake.

The next one sported a neckline that would probably dip to her belly button. No go.

"This is gonna take awhile, isn't it?" she asked.

"Looks that way." He sighed. "Hanging out with you was easier when you were little and I could get you to do things I *understood*, like fishing."

Next, a red dress that sparkled and looked too much like the one they were returning earned another definite head shake.

"Probably should have asked Trish to come with us," Joe said. "She'd be better at this than I am." On the drive over, Carissa had asked about the girl Joe'd been seen around with, so he'd filled her in. Not on everything, of course—just that his high school sweetheart was back in town. From there, Carissa had prodded and asked questions, but he'd kept his answers short and vague.

Even so, he must have somehow said more than he'd meant to, since Carissa abandoned the dress rack to say, "So this whole romance thing never gets any easier, huh?"

Joe tilted his head, thinking. "It must for some people. Kenny and Debbie are happy. Seems easy enough for them." But then he found himself remembering big fights they'd had from time to time, major disagreements over something to do with one of the boys or the fact that they often had a hard time making ends meet, and added, "Hell, Care Bear, it's probably something you always have to work at."

She held up an electric blue dress that made his eyes hurt and he shook his head. "How do you work at it?" she asked.

He raised his eyebrows, casting a dry look. "You're askin' *me?*"

She shoved the blue dress back on the rack with a shrug. "Somebody as old as you surely has to know *something* about it by now."

He gave her only the slightest hint of a wry grin, then summoned an answer. "All right, here's my advice. Your love life will be easier if you make sure you . . . never hurt the person you care about."

"How'd you hurt her?"

"None of your business."

Carissa's eyes widened. "Wow, you must have done something *awful.*"

If she only knew. But he sure as hell wasn't going to tell her. "Let's just say . . . if any guy does to you what I did to her, he won't live to talk about it."

He expected her to pry further, or at the very least roll her eyes at his dramatics—but instead, she stepped forward, into his arms, for a small hug.

Hell, maybe, despite his mistakes in life, he *had* done one or two things right along the way.

After scouring at least ten dress racks, he'd approved a whopping five for her to try on, but he didn't hold out much hope, and he didn't think she did, either, judging from her slightly downcast eyes. Waiting for her to change, he wondered what time it was and how many other stores in the outlet mall had fancy dresses.

That was when she stepped out of the dressing room in a sophisticated-looking, layered sort of dress that stopped just below her knees. The fabric underneath was pale pink, but the filmy black overlay turned the whole dress a warm, rosy, glowy color that reminded him of the sunrise he'd watched with Trish that morning. Black beads sprinkled the top, near her chest, which showed only a hint of cleavage, and pink ribbons served as shoulder straps. "Wow," he said.

Her eyes narrowed. "Good wow or bad wow?"

"Good wow," he said with an emphatic nod.

"Yeah?" She smiled. "'Cause I like it, too."

"You still look older, though."

She frowned. "I thought that was bad."

So had he. "But this is different. It's older in a . . . classy way. You look . . . really pretty, Care Bear."

"I was afraid you'd say it was too tight."

And yeah, in a perfect world, it would have fit her looser. But the world was far from perfect, and all things considered, she looked gorgeous and it would be a sin for her not to wear that dress. "Nah," he said. "You look too good in it for me to nitpick about that."

Peering up at him with an earnest expression, she bit her lip. "You want to hear a confession?"

"Sure."

"I love this dress *way* more than the other one. I guess I . . . *feel* kinda classy in it or something." But when she reached down to check the price tag dangling beneath her arm, her happy expression disappeared. "Holy crap."

"What?" he asked calmly.

She let out a huge sigh. "It's a hundred and forty dollars."

He gave his head a short, decisive shake. "No problem, Care Bear."

But she didn't look relieved. "That's a *lot*, Joe. I'd feel *cruddy*."

"Don't. It's a gift."

"Still . . ."

He decided to end this by changing the subject. "Want to pay me back? Tell your friends I'm giving away free kittens."

Her eyes widened in girlish delight as her mouth formed a large O. "You have kittens? Why didn't you tell me?"

"Guess I forgot." What he'd actually forgotten until this moment was that she'd had the exact same reaction the *last* time Sunshine had dropped a litter. Man, girls and kittens—what was the big attraction?

"You think Mom would let me have one at the apartment?"

He shrugged. "You'd have to ask her."

She grimaced instantly. "She'll say no. Because we're not there all day and it'll scratch stuff up."

Joe thought through it a minute, then decided he was going way too soft even as he said, "Tell you what. Maybe I'll . . . keep one at the house, but it can be yours." And it had nothing to do with Trish saying he shouldn't give away all of Sunshine's babies.

She looked like he'd just handed her a million dollars. "Really? Could I come visit?"

He rolled his eyes. "Of course you can come visit. That's the whole point. And there's a little black one that's got your name written all over it."

A huge smile took over her face. "I *love* black cats!" He knew that, of course. "I'm gonna name him Midnight!"

But then—again—she looked slightly deflated. "I still haven't exactly paid you back for the dress, though. I've just made you adopt your own cat for me instead."

He laughed softly—yet he always appreciated that she understood the value of money, so he made her an offer. "How about this? You really want to pay me back, you start stopping by the garage two or three days a week after school. I've been thinking I could use some help in the office. I could train you, you could see if you like it. Then after you've worked off the dress . . ."

She tilted her head. "I could work off everything else you've ever bought for me?"

Joe sighed. "No, dummy. I was thinking I could pay you."

Carissa blinked, and he didn't think he'd ever seen her look so stunned. "Really? So it would be like . . . a real job?"

"Sure. But only if you like doing it and your mom says it's okay."

Carissa hugged him again, and as they exchanged the old dress for the new, then climbed into Joe's truck and hit the road back to Eden, he realized that despite the exhaustion beginning to set in, it had been a pretty damn good day.

"Bride's side or groom's?" asked a bald, burly guy wearing what had to be an XXL tux. He sported three diamond studs in one earlobe.

"Bride's," Joe bit off, adding, "I'm her brother."

"Joe, right?" the big guy asked with a smile.

Trish could tell it took him by surprise. "Uh, yeah."

"Jana wants you right up front," the usher said, then seated them in the second row of white chairs situated before a picturesque gazebo twined with flowers. A pristine lake in the background came complete with two regal swans.

"Probably a bouncer at Vinnie's bar," Joe growled after the guy walked away.

Trish shrugged. "Bars need bouncers. Come on, lighten up and try to enjoy the day." She knew Joe didn't like Jana marrying this guy, but she was beginning to think he was overreacting.

The weather was lovely for a wedding—temperatures in the seventies with a soft, gentle breeze—and despite Joe's tension, things were going smoothly enough. Of course, they'd not yet spotted the bride—or the groom.

Trish hadn't had anything appropriate to wear, but rather than make the trip home, she'd stopped at The Daylily Boutique, adjacent to the diner on Main Street. She'd found a lovely pale yellow dress with rusching below the bustline—and now that they'd arrived, she thought she'd made a good choice for the setting. Joe sat with his arms balanced across his knees, fingers threaded, looking uncomfortable but still handsome in crisp khakis with a dark sports coat over a blue button-down.

Only . . . as other guests began to trickle in, Trish began to notice that not everyone seemed dressed in what she thought of as normal wedding attire. Two young women, one blonde, one redhead, both with hair that hung long and voluminous down their backs, wore low-cut halter dresses without anything remotely resembling a bra underneath. Then a couple arrived—a handsome guy sharply dressed in a black suit, black shirt, and black tie, with numerous earrings in both ears, and a woman in a frighteningly short, off-the-shoulder dress—also sans bra, noticeable mainly because her breasts were so voluminous. Her earrings dangled to her shoulders and she sported a mane of thick raven hair that draped nearly to her hips.

When other people took seats around them and Trish witnessed still more scant, often sparkly dresses and amazingly high-heeled—and also sparkly—shoes, she couldn't help turning to Joe, speaking quietly. "Is it me, or am I underdressed?"

She could tell he'd already taken in the same phenomenon. "It's not you, honey. You look beautiful."

She didn't want to judge Jana's friends harshly, but she was reasonably certain she was the only woman in attendance wearing anything that descended past midthigh. And sure, she'd worn a dress like that *recently*—to Joe's house, but that had been for *sex*. This was a *wedding*. She also couldn't help realizing the other women were all drop-dead gorgeous and seemed to possess especially large breasts. Trish squinted, turning it over in her head. What were the odds that one girl's friends would *all* be so well endowed and beautiful?

She couldn't help being aware of too much perfume scenting the air as her eyes dropped to the monster platform heels—silver and glittery—on the woman who'd just sat down next to her. She had great legs—shapely and tan. Trish knew because the woman's hot pink dress rose right to the top of them. Yeesh.

She was still trying to piece it all together when Joe said softly, voice strained, "I think we're at a stripper wedding."

Trish gasped, albeit more in shock than doubt. "You're kidding!" Okay, so maybe he hadn't been overreacting.

Joe's mouth pressed into a flat, grim line. "Nope, I think my sister's a stripper. And all of her friends are strippers. And I think Vinnie's in the mob, and that all these guys dressed in black break people's fingers if they go bad on a debt. That's what I think."

Trish tried to scan the area again without being too obvious, and without letting her jaw drop. A stripper wedding? Really?

Beside her, Joe released a heavy breath, looking angry. "I've had suspicions about Vinnie's bar and what exactly Jana does there, but I didn't ask . . . because I didn't want to know. But don't these people look like strippers and mobsters to you?"

She pursed her lips, wishing she could argue the point, for Joe's sake, but she couldn't. "Well, um . . . yeah."

Just then, an Italian-looking guy appeared near the gazebo

to start greeting people. His thin hair was pulled into a low ponytail and he sported a small silver hoop in one earlobe. If he weren't smiling, he would have looked scary.

"Could that be . . ." Trish began, but she trailed off as a large shadow fell over them. Glancing up to see the bald bouncer/usher back at their side, she nearly flinched, wondering if he really broke people's bones.

"Joe," he said, leaning over. "There's a little problem. It's past time to start, but your dad hasn't shown up."

"Bastard," Joe muttered, eyes darkening, and Trish felt just a hint of what that sort of abandonment must be like. And to think Joe had been carrying the burden since he was eighteen.

"Jana wants to know if you'll give her away."

Joe pushed to his feet without hesitation, looking instantly like he'd mow down anyone who tried to hurt his sister. "Hell— of course I will." He squeezed Trish's hand in parting, then followed the big usher down the grassy aisle.

When Joe made his way into the little white tent erected behind the chairs, his sister leapt up from a small dressing table and ran toward him. His first thought—she looked beautiful in her strapless white wedding gown, even with the blond hair. His second—she also looked like she was about to burst into tears.

"He didn't come, Joe! He didn't come." She threw her arms around his neck and he hugged her to him, wishing what he'd always wished from the time she was a little girl—that he could somehow hug her pain away.

"You know he's an asshole, honey, so forget about him. *I'm* here. *I'll* walk you down the aisle."

Jana pulled back to look him in the eye. "I should have asked you in the first place. I'm sorry I didn't, Joe. I was just . . . afraid you wouldn't."

Hell. Maybe, if she'd put forth that request a week ago, he *would* have turned her down. But now he just wanted to make his sister happy. He lifted a hand to her cheek. "Of course I'll do it. Now let's get going before people think there's something wrong."

She nodded. "You're right. I want this to be perfect."

And that's when it hit him. God, no wonder she wanted to get married. She wanted some *security* in her life; she probably wanted a *normal family*. And Joe had no idea if Vinnie Balducci could give her either of those things, but for today, he had to believe the guy would.

Soft guitar music began to play as Jana looped her arm through his and they stepped from the tent out into the bright sunlight. Walking his sister up the aisle between a hundred strippers and mob guys felt a little surreal, but Joe had bigger things to concentrate on—like making sure Jana stayed balanced in her ridiculously high heels in the grass. She clutched tighter at Joe when the crowd turned to watch her make her way toward her husband-to-be, and he instinctively covered her hand with his.

At the foot of the gazebo stood the guy with the ponytail he and Trish had seen a few minutes earlier—and Jana beamed at the sight of him. Three more guys—who looked a lot like the groom—stood next to him, all in black. That's when Joe noticed the bridesmaids, revealing dresses and all, who he figured performed at seven, nine, and eleven nightly.

When the justice of the peace—who looked like he might also be a bouncer—asked who gave this woman, Joe said, "I do," then kissed his sister on the cheek.

The way she smiled at him tightened his chest and made

him damn glad he'd been there for her. Hell, no matter what she chose to do with her life, he knew he *would* be. He just *would* be.

Of course, as he sat back down beside Trish, his mind reeled. The stripper thing was still a blow. Sure, he'd sown some wild oats in his day, but there were some things he was real old-fashioned about, and one of them was that his *sister* should not *take her clothes off and dance naked for strange men*. But he couldn't think about that now.

No, right now, he had to watch the union to which he'd just given his blessing take place, whether he liked it or not. And a few minutes later, as Vinnie Balducci gave his sister a way-too-long kiss, the kind Joe reserved strictly for the bedroom or the Cobra or someplace where he was getting ready to have sex, Trish said, "You know, they look really happy."

"I guess," he said stiffly.

"Maybe he really loves her—maybe they're going to have a great life together. And . . ." She paused to study the crowd, who was now cheering and applauding at the kiss. "Their friends all seem really happy *for* them. So maybe this will all be okay, Joe." She squeezed his hand and he thought—*Oh shit, I'm crazy about this woman*. But that was one more issue he couldn't deal with right now.

Next thing Joe knew, they were standing in a line, waiting to greet the bride and groom. When he finally reached his sister, Jana threw her arms around him again. "This is Vinnie," she said at the end of the embrace, still gripping Joe by the wrist as she drew him closer to her new husband. "Vinnie, this is my big brother, Joe."

Joe knew he sounded too brusque when he said, "Nice to *finally* meet you."

Vinnie took his hand in a firm handshake and Joe liked realizing he had several inches on the guy. "Joe, my girl here talks
about you all the time. I'm sorry we haven't met before now."

Joe narrowed his gaze. "Well, I'd hoped to on the day you guys
brought my car over."

Vinnie nodded in reply. "That was my fault. I was having a
bad day, some business problems, and I didn't want to meet you
when I was in a sour mood. I'm sure you understand."

*Not really.* But Joe held his tongue, so Vinnie went on.

"I hope we can get to know each other *now*. I know Jana would
like nothing more."

Joe didn't respond to that, but before letting go of Vinnie's
hand, he leaned in closer, met Vinnie's dark eyes, and said, "Take
care of my sister. Make her happy."

Vinnie didn't pull his gaze away, didn't look bothered or
threatened at all, which kind of disappointed Joe. But he also
didn't look angry. Instead, he just said, "You've got my word."

"Good."

So he'd come to the wedding he'd dreaded, and he'd taken
care of his little sister one more time—either that or he'd given
her to a thug. The only thing left to see now, he supposed, was
just how good Vinnie Balducci's word was.

"Listen—a whippoorwill." Darkness had long since fallen and
Joe sat with Trish on her parents' screened-in porch. They'd
left the wedding reception right after the cutting of the cake—
he hadn't been able to stand it any longer—then driven back
here, grabbing dinner on the way and arriving just in time to
say goodnight to Mr. and Mrs. Henderson as they were heading
up to bed. Strange how comfortable he was with them again
so quickly, now that he'd made peace with Trish's dad. Strange

how much better he felt walking into this house than his own sister's wedding.

Trish smiled up at him as the whippoorwill called again. "I haven't heard one of those in a very long time."

"Stick with me, babe," he said, "and I'll keep you in whippoorwills."

She laughed softly and he tightened his arm around her.

Then lowered his voice. "And by the way, thank you."

She lifted her head from his shoulder to look up. "For what?"

"Going with me today. It was a nightmare. But less of a nightmare with you."

She gave him a teasing smile. "I'd have thought it was a dream come true. How often do you find that many scantily clad women with fake boobs in one place?"

He grinned—and held in the reply that came to mind. *Who needs scantily clad women when I have you?*

And instead of asking him what was wrong or why he was looking at her so strangely, she simply reached both hands up to his face and kissed him. Nothing heated, just a soft, chaste, sweet kiss—and he wondered if she could feel the weird pain running through him right now.

And the strangest part was—he suddenly wanted to tell her. He didn't know why. Hell, just two nights ago, he'd worried what she'd think if she knew. But Jana's wedding, along with wondering if the path she'd taken had been his fault, had some old, hard memories bubbling to the surface. Trish's return to his life had brought them back, but Jana's wedding was bringing them *out*. "I need to tell you," he heard himself say.

She looked up. "What?" He supposed he'd sounded abrupt, maybe a little reckless.

"I need to tell you," he said, softer this time, "about the night my mom died."

Her eyes went round and sad, and even in the dim lighting he could see her heart welling in them. "Oh, Joe. When it happened, I knew . . . I knew I should have been there for you. I cried and cried, so sad for you, and feeling like I should have been at your side. I'm sorry. That I wasn't."

He blinked, amazed. He'd never even thought about what she might have felt when she heard about it—hell, he'd been pretty wrapped up in his own troubles at the time. "You don't have to be sorry, Trishy. We'd been over almost a year by then. And the truth is . . ."

He heard her swallow. Felt the heavy knot growing in his own throat, too.

But he had to get these words out. Just had to *tell* her, tell *somebody*. "The truth is, I didn't deserve sympathy. Because it was my fault."

"What?" Shock reshaped her pretty face, but it still stung because he knew he was about to shock her in a much worse way.

He stared out into the darkness, remembering that night over a dozen years ago—but sometimes it felt like yesterday. He'd spent a damn lot of time wishing he could take it back, make things like they were before, bring his mother back to life. Crazy, but some mornings he'd wake up half-forgetting that she was gone, dead—and even after he'd remember, he'd lay in bed pretending it wasn't true, pretending she was out in the kitchen making coffee, stuffing bread in the toaster, about to yell through the house that they'd all better get up if they were gonna get to work and school on time.

"On the night she died," he began low, still peering out

through the screen into the blackness of the backyard, "she and my dad had a fight, a bad one. They fought a lot, especially if they drank too much."

Trish's voice was barely audible above the songs of crickets wafting in. "What were they fighting about?"

He gave a short, cynical laugh. "Who knows—could have been anything. Money. Me or Jana. Anything. You probably never really knew . . . how much my mom drank."

She blinked, clearly taken aback. "No. I guess not."

He choked back his pain. "I guess she kept it kind of hidden, but some mornings I'd find her asleep on the couch with a glass or a can still in her hand. Not every morning—just . . . pretty often. And on the weekends, she and dad would both drink all day. It wasn't until I started spending time at other people's houses, like yours, and Kenny's, that I started realizing not everybody drank that much.

"Anyway, she was drunk—both of them were. And screaming their damn heads off when I came home that night. It was a Saturday in June—hot as hell, and no AC back then, so I remember walking in to find them both dripping with sweat, yelling at each other. Jana was barricaded in her room. I was about to go barricade myself in mine—and remind myself that I needed to save enough money to move out so I didn't have to listen to it anymore.

"Then Mom started screaming that she was leaving, that she wasn't putting up with his shit. She started for her car keys, but I picked them up first."

He stopped then, sighed. God, remembering it made him weary.

"So suddenly I was in their argument. She was screaming at me, wrestling me for the keys, telling me I had no right to take them, asking me who I thought I was, threatening to throw me out of the house, you name it. And Dad—hell, he didn't do much of *anything*. He just stood back and let her take her wrath out on me."

"God, Joe." Trish touched his thigh. "It sounds awful."

But she didn't know the half of it yet. And the hard part was coming. "So . . . I told her she was too damn drunk to drive. I called her an alcoholic. And she slapped me. Hard.

"My mom had never hit me before. With my dad, it was different—he'd taken the belt to me when I was a kid and got in trouble. He'd never had a problem shoving me around if he thought I'd done something wrong. But with my mom—I never saw it coming."

He felt almost out of breath, but knew he had to keep going now. "So she slapped me and yelled that I'd better give her the damn keys. And I was so mad that I said, 'Fine, you want to go out and kill yourself, do it,' and I threw the keys at her and went in my room and slammed the door." It was difficult to talk now—his throat had started closing up. "And that's exactly what she did. She got in her car, drove up the road, missed the turn by Pollard's barn, and hit that big oak tree on the curve."

"Oh, Joe."

He heard Trish's voice—but it sounded distant somehow, as if he were in a bubble by himself. He pushed back the huge lump blocking his airway and blinked to keep any wetness from leaking from his eyes. "She wasn't perfect, but she was my mom, and I loved her. And I let her get behind the wheel of a car when I knew she was drunk. It was like . . . I killed her myself."

"No, Joe," Trish said, her voice sharper now, cutting through the fog surrounding him. "You were a kid, and she put you in an awful position—and she *hit* you, for heaven's sake."

He pulled his gaze from the darkness finally, meeting Trish's. "But I still didn't have to give her the damn keys."

"You just reacted, that's all. It was a horrible situation, and you wanted out of it, and that makes sense. It's not your fault she drank, or was angry, or drove. If you hadn't been there, the same thing would have happened."

His chest hollowed and he felt eighteen all over again. "My dad said if I hadn't been standing between them, *he* would have gotten the keys first, and he wouldn't have given them to her for anything."

Trish's eyes widened, her face painted with something like horror. "Your father blamed you?"

Joe tried to explain, but his mouth felt weird, numb. "He never told anybody else about it. But when I said it was my fault, he said it would've been different if I hadn't come home when I did, or if I'd just stayed out of it."

Trish feared her heart would burst in her chest. In that moment, she hated Joe's father with everything inside her. And she hated that Joe had been put in that hideous position and had been carrying this weight around with him, blaming himself for something that wasn't his fault.

She considered trying to absolve him some more, to make him understand, but she feared he wouldn't be able to hear, to absorb her words, right now. Still, she desperately needed to comfort him. "I don't want you to hurt anymore," she said softly, then lifted her hands back to his stubbled cheeks and kissed him again—but deeper this time, because she had to take him far away from those memories, to someplace much better.

Below the occasional call of the whippoorwill, the low trill of crickets still emanated from the shadowy trees beyond the yard. Even from the enclosed porch, she could see stars twinkling above the treeline amid a darkness so thick and velvety she'd forgotten it could exist. The rich, fecund scent of earth and grass and pure summer night filled her senses. And Joe filled her senses, too.

Ending the kiss, she drew back to look at him, take him in completely—the dark beauty of the man he was, with all his hurts, all his regrets, all his brusqueness and anger and gentleness and sweetness, everything.

When *he* leaned slowly forward to kiss *her*, only their tongues met—somehow tentative yet utterly sensual. But then his mouth closed back over hers, warm and exciting and as new as if it were the very first kiss they'd shared since high school, and she sank into it completely. She might not be willing to surrender her heart to him—but she seemed to have no control over her body when he touched her.

His breath grew labored as their kisses deepened, and she soon found herself trembling in his arms. *Because* it felt new. But it also felt old, ancient—primal.

"Need you, baby," he murmured against her neck, his hand rising to the side of her breast to mold and caress—and before she knew it, the intensity of the moment gave way to baser instincts, hard raw needs, and all trembling disappeared as he pulled her over to straddle his hips on the couch. They moved together in that rhythm as old as time itself, and she bit her lip and peered deep into his eyes as she undulated against that sinfully hard part of him in tight, hot circles.

"God, you're beautiful," he whispered, sliding both hands tenderly to her breasts, his thumbs stroking over the nipples, hot, sensual. She'd been unaware that her breasts were aching for his touch, but now she knew they had because it felt so good.

She sighed, whimpered—so ready for more that she could taste it. Still . . . "We can't do this here," she reminded him.

"I know," he agreed. "But it's your own fault for kissing me like that." God, his voice was sexy.

"I couldn't help it," she breathed.

"And *I* can't help *this.*" With that, he pulled her close, leaned in, and gently bit at the crest of one breast.

Shivers of pleasure rippled through her as a ragged moan escaped her lips, but she had to get hold of herself here. "My parents are upstairs. We can't let things get out of hand like the last time we were out here."

He released a low groan, then whispered throatily, "Let's go outside."

She pulled back slightly. "What?"

His eyes reprimanded her, his voice coming on labored breath. "Don't look at me like I just suggested we do it in the middle of Main Street. If we take a blanket way out in the yard, by the woods, nobody'll hear." When she hesitated, he added, "The only other choice is to stop." Then he nipped at her other breast, which had just grown more sensitive than ever in her life. "And you don't want to stop, do you, cupcake?" He looked positively wicked, determined.

Trish glanced down between them, at the way she straddled him so lustily. No way could she say no—the need burned too hot, the pulsing between her thighs echoed too urgent. She was lucky she'd managed to resist letting him rip her clothes off right there on the porch, parents or no parents.

But—oh God, she wanted him just as much with her heart as she did with her body. Because he'd just bared his soul to her. Because she was leaving soon and who knew how many more nights they'd have like this. And because—yes, *she loved him.* She still couldn't *tell* him—but in that moment, she knew she loved him with every fiber of her being.

She didn't say a word, simply climbed off him and reached into a wicker trunk to draw out an old quilt her family had always used for picnics. Then she took his hand and led him out the door, making sure not to let it bang, and she let the splendor of the night, and him, fill her as they strode hand in hand through the big yard toward the woods.

A certain tension built between them as they walked in silence. Anticipation, heat—but more than that. Something deeper that had no name.

As they ducked under the canopy of the trees, Joe stopped and turned to face her. Even in the lush darkness, she could sense the weight in his expression. "Trish, I . . ."

Her veins surged with emotion. "What?"

He hesitated, his voice wrenched. "I just want you so damn much."

They didn't take another step. He pulled her close and she arched her neck for his tender kisses. His hands roamed her body with a sweet, thorough slowness that buried all thought or decision and left only sensation. When his touch finally came to rest on her breasts, their mouths met in a series of hot, hungry kisses that—like all else between them at the moment—soon slowed into something softer, sweeter.

Wordlessly, they peeled off each other's clothes, letting them drop on the forest floor. Joe spread the blanket on a bed of wild ivy, then gently pulled Trish down with him until they lay side by side, touching each other and drowning in each other's gaze. Moonglow sifted between the heavy branches and thick leaves to spread a kaleidoscope of light across their bare skin.

When she could wait no longer to soothe the ache between

her legs, she reached for him and drew him into a long tongue kiss that culminated in her climbing on top of him and lowering herself warmly onto his erection. "Oh," she breathed as he filled her. She moved on him—more of that lovely, timeless rhythm—but so much deeper now that their bodies were connected. She whispered his name. "Joe. Oh, Joe." She loved him. So, so much. How could she possibly be planning to leave him? In that moment, it seemed crazy.

"Come for me," he whispered up to her. "I want to watch you come."

A breeze rustled leaves and cooled her hot skin, tightening her already beaded nipples as she continued to rock on him in heated gyrations.

"Come for me," he said again. Lower, huskier this time.

She moved harder against him and sensed it building, the glorious release.

"Oh *baby*," he groaned, almost as if he could feel how close she was getting.

And then it happened, like a sweet explosion, her body shattering into pieces, each of them filling with so much pleasure that they were forced to split again and again, like a tiny atom bomb going off inside her.

She clung to him when it was done, clung to him like maybe he was the one safe, dependable, loving part of a world gone mad. And maybe he was. Maybe her world *was* mad. Was it mad to live in a big city when you loved the country? Was it mad to feel compelled to climb the ladder in a job where you doubted those you worked to save? Was it mad to run away from the one man who made you feel brand new every single time he made love to you, to run away from the one man whose touch made your skin seem to breathe with energy and life? Oh God, maybe it *was* pure madness, but she couldn't dig through it all right now. She could only clutch at him like a lifeline as he held her tight and whispered in her ear.

"I want to be on top of you," he said. Just like before, that first night, on his couch. She'd been the crazy, wild seductress—and yet even then, somehow he'd managed to control her because that's how much of herself she surrendered to him when they got this close.

Wordlessly, they rolled together, their bodies still as one. And then he moved inside her—each stroke slow and deep, so slow that she could feel every bit of friction as he slid in, then back out. And again . . . and again. They writhed together naked on the ground, their movements like slow motion, coming with an intimacy that somehow surpassed any hot, frantic mating they'd shared before. His tenderness astonished her as he whispered, "I love you, Trish."

Every muscle in her body tightened. He'd said the words a million times when they were young, but this was . . . a hell of a lot different. Her lips began to tremble, her whole being suffering a thousand beautiful, stunning, tingling sensations as the words filtered through her.

She wrapped her arms around his neck and drew him down until their bodies crushed flat together and she absorbed his warmth from head to toe. She could feel his breath on her neck. And she could hear the pain in his voice when he said, low but firm in her ear, "Forgive me, Trish."

She pulled in her breath. Said nothing. Just felt the plea melt into her.

"Please," he whispered. "You have to forgive me. I *need* you to forgive me. Finally."

Oh God. They'd shared so much the last few weeks. Been so

close. He'd bared his soul to her, told her his secrets. She'd tried to do the same, as much as her heart would allow. And she'd fallen in love with him again—or maybe she'd never fallen out of it. But either way, she loved him, too. Her heart was as full with him as her body. And maybe it was only her head—her damned, logical, analytical, frightened head—that had held her back from this moment. Because she knew now that, deep inside, she'd already done what he asked. She'd already forgiven.

"I do, Joe. I forgive you. I promise."

He let out a heavy breath and seemed to sink deeper onto her. She felt his relief echo through her, felt a measure of tension leave him which she hadn't even realized had been lingering there all this time.

"And I'm sorry," she said. "Sorry it took me this long. Maybe in the beginning . . . I *was* trying to hurt you back, somehow— I'm not sure. I thought I was so mature, so grown-up, yet maybe I was just lying to myself. But I don't want to hurt you anymore, Joe. I want to love you."

"Aw, God," Joe said, and Trish let a whimper leak from her lips. She began to move harder beneath him, wanting to feel him inside her more forcefully, maybe wanting to make sure that this was all real, that *he* was real, that his words were real, that none of it was a dream.

"Oh my God, baby," he moaned, and then he thrust inside her with all the power she needed from him, and together they cried out softly as he emptied himself there. And the knowledge of it—of him leaving something from his body in hers—somehow made her whole.

They lay together after for a long moment, bodies still joined, not moving. It felt strangely as if the world had stopped spinning, as if only the two of them existed in their private hideaway in the trees. Trish became aware again of the pungent smell of earth beneath them, all around them. And she felt as connected to this place as she did to him.

"Stay," he said.

She sucked in her breath—hard. "What?"

Gently, he rolled off her, his hand splaying large and warm across her bare stomach. "Stay here with me, Trishy. Don't go back to your old life. Make a new one, here. With me. I know it's a hell of a big thing I'm asking—but I'm asking. Stay."

**Verdict:** the judgment of a jury or judge that determines the guilt or innocence of a criminal defendant; _or_ a decision.

# Thirteen

Trish let out a deep, trembling breath. She barely knew how to answer, and she certainly hadn't seen this coming. "Oh, Joe," she murmured. "I don't know."

"You still doubt me," he said.

"It's not that. It's not. It's just . . . everything. My job, my life. It would be a lot to give up. And you and me—isn't this . . . kind of quick?"

He looked almost dumbfounded by the question. "Quick? No, honey, I think fourteen years is more than enough time to lose. And if I thought you wouldn't be happy here, I wouldn't ask—hell, I'd follow you to Indy. But I see you here, with your parents, and fixing up the diner, and . . . you _fit_ here, cupcake. You _have_ to know that. You fit here. With me."

Trish swallowed hard—at a memory. She didn't want to still

be feeling this, but since she was, she figured she may as well put it out there. "Joe, I do forgive you, I meant that. But . . ."

He leaned over, peered down into her eyes. "But what? Tell me."

She pushed him up so that she could sit upright, too. She pulled her knees to her chest. She didn't feel the fact that they were naked—it had quickly grown natural, easy, to be that way with Joe—but she felt the hard truth bubbling up inside her. "Remember when I said you should have come after me?"

"Of course."

Damn, it had been a heavy night—and she wasn't really up for more, but he'd opened this can of worms, so now she was going to spill them all out. "I still *feel* that you didn't. To hear you say you love me just now was . . . incredible. But I have no idea how much faith to place in that love, how deep to believe it runs. And I don't know how I could leave my whole life behind for something that—amazing as it's been—feels . . . uncertain to me."

"Trishy, what I just told you on the porch before . . . about my mom?"

"Yeah?"

He gently shook his head. "Nobody knows that. Not Kenny. Not Jana. Nobody. Because I never had the courage to tell them. Because I was so ashamed. But I wanted you to know, *needed* you to know . . . because I love you. And because I . . . didn't want anything, any secret, standing between us.

"I was scared as hell to tell you. I was sure you'd see me the way . . . well, the way a lot of this town always used to see my family. But I still *needed* to tell you. I needed you to know *all* of me, the good parts *and* the bad.

"And you . . . somehow you made it okay. I mean . . ." He shook his head. "It'll *never* be *okay*, but . . . maybe I should have known you'd make me feel better about it." He sighed, looked her in the eye. "Because you *always* made me feel good about myself—in a way nobody else ever did."

He stopped, pulled his knees up, too, and bent over. "Hell, Trish. I don't know how else to say this. The last time I tried to let a girl know how much I cared for her, she was . . . you. I haven't had a lot of practice. I just know I'm happy when I'm with you, and I think you're happy with *me*. So I'm just asking you to think about it. Just think about it. That's all I can do."

Trish listened to the crickets, felt the thick night sounds. Then slowly, softly, told him her own truth. "I'd been trying to figure out how to tell you I was leaving. Probably in a few days. The diner's almost finished, and I'm planning to call Lois Faulkner on Monday to get it back on the market. And I have cases to work on, people who are depending on me—you remember, the Richie Melbourne case, the college kid accused of rape." Her voice went softer then, without planning. "I didn't want to tell you, because I'm going to miss this, miss *us* . . . but I have to go. Surely you know that. I mean, it's not like you could just walk away from the garage tomorrow if the situation was reversed."

"But I would." He said it without hesitation, like it was easy. "If I thought you were really, truly happy in Indy and you asked me to come there, to be with you, I'd sell the garage."

She blinked, amazed. "Really?"

"Trish, I messed up our lives a long time ago. If you gave me a second chance to be with you, I mean *really be* with you, *forever*, I wouldn't mess up again."

The sureness in his voice left her speechless. Numb. But also torn inside, even if she didn't want to admit it to herself. She'd not wanted to admit, the whole time she'd been home, that she still loved him. And now she didn't want to admit that staying here with him, in this world where they'd *first* fallen in love, sounded . . . good.

"I can only promise . . . to think about it." Yeesh. She couldn't believe she was saying even *that*. Or that she *meant* it.

But she did. She hadn't considered it until this very moment—and yet now, suddenly, it almost seemed within the realm of possibility.

"Thank you." He eased his arms around her, pulling her close.

Her whole body tingled with the scope of their conversation. "I can't believe this—it feels surreal to me."

"What?" he said on a short laugh, suddenly seeming happier than he had in a while. "The idea of staying with me? Or that we're sitting in the woods stark naked like it's normal?"

She smiled. "Both."

"I *love* you naked, honey," he said, his voice gone leathery and hot.

She found herself running her hand up his thigh and thinking about what lay mere inches higher. "I like you naked, too."

"But don't let that make you think I got enough of you in your naughty little lingerie. I've been thinking about that. Thinking you looked goddamn phenomenal in it, and that I wouldn't mind another chance to take it off you again—more slowly this time."

Another chance. For lingerie. For love. One so playful, one so serious. Still, they coincided perfectly. And at least in that moment, Trish's doubts—so deep-rooted and long-standing—finally began to melt away. She was supposed to be with him. She'd known it with certainty at seventeen. And it had taken her a hell of a long time to accept that she'd been wrong about that. Maybe she hadn't been.

And yet, she had to be smart here. Smart and safe. Well, as safe as she *could* be. She locked those words in her mind and tried to focus on them—*smart and safe, smart and safe*—even as she suddenly became aware that, like almost everything else about the person she'd grown into over the years, it was just one more defense mechanism, one more routine designed to keep anyone from hurting her.

So, for just this moment, she allowed herself to abandon *smart*, abandon *safe*, and just go for *sexy.* "Well, maybe if you're a good boy . . . you'll get that chance."

"Mmm," he growled, sounding pretty sexy himself. "I think I'm sensing a little of that biker chick in you, cupcake. I sure would like her to come out and play."

The crux of her thighs rippled softly and she flashed her naughtiest smile—something she'd never even possessed before Joe had come back into her life. "Like I said, if you're a good boy . . ."

"You'll be a *bad* girl?"

"Something like that. But . . ."

"But what?"

*But the time for dirty talk is over and the time to come back to reality is now.* Because one minute of lingerie chat hadn't quite made her forget the much more serious words they'd just exchanged. "But I think we should get dressed and you should go home," she said quietly. "I need to think."

Joe nodded, then wasted no time passing her panties and reaching for his briefs. "Take all the time you need, cupcake."

Trish felt darn proud of herself for backing away like this, putting some distance between them, instead of simply throwing herself wildly into his arms and professing her undying love. Even so, as she slipped on her underwear, she watched him in silence, drinking in the beauty of his body in shadow, and as she eased back into her dress, she couldn't help feeling a bit sad that their tryst in the woods was coming to a close.

A minute later, Joe gathered the quilt in one arm and, with his other hand, reached for hers. Their fingers laced as he led her quietly from the trees and up through the big yard, finally stopping at the back door. "I was wrong," he told her, leaning his forehead against hers. "I thought if we went outside and had sex, it would make it easier for me to go home without you. But I still don't want to."

She tried to smile, yet the emotions between them right now simply ran too deep. All smart and safe tactics aside, she didn't want him to go, either. She lifted one hand to his cheek, felt the stubble bristle against her palm. "I know. But we'll . . . talk soon. And you know . . . well, you know you'll be on my mind. A lot." *Every second. I want to kiss you from head to toe right now. I want to wrap myself up in you.*

She caught her breath, wondered if her skin was flushed.

But then she realized there was one more thing she needed to say—something dreadfully important. "What you told me about your mom, Joe—please, please know you aren't responsible."

He looked down toward their feet, then raised his gaze back to hers. "One of the hardest things is . . . that's my last memory of her. That we were screaming at each other. That she hit me and I threw those damn keys at her."

Seeing that pain etched into his handsome face, Trish still wanted desperately to fix it, at least ease it somehow. "I hope you have more *good* memories of her than bad ones. I hope you can focus on *those.*"

He glanced toward the ground again, but a hint of a smile re-shaped his face. "Do you remember the time she got the bright idea to make M&M pancakes?"

Trish laughed. "God, yes. What a mess." They'd discovered that M&Ms and hot griddles didn't mix.

"That's the kind of stuff I try to remember," he told her, but then grew solemn once more.

"She loved you. You know that."

Joe looked into her eyes, and she was struck, as she was so often, by the way they penetrated her every defense. "And *I* love *you*, Trish," he whispered. Then kissed her on the forehead and disappeared into the darkness.

A short while later, she turned back the covers and lay down. Time felt strange—slowed, her movements mechanical. So much hinged on the coming hours, days, weeks. She knew she had to go home—to Indianapolis—there was no getting around that. But the question now was—would she stay there? Or would she change her life radically, irreversibly, and come back here to her hometown, to her family and friends, to Joe?

As she lay looking up through the leafy branches of the oak tree just outside her window, she found herself searching out the moon. It was difficult, but she finally caught sight of it and was surprised to be reminded how bright it shone when it managed to weave its beam through the thick leaves and heavy limbs. It made her think of all the muck she'd had to look through to really see Joe, and how tonight she'd seen so much more of him than ever before—the heart-and-soul part.

She closed her eyes, remembering all the other nights she'd lain in this bed thinking of him. In the past, it had been girlish passion and excitement over what to wear on their next date.

They had already promised to marry each other then, yet this somehow seemed much more serious. He was asking her to stay. To give up the life she'd built on her own and stay here to be near him.

It was scary how much that appealed to her—in so many ways.

The fact was, she would love being close to her parents. She could eat her mom's home-cooked meals. She could help her dad with farm work, and she knew Joe would, too. She could . . . simply be a bigger part of their lives.

And then there was the diner. Which, frankly, just *wasn't* a diner anymore. She'd felt some separation anxiety coming on the longer she'd worked on it, and once or twice she'd even found herself imagining if she kept it, ran it. She knew exactly how she'd do it, too. It would become Trish's Tea Room and Café. Mornings would feature muffins and danishes and coffees. Lunches would be deli sandwiches on specialty breads, and salads made to order. A wide menu of teas and coffees would be served all day, with an easel out front featuring the day's special in colored chalk. She'd close early on weekdays, like the rest of Main Street, but weekends drew more people through town, so she'd stay open as warranted then, especially in the summer. When she imagined someone else running the place now, it seemed like, well . . . sort of like giving birth to a child only to let someone else love and raise it.

And maybe she could still use her legal expertise, too—in small ways, working out of the back office privately, taking on cases like Marjorie and Jeremiah's.

Oddly, she thought it was . . . exactly the existence she might have had—minus the law work—if life had gone as planned, if she'd come home from college and married Joe. And maybe that should sound disappointing on some level, like a step backward, but it didn't. As proud as she was of her achievements, was there something . . . wooden about it all? Perfunctory? Had she gone through the motions of law school and building her name as a defense attorney *only* because she'd been running away from everything that hurt, every plan that had gone awry, to become someone completely new? Someone who *couldn't* be hurt? Someone who built walls around herself? Maybe her whole adult life had just been about building walls, making sure no one ever hurt her again.

She'd never planned on a law degree; she'd had an eye more toward retail and marketing. But somehow she'd drifted right into law school after running away from Eden. She supposed after what had happened with Joe that she'd just been unable to see herself coming back here, being that same small-town girl. She'd needed to reinvent herself—make herself into a city person, a career woman, someone who didn't need a man, didn't need a home, didn't need anyone to lean on.

She recalled the words that had almost slipped out when she'd been explaining her job to Joe that night at the Burger Barn, when she'd been telling him it was only about winning, about being competitive, that she didn't care about anyone's guilt or innocence. She'd nearly said, *Being a lawyer keeps my head and heart separate.* She'd stopped herself, though, because the truth in it had struck her.

Maybe that was why she'd turned to law, because it was so cut-and-dried, because maybe that had helped her not feel things quite so much as she had as a girl.

Only . . . since she'd come home, she'd started feeling things again. And maybe, just maybe, that was okay.

And to think Joe had said he would leave Eden and come

with her to Indianapolis if that was what she wanted! It had floored her. But it had also instantly felt so wrong—she would never take Joe away from fresh air and open roads. She would never take Joe away from the business he'd built and was such a part of. The moment she'd seen him in the garage bent over that fancy car, she'd understood he was part of the fiber of the place, as integral to it as the tools or the lifts or the building itself.

It wasn't that way with her and Tate, Blanchard & Rowe. She worked hard, she did a good job, she was a valued member of the team. But even if she made partner—well, it wasn't the same. It just wasn't part of her soul.

She hugged a pillow to her chest, aware she was on the verge of making the biggest decision of her life. *Please, God, help me make the right choice.* She didn't pray much—her life in the city kept her too busy and on edge to remember even the occasional silent plea for help. But here, it was easier. *Everything* was easier.

On Sunday morning, Trish went to church with her parents— for the first time since high school. Partially, it was an appeal to God—to forgive her for not going to church forever, and to remind Him she was in need of His help at the moment. She sat in the pew, praying silently. *I know, God, I know, it's been way too long and I wouldn't blame you if you struck me down with a bolt of lightning or sent a pox upon me or something. But I've mostly been a good person all this time, and now I'm trying to figure out the best way to live the rest of my life. And yeah, I know I've been having a crazy amount of sex with Joe out of wedlock, but . . . does it help that I love him? And that I probably always have? I'm hoping that earns me some points, since I really need some guidance right now. I'd be giving up a lot to come home. But I'd be gaining a lot, too. So . . . if you could just send me a sign or something, that would be great. And I promise I'll try to get back here before another fourteen years go by.*

Okay, so she was rusty on praying. But at least she was trying.

She'd also gone to church because she knew it would please her mother. And it had.

What she *hadn't* expected were all the people from her past—older now, of course—who wanted to give her hugs and say they'd missed her and how wonderful it was to see her. Old Mrs. Whitaker from her Sunday school days, Mr. and Mrs. Greenwell from up the road, Reverend Harris and his daughter, Melissa—whom Trish used to babysit on occasion, but she was all grown up now. The greetings truly warmed her heart and reminded her how much she missed the sense of community a small town provided.

After church, she took her parents to the diner. She wasn't exactly looking forward to it, but the time had come to unveil her work. She spent the drive preparing them for the changes, explaining her views on shifts in the area's consumer base and what would work best with the other businesses currently residing on Main Street. But when the three of them stepped inside, the bell above the door tinkling, her mom and dad still couldn't hide their shock.

"Well, I'll be horn-swoggled," her dad said. Since she'd never heard him be horn-swoggled in her whole life, Trish knew he was stunned.

"This is . . . different." Her mother looked like she might faint.

Despite herself, Trish's stomach churned with defensiveness. "It's *supposed* to be different. More modern. More of a café or coffeehouse. Don't get me wrong—I loved the old diner. But the current vibe in the area calls for something updated—a friendly, funky place you can pop into for a quick drink or snack or sandwich."

"Funky," her father repeated numbly. Another word she'd never heard him use.

"I really think this will work," she went on—without adding that the changes would garner a quicker sale, since at the moment, she wondered if *she* might be the buyer. She didn't want to tell them yet and get their hopes up. So she changed the subject instead.

The only real remaining fixture from the diner was the old jukebox. "I think you guys should take that home," Trish told them, pointing at it, "find a place for it, and think of it like a souvenir from all the years you ran this place."

Her parents exchanged looks and she suspected they liked the idea—better than they seemed to like her alterations. "Guess we could find a spot for it," her dad said.

"There's that alcove off the dining room. We've been meaning to get rid of that old table there," her mom chimed in.

Then her dad smiled. "We could listen to Hank Williams and George Jones while we eat."

And suddenly, her parents seemed at peace with the changes—Trish supposed it had just taken a few minutes to sink in. Or that taking home the jukebox somehow provided the closure they needed to let the diner go.

After driving them home and eating a Sunday dinner of pork chops, baked beans, and cornbread, Trish changed into shorts to head back to . . . the *café*—no longer the diner. Of course, there wasn't much left to do—the whole place was painted from top to bottom, the booths were back in place, and tables now dotted the previously wasted floor space. Bold new curtains draped the windows and the old gold paint had been chipped off the glass. The counter, display case, and kitchen were spotless, and the old menu boards had been taken down, the bare place on the wall just waiting for a new one.

So she supposed she'd come here just to think . . . and feel.

She ran a Coke from the fountain and sat down in a plum-colored booth, facing the front window, peering out at the empty storefront across the street. Sherry McClain, a friend of Marjorie's, had come by a few days ago to say she was considering opening a scrapbook store there, and that her mother-in-law might take the smaller shop next to it—Mother McClain's lifelong dream was to open a yarn store called Knit Wits. Sherry seemed to think turning the diner into a café would be a big draw for the specialty shops popping up on Main, and inside, Trish beamed.

Staring out at Main Street now, the wheels in her mind began to spin. Perhaps all the shop owners could start working *together*—they could host a Christmas walk some Saturday in December, offering free cookies and punch, playing Christmas music in each store. Heck, maybe it if went well, she could talk the town council into starting a new tradition, a holiday parade or something. Of course, that meant she'd have to get *involved* in the town council. But after some of the things she'd wrung from witnesses, and even judges, winning over a small town council should be cake.

Come April, they could hold a Spring stroll. She could give away a free seed packet to everyone who came in. And maybe even Hamler's Hardware, the last remaining business from the old days, could get into the spirit—they sold plenty of gardening equipment.

Just then, the door opened and a clean-cut teenage boy stepped in. "Trish Henderson?"

She nodded, surprised. "Yes, that's me."

That's when she realized he was holding a clear glass vase, and from the top sprouted . . . dark pink tulips.

After the delivery boy departed, Trish sat down to read the attached note.

*Trish,*

*Jeremiah and I can't thank you enough. It's so good to have you back in town, and you're doing great things with your parents' place. I know you have a job to get back to, but we'll miss you around here. Wish you could stay. You sure made a difference for me and Jeremiah. Every time I see these tulips, I think about you.*

*Marjorie*

Trish let out a thoughtful sigh.

Not three hours ago, she'd asked God for a sign.

Pink tulips could be a sign.

Of course, she'd *asked* Marjorie to send her flowers if they won the case. And she knew Marjorie had these tulips in mind for her wedding, so she realized she was stretching it to believe—

But wait. Maybe *that* was the sign. Flowers for her wedding. Delivered to her.

Sitting right in front of her.

Making her envision walking down the aisle to Joe someday.

She had to stop, catch her breath.

*Walking down the aisle to Joe.* The picture in her head made her dizzy, a little shaky—but in a good way.

Oh God, she'd become *such* an untrusting person. Because of one thing that had happened a million years ago.

And she had to *stop*. Just like Joe had said she *had* to forgive him. Now she *had* to stop distrusting people, expecting them to hurt her. She *had* to quit fearing *Joe* would hurt her. She had to trust him. Believe in him. Finally. All the way.

Standing up, she walked to the back of the café. And then she realized . . . she was thinking of it as *her* café. She envisioned the muffins and scones and danishes in the display cases, then lifted her gaze to where she would soon place colorful menus.

Wow. She was doing this? Really doing it?

Giving up her shot at partner in Indianapolis's most prestigious legal firm?

Running a café?

Coming home to Joe?

"Yes," she said aloud to no one but herself. "I'm really doing this. I'm really doing it."

And then she started to laugh, the kind of laughter that might have sounded slightly crazed if anyone else had been around—but she didn't care. Because she felt . . . *happy. Free. Excited. In love.*

"Holy crap," she said at the realization, then laughed again, plopping into a yellow booth.

Part of her wanted to pick up the phone and call Debbie. Or drive home and share the news with her mom and dad. But she knew in her heart that she needed to tell Joe first. And she knew just how she was going to do it.

He wanted more of her inner biker chick?

He was going to get it.

She was in the mood for a cupcake—and not the cake kind.

Joe sat in his truck at the Burger Barn, eating a deluxe burger and fries, trying to clear his head. The last twenty-four hours had him reeling—yesterday had been so packed with good and bad that he could barely sort it out. His sister was a stripper. He'd told Trish his darkest secret and she still cared for him. And damn—then he'd asked her to stay.

He hadn't planned it—but he'd meant it. He didn't want her to go. And he loved her. Still. Always.

Part of him didn't think she'd say yes—but he held out hope simply because of the way she clung to him every time they were close, moving together. No other woman had ever held him that way, so tight, warm, desperate. No other woman had ever *needed* him as much as he felt Trish needing him when he was inside her.

Just then, the passenger door opened and Carissa climbed in.

His heart went a little warm just seeing her. "Hey, Care Bear, what's goin' on?"

"Grandpa and me are having lunch. I saw you over here, so thought I'd say hi."

Joe glanced inside the small octagonal building at the center of the lot and spotted Willie at the counter. "So," he said, "how was the dance?"

Her smile stretched from ear to dainty ear. "The dress was the bomb. Everybody loved it! And when Justin came to the door, I could tell he thought I looked hot."

Hot, huh? Not exactly what Joe was hoping for, but he tried not to let that show. "Then you had a good time? Did he behave himself? Or do I need to kick his ass?"

She rolled her eyes as if he were crazy. "He was totally nice, Joe."

"Promise?"

Another even more exaggerated eye roll. "Yes, already."

After that, Carissa regaled him with details of all the teenage drama that could take place at a dance—one of her friends had broken up with a guy and it was "tragic!" and another girl had cried when the heel snapped off her shoe. Joe did a lot of nodding and trying to pretend he was engrossed, but when she finally took off to eat with her Grandpa, he realized that just talking to her for awhile had made him feel more relaxed than when he'd arrived.

That afternoon, he mowed the yard, fed the cats, took a shower, and hung out on the front porch swing with Elvis, who curled up at his feet. He considered calling Trish, but decided to give her some time. He wasn't gonna pressure her—he only wanted her to stay if she really wanted to.

About the time he was going to pull a frozen dinner from the freezer, Kenny called, and Joe found himself over at Kenny and Debbie's for chicken on the grill. They ate on the small deck that he and Kenny had built onto the back of the house a few summers ago, and as soon as the two boys finished their dinner and took to the yard with a baseball and gloves, he heard himself telling his friends he'd asked Trish to stay.

He thought Debbie's eyes would pop out of her head, and Kenny's jaw dropped to the table as he said, "Bud, you work fast."

Which is when Debbie hopped to her feet. "I'm gonna go call her."

But Joe grabbed her by one wrist and Kenny by the other before she could get away. Joe said, "I totally forgot who I was confiding in here or I would have kept my big mouth shut. Deb, please, if *ever* in your life you wanted to help me out—don't call her. Okay?"

Debbie appeared totally deflated, but sat back down, parking her chin dejectedly in her fist.

"And don't do it after I leave, either," he said, pointing a finger at her.

"You take the fun out of everything."

"Trish wouldn't agree," he said matter-of-factly.

Then Debbie pushed up her glasses and smiled. "God, I hope she stays. Just think—we could have cookouts, and parties, and big family dinners, and . . ."

Joe just let her ramble on—and tried not to think about how nice it sounded.

And then he went home . . . and waited for something to happen.

Trish felt positively adolescent as she left the house in jeans and a tee, claiming that the shopping bag in her hand contained clothes she'd borrowed from Debbie. In reality, the bag contained her inner biker chick—the whole ensemble she'd worn to seduce Joe that very first night. She was going to change in the car. And she knew it was silly, but also a necessity—no matter how old you are, you don't let your parents see you walk out of the house looking like a prostitute. No, you only let the man of your dreams see you like that—and that's exactly what she was going to do. Give Joe his biker chick fantasy, and then give them both a new reality by telling him she was going to come home, run Trish's Tea Room and Café, and be with him.

Night had fallen, which made changing in the car easier even if still challenging. She drove behind a neighbor's barn and made the transition into bad girl—then felt a giddy little smile grow on her face as she pulled back out onto the winding country road, headed to Joe's.

She'd have expected to be nervous about this on some level— not the sex, but the decision. Yet she didn't feel nervous at all. She simply knew it was right.

Joe sat munching potato chips, watching an old Bill Murray movie on cable, and wondering what Trish was doing—when the doorbell rang.

It had to be her.

Of course, maybe she hadn't made up her mind yet—maybe she was just coming over.

Still, his heart beat a little too fast as he muted the TV with a click of the remote, set his chips on the coffee table, and rose to get the door.

Drawing in a deep breath, he grabbed the knob and pulled it open—to find Beverly standing on his porch in her Waffle House uniform. Christ. "Bev," he said, taken aback.

Her face looked drawn, tense. "Can I come in, Joe? I need to talk to you."

Shit. Was something wrong with Carissa? He stepped back and let her inside. She'd never come here before, and he'd always appreciated that she had the sense to respect his boundaries— but if something had happened to Carissa, that was different. "Is it Carissa?"

She let out a heavy breath, meeting his eyes as the screen door fell shut behind her. "Yes," she said. "And no."

Hell. "What does *that* mean?"

She walked around him, moving toward the couch, finally turning back to face him. "Joe, you're so good to her."

He leaned forward slightly. "And?"

"And . . . she needs a father, Joe."

He shook his head slightly. What the hell? "I don't know what you're getting at, Bev. I do the best I can, under the weird circumstances."

Her eyes widened, her lips parting, as she reached out to grab both his hands. "Of course, I know you do. You're wonderful to her, Joe. It's only that . . ."

Okay, now he was starting to get pissed. He pulled his hands away. "What's going on, Bev?"

She pursed her lips, almost looking sheepish—but not quite. "I've been thinking a lot about this, Joe—about you, and Carissa, and about *me*. We're missing out. We're . . . wasting time. We could be happy, Joe—the *three* of us."

Aw, shit. "*Bev*," he chided her. "My God. Are you serious?" She'd come to put the moves on him?

"Of course I'm serious. I love you, Joe. I always have. And I know you love Carissa and she loves you. But the one thing I've always wanted to give her that I can't, more than anything else, is a normal family. You and I could give her that, together—and we could be happy." Slowly, her voice dropped to something sultry, more seductive than he'd ever heard from her. "I could make you happy, Joe—just let me try."

He could've turned her down in a million different ways, but he figured it would be most effective to keep it simple. "Bev, I've been seeing Trish. And it's serious."

Resentment flared instantly in her eyes. "That girl will never give you what you need—she doesn't want the same things you do." Then her voice softened—back to seduction. "But *I* can give you what you need. I can be a wife. A mother. A lover. I can be a *hell* of a lover, Joe. Let me show you how good I can make you feel." With that, she reached up to yank at the front of her uniform blouse, opening it swiftly to the waist. She wore a black lace bra underneath, and she stepped toward him, pressing her hands to his chest.

Joe grabbed her wrists, eased her back. "Bev," he said through slightly gritted teeth, "this isn't gonna happen. Ever. Why can't you get that?"

But she still peered up at him, sex in her eyes, lips pouty and anxious. "Because it makes so much sense, you and me. Just one night, Joe. Give me just one night to show you I can make you happy."

"It takes more than sex to make me happy. It takes Trish."

He hadn't exactly planned to say that last part, but there it was. Other parts of his life were satisfying—but Trish fulfilled him in a way nothing else ever had.

He released Bev's wrists so she would leave. "Button up," he said.

But instead she undid the last button on her blouse and let it fall to the floor behind her, still flashing her come-hither look. She smoothed her palms up her stomach and onto her breasts, pushing them together. "Touch me, Joe," she purred. "Make me feel good."

For God's sake. He didn't know what to do, how to get rid of her. If she were a guy, he'd have just tossed her ass out the door and been done with it. But what did you do when a woman you didn't want wouldn't leave your house?

For the most part, he and Bev had always had an amiable enough relationship, though he tried to keep it a distant one—and for Carissa's sake, he didn't want to ruin that. Hell, play this wrong and for all he knew, Bev would suddenly decide Carissa couldn't see him anymore.

So he decided the best route here was to be gentle—something he wasn't skilled at, but he'd give it a shot.

Stepping forward, he drew her hands from her chest down into his, then looked her in the eye. "Beverly," he said slowly, trying to sound kinder than he felt, "I'm in love with Trish. But even if I wasn't, you and I . . . would never happen." He shook his head once more. "I just don't feel that way."

Trish sucked in her breath, watching through the front window.

She'd seen a strange car in the driveway, so given how she was dressed, she'd peeked to see who was inside before knocking.

Joe held Beverly's hands, squeezing them in his as he peered into her eyes. Half undressed, she gazed up at him with such hunger that it gouged a hole in Trish's heart.

Finally, Trish spun, turning to lean her back against the siding.

What had she just seen?

Was it the way it looked? Were they about to have sex? Was there more between them than he'd admitted?

Or maybe he was turning her down, for all Trish knew.

But *whatever* was happening in there, it was twisting her stomach into knots, thrusting a huge, horrible lump up into her throat, and making her eyes ache with the effort of holding back tears.

Whatever was happening in there—it hurt too much.

Trying to push back the pain, she silently scurried down the porch steps, careful not to let her heels make noise. Then she sidestepped the front walk and took to the grass, so she could run in earnest without being heard. Tears blinded her by the time she made it to the driveway, and she forgot all about being quiet as she slammed her car door, started the engine, backed haphazardly out into the road, then raced off into the night, thinking—*I can't do this. I thought I could, but I just can't.*

**Convict:** to prove or declare guilty of an offense or crime after a legal trial; _or_ to impress with a sense of guilt.

# Fourteen

On Monday morning, Trish sat at the little white wooden desk in her old bedroom, working at the laptop. But suddenly, the laptop was the only thing around her that felt familiar at all—the rest of the daisy-laden room seemed as foreign and distant to her as when she'd first arrived.

Not that she was thinking about her feelings. No way—she couldn't afford to. It was a lot easier to just shove them aside.

Take care of business.

Focus on things she could control.

She'd already done her crying last night while she'd been sitting behind a barn in the dark, struggling her way out of a corset dress and back into a pair of jeans while cramped behind the wheel of her Lexus. It had seemed surreal. And humiliating—even if no one knew but her. What had happened to her self-respect? Maybe she'd left it in Indianapolis. She'd been behaving like an entirely different person ever since she'd left, after all.

Of course, thinking about that moment brought it all flooding back—that sense of emptiness and despair. Betrayal? Of that she wasn't sure. But it didn't even matter. She couldn't take that kind of uncertainty, the desperate small-town drama that occurred when people decided they were bored with their lives and were going to change it, no matter whom it hurt or affected. A heavy knot settled in the pit of her stomach, leaving her nauseous.

But then she pushed it away again. She would not be a victim. She had a real life, far away from here, a job she was good at, people who appreciated her.

Case in point, when she pulled up her e-mail, she found one from Kent and clicked immediately to open it.

> Hey, beautiful, are you ever coming home? I'm getting tired of chugging those mega-margaritas by myself. That's what they have at Burrito Bob's, Trish—MEGA-margaritas! I've got at least 3 megas worth of good office gossip saved up, but if you don't come back soon, I'll have to tell it all to Burrito Bob himself—which will suck, since he won't get most of it ; ) You've got a handsome (if I do say so myself) guy here dying to buy you lots of drinks—how much longer can you resist?

She sighed. Dear, sweet Kent. He *was* handsome. Charming. A catch.

Anyone would think so.

Maybe she *was* a fool for still being here.

After all, Kent and she actually had things in common. Their work, for one, which was huge. But other things, too. They both liked margaritas, after all. And they enjoyed dinner parties. And foreign films— it had been Kent who'd first recommended *Life Is Beautiful* to her, and they'd been discussing foreign movies ever since. Kent jogged in the park on Sundays, and Trish kept *meaning to jog*—so that was sort of like a common activity, wasn't it? Maybe if she dated Kent, it would motivate her to start jogging once and for all.

And what did she and Joe really have in common besides their backgrounds? The sex was good, of course. Okay, that was a lie—the sex was *great*. And they both liked pancakes. And her mom's home cooking. But at the moment, that didn't sound like a lot.

Unless she remembered that one warm pink tulip in the bouquet he'd bought her—how it had somehow drawn him, made him think of her.

The knot in her stomach expanded then, growing into something wider, rounder, threatening to become the biggest part of her.

*Stop thinking about him. Now. Get back to work.*

She closed Kent's e-mail, feeling guilty for not answering, but she didn't think she could muster the strength to flirt about margaritas at the moment.

That's when she spotted a message from Elaine at work, with the subject line: Melbourne DNA Results.

Finally—it was about time. She clicked to open it.

Bad news on this, Trish. Dankins says traces of Richie Melbourne's DNA were found on the cups retrieved from the rape scene. And on the victim's underwear,

too. Even worse, the ratio of X to Y is 3 to 1—one male
and one female, and the alleles showed only two con-
tributors to the sample. Dankins will e-mail you his full
report later today, but that's the gist of it. Sorry to be
the bearer of bad news.

Trish let out a heavy whoosh of breath, then closed her eyes,
suddenly dizzy. She tried to shut out the vision of Richie raping
that girl. Oh God. *Oh God.* Richie was *guilty?* Richie, whom she'd
believed in so much? Whom she'd been so anxious and determined to defend, to save?

She curled her hands into fists, fighting the strong urge to
fling her laptop across the room and watch it bust into a million
useless pieces.

*This is what you get, Trish, when you trust someone, when you believe
in them with your whole heart, with no doubt.*

She clenched her fists so tight that her fingernails dug into her
palms, but she managed not to throw the laptop. What Richie
had done was ugly and a world apart from her little yellow-and-
white daisy room—she couldn't let that ugliness completely
take her over, especially not here.

*Get calm. Take deep breaths. Then* stay *calm.*

*Quit feeling it. Quit feeling anything.*

*Be the old Trish. You got by fine that way for a lot of years, after
all.*

So she blew out long, relaxing breaths until her heartbeat
slowed, but she still felt sick to her stomach. Then she com-
posed an answer to Elaine, simply thanking her for the information and indicating they would need to swing their defense in
an entirely different direction. Now, they would refrain from
introducing the DNA evidence themselves, but they'd still have

to come up with a supposition as to how Richie's DNA ended up in such damning places if he wasn't guilty, since surely the prosecution would have their own experts examining the evidence.

She knew how to play it, of course. Make the *girl* guilty.

She'd left a party, drinking and possibly drunk, on the arms of two different guys. Anything could have happened. She could have taken the drug found in her system completely willingly. She could have invited one or both of them into the bushes with her, then cried foul when it was over.

Trish didn't believe for a second that was what had happened, but it was no longer about what she believed. It was back to being about what it was *always* about—how to get her guy off. How to get her guy—a stinking, lying, sniveling, raping little bastard—off, so that he could go out and do it again.

She hit Send. Took a deep breath. Closed the laptop.

And with it, she closed up the part of her heart she'd been foolish enough to open way too wide the last few weeks. If she'd needed proof, this was it. Screw the flowers—*this* was her sign. And it said, loud and clear, that appearances were deceiving, that no one could be trusted, that you couldn't put faith in anyone without making yourself vulnerable.

A mistake it was high time she stopped making, once and for all.

Another Monday afternoon at the Waffle House, and Carissa sat in a booth in the corner doing homework while Beverly served up yet another plate of food. It was finally September, and brutal summer seemed to be over at last. Something to be thankful for. That's what Beverly was seeking out today, things to be thankful for. To help her forget what she'd done last night.

Even as she set a plate of eggs and grits before a trucker at the counter, her face warmed with humiliation and regret, re-membering. She wasn't sure what had made her do something so stupid, so desperate. She'd just wanted Joe so bad. And she'd tried so hard. She'd really believed she could make it happen, through sheer will, if she just kept trying.

Tossing Butch out of her life had been smart, but had also left her vulnerable, and lonely. Going to Joe's house had been an ill-thought-out, split-second decision—she'd literally been driving home from work, feeling sorry for herself, and it had hit her that maybe if she just put herself out there, told him how she felt, it would magically change things.

When would she ever learn that sex wasn't the way to a man's heart? The whole world seemed to think it was. She'd been sure of it as a girl. But she'd had sex with a lot of guys over the years, and not once had it reached anyone's heart but her own.

What did men want?

She simply didn't know.

Maybe it was time to just give up, quit trying to understand. Just accept that it was her and Carissa against the world.

Just one problem with that, though, she thought as she waved to an older couple, regulars Mabel and John, as they came in for their afternoon coffee and pie. The problem was—she *wanted* a man. She wanted love. A sense of security. Someone to lean on when she was feeling weak. And to take care of when she was feeling strong. She'd yearned for that kind of connection with a man for as long as she could remember—and she'd never, ever had it. Not for more than an hour or two anyway.

"You okay, Bev?" She looked up to see Floyd at the griddle, leaving everything to fry and sizzle on its own for a minute to glance her way. "You look like you don't feel good."

He was a sweet old man, Floyd. Surely he knew what she did

when she disappeared out the door with Butch for half an hour, but he never judged her. They'd worked here together for over ten years—she wouldn't start dragging him into her troubles now. "No, Floyd—I'm fine, thanks." Then she pointed to the griddle. "Don't let those hash browns burn now."

*Pull yourself together. This is just like any other day. Nothing has changed.* She just hoped Joe didn't hate her too much now. And she tried not to remember the awful moment when she'd finally realized that he *really, truly* didn't want her, when she'd had to put her blouse back on and slink away into the night, defeated and alone.

The Dixie Chicks started singing "Cowboy Take Me Away," as the front door opened to bring in a tall, clean-cut man with short blond hair—military short, although he wore civilian khakis and a plaid shirt with the sleeves rolled up. Handsome and lean, confidence filled his brown eyes.

Brown like Carissa's, she thought, and that's when her gaze stuck on him, and it was as if he moved in slow motion toward the counter.

He was . . . the spitting image of her daughter. Almond-shaped eyes the color of milk chocolate, thin nose, wide mouth, slightly pointed chin.

Holy shit.

Could he be . . . ? Was it possible?

He *was*. She knew it without doubt, that fast.

He was her long lost Dairy Queen lover.

He was . . . Charley.

Her heart nearly burst through her chest, but she held herself steady, tried to stay cool. Tried not to wonder too hard how this could possibly be. How this man, of all men, could come waltzing into the Waffle House fourteen years since she'd last seen him.

"What can I get you to drink?" Her voice didn't quiver. Good.

"Coffee, thanks." He smiled kindly into her eyes. A familiar smile. Her daughter's smile.

*Shit, shit, shit.* This was impossible. Wasn't it? She turned away, pouring a cup, careful not to spill it, since her hands were trembling.

Facing him again, she watched him perusing the menu as she gently lowered the cup before him. "Know what you'd like?"

He placed the plastic-covered menu back in the holder at the counter's rear edge. "I'll have an egg and bacon wrap with some hash browns and toast."

Beverly wrote it down in a shaky scrawl, calling it to Floyd around the lump in her throat. Then she lifted her gaze back to the man before her.

*Is it really him? Are you sure?*

Yes, no doubt.

"I . . . think I know you," she said, trying her damnedest not to sound nervous. "Is your name Charley? With an e-y?"

He smiled uncertainly, clearly not recognizing her. "Yeah. But I'm not from around here." Then he pointed vaguely eastward. "I was just visiting my uncle over in Versailles on my way home to Terre Haute. Just got back from Iraq and decided to drive home from Ft. Benning, see some folks along the way."

She smiled, remembering how he'd been heading off to the Marines that night fourteen years ago. "But you passed through here once before," she reminded him. "A long time ago. You stopped at the Dairy Queen. And asked for extra whipped cream on your sundae."

Charley studied her a minute, and then the light of recognition slowly dawned in his eyes, even as he lowered his chin in disbelief. "No way. Are you . . . Did we . . . ?"

She drew in her breath, trying to look more sheepish than she actually felt. "Yes. And yes."

He spoke quietly, a soft grin unfurling. "Well, I'll be damned. What a coincidence."

Sort of, she thought. He'd traveled the world, but she'd barely moved an inch the whole time he'd been gone. She could see the DQ out the window across the highway.

"Um . . . Beverly. Am I right?"

She smiled, glad—even if a little surprised—he remembered.

She nodded and said, "It's . . . nice to see you," not sure where to go from here.

Just then, Carissa called out from the corner, filling the awkward moment. "Mom, I need help with my algebra when you have time."

As if she knew anything about algebra. "All right, honey. I'll be over shortly."

But when she turned back to Charley, his gaze was stuck on Carissa, even though her daughter looked back down now, scribbling in a notebook. And Beverly's whole body froze up. Because he saw it, too. That unmistakable resemblance. So obvious that a person would have to be blind to miss it. "That's your daughter?"

Bev worked hard to meet his eyes as she nodded briefly.

He stared at Carissa a moment more before speaking. "Uh . . . how old is she?"

Her chest contracted as she answered. "Thirteen."

Charley's jaw dropped slightly as he let out a long, whooshing sigh, his eyebrows knitting. And Bev's stomach hurt—like a bag of rocks was tumbling around inside it.

"Am I crazy," Charley said, "or . . ." He blinked, stopped, seemed at a loss.

"You're not crazy," Bev let out on a heavy breath. She feared she might faint. Carissa was in the same room with her father and didn't even know it. He was really *here*—suddenly, out of nowhere.

"My God," he said.

"I'm sorry," she told him quickly. "I had no idea how to find you. I didn't even know your last name. And . . . hell, I didn't even know you well enough to know if you'd even want . . ."

The poor man looked shell-shocked. And maybe he had no interest in a child; maybe this was the worst possible news he could get. Either way, it had to be a blow.

"Hey," she said softly, reaching to touch his hand where it rested near his coffee cup. "If you want to pretend you never came in here . . . it's okay. We're fine, Carissa and me."

"Carissa?" he asked, hearing her name for the first time.

Bev nodded.

"Are you . . . married?" He swallowed visibly. "Does she have someone . . . someone she thinks is her dad?"

"No, I'm not married." But the rest was, of course, complicated. "And, well, there's a guy who . . . spends time with her, and is sort of a father figure, but . . . she's never asked who her dad is."

Charley peered long and hard into Beverly's eyes. The jukebox still played, and bacon sizzled behind her, but she was aware of nothing but him. When he said no more, she spoke quietly. "It's okay. Really. If you want to leave." She'd never said harder words.

But Charley sat before her, still looking just as dumbfounded, even as he began shaking his head. "That's just it. I don't think I can. I don't think I could walk out that door and not look back."

Beverly nearly collapsed with joy, but held strong and managed to say, "She's a great kid." *And you're a good man.*

"Order up, Bev!" Floyd called, and she flinched, and both she and Charley laughed nervously.

And she knew this was going to be tricky, and huge—suddenly introducing Carissa to a father. And she realized that she didn't know him at all, not really. But she had the same feeling she'd had that night fourteen years ago—that he was a man she *wanted* to know, and now a man she wanted her daughter to know.

And she wouldn't do anything to ruin this. She wouldn't be clingy. Or act crazy. Or even make a move toward him. Even if, that quick, she had a feeling Charley could truly make her happy. If anything good happened between him and her—well, it would have to happen naturally, because *he* wanted it to, because no way would she risk messing this up for Carissa.

And somehow, suddenly knowing Carissa would have her real dad in her life made her feel so strong, so stable, that at least for now, that alone was enough.

*Concentrate, man.*

Joe bent over the engine of a 1999 BMW 740i, putting a crank case vent valve in the back of the intake manifold—a task that took all his attention. So it was bad he was thinking about Trish instead.

He kept replaying last night in his head. He'd been trying his damnedest to be gentle with Beverly when he'd heard a door slam outside just before a car went squealing out of his driveway, gravel crunching beneath the tires. No doubt who it was.

He'd called her cell, her mom, Debbie. He'd had no luck reaching her, though, so once Beverly was buttoned back up and on her way, he'd gone out driving, looking for Trish's car.

He'd tried her cell again, too—but soon it had gotten too late to do any more, so he'd spent a sleepless night wondering exactly what she'd seen and exactly how awful it had looked.

Now it was Monday afternoon and she still hadn't contacted him. After work, he was *going* to find her—he'd start at the diner, then go out to her parents' place. Shit. His stomach churned. He hated—*hated*—the idea that he'd hurt her again, even if it wasn't his fault. But he also wasn't crazy about the idea that she'd jumped to conclusions and clearly *still* had so little faith in him.

He was tightening the valve when, somewhere on the periphery of his vision, a car pulled in the lot, right up to the bay where he was working. He was still trying to concentrate, but lifted his gaze—to see Debbie walking toward him. She looked . . . grim.

He abandoned the valve and stood up straight, his back going rigid. "What?" he said. He lowered his wrench to a shop towel on the fender, then stepped toward her.

"She's gone," Debbie said quietly.

Jesus. Joe's chest tightened, and damn it, a lump rose to his throat. He pushed it back so he could talk. "Just gone?"

"She got a call this morning from someone at her firm. She made partner. So she had to drop everything and go back."

He let out a breath, pissed and hurt. "Including me."

"She wrote you a letter." Debbie reached in her purse and fished out a flowery piece of stationery Trish's mom probably used for corresponding with old friends.

"A letter," he repeated, numb, and thinking it sounded too damn familiar. Not to mention feeble, considering all they'd shared.

Debbie sighed. "She said she didn't have time to explain it all in person."

Yeah, right. Joe took the letter and read.

Dear Joe,

I'm sorry to leave like this. Don't hate me. I just found out I made partner and it's a big deal, so I have to go back to Indy right away.

About last night, I saw you with Bev, and yeah, I ran. And I'm pretty sure you weren't doing anything wrong, but the problem is—I just can't live like that. I can't live in a fishbowl with you and Beverly and all these people who know what you once did to me. I can't take the drama people like her foist into life. I can't live with even one moment of doubt, like I felt looking in your window last night. I knew almost as soon as it happened that it wasn't your fault, but that almost didn't make any difference. I couldn't stand seeing her with you like that. I couldn't stand the few seconds of shock, of wondering what the hell was going on.

I know our breakup was a long time ago, ancient history. I know you were just a kid, I understand why it happened,

*I get all that. But it's still there, it still occurred. It makes what happened last night an entirely different event than if it had never taken place.*

*And so, I guess what I really can't live with is . . . wondering, fearing . . . that someday, somehow, I'll discover all over again that I really don't know you, that you're capable of things I never believed. And I can't live with wondering when that will be.*

*This isn't your fault, I promise. It's me. Last night hurt. And it felt like old times. I worked long and hard to quit feeling that pain when we were younger and I can't go down that path again.*

*The last couple of weeks with you has been truly amazing. But I have to get back to my real life now.*

*Forgive me. And be happy.*

*Trish*

Joe's stomach dropped. He understood that he'd shattered her sense of security fourteen years ago. But Jesus Christ—what more was he supposed to do? How was he supposed to redeem himself? He'd thought the time they'd spent together had changed things, but apparently it hadn't.

And now *she* was the one asking *him* for forgiveness?

Ironic, since this pretty much meant she still *hadn't* forgiven him for the past, no matter what she said. At the very least, she still didn't trust him.

Amazing, huh? So amazing that she'd just dumped him without even blinking.

He almost couldn't breathe. He'd been so close, so close to having what he really wanted deep down inside. Trish. Just Trish. And now she'd just fucking disappeared from his life without so much as a kiss good-bye.

"She put the diner on the market today before she left," Debbie told him.

"Good," he said, angry.

Debbie spoke quietly. "I had thought, hoped, maybe she'd keep it, you know?"

"If she doesn't want to be here, I'm glad she's gone."

"*Joe*," Debbie gasped as if he'd said something awful.

And the truth was—the only chance he'd ever had to feel a real, deep connection with a woman had just walked out of his life. But he refused to let himself wallow in that, even for a minute—he was too mad. "I gave her everything I had to give, Deb. It wasn't enough. End of story."

With that, he headed back to the BMW. He didn't mean to turn his back on Debbie, but hell—he couldn't talk anymore. He needed to be alone. He needed to get back to work, concentrate on something solid, something that made sense, like the engine of this car.

"Take care of yourself, Joe," Debbie said softly behind him. "We'll call you in a couple days."

He only grunted his reply around the damn lump in his throat. He focused on the intake manifold but couldn't really see it, hard as he tried.

He'd done nothing wrong here. His last crime against Trish

had been fourteen years ago, and if she intended to make him pay for a lifetime, well . . . hell, maybe she was right to go. If she couldn't trust him, couldn't believe how much he loved her, maybe he was better off alone. In fact, he wished she'd never come back to Eden, never shown up at the bar that night.

Gary Allan's "Best I Ever Had," sounded over the speakers and echoed through the garage as Joe gave up on the BMW and walked into his office, letting the door slam behind him. He plopped down behind his desk and ran his hands through his hair, then closed his eyes against the pain behind them. If he was so glad she was gone, why did it hurt like hell?

**Redemption:** a procedure in a Chapter 7 case whereby a debtor removes a secured creditor's lien on collateral by paying the creditor the value of the property; _or_ atonement for guilt; deliverance; rescue.

# Fifteen

Joe sat on the front porch drinking a beer, hanging out with Elvis, who lay plopped at his side. He scratched behind the dog's ear. "I was fine enough without her. Wasn't I?"

He'd always _thought_ he was. A shame she'd had to come back and remind him just how good things could be.

"But hey," he said, glancing down to the dog, "what do I need with a woman who doesn't trust me? That's the good part of not having one at all—you don't have to worry about crap like that. You just live your life, go your own way. Eat when you want. Sleep when you want. Nobody doubting you or arguing with you. Keeps life simpler."

Of course, the words didn't make him feel any better. But he had to snap out of this, get back to normal. He had a life to live, a business to run. An almost-daughter to look out for.

When a car slowed down, then pulled in the driveway, he looked up to see it was Beverly's. She got out, wearing her Waffle House uniform as usual. He hoped she'd keep it on this time. And as he restrained himself from saying, *What the hell are you doing here?* he also hoped she didn't feel free to just stop by anytime she liked now. "What's up?" he asked. Didn't smile.

"I'm sorry for coming here, Joe," she said, sounding contrite. "But I need to talk to you. About something important."

He pushed to his feet. "What's going on?"

"You may want to sit down."

Damn. She really sounded serious, much more than when she'd pulled that stunt the other night. He lowered himself back to the porch.

When Beverly took a seat on a step just below him, she looked worried, and he narrowed his gaze on her, silently telling her to start talking.

"Joe," she began, "I don't know how to tell you this, so I'll just say it. Carissa's real father is in town, and he wants to be in her life. He's meeting her tonight, in fact."

Jesus Christ. Had he heard that right? The news hit him like a boulder to the chest.

"I'm sorry," Bev said, and Joe didn't even care when she reached out to touch his knee in solace, too stunned to object.

"How the hell did *this* happen?" he managed to ask.

Then listened as Beverly told him about how the other guy she'd slept with just after him had miraculously walked into the Waffle House yesterday afternoon and seen the unmistakable resemblance. She claimed he was a good guy, just out of the Marines, who wanted to know his daughter, and maybe even move here.

The light of infatuation shone in Beverly's eyes, making him wonder if there was any chance this guy could give Bev that family she'd always dreamed of for her and Carissa. It was hard not to want that—for both of them. But shit. At the same time he felt . . . weirdly displaced. And hell, there was the chance, too, that the guy would be a jerk, or that Bev would manage to drive him away, that this would all turn out to be a big disaster.

Despite the doubts, though, he heard himself asking, "Can I still be in her life?" He found himself pointing vaguely over his shoulder. "Because I promised her this cat, but told her it could live here and she could come visit, and . . ." It was the least of the reasons he wanted Carissa around yet had somehow been the easiest to toss out.

"Of course," Bev said with a calm, sure clarity he'd seldom heard in her voice. In fact, she'd sounded that way since she'd arrived. As if she suddenly had a handle on life.

He felt his eyebrows knit. "Will that be okay with *him?*"

She nodded. "I'll *make* it okay. I swear, Joe. I've made a lot of mistakes, but cutting you out of Carissa's life would be the worst."

On Wednesday afternoon, Carissa came to the garage for her first training session in the office. It turned out to be more of a talking session, but that suited Joe fine. She told him about her "brand-new dad," who she described as "tall and really nice." She said her new dad Charley had decided to move here from Terre Haute. He'd been a surveyor in the service and planned to look for similar work in the area.

"I told him all about you," Carissa said, sitting in a chair next to him at the desk.

"Yeah? What'd you tell him?"

"That I always kinda thought *you* might be my dad."

Joe's stomach dropped as he looked into her sweet eyes. He supposed she'd probably wanted to bring this up for years. "Truth is, Care Bear," he said slowly, "I always kinda *wanted* to be. But I didn't want to lie to you about it. And now I'm really glad I didn't, or you'd be confused as hell right now."

She shrugged, looking cheerful and acceptant. "Good point, I guess. But can I ask you something?"

"Sure."

"If you're not my dad, who are you? I mean, why have you always been there, hanging out with me, giving me stuff?"

He swallowed. Every damn day of this week just kept getting more and more complicated. "I suppose you're old enough to hear the whole truth of it, Care."

"I'll be in high school next year, you know."

He couldn't hold in a soft grin. Woman of the world. "Truth is, when you were first born, I thought maybe I *was* your dad. So I got attached to you and the way you smiled up at me when I was changing your disgusting diapers." They both laughed. "So even when I found out I *wasn't* your dad, I just . . . didn't go away."

She bit her lip, her eyes wide, but her voice quiet. "That was nice of you."

He shrugged. "It worked out good for both of us."

"Definitely," she said, nodding. "Is it still cool for me to work for you?"

"Damn straight. Look at this place." He motioned around them to the piles of invoices and other paperwork littering his desk.

"You're right, it's a mess. You need me."

"Yeah," he said softly. "I need you."

By Thursday evening, Joe was spent. He went through the days as normal, working at the garage—that afternoon he'd actually given Carissa some training on the computer—then coming home at night, feeding Elvis and the cats, finding something to pass as dinner, and relaxing in front of the TV a while before heading to bed. Which was what he was doing right now. But it had been a hell of a week. A hell of a *few* weeks, actually.

Now that he'd had a chance to digest the news about Carissa's dad, he was glad. He still wanted to meet the guy soon, see what he thought of him, but he had a good feeling about it. Maybe he'd miss not being the number one man in her life, the guy who ate waffles with her or took her dress shopping, but he'd figure out his new role as time passed, and she'd be better off for having a real father.

What had happened with Trish, though, continued to eat at him. He'd been so damn mad at her for *still* not trusting in him. But now, as days began to drift by, he found himself remembering the conversations they'd had about the past, and how, each time, he'd felt the pain just pouring from her. He'd truly begun to see the depths of how he'd hurt her.

*You should have come after me*, she'd said.

When he envisioned his young, pretty, eighteen-year-old Trish sitting in some dorm room waiting for him, waiting and waiting, and him never coming, it tore him up. If only he hadn't been so young—and stupid.

When the doorbell rang, he muted the TV, but by the time he rose to answer, the screen door had already opened. Jana stepped inside, looking . . . a lot less scantily clad than usual.

She wore a simple pair of shorts and a fitted tee, the word "Angels" emblazoned across her chest in tiny red rhinestones. Beneath it, an Ohio address. It took him only a second to conclude it was probably the establishment where her husband paid her to take her clothes off for other men. Man, he was *not* in the mood for this.

He got even more miffed when Vinnie himself stepped in behind her. Joe had made some peace with Jana on her wedding day, felt closer to her again, but he'd also made a point of not letting himself think about what she did for a living since then.

"Hey," Jana said, lifting her hand, flashing a smile.

"Hey," he returned, figuring he looked ready to kill somebody.

Vinnie's eyebrows knit, but he reached out a hand toward Joe.

Surprised, Joe took it, shook it. It was either that or punch the guy out.

"Good to see you again, Joe."

A *You, too* was more than Joe could muster, so he settled on, "What brings you by?" Especially two and a half hours away from home.

"Kittens," Jana said with a girlish sparkle in her eyes. Then she looked over at her husband, as if they shared a big secret. "Vinnie and I want the twins."

Joe's eyebrows shot up. It was a little thing, but about the first to go right for him since the weekend. "Great, they're yours. Only they're probably not weaned enough to leave yet. Might want to give them another couple of weeks."

A slight frown reshaped her face. "Oh, crap. I didn't even think about that." Yet just as quickly, she smiled again, a strange look of contentment coming over her as she reached out and took both his hands. "But there's another reason we're here, Joe. A bigger reason. A lot has happened today and . . . well, you were so great at the wedding, stepping in and getting me through being upset about Dad, so I . . . just wanted to tell you my news in person."

Joe let out a heavy breath. More big news—not exactly what he needed. Running a hand back through his hair, he simply walked back to the couch, sitting down at one end. Jana followed, settling next to him, and Vinnie wisely took the easy chair in the corner.

"Start talking," Joe said, seeing no reason not to get to it, whatever *it* was. He supposed maybe his sister was going to admit what she did for a living now, and he only hoped he could keep himself from beating Vinnie to a pulp before the conversation was over.

Jana pursed her lips tightly, dropping her gaze between them, and Joe's chest tightened. Over all of it. Her being a stripper. And that she was going to tell him. And that it was hard for her to say. And that maybe it was all his fault because if he'd held onto those keys that night a long time ago, Jana's life would have been different.

"The thing is, Joe," she began very quietly, "I haven't been completely honest with you about my job at Vinnie's club."

"I know." He tried not to sound too brusque.

She looked up, surprised. "Oh. So you *did* figure it out."

"Lotta sequins and silicone at the wedding, hon," he said softly.

She nodded and looked like she might cry. "I guess you're really disappointed in me."

Joe sighed and his stomach churned. He wasn't sure what to say, so went with simple honesty. "I . . . want better things for you, Jana, that's all." He couldn't have cared less that Vinnie the Stripper Boss was sitting there listening.

Jana's lips drew together tightly. Then she blinked, her eyes pretty even if glassy with unshed tears, and she even managed to smile. "Thing is, Joe—that's why I'm here. Something happened today that changes everything."

She glanced over at her husband, so Joe did, too—and if he wasn't mistaken, he saw true affection for his sister in Vinnie's gaze.

"I'm pregnant, Joe. And the doctor thinks it may be twins." She laughed giddily, even as a tear rolled down her cheek, and Joe went numb. "That's why we decided to take the cats. We thought each baby could have his or her own kitty—you know? But the bigger thing is, we had a long talk and we both agreed that we need to make a change in our lives. So tomorrow morning, Vinnie's going to put the club up for sale. He's already got his eye on a sports bar close to home that went on the market a couple of weeks ago. So"—she looked up hopefully—"what do you think?"

Joe had seldom been more utterly floored. He raised his eyebrows. "I'm gonna be an uncle?"

She nodded, looking at once nervous and excited. "*Twins*, Joe! I'm having freaking *twins!* Can you believe it?"

A light laugh escaped him, trying to imagine Jana handling one baby, let alone two. "You'll be a great mom, Jana. And . . ." He glanced over at Vinnie. "It's a good decision. About the club."

Vinnie nodded, and Jana smiled—then threw her arms around Joe's neck. "I'm so glad we came over. So glad we got this cleared up. I hated keeping something like that from you."

He wasn't sure they'd really cleared much up—it had been a

pretty short conversation. But a warmth he hadn't felt from his sister in months radiated out of her and into him, and maybe that was enough. He hugged her back, gently at first, but then, on impulse, harder.

She must have felt it, how firmly he was holding her, or somehow she sensed the heavy stuff going on inside him, because she pushed him back to arm's length. "What's wrong, Joe?"

He sighed, still trying to smile. He could tell her, but it wouldn't fix anything. And he didn't want to rain on her parade. "Nothing. Everything's fine." And even though it was a lie, at least a *few* things were fine. Finer than they'd been before anyway.

And by the time Jana and Vinnie departed a little while later, Joe felt . . . strangely at peace. At least about his sister. And even about her husband. He still wondered about a mob connection, but he was convinced that Vinnie loved Jana and maybe he'd do right by her from this point forward.

And hell, Joe was going to be an uncle. He already had visions in his head of taking two little boys fishing. Or girls. Dress shopping. And he even had to admit to himself that something about this news took a little of the sting from no longer being Carissa's "sort of" father.

God, he wanted to tell Trish. All of it. About Jana's sudden turnaround. About Carissa and her dad and how weird it was going to be until they all got used to it. Hell, even about the fact that he'd unloaded two kittens and promised to keep one for Carissa—and now only Pepper's fate remained to be seen.

Heading to the bathroom to wash up, he looked at himself in the mirror, at the dark stubble dusting his chin, at the faint lines starting to appear at the corners of his eyes. He needed a haircut. Hell, he needed a lot of things he didn't have at the moment. *Is Trish sitting somewhere in Indy waiting for me right now, waiting for me to come for her? Am I being a fool to just accept her decision, to let her run from me again?*

Everyone around him, it seemed, was finding what they needed to make them happy, complete. For Carissa, for Beverly, for Jana, all the little blank spots in the pictures of their lives were suddenly being colored in, every white spot filled.

So everyone had what they needed now.

Everyone but him. And Trish.

"Thanks, that's great. I'll talk with you soon."

Trish hung up the phone. Lois Faulkner had called to say she had serious interest from a new buyer only four days after putting the diner/café back on the market. It hadn't hurt, she'd been told, that the two storefronts across the street had just been leased yesterday—the scrapbook store and yarn shop were moving in. Lois expected an offer by Monday.

Trish pushed down the wistfulness that grabbed her at the very thought of the café, then slipped into her favorite little black dress. It was Friday evening and she was hosting a party. Just twenty or so friends, mostly from the firm. She'd had to throw it together quickly, but a soiree had simply seemed in order after learning she'd made partner.

The thrill of achievement rushed through her even now as she hooked a black pendant around her neck—a tiny black cat's face with diamond eyes and nose. The thrill of achievement . . . kind of like she'd felt upon completing her café renovations last weekend. Yeesh, things had changed so fast—it was like riding a crazy roller coaster. *But you'll reach the end now, the part where the hills get smaller and then level out. You'll get back to focusing on your work, your cases.*

Why did that suddenly sound boring?

It didn't matter. For tonight, she refused to allow any negative thoughts to enter the picture—tonight she was the celebratory party girl, partner at Tate, Blanchard & Rowe. And God knew she needed a party.

She missed Joe. She hated it, but she couldn't deny it. She thought about him all the time and constantly wondered what he was doing—working in the garage, playing with the kittens, eating a pizza, hanging out with Debbie and Kenny? She never once wondered if he was fooling around with Beverly Rainey—because she simply knew he wasn't. At the moment, she wondered if he might wander into the Last Chance tonight to watch Kenny shoot pool.

She also wondered if he hated her for how she'd ended things. She knew it was weak, just like she knew it was weak fourteen years ago—but she simply hadn't had the strength to face him. She'd been sure she'd break down into a weepy, sobbing mess. And she'd been just as sure of her decision—sure she needed a life that was steady, dependable, and completely within her control. When she'd gotten the call about making partner, she'd decided *that* was the sign she'd been waiting for. So she'd taken the easy way out. She'd left him.

Just like his father had. Just like Jana had, too. And even his mom, in a way.

*Stop it. Right now. He's out of your life. You have Kent.*

They'd gone for margaritas. And they'd laughed and gotten caught up on each other's lives—minus the Joe part—and Kent had been dumbstruck to hear she'd overhauled an entire restaurant in the time she'd been gone. He'd said, "Wow, I didn't know I had such a multifaceted woman on my hands. Makes me wonder what *other* talents you possess that I don't know about."

More flirtation. And it was getting more serious—as in more sexual. She'd done her best to flirt back.

Of course, he'd be here tonight. And maybe . . . he'd stay until everyone else left, under the guise of helping her clean up. Maybe then he'd start to kiss her, and maybe they'd even end up in bed.

She let out a heavy breath. That would be great if she had any desire to touch anyone but Joe.

*That boy's trouble. Pure trouble.* And it just kept escalating, it seemed, even from a distance.

*But you'll get over that. Soon. You have to. Your real life is here. And he's there. And Eden might as well be the moon for all Trish the High-Powered Attorney has in common with Trish the Café Girl.*

*It will all be fine—you'll learn to love your life and your job again. You will.*

Just then, the doorbell rang. First guest.

Smoothing her dress, she rushed to answer and found Kent on the other side, bearing a dozen red roses and a bottle of champagne—the perfect date. "Hey, beautiful—heard there's a party here tonight."

Sometime after nine, the doorbell rang—again. Trish looked up from where she stood at Kent's side in a circle of coworkers, all toasting her rise to partner. Other guests dotted the loft—seated in the living area, or mulling about the spread of finger food spanning her dining table. The party was a grand success, and she was even having a good time—something she'd feared wouldn't happen.

"Want me to grab it?" Kent asked.

She shook her head, replying with a teasing smile and a line from an etiquette book. "A good hostess always greets her guests personally." She whisked toward the door, champagne flute in hand, then pulled it open.

Joe stood on the other side. Instead of roses and champagne, he held dark pink tulips and a gray kitten.

Oh boy. She nearly fainted.

"Hey, cupcake."

"Uh . . . hey."

He blinked, looking uncharacteristically uncomfortable as he said, "Did I . . . come at a bad time?"

"Um . . ." He looked *so* good. He wore his usual faded jeans topped with a slightly snug tee, this one bearing the Jaguar logo. His snake coiled beneath one sleeve. "I'm kind of . . . having a party."

"Oh."

Oh God. He was just standing there, wondering what to do—and she was letting him.

"Come in," she said.

"I don't want to interrupt your party." She could hear the rest of it, the unspoken part. *Your party where everyone is wearing a suit or a fancy dress and looking so different from me.*

"You're not," she promised—even though she knew she sounded awkward, because suddenly everything *was* awkward. Because her earlier thought had been right— nothing about Eden, including Joe, fit with her life here. Eden and Joe, Indy and Kent—two opposite ends of the spectrum.

"I came . . . because I need to talk to you."

Her eyes dropped again to the tulips—and Pepper. The more she absorbed the sight, the more speechless she grew. So she followed her gut impulse to pull him in the door and through the large, open loft to her bedroom, only glancing over her shoulder toward her stunned-looking friends to say over strains of Beethoven, "I'll be back in a minute. Keep having fun."

She shut the door behind her as soon as they were inside.

Joe turned to face her, still bearing what she couldn't deny were the most perfect gifts he possibly could have brought. His eyes shone on her as blue and seductive as ever. "This is me . . . coming after you," he said.

His words swept down through her, leaving her breathless. "What?"

"You told me I should have come after you all those years ago, and you were right. I was an idiot to ever let you go. So here I am. Here to tell you I love you, and that you can trust me 'til the day we die, and that there's nothing I want more than you. I'm here to make you mine again—for keeps this time."

Whoa. She reached a hand to the dresser to steady herself. He was saying all the right words, but . . . what about the roller coaster? About the hills getting smaller now? She wanted the smaller hills, had been *counting* on the smaller hills. Her heart beat a hundred miles an hour and her whole body felt energized simply by the sight of him, but . . . oh God, so many questions bubbled inside her. Not to mention the pressure of having a whole loft full of people just outside the door waiting to celebrate the new beginning of her career.

She dropped her gaze to the kitten in his hand, furry front paws waving cutely through the air. The cat's sweet little face peered up at her as he released a tiny mew that clawed at her heart. "Why did you bring Pepper?"

"To help me convince you. I wasn't sure you'd want to see me, but I figured *him* you'd have a hard time turning away."

She smiled despite herself—he knew the way to her heart. "He's pretty adorable."

Joe tilted his head, eyes determined. "Is he convincing you yet?"

She sighed, stomach churning. "Joe. Oh, Joe." Leaving him had been so hard, but she'd done it. And she'd felt . . . *safer* since returning here. Bored in ways, and wracked with a sadness that wouldn't quit—but still safe. She hadn't expected to be face-to-face with the man she loved so soon, and she'd quickly forgotten how he affected her. She'd never felt so torn between safety and . . . soul-stirring passion.

Joe stepped forward to lay the flowers on her dresser and pull open a deep drawer, lowering the kitten inside—so Pepper wouldn't get lost, she presumed. She couldn't help quirking a grin at the bizarre sight of a tiny kitty resting among her casual cotton undies.

But Joe didn't look even slightly amused. No, Joe looked the way he had on the first night she'd met up with him back in Eden, like a man who knew what he wanted—and was about to take it.

"If he can't convince you," he said, "maybe this will." And with that, he lifted both work-roughened palms to her face and brought his mouth down on hers, firm and hot. His tongue pressed between her lips and the sensation of being entered by him, even like that, sent a shiver rushing the length of her body.

And then—oh God—she succumbed. Simply succumbed.

Her arms circled his neck as his hands splayed over her hips, drawing her to him, warm and snug. "You look beautiful," he breathed in her ear, and her whole being rippled with unstoppable desire.

"Take me," she whispered back.

"What?"

She'd shocked him, but she didn't care. Because that fast, she had to have him, *all* of him. "Take me, Joe. Please. Hurry."

A groan erupted from his throat, his expression blazing with exactly the kind of heat that released her inner biker babe. His palms closed firm over her bottom, pressing her to the delectable hardness behind his zipper, and—oh God—she began to writhe against him without thought or decision, her body simply responding.

But then he began gathering the skirt of her dress in his hands, pulling up more of it, higher and higher, until there was nothing between his fingers and her rear, since she'd worn a thong to avoid panty lines. His breath echoed hard as he kneaded her, slowly beginning to back her toward the nearest wall.

He didn't ask this time if it was okay to rip the panties—just gave a firm yank. She heard the lace tear, felt them fall away from her. Their eyes locked and her whole body tingled.

Through more hot, punishing kisses, she found the presence of mind to reach between them, unzip his jeans. When she reached inside, he moaned, and so did she.

Pushing her back against the wall, he lifted her, hands cupping her ass, and she scissored her legs around his hips as he pushed his way inside.

"Oh . . . Oh God," she breathed as a raspy growl left her lover.

Their eyes met, his that same beautiful, almost shocking blue that she never quite got used to, no matter how many times she looked into them. He moved in her, slow, deep, their faces only a few inches apart. Classical music from the party echoed through the nearby door, reaching a loud crescendo, but the only real sound in the room was their rhythmic, labored breathing. Trish arched against him, taking him deeper, letting her eyes shut for just one moment of heady bliss before she reopened them because she wanted to see him, *needed* to see him, feel every *nuance* of him, here with her, *in* her. Her whole being felt liquid, moving against him, like one with his body as his fingers curled tight into her bottom, somehow seeming to stretch her, pull her, open her to him even further. All the pain she felt surrounding him mixed and mingled with all the ecstasy, all the blunt lust and heat, nearly blinding her with emotion. She'd never experienced anything so intense with another human being as in that feral moment.

His breath came warm on her neck. "I thought . . . I'd never . . . feel you . . . again."

"*Ohhh.* Oh, Joe." *Her* breath turned thready, ragged.

"So warm for me, baby. So tight."

*Yes, yes.* She arched against him, pleasure opening up inside her, wider and wider, blooming like a flower beneath the hot rays of the sun. "Oh God," she whispered, desperate and close, and then the climax crashed through her like a storm. She bit her lip, hard, trying not to whimper too loud, or—dear Lord—not to scream, thankful for the music beyond the door.

A few seconds later, she opened her eyes to find Joe's hard gaze still pinned on her, still fueled with passion as he carried her to the bed to lay her on her back. His thrusts inside her came harder, faster. Somewhere on the other side of the room, Pepper mewed. She bit her lip, more, more, wanting to cry out beneath the power of his slick strokes. Her fingers raked through his hair, over his back, then found his face, touching the dark stubble. "Ah. God. Now," he said, and his eyes fell shut as he plunged hard, coming deep inside her, clearly trying to keep his own groans quiet, too.

They lay silent, recovering, when a knock on the door made them both flinch.

"Trish, is everything all right in there?" Oh God. Kent. She slapped her hand across her forehead. Dear Lord, how had this happened? If ever two opposing worlds had collided, this was that moment.

"Yes. Just fine," she called, but she wasn't sure she *sounded* fine. "I'll be out in a minute—I'm just talking with an old friend in here." *On my back. While he's inside me.* Yeesh.

"That guy—is he . . . somebody important?" Joe's deep voice drew her focus back to his eyes, mere inches above her.

How to explain? Especially considering how dazed she felt at the moment. "No. Yes. I don't know." She shook her head. "We've never . . . done *this*, if that's what you mean."

"Good." His voice came low, possessive.

And Trish began to slowly return to herself, leaving the fog of orgasm and easing Joe off of her until they both sat up on the bed.

She felt his gaze. "Old friend, huh?"

She sighed. "Joe . . ."

"What?"

"I love you, I do. But—"

"But what?"

Her heartbeat hadn't slowed, even after sex. Because this was about so much more than that. This was about . . . reality. Life. Forever. This was about . . . trudging on through the life she knew, where it wasn't always pretty, but it was safe, because the only people who ever got hurt here were the people she defended or their accusers. For *her*, nothing was really ever at risk. And maybe she liked it that way. She must—or why had she come back?

"Joe, I . . . I can't leave with you. I just made partner at my firm. Partner, Joe—do you have any idea how huge that is?" She shook her head. "I . . . can't leave now, Joe. I can't give that up.

This is a huge achievement, too huge to walk away from. It's everything I've worked for suddenly coming to fruition. And I told you, even if parts of the work aren't satisfying, I make it that way . . . by doing my best at it."

"Cupcake," he said, looking her in the eye, "I'm not asking you to leave anything."

She let out a breath, confused. "You're not?"

"I called Lois Faulkner today."

Her parents' real estate agent? She knit her brow. "About the diner?"

He shook his head. "About the garage. I'm putting it up for sale."

What the hell was he talking about? "What?"

"I'm putting it up for sale so that *I* can come *here*. To be with *you*."

She simply gaped at him, stunned. Was he crazy? He couldn't leave the *garage*—he just couldn't.

He *was* the garage—it was his heart and soul. He'd never told her that, but she knew it—nothing had ever been clearer to her. For him to leave it made no sense.

"No, Joe," she said simply.

He just looked at her. "No?"

She had to make him see. "I won't let you do that. I don't *want* you to sell the garage. Please don't."

Next to her, he just sighed—and started to look mad. "You don't want me to sell the garage," he repeated.

She peered helplessly into his eyes. "Of course not. You *can't*."

"Fine, damn it," he bit off. "To hell with it then."

Trish watched, stunned, as he got to his feet—zipping his pants—then took the few steps to the dresser, picked up Pepper, and said, "So much for a grand fucking gesture." Then he opened the door and walked out. That quick.

To leave Trish staring at an abandoned bouquet of tulips, numb and confused, as Kent came to the bedroom door. "Who was that guy? Are you okay?"

*I don't know.*

*I don't know anything anymore.*

**Tort(e):** a civil injury or wrongful act to someone or their property; _or_ a rich cake, usually made with eggs, ground nuts, and bread crumbs—and on the menu at Trish's Tea Room and Café.

## Sixteen

_Okay, wait a minute. I'm sitting here alone, with a bunch of pink tulips he drove two hours to give me. And he just offered to sell his garage and move here with me. And he thinks I just rejected him, even though I was only trying to keep him from making an unthinkable mistake. And he's gone._

Of course, she wasn't _really_ alone. Kent stood staring at her. And a roomful of people were probably just outside the door waiting to see what was going on. And she cared for Kent. And her work friends. She really did. They were good people.

But they weren't Joe.

And what Joe had just offered to sacrifice for her was . . . freaking _astounding!_ And insane. Insane that he would give up his business for her. For her and a job that . . . _oh my God, that I don't_ *even like!* Who cared that it was an achievement and an honor? What difference did it make if she didn't even *like* it?

And sure, she was scared of giving up her life here. She was scared of how good she and Joe were together and how much it would kill her if they ever split again. And she was scared of . . . going after the life she really wanted deep down inside. A simpler life. With Joe.

But he was willing to give up everything for her. His work. His home. Being near Carissa. All of it. When all she needed to do to make them both happy was . . . be brave, take a risk, for once in her life. And go home.

"I have to go," she said, pushing to her heels.

"Go where?" She had the vague impression Kent looked worried, but she hadn't actually met his eyes, so she didn't know for sure. She was a little wrapped up in herself at the moment.

"*Oh,*" he said then, so dramatically and disheartened that she followed his gaze to his feet, where a torn black thong lay.

"Oh," she said more softly in reply, then looked up. "He was . . . my old boyfriend."

Kent stood nodding, his expression decidedly let down. "Maybe not so old?"

"Maybe not," she answered on a sigh, then took a brief moment to lift a short kiss to his cheek and say, "I'm sorry."

Five minutes later, she was behind the wheel of her Lexus, wearing fresh underwear, with a bouquet of pink tulips at her side. Hitting the city streets, she headed for I-74 and drove like a madwoman, just praying that the speeding gods were with her and she wouldn't get a ticket—because she needed to get home to Eden.

As she traveled through the dark Indiana night, the Bellamy Brothers began to sing an old song from her childhood—"When

I'm Away From You"—on the radio, and tears began rolling down her cheeks, one after the other.

She'd been so, so foolish!

Not just about Joe and the last few weeks, but—dear God, she'd let something Joe did fourteen years ago color her lifelong opinion not only of *him*, but of *everyone!*

When was the last time she'd trusted someone new in her life in a deep, *real* way? Or anyone other than Debbie or her parents, for that matter? As for the friends she'd just left at her party, they were lovely people, but they weren't people she considered life-lasting friends. And her relationships with men generally went nowhere. And this was why!

She couldn't even blame Joe. He'd made one mistake—an awful one, yes, but she'd closed herself off from people, from feelings. Hell, no wonder she was such a good defense attorney.

And Richie, well, he was the first defendant she'd allowed herself to feel any emotion for in quite a while, and her trust had been misplaced. And that stung on a lot of levels, but she'd let that influence her decision not to trust in Joe, and that made no sense. Joe and Richie were like night and day.

Now, thoughts of her job, her new responsibilities, and Richie's upcoming trial—which started next week—filled her with a slow sense of emptiness bordering on dread. Oh God, when had *that* happened? At the diner, when she'd discovered she was attached to the place and wanted to run it? Or while spending time with her parents? Helping her mother cook—albeit poorly? Helping her dad with the hay? Or had it been doing something pure and simple and good with her law degree—getting justice for Marjorie and her little dog?

Or had it been when she was with Joe, letting him remind her of a time when she wasn't so afraid of her own emotions that she'd choose to wrap herself up in other people's problems for a living?

Oh God, she *hated* it. Really *hated* it!

She hated the slick, black, modern furniture in her new office.

She hated arguing with judges and other attorneys.

She hated making it so criminals were free to rape, rob, and hurt people again.

She hated her suits and high heels.

Okay, wait. She didn't *really* hate her high heels—that was going too far. A girl was allowed to love her shoes. But she also wouldn't care if she didn't have a reason to put them on very often. In fact, jeans and flowing skirts had started feeling all too comfortable lately, and panty hose were a drag.

So it boiled down to this: She hated what she'd chosen to do with her life.

Which was sobering.

And maybe a little crazy.

But she reached toward her purse, fishing out her cell phone as she drove, to call Elaine. No answer—just a recording. Not a surprise, given that Elaine was actually at Trish's loft, probably still helping Kent figure out what to do with all the tiny crepes and mini-cheesecakes. But she had to unload this from her heart *now*, so she left a message. "Elaine, I'm so sorry to do this to you, and I'll explain later, but I need to let you know I can't defend Richie Melbourne. You already have all the paperwork associated with the case, and this will be a great opportunity for you. I'll talk to Mr. Tate first thing Monday about making you first chair. I know this comes as a surprise, but . . . I'm officially removing myself from the case."

And the firm. But she'd have to deal with Tate, Blanchard

& Rowe later since there was only so much business you could do after ten o'clock on a Friday night. For the moment, at least she'd disassociated herself from Richie, and if he was set free to rape again, it wouldn't be her fault.

No, there wasn't much *business* you could do at this hour—but there was *pleasure*.

And before pleasure came . . . fixing what she'd messed up so horribly.

She squealed into the parking lot at the Last Chance at nearly 11:30. The bar happened to be on the way to Joe's house, so she figured she might as well check there first. It took only a glance to spot the big pickup with naked women on the mudflaps—and her heart went wild in her chest.

Only as she got out of the car still clad in her cocktail dress, a bouquet of tulips clutched in her fist, did she realize what a spectacle she was about to make of herself. But she supposed it would be no different than Joe walking into her party tonight, so she never slowed her stride as she headed toward the big steel door. She'd told herself she had to be brave and this was a good time to start.

When she pulled it open, "Must Be Doing Something Right"—the same song she'd danced to with Joe on that very first night—spilled out. Stepping inside, she scanned the room. Thirty sets of eyes looked her way, and two of them belonged to Kenny and Debbie. Kenny smiled. And Debbie's jaw nearly hit the floor, but her eyes filled with glee.

A sexy, dark-haired man with a cobra tattooed on his arm sat at the bar, a beer bottle in his hand. He didn't look up until she grabbed onto his wrist and said, "Dance with me."

He blinked, mouth open, eyes caught somewhere between pissed off and stunned.

"Please," she said. Willing to beg him now, if that's what it took.

Wordlessly, Joe set his beer on the bar, climbed down from his stool, and accompanied her to the dance floor. He took her in his arms in that old, intimate way of slow dancing she remembered from their first encounter—but he didn't meet her eyes, and even as close as he held her, she felt the distance she'd put between them hours earlier.

So here she was in a cocktail dress, dancing with a man who didn't really want to be dancing with her at the Last Chance Bar in Eden, Indiana. There was a hell of a lot wrong with this picture—but once and for all, she was going to make it right, and she wasn't going to waste any more time.

"I screwed up when I left you," she told him. "But tonight, you misunderstood. I'm moved beyond words that you would leave the garage for me. But the reason I said I didn't want you to is because you *belong* there, it's a part of you, and it would just be wrong. What would be right is *me* coming *here*, to be with you."

"What about making partner?"

"Screw making partner," she said. "I figured out as soon as you left that there are things I want a hell of a lot more. I want *you*. I want *Pepper*. I want the *café*. I want it all, Joe."

He gazed down at her then, but his eyes didn't soften—in fact, they sliced right through her. "How do I know you won't just change your mind again tomorrow? How do I know you'll really come home, really stay? How do I know you'll finally trust in me, Trish?"

She peered desperately up at him, willing him to believe. "Because I *do*. I do trust in you. I swear."

"All I know is, I've apologized for my mistakes and promised

I won't make them again. I did what I thought you wanted tonight, I made the grandest gesture I know to make, and I left there feeling like a fool. How can I trust *you* now, Trish? *How?*"

Oh boy—this wasn't going well. What if she'd *really* messed up? What if he *really* wouldn't believe her? What the hell was she going to do to make him understand, make him *know* that she would love him forever?

Then his determined plea in her parents' yard came back to her. She felt just as desperate now as he'd been then, so she gazed into his eyes, pressing her palms to his chest. "Forgive me, Joe. You *have* to forgive me. You *have* to."

Because nothing else made sense. She'd understood his simple, needful words when he'd said them, that forgiveness between them was the only way to ever make things right and as they should be—and now she stood in his arms, praying he'd give her another chance, too. She'd finally realized that life came with no guarantees, that she just had to put herself out there and *trust*. Now he had to do the same thing.

His response came silently, softly— he simply leaned his forehead over against hers. They no longer moved to the music, the only two people on the dance floor, and the lack of pool balls clacking together probably meant everyone was staring at them, but she didn't care. She drew her hands from around his neck to his face and tenderly kissed him.

She still clutched the tulips in one hand, the petals now brushing his cheek. He drew them down to look. "You brought the flowers."

"That's because they're beautiful and I love them and they're the flowers I'm going to carry when I marry you."

He went utterly still, lifting his eyes from the tulips to her face. His lips trembled slightly, but his voice came deep and steady. "Is that a proposal, cupcake?"

Wow. It had sure sounded like one. And she hadn't exactly planned that, but . . . just like forgiveness, nothing else made sense. "Yeah. I think it was."

In response, he grabbed her hand and pulled her toward the door—and straight out into the parking lot! She'd been thinking they might announce the news to the bar, perhaps be the center of some applause, of some grand ending worthy of a romantic movie—but apparently not. "What are you doing?"

As he led her to his truck and opened the door, he said, "That's a pretty untraditional marriage proposal. So I'm gonna give you a pretty untraditional acceptance."

The word "acceptance" was just registering in her mind as he climbed inside and pulled her into his lap. Settling his arms around her, he delivered a long, slow kiss to her mouth.

"So," she said, a bit breathless, "is that a yes?"

He nodded. "Mmm hmm. And here's another one." He kissed her firmer this time, lifting one hand to her cheek, touching his tongue to hers and igniting a fresh fire inside her.

A few minutes later, the kisses had deepened and the crux between her legs rippled as he slid one hand to her breast, stroking his thumb across the nipple through her dress. Trish considered her marriage proposal fully accepted now as they both sank deeper into more of the pleasure portion of the evening she'd been anticipating ever since leaving Indy. "I can't believe," she purred, letting out a small laugh, "that I'm making out in a truck with naked women on the mudflaps."

"They're silhouettes," he said low and sexy between kisses. "You don't know for sure they're naked. It's . . . mysterious."

Smiling at her lover, she curled one arm around his neck and gave him a short but heated open-mouthed kiss. "I would never try to change you, Joe—I love you just the way you are. But surely you realize . . . those mudflaps have to go."

He answered with a playful grin, their faces close. "You ask a lot, woman."

"This will be my only major request, I promise."

"What do I get in return?"

"My inner biker chick?"

"Done. Next time I'm in the accessories store, I'll see what I can find in a nice Yosemite Sam."

She smiled. "Your biker chick thanks you."

"She's gonna have to do better than *that*."

She heard a hot, sexy moan escape her—the first sign of the biker babe—but then found herself looking around the truck's cab. "Hey, where's Pepper?"

"He's too young to drink, so I dropped him off with his mom before heading here."

A soft smile stole over her, an incredible sense of *rightness*. "So he'll be at home waiting for me when we get there."

"Yep. Along with Midnight, Carissa's cat, who I promised could stay. And the yellow twins—although Jana is adopting those two for her *own* twins, which are due sometime next spring."

Trish's eyes flew wide, and Joe simply said, "Lots to tell you, cupcake."

And the rightness grew, because she knew Joe needed her just as much as she needed him. She kissed him again and felt a fresh burst of amazement deep in her soul. "I can't believe this," she said, growing more serious. "I can't believe that finally, after all this time, I'm home, where I belong."

"Everybody will be glad you're back, Trish."

But she shook her head. "I didn't mean Eden. I meant . . . you. *You're* home to me now, Joe. *You're* home."

"Oh *baby*," he growled, "I love you. And I'm in the mood for a nice . . . moist . . . messy cupcake."

She let a wicked smile unfurl as she made him a promise. "Mmm, Joe—I want to eat cupcakes with you all night long, every night, forever. And I want fudge, too. Lots and lots of fudge. Because I used to be allergic to fudge, but I'm not anymore, and I want all of it I can get."

He drew back to look at her. "I know cupcakes mean sex, but I don't have any idea what fudge means. Sounds like it might be kinky, though, so okay." Then he shut her up with another kiss and they had cupcakes.

*Toni Blake*

**TONI BLAKE**'s love of writing began when she won an essay contest in the fifth grade. Soon after, she penned her first novel, nineteen notebook pages long. Since then, Toni has become a multipublished author of contemporary romance novels and had more than forty short stories and articles published. She has been a recipient of the Kentucky Women Writers Fellowship and has also been honored with a nomination for the prestigious Pushcart Prize. Toni lives with her husband in the Midwest and enjoys traveling, genealogy, crafts, and snow skiing.